The Couple

The Couple
Woman in Progress 3

by
Victor Margueritte

translated, annotated and introduced by
Brian Stableford

A Black Coat Press Book

Edited by Peter Gabbani

English adaptation and introduction Copyright © 2015 by Brian Stableford.
Cover illustration Copyright © 2015 Mike Hoffman.

Visit our website at www.blackcoatpress.com

Introduction

Le Couple by Victor Margueritte, here translated as *The Couple*, was originally published by Ernest Flammarion in 1924. It was advertised as the concluding volume of a trilogy collectively entirely *La Femme en Chemin* [Woman in Progress], following *La Garçonne* (1922; tr. in parallel with the present text as *The Bacheloress*) and *Le Compagnon* (1923; tr. in the same set as *The Companion*), although the two earlier novels had been initially planned as a couplet. The decision to add a third element was a belated one, albeit an entirely logical and appropriate one, given the futuristic hopes and expectations elaborately developed in *Le Compagnon*.

Le Couple features the characters from both earlier novels, although it reduces the importance of the supposed overall theme of the trilogy considerably, dealing extensively with the ideas of socialism and pacifism and paying only corollary attention to feminism. The novel is, in fact, a speculative account of the ultimate crisis of capitalism and the possibility of an international socialist revolution; it is not so much a *roman de moeurs*, as its two predecessors were, as a thriller in which disadvantaged heroes must work against the odds to thwart a conspiracy of evil capitalists plotting to contrive an international war, in order to give them an opportunity to crush the forces of socialist protest once and for all. The fact that the period in which the story is set—1943-44—eventually turned out to be contemporary with an actual war makes the comparison between the hypothetical history and the real one an interesting exercise in stark contrast.

Le Couple features both of the couples formed in the course of the earlier novels—Monique Lerbier and George Blanchet from *La Garçonne* and Annik Raimbert and Amédée Jacquemin from *Le Compagnon*—but focuses primarily on their children, each of the original couples having brought up a boy and a girl, who are clearly meant by destiny to form two couples of their own. Since novels cannot work without catas-trophe and suspense, however, one of the nascent couples is afflicted by a stubborn failure on the part of one component to accept that destiny until the last possible moment. The charac-ter guilty of the misunderstanding, Annik's son, Claude, inevi-tably becomes the central character of that plot-strand, but his amorous dilemma is complicated by the question, generated by the broader plot-strand, of how he ought to react, as a committed pacifist, when he is conscripted for military service in the corrupt war contrived by evil capitalists eager to recover the Golden Age of Profiteering provided by the war of 1914-18.

It is presumably no coincidence that Claude is supposed-ly twenty years old when the novel begins: the same age at which Victor Margueritte attempted to follow in the footsteps of his father, an army general, and joined the Spahis. That was a decision that he presumably repented just as much as Monique Lerbier repented her brief career as a slut, albeit more belatedly; at any rate, he abruptly abandoned his military career after ten years in order to join forces with his older brother Paul as a writer in the Naturalist tradition pioneered by Émile Zola.

The romantic strand of the plot of *Le Couple* also makes much of the agonies suffered by Sylvestre Blanchet because of her seemingly-hopeless love for Claude, whose misguided infatuation with Marise Cervier is further complicated by the fact that she is the daughter of a filthy capitalist, who is one of the novel's archetypes of evil. The novel is able to achieve a melodramatic pitch more intense than its predecessors be-cause, even more so than *Le Compagnon*, it does not equivo-cate on the characterization of its archetypes of evil, which is exaggerated to the point of caricature. The banker Jean Cervier and his co-conspirators, the politician Max de Laume (no longer the "Antinous" of the earlier novels) and the news-paper proprietor Paul Turbot, are credited with every imagina-ble corruption and degradation, and not permitted a single redeeming feature—but such is the way of political and moral propaganda, which cannot afford to pull its punches in the fierce battle for hearts and minds.

The extremism of the novel's representation of its evil characters and their virtuous counterparts has the probably-unintended side-effect of making Marise a uniquely interesting character in the story, because she is the only one possessed of any real ambiguity. Although it is starkly obvious that she is a victim of circumstance, and is not much different in her actions and opinions from Monique in *La Garçonne*, she is treated very differently by her creator. Whereas Monique was given the chance to redeem herself, to the eventual extent that she is explicitly credited with metaphorical sainthood in the present story, Marise is condemned by the logic of the narrative to a different fate. Readers will doubtless make up their own minds whether the treatment meted out to her by Claude—and, more fundamentally, by the author—is more or less cruel and perverse than the treatment meted out by French moralists to *La Garçonne*, whose hate-campaign against it not only boosted it to massive best-sellerdom but drew vitriolic criticism in *Le Compagnon*, where the artist Jean Roussot is subjected to similar persecution for allegedly similar reasons.

Marise is, in any case, a greater asset to the author in *Le Couple* than her father and his partners in crime; whereas they only provide him with the clay required to excite revulsion and indignation, she gives him the opportunity to include two lurid orgy scenes, which permit him to titillate his readers, as he had in the earlier novels, while posing as an outraged moralist. He does so more discreetly than in the earlier novels, however, and he gets just as much narrative mileage out of Claude and Sylvestre without any recourse to shady tactics, by contriving problems that persecute and torture them to the extent of driving them both to the brink of suicide. Whether or not that raises moral questions about the authorial sadism required in such maneuvers, and the reader's glad participation therein, is probably a moot point, given the story's assumption and assertion that such personal troubles ought to fade into insignificance by comparison with the novel's other main theme: the necessity for progress toward a more egalitarian society, and the extreme difficulty of finding an appropriate strategy for that progress, when the enemy will stop at nothing to annihilate it.

Given *Le Couple*'s date of composition (specified at the end of the text), it is interesting that the author and his most favored characters take such a strong interest in the philosophy and political strategy of Mohandas K. Gandhi, whose career as a pacifist liberator still had a long way to run in 1924—he had become leader of the Indian National Congress in 1920—and had not reached its climax even in 1943, the year in which the story is supposedly set. Although not "prophetic" in the vulgar sense that the events it describes bear any resemblance to the actual pattern of political circumstance in 1943-44, the story does show considerable anticipatory flair in placing the philosophy and practicality of Gandhi's strategy of passive resistance at the heart of its thought-experiment.

As a futuristic novel, *Le Couple* is also interesting in its notion of the likely sophistication of technology during the two decades separating its writing from the notional date of the story. In that respect it follows lines that had become conventional in French futuristic fiction, largely thanks to the enterprising imaginative endeavors of Albert Robida, featuring personal air travel, videophones, conveyor-belt sidewalks and the like, but it deploys those technologies in a fashion that is dexterous by the relatively inexperienced standards of the day, both in terms of integrating them seamlessly into a future social order and in terms of the narrative strategy of their referencing and description. Like almost all French futuristic fiction of the previous half-century, however, it also foregrounds the likelihood that new technologies will provide the combatants in the next war with unprecedentedly powerful weaponry—in this instance, as in many others inspired by the dire example of the Great War, a new species of poison gas designed for distribution by aerial bombing—and similarly handles the idea with a deft combination of horror and irony.

By virtue of its complexity and its ambition, *Le Couple* might have seemed to its contemporary audience to be a rather awkward hybrid of the *roman de moeurs* and the more melo-dramatic variety of *roman scientifique*. In both critical terms and in terms of its sales, it seems to have fallen between the two stools, failing to attract much admiration from either di-rection, and selling moderately in spite of being a sequel to a huge best-seller. It has been virtually forgotten in the inter-im—although *La Garçonne*, like many once-scandalous nov-els that eventually came to seem tamer as the bar of scandalousness was inexorably raised, has also been largely forgotten. The neglect of both texts is, however, unjustified, and the hybridization of *Le Couple* can be seen in retrospect as an interesting and valiant attempt to tackle a problem of narra-tive strategy that has never gone away, and has rarely been solved in a satisfactory manner. Although the story cannot be regarded as a complete success in that regard, remaining something of a hopeful monster, it certainly ought not to be reckoned a failure, retaining a great deal of narrative energy as well as commendable enterprise and sterling ambition. In all probability, few of today's readers will regret that history did not work out the way the story's heroes wanted it to—but the filthy capitalists who actually won the war that was raging in 1943, and continue to win them all, would want everyone to think that, wouldn't they?

It might be appropriate at this point also to mention an interesting feature of the story's chronology. In a footnote to the translation of the first volume of the trilogy I pointed out that the only reference in the plot to a datable event other than the Great War of 1914-18—the engagement of Princess Mary, the daughter of George V, to Viscount Lascelles—was incon-sistent with the internal chronology of the plot as calculated from its references to the war. Those references make it per-fectly clear that the action of the novel begins in 1920, and adding up the time elapsed in the plot establishes that the events detailed must have concluded in 1925. There is not a

9

single reference in *Le Compagnon* to any independently datable event, and even its internal references to the ages of its characters and the births of their children are slightly confused, but it carries forward the sequence of events in such a way that it can be determined by calculation that the time-scheme in question must extend into 1930.

That calculation is, however, blatantly inconsistent with the time-scheme explicitly set out, with dates, in *Le Couple*. According to the extrapolated time-scheme of *La Garçonne*, Georgi must have been born in 1927, Sylvestre in 1928 and Claude in 1929. If that were the case, however, Claude could not possibly be twenty years old in 1943. As the dating of *Le Couple* is entirely arbitrary, however, it would have been perfectly possible for the author to have said that it begins in 1949 rather than 1943, when Claude really would have been twenty, in accordance with the apparent time-scheme of the first two novels. The fact that he did not do that, however, is probably not a mistake, but an illustration of an interesting feature of novelistic time.

Fictional time does not, of course, always run parallel to real time. There are numerous examples of fictional series in which the featured characters always remain the same age, even though the world around them changes—the long-running TV series *The Simpsons* is perhaps the most familiar contemporary example. What happens in Margueritte's trilogy is the opposite: the characters get older, but the world around them does not. Thus when the reference to Princess Mary's engagement implies that it is still 1921, even though Monique has clearly aged nearly four years since she was introduced at the age of twenty, more than a year after the end of the war, it is not necessarily an error. Even though she is four years older, there is a sense in which it is still 1921 in the historical backcloth of the novel, because the novel was written in 1922 and nothing within its background, no matter how long the events described take, in terms of the aging of the characters, can move out of the past relative to the time of writing.

In the same way, although the time-scheme calculated from Monique's aging places the principal action of *Le Compagnon* in 1928-30, the world in which the novel is set is still stuck, implicitly, slightly behind the time-period in which it was written, in two drafts in 1921-23. Thus, although Claude is not born until Monique is nine years older than she was in 1920, he is, in fact, "really" born in the present day in which the final draft of the novel was written—1923—and thus he actually is twenty, and not fourteen, in the hypothetical 1943 of *Le Couple*. Perhaps oddly, this temporal paradox is a side-effect of the author's obstinate Naturalism, which insists on letting the events of the plot extend over their natural time span, while refusing to allow their narrative context to advance beyond the moment of composition. It is, in fact, a matter of relativity—which was, of course, still a big idea in the early 1920s, following Arthur Eddington's supposed proof in 1919 of the general theory of relativity published by Albert Einstein in 1916.

This translation was made from the London Library's copy of the Flammarion edition of *Le Couple*.

Brian Stableford

THE COUPLE

FOREWORD

It seemed to me, as I wrote the final pages of *Le Compagnon*, that *La Femme en Chemin* would remain half-done if, after the phases mapped out by Monique Lerbier and Annik Raimbert, I did not clarify, in a third volume, the objective glimpsed when I sketched the plan for the first two in 1921.

La Garçonne, by incarnating, in a type of modern young woman, the feminine right to equality in amorous matters, and *Le Compagnon*, by demonstrating via a free union the impossibility French wives and mothers still have in having their equality recognized in marriage and in the education of their children, only claimed to depict post-war mores with sincerity, and also with a bitter concern for justice.

Will the women who are prevalent in twenty years, thanks to the generations of dance halls, stadia and affairs mark, with the end of one society, the commencement of a new order? Shall we see a better future, a less unhappy humankind, thanks to a more equitable and more elevated conception of amour? In sum, will mothers still tolerate the brutality of a few men making their daughters pleasure-fodder and their sons cannon-fodder?

Such are, with the postulate of virginity and fidelity for men as for women, the questions posed in *Le Couple*.

My heroes will not fail to excite a facile animation. Is not preliminary experience, not to say male satiety, along with adultery, one of the safety-valves of marriage?

Let those who mock remember Victor Hugo, marrying Adèle Foucher at the age of twenty. *I would only consider*, the poet wrote to his fiancée, *as an ordinary woman—which is to say, a trivial one—a young woman who married a man without being morally certain, by virtue of the principles and known character of the man, not only that he is virtuous, but also, and I employ the word in all is plenitude, that he is virginal, as virginal as herself. I also think that the most severe modesty is no less obligatory a virtue for a man as for a woman; I do not understand how one sex can repudiate that instinct, the most sacred of all those that separate human beings from animals.*

And if one raises the objection of Sainte-Beuve and Juliette Drouet,[1] I respond that an error of choice is not sufficient to cripple an ideal. Untiringly, I shall repeat: The same right and the same duties for all is a condition of equilibrium, progress and human happiness.

V.M.

P.S. It is appropriate, with regard to the title of this book, that I thank Madame Aurel, the well-known novelist and feminist.[2]

---

[1] Charles-Augustin Sainte-Beuve became famously infatuated with Victor Hugo's wife, pouring his frustrated and guilt-ridden sentiments into the novel *Volupté* (1834), which became a key document of the Romantic Movement and an important influence, via the admiration of Charles Baudelaire, on the Decadent Movement. At the same time, Hugo became infatuated with the actress and courtesan Juliette Drouet, who gave up acting and whoredom to become his mistress, secretary and travelling companion—a relationship that became equally notorious, of which a record was similarly preserved in her published love-letters. If ever there was an "error of choice" capable of crippling an ideal, the resultant mess was surely a prize specimen.

[2] Antoinette (or Aurélie) Mortier de Faucamberge (1869-1948), who signed her literary works "Aurel," had published *Le Couple: Essai d'entente*, in 1911. She hosted a significant literary and political salon while married to the journalist and

She has been kind enough not to accuse me of plagiarism in seeing me take up an appellation already marked by her talent. In any case, since Adam and Eve, is there another term to define the creative union more harmoniously?

Le Couple! You will find therein, along with the main characters of *Le Compagnon* and *La Garçonne*, the children of both. My readers will remember that after her dolorous "bachelor life," Monique married Professor Blanchet and that a son, Georgi and a daughter, Sylvestre, completed their happiness. They will also remember the free union of Annik Raimbert, the companion of Amédée Jacquemin. Their son, Claude and their daughter, Gine, continue here, with Georgi and Sylvestre, the endeavors of their parents. Born of their suffering and their faith, they go further than them along the route that the Wife and the Mother are traveling. Is not education the entire secret of the future?

New couples, makers of Tomorrow...

---

dramatist Alfred Mortier (1865-1937), which the Margueritte brothers might well have attended. She had previously been married to the landscape painter Cyrille Besset. She published numerous *romans de moeurs*, and her *Le Couple* was reprinted several times.

PART ONE

I do not bend a docile knee before idols.
Lord Byron.

I

"You know, Maman, I'm leaving shortly with Claude."

"You're leaving. All right, my daughter."

Without astonishment, Annik Raimbert enveloped Gine's blonde body, striking health and decided grace with an affectionate gaze. Standing in front of the helicopter, with one arm raised and the hand on the edge of the wing, the child seemed, with her breasts uplifted, a little Victory ready to take flight.

So modern, in her delicate tremulous features! And yet, in those nineteen years, fashioned and hardened by sports, that nobility of an antique figurine! Beside her leaning over his engine, whose exhaust-pipe he was palpating, Claude, sun-tanned and muscular, was the very image of robust and smiling simplicity.

Silently, Jean Roussot admired them, too. He still lived on the same hillside, in his old small country house, the red roof of which was perceptible from the Jacquemin-Raimbert farm in a grove of eucalyptus. As he had grown older, the great artist had maintained the enthusiasm of his faith. He replied to Annik's thought.

"Aren't they genteel? There they go, my Adam and my Eve."

"All they lack is the future city," said Annik, smiling.

Without touching her youth, the years had streaked her short hair with white. She was as alert as ever, but with a greater determination about her, and also a greater softness.

Roussot assembled all three of them in the same amicable tenderness.

"The future! I'm quite tranquil—it will be better. Thanks to them—which is to say, to you…not forgetting Jacquemin."

"Oh, us! Now them, yes…I hope!"

She felt a surge of pride. Her son, her daughter! A true man, and a true woman. The brother and the sister had not belied her hopes. They had launched themselves boldly into life, as they were about to soar into the air.

She scanned the familiar terrace with its large mimosas. The house of happiness! Beyond the sweep of the rocky slopes, the endless sea sparkled in the sunlight, confounded with the azure.

The blaze that had stripped the Maures of their age-old cork oaks and pines in 1923 had only denuded the beauty of the landscape temporarily. 1943! And the mountains of La Gaillarde extended, under the carpet of their new vegetation, the same splendor as before. Twenty years had sufficed for another forest to become verdant.

Every time she came back, Annik admired the untiring force of Nature. Here she retempered, with Amédée, her faith in the life that resuscitates and recreates... Amédée, the dear half of her existence.

Certainly, it had not been without many difficulties and struggles, succeeding where many other, less well-armed, had failed, that they had ended up triumphantly imposing the example of their free union: harmony within independence.

They had also had the sadness of seeing disappear along the way, one by one, the faithful friends of difficult times. Paule had departed first, and then Mérette, bequeathing to Claude and Gine the savings of a life of privations and nobility.

Then, in their turn, the good Zélonoff and Madame Broussat—whose seat on the International Council of Women she now occupied—had been gently extinguished: beloved shades whose memory would live as long as she did. The spirits of the dead are the counsel of the living, when they are able to hear it.

And there, in front of her, the self-embellished image of those two proud, charming individuals, born of their flesh and petrified by their souls. They had an upright stance like the pines, insensibly grown, beautiful trees of the full earth.

Roussot's right, she thought. *Today they'll catch up with us; tomorrow they'll surpass us*. The law of incessant growth, which, far from saddening her, illuminated her: comforting promises in the fire of the daily battle, the perpetual ravages of the conflagration, ever reignited by human Stupidity and Malevolence.

"Do you want anything from Paris?" Gine offered, generously.

"Yes."

"Hurry up and make a list, while I pack my valise."

"How long are you going to be there?"

"Just long enough to run your errands and visit some friends, since Claude has to come and pick you up at the end of the week. Your famous Conference in Budapest!"

A hint of jealousy showed through beneath the smile. Gine would have liked her mother to associate her more often with her propaganda trips, and to employ her, in preference to her brother, in external secretarial tasks. She was good enough to undertake daily correspondence, to dictate to the automatic recorder, to do filing—it was hardly worth the trouble, for that, of having graduated from the École Normale Supérieure! A bureaucrat, when it would have been so amusing, like Annik and Claude, to travel all over Europe, to cast the good grain to the crowds, to go back and forth, intoxicated by space, with the wind whipping her cheeks, breathing in the sky, at top speed, at an aerial gallop!

Annik perceived her regret and, in order to attenuate it, proposed: "If you prefer, you can stay with the Blanchets while we're in Budapest. I'm sure that Monique would be delighted..."

"That's an idea! I love Versailles..."

Claude underlined the remark with hearty laughter. "And you adore Georgi!"

She sketched a dance step, and then said to her brother, who was checking that the wings obeyed the controls properly: "Go on, maniac! For a journey of an hour and a half!"

"I'll be responsible for a donkey," he declared, "since I'm taking you!"

She punched him cheerfully. "Donkey yourself. Given that the apparatus has been tuned up by Georgi!"

The image of Georgi Blanchet, their childhood comrade, was interposed affectionately between them—and at the same time, the silhouette of his sister Sylvestre. The prospect of a pleasant fortnight in the house that she loved suddenly consoled Gine. Let Sylvestre, who would soon be a doctor of medicine, amuse herself playing the conference delegate, at her ease! She no longer envied her.

Claude grumbled, sarcastically: "Obviously, when Sylvestre and you have said Georgi, there's no more to do than take away the ladder. His trickery is good, that's understood—but he's not a sorcerer."

He swung the steering column laterally, in various inclined planes. The pearly wings curved one after another. Then he moved them from down to up, and from up to down, in the vertical plane. When they were raised they gave the apparatus, perched like a great red bird on its metal foot, a vertical oscillation.

"That's splendid!" said Gine. "To have combined the two kinds of flight, sail and motor. No, my lad, you didn't find that. And it isn't with your ground-scraper that you'll advance progress as rapidly as with his cloud-skimmers!"

While inspecting his magneto, Claude said, sardonically: "Daily bread is good, even by comparison with Dr. Lagre's concentrates—a complete meal in a pill!"

"Your turn, Annik!" said Jean Roussot

"Perhaps he'll be content to do as I do one day. Life is short and meals long."

19

"And then there are people whom the earth still nourishes fortunately. Wait until I've brought out my essorette[3]... Gine will see whether or not it's as good as a helic!"

That was one of that perpetual subjects of teasing between him and his sister. Georgi Blanchet, a graduate of the Polytechnique, was already well-known, at twenty-two, for his discoveries in aerial locomotion. Claude, two years younger, yesterday a simple pupil of the Arts et Métiers—as his parents had wanted, in order that he should remain closer to the artisan and technologist—was today a manufacturer, inglorious but assiduous, of agricultural machinery, and also a passionate writer of poetry. He concluded: "Go get ready instead of talking! I have a meeting at six o'clock at the factory."

"And one at five in the Tuileries!"

He looked at her with feigned surprise. "What! What?"

"One knows what one knows!"

He could not help smiling. A mute confession. Well, yes, she had guessed. He intended to be there, at the time announced for the landing of Marise Cervier, returning from New York. And afterwards...?

Gine, satisfied with having guessed correctly, did not persist. "Don't worry—you'll be there. Give me five minutes."

Although the ardor of the September sun was radiating over his vacation and the agricultural machinery could do perfectly well without him, Claude, embarrassed to reveal the true motive for his flight, had found the pretext of making a surprise visit to the factory to make sure that everything was going smoothly.

He was the co-director—with an authority and a competence that was surprising in an adolescent, in spite of the pre-

---

[3] This improvised term has been re-improvised more than once since 1924, but its modern meanings are derived from the verb *essorer* [to wring out or spin-dry]; it is usually used nowadays with respect to salad spinners, but the comparison with a helicopter here implies that the author is deriving it from *essor* [flight, or soaring], and that it is some kind of flying machine.

cocious maturity of his generation—of the great cooperative industry founded at Mantes in 1937 by Baron Plombino, a philanthropic capitalist. Other offers even more advantageous had been made to him. The foundries of Romicourt and Crozat would have liked to acquire Amédée Jacquemin's son; via the young man they would have "had" the father: the Statesman whose character added an additional luster to evangelical socialism...

The international plutocracy and its feudal masters of the world hated the great heir of Jaurès,[4] the savior who, in two terms as President of the Council, had returned the ox-cart of France to the popular path. For a time, the State-Machine had forged straight ahead, modernized in the hands of the meritorious conductor, by virtue of his broad views and generous heart. And then, as soon as the idler kings, the profiteers become Oligarchs, were reinstalled, the grinding vehicle had resumed its zigzags toward the gulf. It was heading there at speed since they had got their hands on power again.

Annik finished giving Claude her instructions in order that he could make the best use of his short stay in Paris…to seek information, cleverly, from Jean Cervier's entourage about the underside of the oil deposit business and the true motive for his voyage to New York.

"Since you're infatuated with his daughter, at least try, when you see her, to find out the hidden agenda of the mission."

---

[4] The pioneering "social democrat" Jean Jaurès (1859-1914) became the leader of the French Socialist Party in 1902, which merged three years later with Jules Guesde's more radical Socialist Party of France to form the Section Française de l'Internationale Ouvrière [French Section of the Workers' International], more usually abbreviated to SFIO. He was a committed anti-militarist, and tried to organize co-ordinated strikes in France and Germany in order to prevent the Great War; he was assassinated on 31 July 1914, the day before the war began, and is the obvious model for Amédée Jacquemin.

Anglo-German finance, it was said, was trying to take possession of the inexhaustible deposits of Provence, recently discovered after those in Forez. In the absence of Amédée, who was away at a pacifist conference in Japan, it was absolutely necessary to obtain information as to which foreign banks were interested, along with Jean Cervier's, in methodically taking over the French oil wells.

Claude promised.

Roussot, whose art was never disinterested in public affairs, added: "If the big eaters have their way, we'll be swiftly devoured, not *à la sauce Anglaise*[5] but in the manner of Anglo-German finance—and without even being aware of it. Fruitful as war might be, from all points of view, for those Messieurs, they'll obtain even more profit, if they can, from making economies therein."

"I'm not so sure about that. Embryonic as it still is, the threat posed by popular organization to capitalist supremacy is increasing by the day. War isn't only an objective for the manufacturers of cannons and gases. For the Finance that leads us, it's the sole means of realizing Thiers' dream: bloodying democracy, not just for thirty years but forever."[6]

Claude shrugged his shoulders. "Right!"

"Oh, I never despair of the future," said Annik. "It's the present that worries me. At the end of this looting of oil there'll be an inevitable revolt of the community, which won't allow itself to be suppressed so easily this time. Then…"

"That's a bold move! Will they risk it?"

"With much less scruple, because their very existence is at stake! And as they think they're the stronger…"

---

[5] i.e. with custard.

[6] Adolphe Thiers (1797-1877) became the president of the Third Republic in 1871, in the wake of the Franco-Prussian War, but acquired the lasting hatred of French socialists by immediately ordering the bloody suppression of the Paris Commune.

Claude cast a glance toward the house. What was Gine doing? Not seeing her coming, he protested: "War against the Profiteers? Impossible! When Europe's wounds have only just begun to scar over! When the democratic movement, everywhere..."

"In a fine state here," jeered the painter, "with the de Laumes and the Solmous in power! It's worse than before, when Perd-la-Victoire[7] or Alexandre Vilfaux was in power!"

"Solmou and de Laume are another accident," said Annik. "Amédée will cure us...but England has fallen under the yoke again! Conservatives and Liberals in coalition against the workers' movement, after its defeat..."

"It's still alive," Claude observed.

"But diminished—and the ultranationalist Prussians and Bavarians are now masters of Germany in spite of our friend Rohn? There, as here, party rivalries have weakened the working class; the bourgeoisie take advantage of that. There's also the obsession with revenge that troubles so many minds beyond the Rhine!"

"Whose fault is it," observed Roussot "that we're taken back the Sarre and that we were only able to free the Rhineland by force? Today we're expiating our past errors and the Imperialist face that the Bloc National had given France with the juridical chicanery of Cibéron.[8] We're expiating—after the

---

[7] Georges Clemenceau, President of the Council during the Great War, was hailed thereafter as the "père de la Victoire" [father of the victory], which cynics dissatisfied with his postwar politics scathingly amended to "Perd-la-Victoire" [Lose the Victory].

[8] The Bloc National was a right-wing coalition that took control of the French parliament after the Great War, riding a wave of nationalist sentiment and winning the 1919 election by a landslide; it was still in power while the author was writing the present novel, although it was defeated in the May 1924 election. It plays a significant role in the political back-

narrow spirit of the Treaty of Versailles, so different from Wilson's great dream, the just peace that people were expecting—our politics of magnificence, all the more stupid because in men and money alike, our meager birth-rate and our shrunken finances don't give us the means!"

"When one thinks," said Claude "that so many millions of men had accepted their sacrifice because they thought they were ensuring a new order!"

"Well, my dear Roussot," said Annik, "have we repeated it enough, that every victory is a catastrophe and that the anthem *War Pays* was the bloodiest of deceptions? Today, as yesterday, war only pays those who count on it, as it will pay tomorrow, if those who prepare it like a coup on the Bourse have their way. And now we're arriving at a moment more critical than that of 1914. It's no longer the emperors of Germany, Russia and Austria, nor French chauvinism, that's threatening the precarious peace: it's the emperors of oil, coal and iron, world capitalism working secretly on its supreme war of conquest."

"Fortunately," exclaimed Roussot, "socialism is ever more alert, and in all countries. I hope that in France, and everywhere else, the sheep won't allow themselves to be led to the slaughterhouse this time."

"You won't have sown in vain, Maman! Today we're the majority and tomorrow we'll be the masters. The bourgeoisie will die, the people will be born."

"The former still have the power!"

"It will break against the energy!" The young man's eyebrows had furrowed harshly. "If a revolution is required, there'll be one. Let the blood fall back on those who cause it to be shed. The evil will disappear, along with the evil-doers." His appetite for risk and audacious youth were trenchant.

"Bravo, Saint-Just!" cried Roussot. He had baptized Claude thus, being fondest, among all the heroes of revolu-

---

ground of *Le Compagnon*, in which its actual leaders are replaced by fictitious characters, including Cibéron.

tionary history, of the archangel with the steely gaze. Saint-Just doubly incarnated, in the gaze of juvenile worship, the virtues with which his name shone: sanctity and justice. The model and the pupil had the same absolute thirst.

Claude was gentler, however. He looked kindly at his mother, who exclaimed in distress: "Blood, what horror! I'll never convince you, then? You don't understand that it fatally summons blood? That it's the provocation of endless massacre? How many times have I told you that violence is the worst of weaknesses?"

"I expect we'll reckon with the vultures without having to wring their necks," Claude said. "What on earth can Gine be doing?" He was waiting impatiently beside his airplane, no longer listening to Roussot or his mother.

"Your efforts won't have been futile," said the painter. "Thanks to your International Council of Women, a universal conscience is awakening, with a clearer sense of progress, an immense need for peace and work..."

"How I wish!" murmured Annik, ardently.

"Now that women can vote all over the world..."

"Except in the Latin countries! What shame, that they're still quibbling over the legislative mandate, as if we female voters and candidates hadn't given proof enough by now in the municipal arena—in hygiene, in welfare, in the management of budgets!"[9]

"Patience! France will end up listening to her prophets. The syndical organization for which you and Amédée have worked so hard is beginning to bear fruit. If the League of Nations has vegetated impotently, it's because it's only an intergovernmental administrative council, and can no more decide to arm itself alone than to disarm everyone else. A new

---

[9] Although women had been able to vote and stand as candidates in French municipal elections since 1872, they were not allowed to vote or stand in legislative elections until 1944, so the author's anticipation that the demand would still not have been met in 1943 was correct.

moral power exists; the League of Peoples. It only has to cry "Peace!" to shut the warmonger up. And tomorrow, instead of the Cerviers having a free hand to fabricate a United States of Europe in their service, with monopolized zones of production, the International Syndical Federation will be able to divide between its participants, like an honest commercial entity, that which is, in the final analysis, the wealth of all. We'll see, Annik, we'll see! Look no further than the imminent elections. If your husband resumes the helm, and instead of the tugboat that she's become, France will reappear as what she was, with a figurehead carrying a beacon at the prow!

"For sure!"

Gine's laughter rang out. "As soon as you're left alone with Saint-Just! Kiss your mother and let's get away. You'll have time to prepare speeches when you're on the way to Budapest."

She bowed: "Madame President, Monsieur Portraitist of the League of Peoples..."

"Little clown!" said the painter, laughing.

With an affectionate caress, Annik stroked the covered head of which only the mischievous eyes could be seen within the leather of the fur-lined helmet. Then, tenderly, she kissed Claude's forehead, before he fastened his safety-harness.

Scarcely had the passengers sat down when the helicopter, with a noise like a rocket, rose up vertically, its ascent so abrupt that it cut short the farewell waves. A black dot, diminishing by the second, it veered vertiginously northwards and disappeared.

Annik and Roussot followed it with their gaze for as long as they could.

II

"There they are—it's them!"

"No!"

"Yes!"

"Which one? The one that's turning on its wing?"

Louise Barlot laughed loudly. "Sylvestre knows what's what! She mistakes a wheezy old rattletrap for one of her brother's aircraft! Listen to that clanking! That's what you make of the silencer?"

That was another invention of Georgi Blanchet's. Louise Barlot, who was infatuated with the inventor, was as proud of it as if the patent had been in her name. Everyone fell silent at the surrounding tables, and they did, indeed, perceive the increasing rumble of the engine. Laughter burst forth.

"That's true," Sylvestre admitted. "Anyway, theirs is white and red. They're late! Are you sure, Georgi, that it's platform B where they're landing?"

It was Louis Barlot who replied, a trifle sharply: "As always—since your friend Gine telephoned him: the Tuileries, five o'clock."

At Gine's name, Georgi blinked imperceptibly. Without departing from his habitual silence, he took little sips of his iced coffee. His was a thin tormented visage, whose concentration of thought impressed Louis Barlot more than anyone, and annoyed her more than usual that afternoon. How could one penetrate the depths of that soul, which seemed absent, or which, for the present, was in hiding? Only Gine could do that! She detested her, deep down, that little Jacquemin-Raimbert—one didn't even know what to call her—and Sylvestre, too; they stank, with their false simplicity! Because the one had passed her P.C.N.[10]—a doctor, no, I ask you?

---

[10] PCN was the standard abbreviation of the *Certificat d'études physiques, chimiques et naturelles*, created in 1893;

27

When one has enough to live on!—and the other had graduated from the École de Sèvres! Prissy, the pair of them!

There was a silence.

"You're not chatty, you know? Is it the waiting, my dear, that's cut your throat?

The daughter of Barlot the elder, of the "Warmobiles," the young millionaires could not conceive that anyone could resist her, nor that one could pretend not to like enjoying oneself like everyone else—"everyone" being, in her eyes, limited to herself and her peers. She was tempted to switch tables and rejoin the gang of the "three Hubertes"—the first and second Poursaillon du Vagan and Jane Hubert, in whose name people pronounced the t, although her masculine appearance made her resemble a man in the company of her two friends...

"There's a crowd today," Louise Barlot observed, nervously.

Platform B at the Tuileries, the terraces of which had been fitted out as landing stages, was situated directly opposite the Banque Cervier, installed in the vast quadrilateral once occupied by the Hôtel Continental. Only a bodega in the form of an Australian ice bar remained, serving demonic cocktails of old port. It was called *La Frissonnière*: a sort of cosmopolitan buffet from which Fashion dictated that one watched the comings and goings of the new aerostation. People watched in summer for sensational arrivals—and more particularly, that day, for that of the Minister Jean Cervier and his daughter, returning from New York.

It was a Vanity Fair to which the piquancy of possible accidents attracted a crowd of idlers. It was also a waiting room of businessmen, and occasional curiosity-seekers like Georgi and his sister. They gazed with an amused scorn at all that prostitution and luxury, shiny with the wrappings of their false glamour, agitating there, from the crested cranes to the young women's last cry. There were few men except for the

---

in our history it was replaced in 1934 by the PCB, which substituted *biologiques* for *naturelles*.

very young and the very old, confused in the same senile puerility, as in the same smug ostentation.

From noon to one o'clock and from four to six p.m.—not a minute sooner, not a minute later—the parade was in full swing. There was more denigration than admiration, with regard to obsolete forms of cockpit, bucket seats like shells, hulls of mahogany and sculpted plumage. Air-taxis and private planes were lined up on the flat turf of the Jeu de Paume, alongside the runways where the multiform swarm of metal birds was incessantly taking off and landing. From the open bays of the bar one could see their web being woven, almost mutely, alongside the buzz of the rolling walkway that extended above the roadway, reserved for cars, all along the Rue de Rivoli.

A piercing exclamation caused heads to turn. It was Jane Hubert, hailing a group of new arrivals: three young people with green-tinted faces, waddling along in overly short jackets, with studied elegance. At the head marched the famous homosexual Paul de Laume, the son of the no less famous Max de Laume, the former Minister of Public Education, presently Minister of Foreign Affairs and President of the Council. A poet and painter from time to time—in the very forefront of Spherism, whose beardless troops were laying siege to the last Cubists[11]—the esthete presented a repulsive lemuroid face, the phantasmal apparition of a shriveled nocturnal ape. In between times he stuffed himself with the new drugs, scopo and ouaba. Paled by the same vices, his acolytes seemed a republic of shades in his wake.

"I adore them!" exclaimed Louise Barlot. "They're charming!"

"You think so?" muttered Georgi.

---

[11] Cubism was already in decline when *Le Couple* was written, but its author could not know that its replacement in the *avant garde* of art was imminent, with the spectacular emergence in the mid-1920s of geometric abstraction and surrealism.

"A little effeminate, perhaps. At least, with them, one can get on, one can chat."

"One is with one's own kind!" he jeered.

"They have the superiority over others," she retorted, "of being polite."

"The last *chevaliers*," Sylvestre put in. "The refuge of old French gallantry."

"Exactly! *Au revoir*, savages. When you're in a better mood..."

She got up with the dignity of a guinea-fowl, vexed, but primarily delighted to claim her part of the celebrity that the company of Paul de Laume would confer on the three Hubertes.

"Bon voyage!" sighed Sylvestre. "There she's in her element. Only Marise Cervier is missing!" An expression of disdain pursed her lips, further narrowing her slender, ardent visage. She was singularly attractive, by virtue of a spontaneity and frankness of gaze that gave her the brunette grace of a young goat. Just as Louise Barlot had no sympathy for Gine, whom Georgi preferred, Sylvestre reckoned as false coin the insolent flirtation that Marise exchanged for the sincere love of Claude.

All four of them, Georgi and Sylvestre Blanchet, Claude and Gine, brought up together in an even narrower intimacy than that of their parents, had grown up side by side, mingling their sentiments and thoughts without taking account of the fact in the fresh vigor of a single thicket, branches so intertwined that their individual personalities could no longer be distinguished from one another—with the result that they were not only brothers and sisters, coupled by family and assembled in the same affection, but, without intending it, powerfully interlinked lovers.

There was only one difference: Gine and Georgi were conscious of their choice, and, without having yet revealed it to one another, were intoxicated by the vertigo of living, in the secret blossoming of their reciprocal desire; whereas Sylvestre was unaware—or, rather avoided the confession—of the passion that drew her toward Claude, while the latter, dazzled by Marise, only saw in his childhood companion a comrade and a friend. The amorous young woman was suffering from that, unwittingly.

Suddenly, at Paul de Laume's table, such hysteria broke out among the enraptured poultry-yard that, disdainful as Georgi was of it, he murmured: "They're exaggerating."

One of the Poursaillons du Vigan—Huberte the first—was standing up, sucking with ecstatically blinking eyes the pipe that the representative of Spherism had just abandoned in the depths of his cocktail. And the whole chicken-run was clucking hectically. Impassively, Paul de Laume deigned to intone a verse of one of his favorite poems:

In the descent
Pick the flower
Of my dolor
Evanescent...

"They make me sick, those petty Messieurs," Georgi declared. "Men, them? No more than those females are women!"

The laughter redoubled. Mademoiselle Poursaillon du Vigan the elder licked her lips with a pointed tongue. Louise Barlot shouted: "Youth is beautiful!"

Georgi turned his back, revolted, and said, loud enough to be overheard: "Youth, them? Oh, no! True youth works, on the land, in an office, in a studio, in a factory...it scratches, for the benefit of that vermin. Their youth! But they're a thousand years old, those lice, if they have any age at all."

Sylvestre calmed him down: "Don't go on about it. Do they even exist? No more than fetuses preserved in alcohol. They're stillborn."

"How wrong you are! Look! Those daughters will produce seed in their turn—and that's the danger! It only takes one sick seed to rot the plant." He took out his watch. "In the meantime, they're still not here."

31

Everyone was following their own train of thought as they passed in front of the travelers. Sometimes, they were enraged by overhearing what their neighbors were saying, without intending to listen. The poultry-yard was cackling now in low voices, all the heads leaning over their table as if over a platter of gossip. Paul de Laume was dominant, hieratical, nodding his already-balding head. Solemnly, for the third time, he had resumed, in the midst of general inattention: "*And breathe in...very softly...until vertigo...the bleak stem.*"

Meanwhile, Henri Chanteroy, an amateur but skilled musician, was receiving an offer from the sixteen years of Jean de Rancis, a buyer and seller of everything: "Five hundred tons of Chilean guano."

"And you!"

"Idiot. And the boat, too, if you want. Arrived from Valparaiso, in dock at Libourne."

"No thanks. There's nothing like artificial fertilizer. Ten thousand tons of superphosphates, at your service?"

"No? A pearl necklace then? A bargain! Paid five hundred thousand..."

"What is it selling for?"

"Two hundred."

"Have to see..."

Jean de Rancis, sensing a bite, pounced. "A hundred and eighty perhaps...for you, who's a fine lad, the woman included...and that's a boat, old chap!" Jean de Rancis designed a balloon with his two arms. "A model for Paul, I tell you."

But Henri de Chanteroy pulled a face. "No thanks, I don't use them..."

"You don't know what you're missing."

The precocious salesman was in the process of giving details—"Luce Dantin, former mistress of Solmou, pinched by a boxer"—when prolonged *Ahs!* cut the conversation short. All heads turned. Everyone around the tables stood up.

"It's Marise!" Louise Barlot proclaimed, enthusiastically.

As straight as an arrow, a large blue and yellow hydroplane appeared over the courtyard of the Louvre and headed straight for the roof of the Banque Cervier, returning to its garage. It was a hundred meters away when a parachute was abruptly detached from it, immediately deployed above a slender human form.

Propelled by a miniature dynamo, the automatic lander passed gracefully over the rolling sidewalk and came to alight, with its passenger, on the very threshold of the bar. The apparatus was still sufficiently unfamiliar for discreet applause to salute Marise's arrival. Porters from the bank, who had come running, immediately took possession of the parachute, which one of them folded up, and the traveler's cloak and breathing mask, which another carried away.

She shook the bushy gold of her short hair and straightened up, as svelte as a page-boy, in her gazelle-skin suit.

"A harmony in *fauve* minor!"[12] exclaimed Paul de Laume, kissing her hand. "Bonjour, my beauty. Are you arriving from Kamchatka?"

"One gets cold at four thousand meters at that speed! New York to Paris in five hours. It's a record!" Proudly, she threw the news to public admiration, and shouted: "Waiter! An uppercut!"

A cocktail hammer-blow: she emptied it in one gulp, so thirsty that she ordered another and, in the meantime, drank the glass of iced Vittel water with which Jane Hubert was stemming her perpetual ardor.

"That's better!"

Curiously, after exchanging a little nod of the head, Sylvestre listened to the traveler pontificate.

"And your American?" said Huberte.

"One offered to marry him."

"Why?"

---

[12] The wordplay exploits the double meaning of *fauve*, which can refer to a color—as, for instance, with regard to "tawny" hair—and also to a predatory wild animal. The author would have been very familiar with the "Fauvist" style of painting briefly fashionable before the Great War.

"To see whether he'd get a divorce. It's a proof of love. He's wife is richer than me."

"Did he accept?"

"No, fortunately."

"So?"

"One spent a night together anyway, in order to leave him with regrets."

"Regrets?"

"Of course. What did you think? One only had supper. Nothing but *hors-d'oeuvre*, until dawn. Delicious, moreover. I didn't want anything else, and for his part, he's quite content. He has soup and beef at home..."

The three Hubertes giggled and the three Spherists were condescending, with superior expressions. Louise Barlot approved: "*Hors d'oeuvre*—nothing like them."

"As you say, Saint Touch-me-not!"

So saying, Marise had risen to her feet. "With that, my children, I need to take a shower. Come to my place at Garches tomorrow, at five. The old folk won't be there, we'll have fun. I invite you all! We'll eat, dine and...sup...in the American style. Ah, bonjour Monsieur Jacquemin, bonjour—where did you spring from?"

Claude, his helmet in his hand, bowed and smiled. "From the Midi, to have the pleasure of greeting you on your arrival."

"That's nice! That merits a reward. Well, come to Garches on Tuesday for a bite to eat...unless you think you're too serious for our crazy gang?"

Neither Georgi nor Sylvestre, listening to what the gang were saying, had noticed that Claude and Gine, having flown over the Place de la Concorde, had landed while Marise Cervier was monopolizing all gazes. A hand on Georgi's shoulder had made him jump and get up, confused.

"Oh!" exclaimed Sylvestre. "Here they are!"

But, having only taken time to shake hands, Claude had drawn away, while Gine, entirely focused on Georgi, sat down next to him, in the seat vacated by Louise Barlot.

Sylvestre, entirely at her leisure, was able to observe to herself: *He thinks about nothing but her, and yet, she's only making a fool of him!*

Marise, a cold temptress, made her voice seductive: "Will you come?"

"Gladly."

"Tuesday, then, good."

They exchanged a handshake. He tried to squeeze, to retain her slender fingers, but they had already been withdrawn. To steal Marise from those puppets! He replied coldly to their greetings. She, enjoying herself with such cretins!

He had scarcely turned away when, pulling a mischievous face, she stuck out her tongue at him. He annoyed her, with his blank gaze. Oh, if "the Boss" hadn't instructed her to be pleasant...

No, but what is father thinking, taking an interest in those people? He'll never get anything out of them, such fanatics...

She ended up tearing herself away from the amorous adieux and set off at a sprightly pace to reach the door of her private apartment in the Rue Castiglione.

Standing near Sylvestre, without hearing the affectionate questions she was addressing to him, Claude followed the red-haired silhouette and the strange bare head with his eyes.

The door closed again. He emerged from his dream.

III

"You must be mad, Andrée, to arrive at such an hour. As if you didn't know that I have to be in Royat this evening."

The person addressed, who had just silently opened Madame Simone Cervier's bedroom door, raised bovine eyes toward the tyrant timidly. What was she going to put her through now, la Mounine? And to think that they had been childhood friends, having worked on the same farm, she and Simone—Moune in private, Mounine, meaning she-monkey, in the parlor…that was what a Cévenole cook had baptized her, a nickname adopted thereafter by the entire stuff.

Had she not, however, just like her, Andrée Loriet, milked cows before extracting her fortune from men? Oh, some people had all the luck! While Simone, a notorious courtesan before becoming an actress, had ended up, at thirty, hooking up with the fat Cervier, she had known all the miseries of sales by auction, and sleazy hotels that rented rooms by the hour—until the day when, attached by hazard to a shady businessman, she had rediscovered her old friend, now the distant Madame Cervier.

Was that good luck or bad luck? Andrée Loriet—"Madame Andrée" to the staff—felt differently about it at various times. Twenty years of it and not yet sure…

She loved Simone because, when she had been dumped by her "fellow," Moune had given her some money, and then, eventually, taken her on as masseuse, pedicurist, manicurist, secretary, general gofer and confidante…

And she hated Madame Cervier because, while leading a life of idleness alongside her, in material security, and throwing her the crumbs of her luxury, she made use of her as a laughing stock.

At the moment, she no longer felt anything but her accumulated rancor. Knowing Moune, however, she bowed her head before the threat of the storm.

It was necessary for Madame Cervier, a born coquette and harpy, to have someone to persecute. She had always been in search of slaves. For a long time she had contented herself with animals—dogs, cats, parrots—for want of the lovers she drove mad with the cold shower of her kisses or insults, when it was not actual blows. Suddenly subdued by Jean Cervier and his bestial sovereignty, she had tried hard to take her revenge on her daughters —"the Boss" detested animals—but the daughters took after their mother, and had thus escaped her. She had fallen back on Andrée Loriet, who had surged forth at the opportune moment, and, blowing hot and cold by turns, she martyrized the poor girl, who, like good clay, allowed herself to be pounded without even taking account of it.

When the door had opened, Moune Cervier had been standing in front of the fireplace in a night dress. Mechanically, she was in the process of picking up scattered items of jewelry and piling them into a cup. *A fine heap of cash*, she thought. At the same time, she cast an anxious inquisitorial glance into the mirror: how many wrinkles? Suddenly, she had perceived, reflected behind her, the timid swollen face of her principal maidservant. She had turned round abruptly.

"Well, no! Do you imagine that I'm going to lodge you, feed you and clothe you, not to mention the princely salary and all the little gifts, for you to keep me waiting when I need you? We're leaving at half past eleven and you come at ten, as if you don't know that it takes me at least two hours to get ready!"

"But you told me..."

"Shut up! No lies!"

"Oh!"

"You make me sick, with your quibbling. Things have to change! I told you: five to ten. From now on, you obey, like all the rest. If not, out! Fired!"

The whipped-dog eyes moistened. Madame Cervier, furious, although the sight of tears pleased her, raised her arms to the heavens. "Now she's going to blub into the bargain! That's good. You'd do better to massage me."

37

Nervously, the gentle creature threw her night dress into the middle of the room and threw herself on the bed. She could have added, if the confession had not been too costly, that the greater part of her anger was much less due to Madame Andrée's lateness than to the painful expertise in the middle of which she had surprised her, in front of the mirror. Faded, withered, old...whatever! She was old, in spite of her surgical operations...

It had been necessary to begin, for the third time, to pull up the skin of her cheeks and neck.[13] And her weary muscles, after scarcely three months, were stretching again! Tamed by unguents and electricity, the marks did not show, beneath the curls of her dyed hair; the skin was giving way on one side of her face more than the other, She had been obliged to yield to the evidence; she had a "lop-sided" mouth. Yes, it was imperceptible, or almost, to others, but one more reprise and the stitching would appear, frightfully—an observation so cruel that Madame Andrée tried in vain to pinch, pound and caress, all in her desire to please, the fleshy body. From the adipose abdomen the skilled hands rose to the creases of the soft and crumpled breasts. And yet attempts had been made, with the scalpel and paraffin wax, to raise them up, too, not very long ago. The scars in the armpits said as much.

One innocent remark unleashed la Mounine. "The down hasn't grown back," observed Madame Andrée. "That's a pity for the neckline."

Arms, shoulders, back and torso, with the natural exception of the sagging breasts—Madame Cervier, docile to fashion, was accustomed to showing them all, all the way to the hips.

"You're deluded. It's growing back very well."

"At the sides, yes, but not on the red line."

---

[13] Cosmetic "facelifts," pioneered before the Great War, became very fashionable in the 1920s, and would have been all the rage when the present novel was written.

"So what? Do what you have to do, instead of meddling it what doesn't concern you. It's your fault, anyway, if I'm going downhill!"

"My fault!"

"If you hadn't pushed me to get my breasts lifted, refusing to try the operation on yourself first..."

"Me! I..."

"It's jealousy, isn't it, that's racking you? Because I still have tits and you've never had anything but tobacco pouches! Jealousy, exactly! I'm rich, honored, adulated and I look ten years younger than you, even though we're both pushing fifty..."

"Moune, I swear..."

"Why didn't you submit to the operation before me? I would have known what awaited me, and then, not been so stupid. Yes, if I'd only made you do it first, for the breasts, as for the stomach! But I was too kind. Oh, be charitable and look where it gets you!"

Madame Andrée's indignation suddenly exploded. "It's too much! No, I've had enough! What, I nearly died, and I'm still half impotent, to get rid of my paunch, as a trial, because Madame wanted to see how it worked first! Well, go find another patient!"

Such ingratitude made Madame Cervier start to convulse violently and suddenly found herself sitting up. She was choking.

"How dare you! Speaking like that to your benefactress! Weren't you perfectly content to pocket the ten thousand francs? And you're complaining! How else could you have earned such a sum in an hour? Your paunch!! In thirty years you've never saved that much! Ten thousand francs! Not to mention the comfortable life I've given you. I'm well recompensed! You've had enough, have you? Well, me, too, my girl. I won't keep you! Get out, and faster than that!"

Madame Andrée, exhausted by the outburst of her unaccustomed revolt, lowered her head, trying to hold back her sobs. The tears flowed silently down her wan cheeks.

La Mounine was sated momentarily by the humiliated rage of her victim. Better, after all, to keep the old fool, who was stupid but devoted…as long as she held her tongue…

Magnanimously, Madame Cervier hedged: "You'd prefer to stay, I see? All right…we'll see. I'm quick-tempered, but deep down, all heart. Now get out! I only have an hour. I'll ring after my bath."

She turned on her heel, nobly.

Without making any response, Madame Andrée was watching the naked mass disappear when she remembered that Madame Brunat, the poultry-keeper from Suresnes, and the lady with the mantle were waiting to be received.

"I'd forgotten! They've been there for half an hour."

Without turning round, Madame Cervier snapped: "They're waiting? Let them continue!"

What did Madame Brunat want this time? As for the lady with the mantle, Madame du Marsoy, the wife of the Head Cashier at the bank—Andrée had had no need to pronounce the name—it would be no bad thing to leave her stewing in her uncertainty. To let go of such a chinchilla at that price, the household must be in dire need of money…

Madame Cervier retraced her steps, and weighed a silky fur displayed on the back of a chair in her hand. A bargain: "A hundred thousand…not dear, eh?" And, serene again, she hastened toward her bathroom, singing the latest popular song, reminiscent of the jerky yelping of mad hyenas.

Left alone, Madame Andrée repeated, without obtaining any relief: "Shrew! Dirty shrew! And to think that I was as venomous as her! She changes lovers like chemises, while keeping her old Guimard flannel![14] Tell Cervier? But he

---

[14] Hector Guimard (1867-1942) was the leading proponent of the Art Nouveau style, whose designs expanded from architecture to furniture and textiles, but one of the two further references in the present text to the same surname cannot possibly refer to him, so this reference is almost certainly to a fictitious namesake.

couldn't care less. He amuses himself well enough. Quit the house…?" She would have liked to break with her gilded existence and run away, but bread and board retained her. Find a shoulder to cry on? She was surrounded by none but the indifferent and the jealous, for, unhappy as she was, her lot seemed enviable to others. One idea consoled her. For want of a sensitive heart she would find an obliging ear in the servants' parlor.

Marie was there, checking the diamond clasps on Madame's shoes. Louis was filling a little golden flask with five-hundred-francs-a-bottle cognac, before putting it in Monsieur's attaché case.

Madame Andrée sat down, looking depressed.

"What's up?" asked the manservant, while taking a hearty swig himself from the mouth of the bottle before recorking it carefully. "La Mounine giving you a hard time again?"

"Let it wash over you," advised the chambermaid. She opened the electric cleaner, placed the yellow leather shoes inside, and switched on the mechanical brushes and cloths. "The rich are all swine, anyway."

Madame Andrée raised her head. "When I think," she moaned, "that I allowed my belly to be mangled to give her pleasure, and that she reproaches me for not having had my breasts butchered in her stead! How I'm the cause of all her ills, while the fortunes she spends to rejuvenate herself are just hot air!"

Marie, revolted, agreed, while Louis, still incredulous, protested: "It's true, then, that she used you as a knife-tester? Marie told me that, but all the same…"

Blasé as they were, because they had seen and come into contact with the repugnant underside of the most sumptuous of lives, those people—in whom the habit of domestic service had only served to whet the appetite for independence and, by dint of bad examples, a taste for the natural and the simple—could not get their heads around it this time.

41

Glad to find, beneath the apparent superiority of Madame Andrée, that she was more subservient than them, they started gossiping. At length, they empted the dustbin of rancor, and exhaled the reek of their plaints, which were touching nevertheless. Louis and Marie nourished, bitterly, their sly hostility to the capricious despots who believed that they were quits when they had paid them stingily. "And he has millions that he doesn't know what to do with. No! Father, Mother and Cervier kids—what a family!"

Suddenly, a bell rang; all three looked up at the indicator. A peg fell, and they heard, as if Madame Cervier had entered in person, her authoritarian summons: "Marie! Send Madame Brunat up, and come and help me get dressed."

The rolling corridor deposited them, a minute later, on the threshold of the small drawing room adjacent to the bedroom.

"Come in, Madame Brunat!" someone shouted. "You can tell me what brings you here while Marie fastens my dress. I'm in a hurry."

Very emotional, but with her face obstinately decisive, the poultry-keeper—a peasant clad in her Sunday best for the visit—resisted, intimidated by the presence of a third party as much as the fancy furniture.

"It's just that..."

"Go on, go on! There are no secrets for Marie." She pulled the maid's hair to testify to her confidence, so forcefully that a dolorous scream protested.

"That's nothing. I'm listening."

Madame Brunat let it out abruptly. "It's about the increase, Madame. We've been waiting two months now for Madame's reply. We're doing all we can, the proof of which is that the hens are laying abundantly. My husband's killing himself with work, since you refused us an assistant. Things can't go on like this."

She had made her claim in a single breath, without looking at Madame Cervier. Amazed—such audacity, and in front of a servant too!—la Mounine pulled herself up to the full measure of her short height, and showed her teeth.

"What! What?"

"We're not animals, though. The place doesn't pay enough, as Madame knows very well."

"What! A nice house with four rooms. And your vegetables! When you only had a hut, and poverty, in your province! Me, who's just placed your brother-in-law with friends! And you're not content!"

"That doesn't prevent life from being too dear. Another two hundred francs a month—what's that to you? When one's so rich!"

"Rich! I wouldn't be for long with poor folk like you. Rich! You're very timely! Look, here's a mantle that I've just been forced to buy, out of generosity. Do you know how much I've been asked to pay for it? I daren't say. Madness! No, no, no increase, Madame Brunat. Nothing, for some time. Don't count on it. I need to make savings!"

Madame Brunat, red with disgust and contained anger, looked her in the eye this time, and replied: "It's take it or leave it. Madame can think about it. Either she gives us an increase, or we're leaving at the end of the month. Response by the end of the week. Madame only has to imagine that she's paying a little more dearly for her mantle, out of generosity."

While speaking she had retreated to the threshold, so effectively that before Madame Cervier, thunderstruck, had time to open her mouth, she had disappeared, with a scornful bow.

Marie was secretly jubilant. The farmer's wife had guts!

"What impudence! Did you hear that? She's taking advantage of the fact that we need her! Oh, humankind isn't very pretty!"

A rapid mental calculation had calmed the first impulse, avarice holding sway over offended pride. The Brunats were worth their weight in gold. And even with the increase, they'd be coming cheap. The produce of Suresnes, which was always winning prizes at shows, was also one of the banker's manias, one of the glorifications of his table.

"There! I'm ready. My hat, my veil...Someone's calling—who is it? Go see."

Marie unhooked the telephone receiver, at the same time as Louis appeared at the other end of the wire.

The machine transmitted: "Monsieur the Minister is with Madame du Marsoy in the small drawing room, and asks Madame to come down, please."

"I'm coming. Put the chinchilla back in its box, Marie, and bring it along. Gently! With respect, my girl—that's worth two hundred bills, if you please."

When the precious package had been set on a stool, Marie withdrew, regretfully. Monsieur the Minister was smiling, his weather-beaten face cleared. It would be amusing to watch the bargaining. In front of the huge old man, with the white whiskers of an old tom-cat—a tiger-cat—the lady could try as hard as she liked to preserve her dignity; she was reminiscent of a trapped mouse, her back broken. Poor thing! After all, it would teach her to deck herself out in fancy furs, when other people only had rabbit. If, at least, for want of seeing it, one could listen in? There—behind the door! Marie took up her position, her ear against the keyhole.

Ah, la Mounine: "I'm returning the fur to you, Madame, regretfully. It doesn't suit me..." Oh, the bitch! That's to get a better price!

"So much the worse, my dear, I've just bought it from Madame." Well, well! "Resign yourself, therefore, to making a good deal as well as doing a good deed." A good deed, the bandit! That would astonish me! They've shut up. What was that? Ah! The mouse is on the run!

Marie scarcely had time to hear a bitter: "It only remains for me to thank Monsieur," before the *chambermaid* bell rang. Having allowed a suitable time for her to arrive, the eavesdropper entered, innocently.

"Show Madame out."

As soon as that was done—the poor thing might try to swagger, but her legs were shaking—she ran back to her post. Then, in spite of her confirmed opinion that "They're capable of anything," she started so sharply in her amazement that the blood rushed to her cheeks. She clenched her fists and repeated: "Oh, the pigs! The pigs!"

La Mounine, with the mantle on her back, was preening herself in a queenly manner in front of a Marie-Antoinette looking-glass.

"Yes, not bad—at the price!"

Jean Cervier, with a habitual gesture, was scratching his head: a supposedly meditative mania by which he thought he was concealing his tenacious eczema. Then he cracked his gnarled knuckles, deformed by arthritis.

"Please!" Madame Cervier begged. "You know I can't bear that. It makes one think of skeletons. You got it?"

"You can believe it. And retail."

"Fifty thousand! It's unimaginable. A chinchilla of that beauty, today, must be worth..."

"Three hundred thousand."

She contemplated it admiringly. "I estimated two. How did you do it?"

He looked at her obliquely, knowingly. "I didn't do anything."

"Don't understand."

He explained: "Du Marsoy would be locked up by now if his wife hadn't been reasonable. By paying her fifty thousand for her mantle, I permit a thief first to make restitution, and then to leave my employ with his head held high. Nobody steals from me."

After reflection, she said, regretfully: "All the same, it's rewarding a crime. We could have had the mantle for nothing. I always say it...we're too generous."

"It's necessary to be indulgent to human weakness," he declared, "to be a good prince—not to mention that Du Marsoy knows too many secrets to be strangled without precaution." While she was folding up the mantle he added: "I'll leave you. Come pick me up at noon at the Ministry."

He promised himself to enjoy this escape, after his fatiguing trip to New York. Five days on the beach at Royat, where he was going to take his wife, the children preferring to remain at Garches.

"By the way, remind Marise to be nice to young Jacquemin, since she's invited him to dinner today. She has my instructions."

Naturally. The confidence, the tenderness, all for Marise. Jealous of the predilection that the boss had for his pet, and suffering also, in her decline from the increasing beauty of her daughter, she affected, out of pride, not to let it show. She limited herself to questioning him with a glance—but he was accustomed to keeping all is business dealings from her. And politics was the key to everything...

The amphib—three hundred horsepower and two fins, rolling or flying—had come to rest silently outside the French window. He kissed his wife on the forehead.

"See you soon, my dear." And, stroking the beautiful fur as he went past, he added: "A true investment for the father of a family!"

IV

"Look out! Here come the kids again."

Mériane had, indeed, just appeared on the threshold of the studio. Marise went toward her.

"This is the third time I've told you—I don't want you coming up to my apartment. Stay in your own."

"How nasty you are!"

"And since you don't do as you're told, I'm going to telephone Miss to tell her to lock you in."

The child stamped her foot. "But I only came up to tell you..."

"Go back and play with your cousins. You can see that I'm with friends."

"...To tell you that the musicians have just arrived. I saw them from my window."

At that word, the gang scattered on the divans manifested their joy with animal cries, while bombarding one another with cushions. "Enough over there!" Marise ordered, and grumbled at her sister: "You only had to let Louis telephone me. You're not a commissionaire, so far as I know. We're going to install ourselves in the château. I forbid you to come, if you don't want to be punished..."

"But you'll have it all to yourself! Mother's house is mine as well as yours."

"Papa and Maman have permitted me, while they're away, to receive guests here. You'll understand when you're older. I'm the oldest. Shut up."

Mériane, while sketching a retreat, stood her ground. "Just because you're older, you don't have more rights than me. And since you're throwing me out, that's all right—I won't make you a gift of the golden box you like so much...the lovely little box that friend Guimard gave me..."

"Well, keep it. And go!"

47

Vexed, the little girl took the large staircase, disdaining the elevator, dragging her heels noisily by way of protest. On the first floor she stopped, indecisively. Should she go back to her guests? They didn't amuse her. Mériane thought that they were too childish, especially today, when there were grown-ups around, who were so much fun: Jean de Rancis, her favorite, and Louise Barlot, so comical, and the three Hubertes. She could hear them shouting and laughing loudly.

Pensively, she sat down on the first step of the landing, and refastened her sandal. No, she definitely wouldn't go back to the little ones. The others would soon come down from up there, via the studio staircase, and go across the terraces. The garden was, therefore, the best observatory for her.

Satisfied with that idea, she made her way outside, hopping from one foot to the other.

The Norman house, the domain of Marise and Mériane, was separated from the château by ample plantations of climbing roses and carved yews. It had originally been the main dwelling. Jean Cervier had bought it in 1918, along with the adjoining land, fifteen hectares of park and woodland, for a handful of figs—which is to say, for next to nothing—at the moment when the foolish were fleeing again before the German advance,

A southerner born to make business deals, he had moved on during the fruitful years of the looting, from the small export business he had had before, to be a major importer of all saleable foodstuffs. A fortunate ambush at the outbreak of hostilities, followed by opportune reforms, had permitted him to make millions.

A hero, in his fashion—because he had not hesitated to use dangerous toxins to give him the temporary symptoms of heart disease—he had since deployed in the quotidian struggle the audacity that had once been absent for actual fighting. Making millions from little people, the Banque Cervier had grown in the same fashion, façade by façade, on the Rues Castiglione, Mont Thabor and Tivoli. At the same time, he had constructed at Garches, on ultra-modern plans of a comfort so ingenious that they had no equal in France, the magnificent palace by comparison with which the Norman house, abandoned to his daughters with its ground floor and two upper floors, was no more than a hovel.

Marise had taken over the second floor, which was more independent and more agreeable, with its immense studio. All that she had in common with her sister were the downstairs drawing rooms and dining room; each of the sisters tyrannized a personal chambermaid, and Miss directed the rest of the servants.

It was a treat for Mériane when, on Thursdays and Sundays, she dined at the château. Everything worked by electricity. In the center of the hall there was an enormous oval table in dazzling wood. By pressing an invisible switch, Maman could make it sink into the floor, and then rise up again with appropriate crockery and new dishes. The wine service was also very amusing; the carafes of water and iced champagne were to the right and left of the glasses. A little crystal button was pushed, and lo!—they poured the desired beverage all by themselves. And the recreation room, with its talking colorama, its boudoirs opening on to the dance patio, and the fountain full of perfumed water!

That was not all; there was also, down below, the subterranean hall with its huge swimming pool—a place of special attraction for the children, even though, one after another, they had remained ignorant of its special purpose for a long time. A steam bath provided a pretext on days when agreeable individuals were invited by the husband and the wife. For years, an appetite for enjoyment, overexcited by their frenzy or luxury, had devoured them. Then, their athletic qualities gradually fading, they had dissociated their pleasures.

It was in that school that Marise had been formed. How many times, on coming to say goodnight to her mother, then a fat flirt, had she had been embarrassed to see her wandering around her apartments in the nude, without caring about what the domestics—male or female—might think. Surprised at first, she had quickly got used to it, to such an extent that at eighteen—the exact age when Moune had quite the natal farm for her first debauches—Marise had naturally imitated her...

In asking for permission to give her friends the honors of the château, she had, in any case, refrained from specifying which part. She could see their indignant faces from here, and hear their loud cries! Her parents believed her to be pure and judged themselves to be above reproach, conserving in the eyes of the world, by means of the minimum of appearances it demanded, the necessary respect for convention.

"That was marvelous!" exclaimed Louise Barlot.

They were emerging from a colorama session. Marise had shown them a certain film that she had borrowed from one of her father's friends: *The Secrets of the Convent*. Red-faced and enervated, they needed air and movement. She gave an order to the musicians, whose little orchestra had been installed in a loggia above the patio, from which they could be heard without being seen. They struck up a lullaby.

The couples were already rotating, but Louise Barlot said, regretfully: "We're not vaporizing right away? That would relax me...your film has jangled my nerves."

"Soon. First dance this caline with me."[15]

Marise drew her into the dance. Jean de Rancis had put his arms around the elder Huberte, but at the first step the latter, crossing the path of her sister, arm-in-arm with Jane Hubert, suddenly let go. "Forgive me, I prefer a man. Jane has more...precision than you. My sister will replace me advantageously."

Left standing, he shrugged his shoulders, muttering an obscenity, and then searched with his gaze for the younger Huberte. Disappeared! He found her lying in one of the bou-

---

[15] As with hypothetical vehicles, new drugs and their paraphernalia, and the steam bath, the author improvises names for new dances, sometimes adapting familiar words, as in this instance—*caline* means coaxing or, more brutally, fondling—but sometimes, as with the following dance, employing a more flexible neologistic method.

doirs on a bed. After all, he preferred her to the other one—a Cossack! The younger, without hating "precisions," had more nuances. And provided that one took her imperceptibly, without appearing to touch her...

"Would you like to finish this caline?"

She stretched herself. "Too late. The next one, if you wish."

Jean, compliant, sat down beside her. His eyes never quit her legs, uncovered by the short skirt. At that persistence, Huberte sensed an emotional disturbance invading her.

"Where do you get your stockings? They're not bad."

She would have liked him to examine their finesse at closer range, but the businessman in him eclipsed the delicacy. He estimated the value of the silk rather than palpating it gently. Aggravated, she decided that he was stupid. A second before she had found him pleasing. She elected to lash him with her frankness.

"A present from my lover."

Far from being shocked, Jean de Rancis approved, sensing a business opportunity.

"Do you know how much he paid for them?"

"I don't pay any attention to prices—as long as he pays."

"It's just that I have some admirable ones for sale, even more beautiful than these"—he felt them—"embroidered with an English needlepoint that once belonged to Queen Victoria. I'll show them to you. You can have a pair, if you like."

The last notes of the show dance having faded away into silence, as a strange drumbeat and an allegro rhythm caused the couples to start. From the first bar, the younger Huberte took possession of Jean.

"A sportva. I adore..."

One might have imagined that the breath of the orchestra whipped up a swirl of dead leaves. The rhythm accelerated again. Amid the exclamations, it was as if the young people were carried away by vertigo.

Eventually, out of breath, they tumbled pell-mell on to the divans.

"Oh, I'm so hot!" declared Louis Barlot. "I'm taking off my dress. It's more comfortable in underclothes—too bad for anyone who's shocked. They only have to look the other way."

As soon said as done; she stepped out of her skirt, which fell around her feet, picked it up and threw it, along with her blouse, into a corner of the room.

Exclamations burst forth. "That's hilarious!"

The body appeared under the transparency of her bloomers; the little suspender-belt at the top of her stockings cut darker lines across her thighs.

Louise feigned astonishment, and opened her eyes wide. "What? What's so funny? Am I not made like you?" She looked down at herself. "Oh, it's my suspender-belt and stockings that amuse you? Al right—I'll take them off. I'll be all the better for it."

"Us, too, then!"

And the three Hubertes were unfastening their garments when Marise stopped them. "Don't do that, I beg you. Don't start your follies again, Louise. We can see everything, you know!"

"You wouldn't want me to wear a chemise like my grandmother?"

"No, but I'd like you to get dressed, because I'm expecting someone."

"Who?"

"You know very well—Claude Jacquemin."

"Her admirer!"

"That's true," said Louise. "I'd forgotten about him! You might have invited mine, too—his friend Blanchet. Anyway, for want of him, I'll be content with yours."

As the young people, profiting for her example, had stripped to their underwear, Louis Barlot took possession of Paul de Laume's jacket, put it on inside-out, and thus clad, strutted back and forth, sticking out her rear. "Do you think he'll like me?"

Everybody laughed, all the more so when, at that moment, Louis announced with reproving gravity: "Monsieur Claude Jacquemin-Raimbert."

Surprised by that unexpected explosion of hilarity, Claude hesitated, not daring to advance. Where was Marise, among all these people buried in cushions, shaken by inextinguishable laughter? Finally, he perceived her as she raised her head. She tried to speak to him, but was unable to say anything except: "Oh, Louise!" Her speech was cut short every time she looked at her in her grotesque pose.

It was Mademoiselle Barlot who, having savored her success sufficiently, advanced toward Claude and extended her hand to him.

"Excuse these children! Bonjour—how is your friend Georgi?"

Finally, Marise was able to make the introductions. Her cordiality could not succeed in dissipating the malaise of the ridiculous welcome. In vain, lying down again, she indicated a small space next to her.

Embarrassed, he fetched a stool and sat down. A chill; a few banal remarks…he felt like an intruder in the midst of that lax menagerie, and suddenly regretted having come. How could she enjoy herself in such company?

Fortunately, the music came to Marise's rescue.

"You dance, don't you?"

"Of course."

Already, the couples, glad to be liberated, had re-formed. He took her by the waist, feeling the young body abandon itself entirely in his hands. How sweet it was to be holding her in his arms like that! He no longer saw anyone else, religiously following the musical ritual, every measure bringing him audacity and a pretext to hold her a little more tightly, to breathe in the perfume of her hair and her skin. Marise's face was so close to his own that he bit his lips in order to resist the mad desire to press them against her smiling mouth. He thought that he no longer had ground to stand on when the music stopped.

"A cocktail?" she proposed.

The band had rediscovered its exuberance. Between dances the automatic bar poured its flames of iced alcohol over the fire, so effectively that, with the aid of the heat and the excitement, they were soon all a little drunk. Maris and Claude looked at one another.

For the sake of politeness, he had invited the two Poursaillons du Vigan to dance, in turn, but, disgusted by their fashion of delivering themselves to the man under cover of surrendering to the dance, he had returned rapidly to Marise, whose restraint charmed him. He did not know that she belonged to the category of those women whose caprice and amorality are capable of anything, even elegance.

For form's sake, she darted a scandalized glance at the three Hubertes, who, decidedly drunk, had begun to intone a song fashionable in the cabarets:

It's our glor-ee
To have a lick-ee
Without getting squiff-ee!

They emphasized the ls, as was appropriate, and finished each line with a shrill cry. The others joined in the chorus. She turned her back on them and, questioning Claude with an indulgent smile, had no difficulty in persuading him to sit down again, this time on the same divan. She contemplated him flirtatiously.

"Come closer, and tell me why you seem sad."

"Sad? Perhaps...mostly astonished."

"You never rediscover your childish soul?"

"Oh, yes—when I'm with my family..."

"Why, with me it's the opposite! It's true that given my mother's character..."

"She loves you though?"

"Y...es—but not as much as a nice dress."

"And your father?"

"More than my mother, less than his money...but I forgot that I'm talking to the son of a political enemy!"

"Here, Mademoiselle, if you'll permit, I'm only your friend—a...fervent friend."

"Oho! You're not going to tell me that you love me?"

"But yes! Ardently!"

"Is that a declaration? Be careful. We mustn't have any ideas in common. It's true that in matters of love, ideas..."

He did not perceive, so blinded was he by the glare of her insolent eyes, the grossness of the implication. He gave it the appearance of his own soul. Intelligent as she was, how could she be disinterested in the very foundation of life, in the substance of all communion?

She went on: "I'm probably shocking you. Aren't you...Paul de Laume told me...a poet?"

"An old-fashioned one, in his view?"

"That's true. You can see that I'm being frank..."

"Frank? You'll answer a question, then?"

A preoccupation was tormenting him—not so much the material instruction regarding the reasons for Jean Cervier's trip to New York as anxiety about a quip by Georgi: "Since you're dining with the Cervier girl, ask her about her American."

Without divining that, Marise was following the labor of his thought. She was wary. "That depends on the question."

"Why did you go to America?"

"Oh! Explanations, already?"

"Was it because of this American?"

The harshness of the tone disconcerted her. In sum, the innocent was baroque, but disagreeable. He really had fallen from the moon. Jealous! It was laughable. Such a novelty, in a young man, was as flattering as it was bewildering, though. It would be amusing to string him along.

She played the innocent, and to begin with, the offended. "What do you think? Stupid gossip. It was simply to accompany Papa that I made the trip. There! Are you content?"

"Not yet. I've been told that it was a matter of a project-ed divorce..."

"Go on!"

"And a possible marriage, subsequently, for you..."

She laughed. The night of the trial, the *hors-d'oeuvre*...

In a sincere tone, she said: "Oh, no thanks! One meeting was sufficient for me."

He breathed out, and changed tack. "Interesting all the same, New York?"

"Very. Not a minute to ourselves. Never left Papa's side: visits to factories, official banquets, business dinners..."

"Really?"

She sensed that he was still suspicious, and wanted to convince him, without perceiving that, in order to conceal her own game, she was revealing her father's.

"Since I tell you so! We stayed with his friend, Cooly, who has power of attorney for the Sudekys. That doesn't mean anything to you? Hartmann and Sudeky—the Austro-German bankers. Entirely a matter of oil...a consortium to form...what do I know? There, you see..."

Claude reflected. She took advantage of that to exchange a glance with Chanteroy, who, with a guitar in his hand, was brandishing it like a tomahawk, as if to bring it down on the head of the bore. She sent him a signal, rubbing her cheek with the back of her hand, and then instantly resumed her pose.

Claude raised his head again. "New York! That's a city I'd love to see with you."

"Papa's going back in a fortnight, for the final settlement of the French debt. We could take you. That would look good in the wireless dispatches: 'Departures: Monsieur Jean Cervier, Minister of Finance, and his secretary, Monsieur Claude Jacquemin, son of the celebrated Statesman...'"

He measured the ditch suddenly excavated, ineptly dis-entangling the offer concealed beneath the joke. Impossible! Everything separated them. And yet, how simple it would be if she were to consent to change camp, to quit this repulsive milieu, this family and these friends, who would have degraded her if her pride had not kept her safe, like a heroine in the mud...

He riposted: "Why not, instead: 'Departures: Monsieur Claude and Madame Marise Jacquemin'?"

She burst out laughing. "You go quickly!"

Maliciously yielding the terrain, Paul de Laume and his two lieutenants had disappeared with Jane Hubert. Marise, while continuing her maneuver with Claude, had observed, anxiously, the successive departure of her guests. The only ones remaining, gathered on the edge of the fountain, where odorous jets of water were falling back noisily, were Louise Barlot and the two Hubertes.

Marise was beginning to find the time hanging heavily. She regretted having invited Claude to dinner. A blunder, with such a fellow—pleasant, but from another age. Oh, without that obligation to be amiable...how could she get rid of him politely?

At the given moment, Louise Barlot came to her aid. She hailed Marise from afar, apologetically. "Pardon me for disturbing your conversation but we have to go—an urgent word to say first to the mistress of the house."

Marise went to join her.

"We've had enough of your Jacquemin! He's intolerable. Send him away—find a pretext. We'll go wait for you at the Vapo. The others are there already."

"You know how to turn up the heat?"

"Don't worry...see you soon." She drew the two Hubertes away. "Adieu, young lovers!"

V

Claude, glad finally to be alone with Marise, took her hand and drew her toward him to sit her down next to him—but with a decisive gesture, she took refuge on the stool. Claude gazed at her profoundly. Bored with the chore that she had to do, she seemed to him to be emotional. She was simply thinking: *Will he cut the bridge?*—and also: *Whether he likes it or not, he has to go!*

A residue, not of modesty but of respect for convention, caused her to desire that Claude remain ignorant, and that only the initiates knew what might go on, with her parents' consent, in the Garches steam-bath. The pleasure that she promised herself there held sway over the new sentiment that Claude's originality had awakened in the depths of her unconscious. She decided to deliver the blow without further delay.

"I'm sorry…I didn't know how to tell you…to apologize…"

He thought that she was making allusion to the strange behavior of her friends, and protested: "I've never confused you with those simpletons. Nothing else matters but the rest of the evening, spent with you…"

She disillusioned him, categorical beneath her simulation of regret.

"Exactly! It's just that it's necessary for us to renounce that little fête for today. I haven't dared tell you yet…a case of *force majeure*: my grandmother is very ill, and Maman, obliged to go away, has asked me to go and dine with the old lady, and to give her news, this very evening.… I've already sent the others away. They don't matter—with regard to you, it's annoying. The first time I've invited you…"

He kissed her hand

"Too bad! You'll compensate me, that's all, by giving me, if I'm not being indiscreet, a few minutes more."

She consulted her watch-ring. "It's just that…I only have ten minutes."

She stood up.

He retained her. "Well, give them to me."

"Gladly," she murmured. *In five minutes*, she thought, *I'll throw him out*. A small ransom, in sum, for her reconquered liberty.

Claude thanked her. The thought that she might be getting rid of him by means of a ruse never crossed his mind. He was so forcefully habituated to truthfulness that in the absence of evidence, he never realized that other people were lying.

Deceit was an octopus devouring the majority of souls, against which his optimism, never discouraged, incessantly collided. His enemies said of him: "He's a courageous imbecile." Only his intimates, and rare individuals not entirely possessed by the demon of egotism, were able to perceive the moral elevation and generosity concealed beneath the candor of solid and charming youth. He always gave credit to begin with, though, and the credit he had opened to Marise was, like his sentiment, unlimited.

"You didn't reply to me just now," he resumed, obstinately.

"When?"

"When I told you that, in my dreams, you accompany my future…"

"Wrong—I replied that your dreams were going very quickly. A veritable lightning bolt!"

"Don't joke," he begged, with all his heart. "I love you…"

He seemed more comical than touching. "How unoriginal you are! 'I love you!' No one says that any longer today. And it means even less. 'I love you!' What does it signify?"

"The entire gift of the self."

"How many times have you repeated that pretty phrase already?"

"Never, Marise!"

"Forgetful? Or deceitful? I'll give you the choice."

"Neither."

"What do you say to your mistresses, then?"

"I have none."

"Are you ill?"

"I don't believe so. Does it seem to you to be absurd that I've never had adventures, and that I don't want to have any other woman than the one I've chosen for life?"

Marise hesitated between shrugging her shoulders and bursting out laughing. She contented herself with interrogation, caught, in spite of herself, by the astonishing unexpectedness of such a revelation of character.

"What a joke! You've never…participated in the act of love?"

"No, Mademoiselle. Have you?"

"I'm a young woman."

"And I'm a young man."

"Exactly!"

"What do you mean, *exactly?* You think that a man can and ought to besmirch his youth before the sanctity of the vital union? You think, because it's the tradition, that it's necessary and just that we wear away before marriage our beliefs, our faith, our enthusiasm to be new, our health, even, against more-or-less withered bodies? I don't have any taste for prostitution, even under the mantle of pleasure. Although I might appear very stupid to you, the most beautiful body wouldn't tempt me, if I sensed that the soul was absent."

Marise was no longer thinking about her friends. Engrossed in the debate, she riposted: "You're behind the times, my dear. Your dreams have got the bit between their teeth, but are going backwards! They're taking you back to Edenic times. By virtue of a woman's sin, or rather a man's—no reproach intended—times have changed. You—oh, not you, but all those who don't resemble you—have ended up, although it took centuries, inculcating your humble slaves, as it were, with a taste for liberty and the means of making use of it. Whether you like it or not, girls have followed the example of boys. They live like them, increasingly. That's a fact to which

60

it's necessary to resign yourselves, you men, since, all things considered, it's your doing. And it's a fact that, the moment it's admitted, does no harm to anyone."

"A fact, yes, but, on the contrary, one that, in lessening the moral value of all, harms everyone—not only individuals, but society in its entirety."

"Does that refer to you alone?"

"I don't have that pretention. I'm counting on good wills like ours, and time, to reestablish the equilibrium that has been broken."

"Which men have broken! And which we'll reestablish in the equality of the sexes! It's funny—here I am, more feminist than the son of Annik Raimbert!"

He looked at her, surprised by such conviction in error. Another Marise appeared beneath the one that had blindfolded him...

He rejected the discovery, and conceded: "An appearance of equilibrium, admittedly—in reality, a profound crisis, but a temporary one, I'm certain. The vicious circle in which the desire of men and the salacity of women turn..."

"Thanks!"

"The bargain of the offer and the demand will disappear, as reciprocal fidelity becomes habitual. The verity lies in both arriving, young and chaste, at the threshold of the regained Paradise. It's in beginning life together, in step and with the same heart. The Couple—there, that's equilibrium! It's in the selection of choice, for the perfection of the species, not in the liberty of dogs in heat. Are you, who proclaim the right of young women to what is conventionally called the bachelor life, going to tell me that you put it into practice?"

"Why not?"

"No!"

"But yes, if it pleases me! My parents, like those of Louise Barlot, are obliged to leave me my freedom. Louise simply does whatever she wants, like a man."

He thought it was bravado, more braggadocio than viciousness. "Get away! Deep down, instinct informs you that to live magnificently, it's necessary not to disperse oneself. A sentiment like love is only powerful if it remains unique."

"Not at all of your opinion! It's necessary to banish love from our sentiments, as it has already been banished from our language, if not our literature. Love? An act, I assure you—a simple act. And which, with a few...precautions, is of no more importance than any other."

"What a paradox! What about the race?"

"What about nature? It doesn't have to be cluttered up with complications in order to endure."

He attempted to show her the absurdity of the illogicality. "Precisely. It endures because it doesn't take the...precautions of which you speak."

"So what? Some misfortune if there are fewer children! You, who have such beautiful machines at Chesnay, it's said, that will do all by themselves the work that once required thousands of hours and hands, can't think that the birth-rate is so important! Let things be! Fundamentally, all men, except for eccentrics of your sort, are adapting very well to our new mores. The exchange before the contract...made, besides, with fewer clauses. Free union—and with fewer consequences, as you ought to be the first to praise—is in the process of relegating marriage to the lumber room of prejudices. There's nothing but pleasure!"

She found his amazement so funny that she burst out laughing. "It's the world turned upside down, isn't it? You remind me of a little girl. And I seem frightening to you, like a boy?"

"A little...yes."

"But there are thousands like that today."

"So much the worse for tomorrow."

"Or so much the better! Be careful—you're swimming in romanticism. Twin souls! What remedy do you offer to those who don't find one? Suicide or religion?"

"Someone once said: 'Seek, and ye shall find.'"

She concluded, provocatively: "We're in agreement, my dear Messiah—save for the object of the search."

The deep-seated incomprehension manifest beneath the superficial gloss of intelligence, and the complete opposition of their views, gradually convinced him. An insurmountable obstacle separated him from loving that lovely body, those bright eyes, those lips whose voluptuous sinuosity stirred him dolorously, in contrast to the hostile voice. So great was his chagrin, though, that he strove not to blame her. Was she not right about one thing? That was the slavery from which license was born; Marise was merely a result of that.

She had stood up. He did likewise.

"You find me quite ridiculous, don't you?" he said.

"No, merely backward. With your unique, durable, definitive possession you put me in mind of a savage who doesn't want to eat out because he has a delicate stomach."

"The simple desire of an absolute being only wanting to live absolutely. I don't suppose you know the saying of Guizot's..."[16]

"The Louis-Philippard! Didn't I say that you're behind the times...?" She had a desire to tell him to go to hell, but, at the same time, was amused by a sharp curiosity. "Say it anyway."

He quoted, with all his fervor: "*I only have mediocre desires and only entertain high hopes. I can do without that which I lack, but cannot be content to lower my ambition.*"

---

[16] François Guizot (1787-1874) was a prominent figure in French politics before the 1848 Revolution, who worked hard to sustain the constitutional monarchy established after the July Revolution of 1930, and was notorious for his opposition to extending the voting rights to men who did not own property. He also remains famous for coining the oft-repeated (albeit with minor variations of timing and political complexion) judgment that a person who is not a republican at twenty lacks a heart, while one who remains one at thirty lacks a head: not a sentiment of which Amédée, Annik or their author could have approved.

"All proud people think that! The difficulty lies in defining what is mediocre and what isn't. Ambition has as many aspects as life. Everything depends on the point of view."

"The higher one looks, the less chance there is of being mistaken..."

Shadow and light, they confronted one another in the disturbance of their sentiments like night and day opposed in the confusion of dusk, in the eternal combat of enemy forces. He sensed that she was so distant that he would have liked to seize her, indoctrinate her, convince her...but in the meantime, a bitterness rose within him, the fear that she might really be what she had just shown him...

"I've given you ten minutes," she said. "And we've talked so long that I only just have time to go and get dressed..."

He saw her lost, clinging on. "Where does your grandmother live? I'd be glad to be able to go with you..."

"It's just that my friends are waiting for me. We have an errand to run together first..."

The patio door, opening noisily at that moment, cut short the: *No, it's too much!* with which she mentally punctuated the dismissal. At the gallop, young men and women, half-naked in towels rolled into loincloths, with their faces masked by washcloths, surrounded Claude and Marise, brandishing a broom, a long-handled brush, feather duster and a watering can. They disappeared as they had entered, all howling; "First warning!"

"What cretins!" she shouted. "They're drunk...I swear to you..."

Mutely, he looked at her so reproachfully that she fell silent, disconcerted. She hesitated momentarily between the utility of soothing a potential adversary and her pleasure...

Bah! If the simpleton suffers a little...

She opted, conclusively, for the vapo. "*Au revoir.* Don't take the trouble to wait for me. I'll go to my grandmother's alone. First, I have to throw those drunkards out."

He persisted, curious to see how far she would take the duplicity. "Do that. I won't go without seeing you again."

She sketched an ironic: "Please yourself," and went out, without paying any further heed to him.

By the time the rolling staircase had taken her to the tepidarium, she was no longer thinking about anything but the relief of her deliverance. Hurrahs welcomed her.

"At last! We were going to come back up stark naked in five minutes!"

"Idiots! I told him that you were waiting for me before going…"

"What have you done with him?"

"He's ruminating upstairs. I suppose he'll go when he's had enough."

She plunged delightedly into her quotidian atmosphere as she relaxed in the humid heat. Already, the Hubertes and Jean de Rancis had assailed her and undressed her. A torpor weighed beneath the low vault. Mist blurred the naked bodies. From the torrid sudatorium, where Louis Barlot was in the process of sweating in air so dry it was burning, the voice of Henri Chanteroy, intoning an Arabic song, became deafening. On the edge of the swimming bath, where the fresh water was quivering, animated by perpetual renewal, Jane Hubert and Paul de Laume were lying fraternally side-by-side on the warm flagstones. They held out their cocktail glasses to Jean de Rancis, recklessly, in order for him to fill them with a further dose of iced scopo.

"How good it is," sighed the esthete, rounding out imaginary spheres in the air with a limp hand. "Speak, Jane."

She had resumed her frightful confidences, amplified by the drug. Paul was listening to them without hearing them. On their worn organisms, its ravages were more terrible than those of morphine or cocaine would once have been. Scopolamine, emptying the souls before the bodies, killed more surely and more rapidly that those outmoded poisons.

Sufficiently degreased, Louise Barlot ran forward. "Pass me the bottle!"

But Jean de Rancis had recorked the precious phial. He could never procure enough of it for Paul de Laume's liking. It sometimes required all the impunity attached to that name for him to succeed in unearthing it without risking prison.

"There's ouabaine,[17] if you want it. I have your box in the left-hand pocket of my jacket...yes, there...and go gently; it's almost as difficult to find..." He had paid a thousand francs a gram for it.

"Ouaba is just as good!" said Louise, offering her box around, after having stuffed her nose. The Poursaillons and Chanteroy imitated her. Only Marise and Jean de Rancis, a shrewd supplier, abstained. She considered that it was necessary to have no imagination to make use of those poor stimulants. In any case, strophanthin, of which that one was full, was dangerous to the heart.

Now, lying on the marble slabs, everyone fell silent, except for Jane Hubert, who was emptying her word-sack without pause. In silence, Marise savored their multiplied drunkenness: a sly silence, as before a storm; an apparent immobility, coupled with sighs, feline stretchings, words as if pronounced in a dream...

Suddenly, a clear protest:

"No! Not that..."

Shoving Jean de Rancis away, Marise activated her flagstone, which slid to the edge of the swimming bath. She leapt in. Jean followed her. Upright in the water, facing him, she no longer feared anything. She allowed herself to be enlaced, as she had some while before for the sportva. They spun, with evident pleasure. One might have thought them two supple beasts, playing without malice.

Marise, still a virgin in the narrow sense of the word, took pleasure in the contact. She had no hidden agenda. Give herself to Jean de Rancis? Never! Nor to any of her male

---

[17] The cardiotonic glucoside ouabaine, or strophanthin, whose principal effect is to slow the heartbeat and reduce blood pressure, has even less obvious potential as a recreational drug than the belladonna alkaloid scopolamine, but whatever turns one on....

friends. She wanted more than their superficial kisses. The image of Claude mingled with the pleasure of the sensation, without her driving it away.

Him, yes, perhaps. Only someone passionate, someone ardent—in sum, "someone," into whom she would dig her claws, to grip him hard...

The arrogant image of Max de Laume passed through her memory. Old, yes, but important! She hated him since he had replied to her advances with an insolent: "Too old for me!" What did he need, then, by way of youth? Mériane?

And she detached herself tranquilly from Jean de Rancis, who had become maladroit again.

"Nothing to do with me, my lad. I buy, I don't sell."

As she emerged from the water, to pick up a peignoir, she could not help hearing Huberte the second, who had just shoved Henri Chantenoy away violently.

"You're intolerable! Be content with what you're given. The rest is private property, my dear!"

"First I've heard..."

"Don't tell anyone about it."

"About what?" asked Marise, who had caught the last two remarks on the wing.

But the younger Poursaillon signaled to her with a pressing gaze. Marise was, in fact, thus far, the only one who knew her friend's secret, and that Jean Cervier had recently made her his wife. She passed on without blinking, thinking about Claude, only saying to herself: *I hope he's gone.*

He had, in fact, gone, after the five minutes he had given her in the hope of seeing her return—but he had run into Mériane, who was emerging, red-faced and anxious, from a door to the basement. Having been seen, she had thrown herself backwards. Hazard had dictated that a discontented voice had called out at the same time from the terraces: "Mériane! Mériane!"

The governess, doubtless.

"I'm here, I'm coming!"

"It's high time! We're eating without you."

The child ran past Claude. He stopped her.

"Pardon me, lovely Mériane. Where's your sister? She invited me to..."

"Oh, if you're invited, I'll tell you. But it wasn't me who told you, you understand!"

He promised.

"Well, she's in the swimming pool, with the others."

"What swimming pool?"

"Ours, of course—in Papa's house, down below."

"Would you be kind enough to tell her...?"

"No! I can't!"

"Why not?"

"They're all naked! They don't know that I've seen them."

"How?"

The child assumed a self-important expression, and, mysteriously, showed him the entrance to the cellars...

"There's a place where there's a crack. One can see everything."

"That's not good!"

"Why not? They're not doing any harm; they're amusing themselves kissing."

Claude received the blow without flinching. A furious disgust filled him...

"Mériane! Mériane!" called the voice again, severely.

"I'm coming! *Au revoir*, Monsieur. I'll tell Marise that I ran into you, but you won't say anything, will you? What's your name?"

"Claude," he snapped, and then, as if tearing himself away, departed so abruptly that the child thought: *Perhaps he's a thief!* Tremulously, she started to run, proud of her adventure.

VI

Claude, having parked his airplane under the hangars of the landing-stage, went in search of Gine and Sylvestre. A childish despair had made his heart swell. He detested, in Marise, the cruelty of love.

He went through the former kitchen garden of the old Blanchet house, transformed into a field of study, with a laboratory and a workbench for testing the motors of the small items of apparatus with which Georgi never stopped tinkering. Claude was hoping to find his sister there. When she came to Versailles she never budged from that corner, taking an interest in the engineer's labors as in the most passionate of pleasures.

The door was closed. No one there! Disappointed, he headed toward the house to make enquiries of the old nurse, Nane, who was now the cook, and who, having seen him, was waiting for him on the threshold of the vestibule.

"The demoiselles are at Buc with Monsieur Georgi."

"Ah!"

"There's only Madame. She'll be happy to see you, Monsieur."

On cue, the door to the small drawing room opened. Monique appeared. Past forty, she was radiant in her maturity, like the mildness of autumn sunlight on the sheen of a beautiful fruit. She kissed Claude on the cheek affectionately.

"I thought that it was my husband. He ought to be returning today after his course at the Collège de France—and it's already almost six o'clock. Will you be dining with us, Claude?"

"If you don't mind...."

"Ceremonious? Since when?" She was about to scold him when, by the tone of bitterness that showed through his remark, she understood that he was upset. Another trick of the Cervier girl? Garches, then?"

69

He made an evasive gesture. She divined that he was so mortified and so sad in his renewed anger that she did not persist.

"A walk in the park? A little music?"

Maternally, she sympathized with the sentiment of the young ones, which he penetrated with the aid of an intuition that was still young, and the memory—so distant now—of her past excitement: lessons of experience that never inform others and from which so few obtain any personal profit. She was not surprised to hear Claude refuse; it was still necessary for him to go to Chesnay.

"...To get news of little Mureau, the daughter-in law of one of my best foremen. A stupid accident...the right thumb severed yesterday."

"One of your machines?"

What was she thinking? She knew, however, that at Chesnay, since he had finished improving the machine tools, there had been no more accidents. He was so proud of that progress! Good business as well as an act of kindness; the return of the new machines increased profits, and the reserve stock was increasing, while the retirement fund...

He protested: "Come on! If the Mureau girl worked at Chesnay..."

"So I thought..."

He explained, briefly: a worker in the Marnand shoe factory...she had been an apprentice there when her mother had remarried...

"She stayed there, unfortunately for her. A nice girl...and as I like Mureau..."

He believed that he had really discovered that obligation, about which he had not spared a thought two hours earlier. An unconscious need for movement, for forgetfulness. His métier was, along with the parental propaganda, the second great interest of his life, and remained to him, he told himself, in spite of Marise—in opposition to Marise.

"Come back quickly! My husband will be glad to have a chat with you before dinner."

Claude promised. He loved, in Georges Blanchet, the philosopher who, succeeding his master Vignabos, whose wisdom he had inherited, sowed bounty and measure. He would have liked him to be a little less skeptical, but how many people were capable of that courage, that generosity to those he cherished and admired above all others? His mother and father! When Claude had said "my elders" he had said it all; when addressed them as *tu* and called them by their fore-names, Amédée and Annik, as if they were friends of the same age, a fervor ennobled his familiarity...

The sudden bound of his apparatus as it took off, the still-vibrant intoxication of the vertical climb—still new—tore him away from his thoughts. He flew at lightning speed over the molehill of Versailles and Trianons, the minuscule check-erboard of châteaux and parks. The automatism of action had gripped him again when, perceiving the large glass roofs of the Chesnay factories, which the setting sun was painting red, he veered almost immediately for the descending plunge.

In the center of the enclosure and the buildings, a vast courtyard offered its sandy carpet. He set down there without a shock. At the sight of him, a boy of about fifteen with an alert expression, pink with cleanliness and health, who was reading a sporting newspaper under the windows of the supervisor's office, leapt up from the stone bench and ran to meet him.

"Bonjour, M'sieu Claude! The team has beaten the Guépards five-three. And did you read about the foot race at Clamart? The factory broke the thousand meter record!"

Fanfan Mureau, known as "P'tit gars," had two dreams: to graduate from primary school to the Lycée and to become a winger at rugby. Claude encouraged him, glad to see in the boy a return of the equilibrium broken by his elders, who were too uniquely sportive: an exclusive cult of strength to the det-riment of intelligence, which so much religious patronage had utilized, capturing the soul via the body.

"Your father isn't here? With your sister, perhaps?"

71

"She has a slight fever. So, as he's taken a quarter of an hour's leave, I've taken his place. Don't worry—I can hear all the telephones from here. Shall I call him?"

They went into the office. The adolescent had already put his hand on the switchboard. He looked at Claude with the assurance of a small adult and the affectionate submission with which everyone at the factory regarded their chief.

"No need, P'tit gars. I'll go over there. Stay at your post."

He stroked the beardless cheek with his hand. He liked it when people served him as he would have done himself, and was not astonished that, following his example, young Mureau took his responsibilities seriously. Had he not, at thirteen, been the editorial secretary of the *Maison de Toutes*,[18] when his mother, with the collaboration of Mademoiselle Hardy, had launched the periodical from which the Work—with its head-quarters of Paris and all the provincial branches—had sprung? A powerful organization that permitted single or unfortunate women to find, in every big city, a temporary roof, the materi-al support and the moral guidance they needed. The others came to it by virtue of the attraction of lectures, the recreation of books, and sports.

At a brisk pace he went to the open-air playing fields, scattered with groups running, doing gymnastics and swim-ming in pools. They were noisy with bathers. He reached the dwellings of the workers. The small houses with their lines of bright facades and pink roofs, in the great orchard of small gardens, the coming and going of men off shift, the house-wives washing or sewing on the doorsteps, gave the customary impression of a peaceful hive. He rejoiced in such order, and

---

[18] This phrase, meaning "a house for all" was adopted by Fourierist utopians from the French version of *Isaiah* 56:7 to summarize their futuristic dreams, and probably made its way into standard French socialist parlance, and hence into Margueritte's work, from there, although it has been employed by other charitable institutions.

darted an amicable glance at the central edifice constructed on his initiative, containing the co-operative stores, the library, and vast lecture rooms and reading rooms, adjacent to the cinema-theater and the gallery for indoor games.

Thanks to his good understanding with the Baronne Plombino's lawyer, Monsieur Lourmal—a blockhead who was director in name only, with a preponderant voice for which Claude was glad to serve as the loudhailer—he had been able to modernize, while humanizing it, the establishment founded seven years previously by the repentant banker.

The principal of such co-operation—the workers owned a third of the capital, in complete liberty, and received half the dividends and benefits, with equal representation on the administrative board—had seemed revolutionary then. Claude had no illusions about the motives of the donor: doubtless a prudent concession to conquering social ideas, insurance taken out against an even more popular future, more than a disinterested creation. Even so, he pardoned the memory of the founder—one of the great profiteers who had flourished during the last war—in favor of such a contribution to the work of peace. After having turned out so many shells, it was a sign of the times that a Plombino, changing objectives, had civilized his steel factory.

He rang the doorbell of a ground floor florid with sweet peas. Mère Mureau, a rounded brunette, lively and energetic, welcomed him like the Messiah. Monsieur Claude had an innate science! And not proud, for all that—for a boss.

"Well?" he asked.

"The physician's been and gone. He says that after the injection he's given her, there's nothing to fear—there's only that poor hand!"

Claude nodded his head; he was already at the bedroom door. With the visual gift that served his memory so well, he registered the neat room at a glance, with its awning, its cleanliness and its white bed. Museum photographs decorated the pink-plastered walls. Hand in hand with in her father, who was standing by the bedside, the injured girl was trying to smile at

73

him. Slightly red-faced, pretty in spite of her tormented thinness, she sat up, straightened up, somewhat confused. He replaced her gently on the pillow, and then turned to Mureau, who was striving to put a brave face on things.

"Bonjour, old chap. I saw Monsieur Lourmal this morning. He's a friend of the Marnands. Your daughter needn't worry. The insurance will pay the maximum. The Messieurs won't mind, in any case..."

"Of course!" said Mureau, who sensed, by the tone of Monsieur Claude's voice, that they were thinking along the same lines. "A severed thumb costs less than new machines!"

Hatred welled up in him, at the contrast between the methods of Chesnay and the primitive routine that subsisted in the Marnands' factory, as in so many others. Many industrialists preferred to keep their old apparatus, so long as they could still sweat gold from fatigue and danger. The misery of others counted for nothing in the balance of their enrichment. The yoke of ancient serfdom, which, to complete the harshness, they thought just.

"You see, Monsieur Claude, "there are those for whom the peace hasn't changed anything. It's just another ongoing war. And it's always the same ones who take the risks!" He indicated, with a sideways glance, his left sleeve rolled up over the stump of his limb.

Amicably, Claude englobed the father and daughter with the same sympathy; he would have liked her to find employment at Chesnay, with her brother, but she had had her habits and her friends at Marnands'. Anyway, there was nothing for it now but to take her away, for the better.

"Don't torment yourselves," he said. "There's a place for you here. As soon as you're better..." He turned to the mother, who was weeping. "Console yourselves with the thought that she might have had a more serious accident!"

He had esteem for those poor folk, and amity for the overseer, one of the best at the factory, active, intelligent and fair. Mutilated at twenty-five, in the second offensive at Champagne in 1918, and gassed so cruelly that he had been tubercular for a long time, Mureau, who was scarcely fifty, would have seemed an old man if the vivacity shining in his eyes had not corrected the roundness of the back and the wan complexion.

"That's what I said to the girl. What's a finger? Me, I left five, and the arm with them, in the saucepans. It hasn't prevented me from keeping ours boiling. Isn't that so, Mélie?"

"For sure," agreed the housewife, maternally.

"We'll find her a little corner in the office," Claude promised, "until she can find, in her own time, the husband of her choice."

Louise Mureau shook her head, her face willful beneath her unkempt hair. She was obstinate in wearing it long, in spite of the gibes of her workmates, most of whom had short curls. "No hurry! And anyway, now..." Bitterness enlivened her gaze, as if some confused chimera had been wounded in her, at the same time as her flesh.

"Be tranquil, now," Claude instructed. "And be brave."

"I am."

He went out, accompanied by Mureau, whose mask of enthusiasm disappeared as soon as they were outside. All the bad luck in his life suddenly impregnated his ashen face, the crushing sensation that he felt, along with millions of others making up the immense, obscure host of survivors, every time he thought about the rolling-press of the war: his youth lost, all of his human existence diminished and soiled...

He apologized. "It's the accident, you see. It reminded me...oh, you're lucky you who won't know that—war!"

"Let's hope so, Mureau."

"You're not sure?" groaned the worker. "Oh, well, let them come back, the flesh-merchants! We'll have theirs first! But no, it's not credible, such a thing, today. If my boy had to..."

The little automated carts extended under the hangars alongside which they were passing, an entire regiment of profound ranks. The long lines of half-harrows offered, in their brilliant networks, the image of fecund furrows to be turned tomorrow. Like Mureau, Claude smiled at the vast future, the labor that would enlarge it further. They had arrived next to the helic on which the apprentice overseer was keeping watch in the center of the courtyard.

"Monsieur Brunet has relieved me."

"Go and play, then, P'tit gars."

Claude took his leave of the father and the son with a cordial wave. He lingered for a minute more, enveloping the monumental courtyard and the silent buildings with a rapid inspection. Only a cheerful whistling emerged through the open window of the office. At that hour, there was no one left in the factory but a duty foreman and the usual watchmen making their rounds.

Thus, reduced to six hours of labor, in conformity with the law proposed by Amédée Jacquemin, the day ended cheerfully for the little people. Instead of an insatiable dream, the hearth juxtaposed with the factory had become, at Chesnay—while awaiting that benefit to spread throughout France—a tangible reality.

Lying at Monique's feet on the grass, like vast lilies, Sylvestre and Gine, patched the fresh green of the grass with the white of their dresses, while the flowers of a late-blooming acacia fell like odorous snow. Their heavy clusters embalmed the gilded evening.

Claude and Georgi were standing nearby, to either side of Monsieur Blanchet. Still sacerdotal, he had grown stouter without losing any of his smiling irony. Happy, since any subject of discontent between his wife and himself had long since vanished, he savored without reserve the sweetness of complete conjugal good fortune, and the pride, no less sweet of having both succeeded in what they, in common with Annik and Amédée Jacquemin, considered to be the most important of human tasks: the education of their children.

There was one single dark spot in their blue sky: the passionate intransigence of Sylvestre's character. Her mother at twenty! If a sentimental injustice, some difficulty in love, were to trouble her, all follies, even the worst, were to be feared. Blanchet, at least, was convinced of that, remembering Monique's errors. How would Sylvestre react? He kept watch with an anxious gaze on the adoration she directed at Claude.

Without noticing anything, the latter was listening for the professor, with regard to Louise Mureau, the latest ameliorations made at Chesnay.

"In sum," Blanchet observed, "you have almost put into practice, in the measure to which it is just, the revolutionary slogan: *The factory for the worker*, which is only one of the articles of the great law summarized by your father: *everything for everyone, and to each according to his work*."

"Justice, in sum!" exclaimed Sylvestre.

Without honoring her with a glance, Claude specified: "No bosses and no workers in the antagonistic sense of old, but bosses and workers reconciled in a single good will, by an equal share."

Monsieur Blanchet applauded: "Who would have expected such an end for Plombino's millions? It's admirable."

"Pooh," said Giorgi. "It's only a beginning. A calming tidbit thrown by way of precaution to the popular appetite. Entire justice isn't in that calculated charity, that half-gift of the rich to the poor. It's the integral recovery and nationalization of all wealth."

"And afterwards?"

"Repartition, in accordance with the sum and quality of the labor furnished."

The father pinched his ear teasingly. "*Teneo lupum auribus!*[19] My son, you can believe in the sovereign virtue of collectivism if you like, and that your own inventions will change the world, but you're still an aristocrat, like your bourgeois father! Will a scientist be more favored, then, in your Icaria[20] than the operators of the digging machines or dishwashers that are gradually replacing, fortunately, the spade of the manual laborer and the cook's dishrag? In the meantime, naturally, when Claude has renewed the face of the earth with his essorette and your friend Poncet and his father have succeeded in compressing the new gases that will take away the appetite for bread from the madmen avid to kill one another, Claude, Poncet and you will doubtless be part of the Government Council of Commissars, since even Soviets need directors! An aristo, I tell you—you're nothing but an aristo, since you admit a difference of appreciation in the very product of labor, and recognize, honestly, that quality balances quantity!

---

[19] "I'm holding a wolf by the ears"—a Roman proverb, cited by Terence, among others, indicating that one is in a hazardous situation.

[20] The reference is to the utopian state featured in a novel published in 1840 by the socialist philosopher Étienne Cabet (1788-1856), which gave rise to an "Icarian movement" that founded several colonies in North America.

Beware of the worm in the fruit: the inevitable inequality in your pseudo-equality."

Sylvestre cried, at the same time as Claude: "Pardon me!"

She backed off, signaling to him to speak first.

He objected: "The absolute only exists in relation to the relative. No ideal is attained at the first leap. We'll put in the time, that's all."

"Oh, yes!" joked Monsieur Blanchet. "With a few millennia, refashioning humankind..."

"And why not?" Sylvestre exclaimed. She had leapt to her feet in order take a stance beside Claude. "Do we resemble the dolls and puppets with whom we rub shoulders?" Claude did not flinch at that allusion. She went on: "Twenty years, Father, and your intelligence, have been sufficient for you and Monsieur Jacquemin, not to mention the determination of our mothers, to enable us to make that progress. Do you deny your signature?"

"Protest, too, then, Georgi!" said Gine, supportively, throwing the engineer an acacia flower that had just fallen onto her bare arm. He caught it in mid-air and sniffed it before affirming: "Science is only at the threshold of its discoveries. Put at the service of reason..." With a gesture, he opened up a limitless perspective.

Gine, as if suspended on the liberating hand, cried: "Bravo!" while Sylvestre continued Claude's argument aloud.

"It's like physical and moral suffering. Pasteur didn't believe, any more than Hippocrates, that we could be delivered from it definitively. Isn't it already very good that physicians, the great and the small"—she bowed comically—"are trying to soothe us?" She enveloped Claude with an ardent, infinite good will.

Monique exchanged an ingenuously proud glance with her husband. She enjoyed seeing herself thus revived in her children, thanks to their having grown up...

"It's necessary to confess," observed the Professor, "that you four constitute a fine bunch of reformers."

"It's a fact," murmured Monique, with a tender glance at Sylvestre, "that compared with Paul de Laume and—forgive me Claude—Marise Cervier..."

"Don't talk to me about her!" exclaimed Sylvestre, violently. "We saw her the other day with Georgi. Fortunately for Father, he has other pupils at the Collège de France!"

"That's true," said Monsieur Blanchet. "Free secondary education, since it has been accessible to everyone, had formed and tempered new forces. An entire renewal of energies; that goes without saying. The spark descends from above, agreed—but the flame rises up from below."

"Of course," said Claude. "The profound fire, the true light-source, is the heart of the people."

A moment before, Gine had made a sign to Georgi to come and lie down next to her. Theories were all very well, but she heard enough of them at home. Why not let herself drift, without thinking, on the current of the moment, so gentle that it might carry one away in a bath of light? Georgi, lying down, looked at her affectionately. They seemed to be, lying in there in bottom of their solitary boat, descending a dazzling river toward the immensity of the sea.

Abruptly, after a whispered understanding, they got up and disappeared, furtively.

Only Claude held firm, supported by Sylvestre and Monique, who had come to link arms with her daughter, attentively.

Monsieur Blanchet went on: "I'm willingly abandon to you all the young guard of our President of the Republic! Byzantium & Co. Solmou only has the zealots he deserves. Literate, those lavatory dregs? Because, after Cubism and Dadaism, they returned to rhyme and the scorn for common sense that was rife forty years ago, they think they're original! With their threadbare slippers!"

"And in painting!" scoffed Sylvestre. "All images of their behinds!"

She would have liked to make Claude laugh, and rip him away from the obsession that was separating him from her, from the profound torment that she divined beneath his feigned detachment, but he merely shrugged his shoulders.

"As for their philosophy"—he said, dismissing it with a brutal sweep of the back of his hand—"they've drunk the post-war vomit. They still believe in the late Mussolini and God! That's just a way of speaking, because, fundamentally, they don't believe in anything, not even the God of Priests and Armies, in whom they only praise a symbol—that of their own authority."

"That's true," observed Monsieur Blanchet. "They've descended lower than their fathers..."

"The 'corporeals,' as they say, sniggering—those pure spirits!"

"And yet," exclaimed Monique, ceasing momentarily to observe Sylvestre's nervousness and Claude's attitude in order to stir her own memories, "weren't they hateful enough, the generation of champions, brutally sportive, and for all their neo-Classicism, esteeming nothing but castor oil and the bludgeon? What a misconception of any true ideal! What scorn, also, for women!"

A triumphal march, suddenly bursting forth from the open windows of the drawing room, interrupted them with a merry racket. It was Gine and Georgi, who, imposing their joy on the gravity of the debaters, had sat down at the piano to play Liszt's *Hungarian Rhapsody* four-handed.

They all listened momentarily to the turbulent rhythm.

Monsieur Blanchet smiled, accompanying the notes with the hum of a connoisseur, while Sylvestre followed on Claude's face, with sympathetic sadness, the aggravation that gradually contracted his features, at the impact of that gaiety with his own torment.

"Play something else!" Sylvestre shouted. "You're hurting our ears!"

The piano fell silent, only to resume almost immediately, mutedly, with Mendelssohn's *Funeral March*.

Monsieur Blanchet, who was thoughtful, turned to his wife.

"What do you expect? After a cataclysm like that of 1914, there are, inevitably, sacrificed generations—and well beyond the apparent term! It's thus that, surviving its accumulation of charnel houses, the war has continued to kill. One by one, almost all of those are dying that it only scratched with its scythe. In the same way, the virus had continued its work unobtrusively. It's not been twenty years, and millions of lost human lives—it's half a century, perhaps, that the incalculable ravages of such scourges—lay low in their passage. It will take a long time for them to stand straight again."

The last measures of the Mendelssohn prolonged their poignant emotion. Claude and Sylvestre were listening, leaning over the edge of the abyss that had suddenly re-extended.

It was Monique who concluded: "At least the Max de Laumes and Jean Cerviers have the courage to show, beneath the varnish of their grand words, what they are: brutes! With their black troops! A fine example of civilization! And they're the masters of the moment!"

Claude declared, resolutely: "Precisely! Those, one can combat, hand-to-hand. The society they personify has thrown away its mask: ferocious egotists and dirty players. We're much more fortunate, who don't let ourselves go!"

However, along with Mureau's growl: "The flesh-merchants!" and his conclusion: "We'll have theirs!" the noble education of Annik's voice, with her perpetual counsel of intelligence and gentleness, was ringing in his ears.

Which of the two was in the right?

Suddenly, in the painful remembrance of his suffering, the image of Marise returned. It was superimposed on that of the banker, and both personified universal despotism reigning over the unhappiness of men. But through the heavy image of the father, he could only distinguish, for the moment, that of the daughter. Neither the questioning gaze of Sylvestre, which he did not see, nor the fraternal presence of Gine, now standing with Georgi on the threshold of the drawing room, nor the happiness shining in Monique's face as she contemplated them, nor even the invisible and constant fire of the idea of the family that animated it, succeeded in calming the pincers that were tearing at his heart. The world was ill-made! And he, in that general joy, was so desolate, so alone!

The dinner bell rang. Nane was pulling the chain rhythmically against the wall of ivy. Two surprised pigeons took off in the old chestnut trees. Claude gazed, as if at a desert landscape, at the intimate frame of the old house, on which was sprinkled, in suspense, a last dusting of solar gold. He shivered.

A hand slid under his arm.

"To the table, Claude!"

It was Sylvestre, who drew him away affectionately.

VIII

Looking through the vast windows of the compartment, Annik and Sylvestre gazed curiously at the landscape coming and going before them. One might have thought it an immense map, through which they were being drawn so rapidly that Hungary seemed to be unrolling steadily.

Ordinarily, when Annik went to Central Europe—the second to last International Women's Conference had been held in Warsaw, and the last in Vienna—she took the Paris-Moscow airbus with Claude, just as rapid and far more comfortable than the helic. This time, Sylvestre wanting to try the experiment of the recently-inaugurated Asia Express, they had decided to leave the aerial vehicle at Strasbourg and take the former Orient Express from there. Since the German frontier, the track had been transformed into a new electric railway.

Via Munich and Vienna, with branches to Berlin, the Reichs and Republics of Austria and Hungary, instead of the narrow double track still in use in France, a quadruple track had been constructed, twice as wide, on which spacious carriages with transversal coupés sped at two hundred kilometers an hour, all the way to Tehran via Constantinople, thanks to relays of ferry boats. All the seats were facing forward, lined up in successive saloons.

A bell tower coiffed with slates in the form of an archbishop's hat disappeared. A village with low roofs perched on a hill...

Already sensible, autumn was announcing itself in the form of a light mist, which fields of wheat and oats punctuated with their russet thatch, over the brown extent of the plain. The Danube surged forth, luminous in the reflection of the sky.

"It's astonishing," Annik said, gazing at the décor flying past at top speed, "what the lure of money can realize." She was remembering the information that Claude had brought back from his visit to Garches. "What a pity that a fine belief can't do as much! To think that that bandit Cervier, once again, is hand-in-glove with Hartmann and the Sudekys, and that the Asia Express is made by the oilmen for their monopolies!"

By juxtaposing the details that Marise had let slip with what she already knew, Annik had reconstituted almost all the threads of the scheme woven by the cosmopolitan filibusters: to take possession of the French deposits, at the risk—or, rather, the hope—of a popular revolt. A good opportunity, under one of the pretexts of national pride, in which an insignificant spark was sufficient to cause the most formidable conflagrations, to relight the fire: a war of definitive settlement, in which capitalist hegemony would crush the people mercilessly.

At the memory of what she had suffered thirty years ago, when she had seen the abdication of mothers before the monstrous massacre of their sons, her heart skipped a beat. She would give her life to prevent such a dementia! She wished that Amédée, already warned of the necessity of hastening his return, were there. She rejoiced in the thought that, in a fortnight's time, when she returned from Budapest, she would be able to press herself against the heart of her great man. He was needed in Paris, especially when the Chambres were not in session.

Claude placed the documents that he was riffling through on his knees and raised his pen like a small weapon.

"The truth will come out eventually, even from those Messieurs' oil wells. And the Asia Express will belong to us. In the meantime, thanks to Sylvestre's good idea, it's not disagreeable to be traveling rapidly in this nice armchair."

She thanked him with a grateful glance. Without a word being exchanged between them on the subject of Marise, she had understood the depth of his distress, and had shared it, without the slightest hint of a selfish hidden agenda. Since the fatality of a sentiment, whose force she measured by her own suffering, pushed him irresistibly toward another person, she wished, with the abnegation of which love alone is capable, that the preferred had responded. To Claude's dismay she sacrificed her own. That did not prevent her from regretting, with an acute bitterness, that the object of such a choice had not shown herself to be more worthy of it.

So, since the departure, she had striven, without appearing to touch it, to bandage the wound that she divined to be open beneath Claude's apparent indifference with her vigilant gentleness. She was satisfied, in that unconscious struggle, by the slightest result. She was glad that he could take pleasure, with her, in the kind of travel that she had wanted.

He continued the theme: "Isn't it! It's not as rapid as going by air, obviously, but it's pleasant, this restfulness..."

"Indeed, yes," said Annik. "It's even surprising, the facility with which one adapts, at least materially, to all the changes of progress..."

"It's so simple!" Sylvestre exclaimed. "Imagine if there were still oil lamps and diligences that took six days to go from Paris to Marseilles, carrying the mail!"

Annik shook her head. "Nothing is simple! You've put your finger exactly on the point that divides humankind into two: young and old, progress and reaction. Half the world remains imprisoned by its past, while the other launches forth, entirely new, from the limit surpassed, toward the next one. That's what's responsible, in spite of the most marvelous inventions, for the slowness with which we actually advance."

"It seems to me," Sylvestre protested, "that I'll never grow old." The future was resplendent in her eyes.

"At a certain age, my dear, one has more difficulty than you think, as a child of today, in keeping up to date. I can still see my poor Mérette undergoing tortures before the telephone. It's even more difficult to get used to the novelty of new ideas than new facts. Good old Mérette! At least she never doubted tomorrow, until her last breath."

Piously, she devoted herself to memories of the old lady: the animator! The school full of gaiety, of singing...the Versailles of her youth and her betrothal. And, because she had remained young at heart, she hoped, like Sylvestre. Internally, she made her act of faith in the perpetual motion of life.

Had Amédée and she not succeeded, by way of their free union and its value as an example, in making a breach in the most solid redoubt of the legal fortress—marriage? Now the ancient prison was enlarged, sanitized, the entrance cleared of inept formalities and exit still possible, through the battened doors of divorce, but also with necessary delays to passing through them. Above all, no servitude, no obedience for the woman: an equality of reciprocal engagements. The family founded, in sum, on justice, with the rights of every birth recognized, to the sacred filiation from which it came.

"It's only stupid people," she summarized, "who cling onto the image of the past. Nothing is immutable! That's why—Claude is right—property will be modified, like everything else. We've already been able to soften it, in the most savage of its forms."

"Do you hear, Monsieur Rohn?" the young man called cheerfully, to a traveler with heavy features, but a gaze brilliant with cunning, who had just stopped at the door open to the corridor and was leaning toward them with friendly solicitude.

"Yes, fortunately!" he said. He spoke French almost without an accent. He was the leader of the German Social Democrats, a distant cousin of the Liebknechts,[21] who, in the image of those superhumans, had refounded and reinspired the disaggregated mass of the party. The corpulent silhouette of his wife, Professor Bertha Rohn, was visible behind him. Blonde and pink, she was attractive in spite of her learned manner. A well-known chemist, she was the German delegate

---

[21] Karl Liebknecht (1871-1919) was the co-founder, with Rosa Luxemburg, of the German Communist Party; both were murdered by the paramilitary Freikorps following the Spartacist uprising of 1919, thus becoming important martyrs to the socialist cause.

to the Committee of the International Council, and was, like Annik, on her way to Budapest.

"Well, Madame President, how's the lunch?"

Annik had complained, in the restaurant car where they had been neighbors at the same table, about the heaviness of the mincemeat seasoned with cinnamon. "It's passing through!" she joked. "What do you expect? It's only in matters of cuisine that I remain a nationalist. In any case, I have a very small stomach. Long live Madame Rohn's tables!"

There was reason to joke; when she was exceedingly busy, she gladly substituted the rapidity of nourishing pills for the slowness and quantity of dishes—those elaborated by the Berlinese chemist or, for preference, the famous condensates of Dr. Lagre.

Monsieur Rohn laughed heartily. "Adaptation! Vital law. By dint of reducing digestion, you'll end up no longer having an intestine. That's what you get for allowing yourself to be captured by the diabolical inventions of sorcerers. Look at my wife—she doesn't use those of her own fabrication! So you get thinner and she gets fatter!"

Bertha Rohn echoed her husband's noisy joy. Annik liked their simplicity, the flower of true intelligence. She had a better understanding with them than Amédée did. He retained an involuntary reserve from the war. Not a hostility, certainly—for, as a fervent admirer of Bayreuth, he was one of those who had most ardently applauded, one Christmas Eve at the Front, the Wagnerian harmonies that had forged a fraternal union of souls even in the bloody trenches. Annik appreciated more equitably what was broadly fecund in German virtues, when, for want of a Beethoven or a Goethe, only a Bebel[22] or a Rohn incarnated them. Whereas Jacquemin remained French, in spite of everything, she strove to raise herself to a

***

[22] The German socialist politician Auguste Bebel (1840-1913), one of the founders of the German Social Democratic Workers' Party.

higher summit, where one could identify oneself, above all, as Human.

For their part, the Rohns, although imbued, by long atavism, with the prejudice of Force, admired in Annik Raimbert the protagonist, in Europe, of the religion of Love, which, resuscitated in Asia for the second time with Gandhi, had triumphed over British Imperialism, as it had two thousand years before, with Christ, over the Roman Empire. They had gradually been convinced that the strongest Force was that of opposing gentleness to violence, and that passive resistance could reason with the power of arms.

"We're arriving," said Bertha Rohn.

"Already!" Sylvestre exclaimed.

"See you later!"

The Berlinese couple returned to their carriage. The train passed like an arrow through the suburban region that encircles all capital cities, a black mass of leprous walls, bristling with factory chimneys, saddened by abattoirs and cemeteries: Death camped at the gates of Life.

They were in the station before they had reassembled their baggage and put on their hats.

From that moment on, Sylvestre had the impression that all three of them were caught in a cinema reel. Simultaneously an actress in and a viewer of a film that flickered incessantly, she surrendered herself, no longer having the time for analysis, to a dispersion whose unexpectedness and novelty amused her all the more because Claude seemed visibly to be distancing himself from thoughts of Marise.

On some evenings, when she got back after a tiring day of visits, banquets and speeches, Sylvestre admired the benefits of that activity. Claude, returned to himself, became cheerful again. Fundamentally, in the so-called fatality of love, was there not a greater measure of auto-suggestion? Although specialized, like all the recruits to her profession—for general medicine was practiced less and less—she was interested in mental hygiene as much in gynecology.

Only timidity had prevented her taking part in the oral communications in her specialization at the Congress. One matter had interested her particularly: the sexual education of young women.

Penetrated by the ideas of Mademoiselle Hardy and Annik, her opinion was that, more than ever, the notions of women, the mothers of tomorrow, regarding the foremost of their functions, were mistaken—no longer, as before, by virtue of ignorance, the fruit of social hypocrisy and Catholic false modesty, but by virtue of a precocious profligacy, both excessive and insufficiently informed, which, believing that it knew everything, thought everything permissible. How many of the young people around her were already depleted in their health! How many fecundities had been compromised by a poorly understood liberty, even more dangerous than the attraction of mystery and the savor of forbidden fruit!

Lodged in one of the large hotels of Brest, it was necessary for them every day to quit the noisy Rácóczy út to traverse the immense suspension bridge to reach the heights of Buda on the other side of the river. The old city had retained from its royal past a severe majesty that chilled Sylvestre, which drove her after the conference sessions, held in one of the old imperial buildings, toward the streets of Pest, lightheartedly. "Up there," she told Claude, "I can feel myself turning into a turnip."

On Andrássy út, everything distracted them: the continual racket of the trams, with their cramped human cargoes, the terraces of the sparkling, swarming cafes. At the Szabadság rakpat, the former Franz-Josef quay, now the Liberty Quay, there was a variegated pedestrian crowd, the anachronism of antique costumes—the Hungarian mantle or embroidered peasant blouse and bare legs—amid the swarm of passersby dressed as in Liverpool or Naples.

"It's via costume," Annik remarked, one evening when they were drinking a *jegeschcaffé* at the Île Marguerite, "that internationalization—oh, what a word!—is making its most rapid progress. What a pity that one can't abandon a prejudice as easily as a mode of dress!"

In spite of the admirable communion of ideals that fused, in a single assembly of efforts, the feminine elite of the world gathered there, Annik, on emerging from the hothouse of Committees, struck by the contrast of people and things when she re-entered the routines of daily life, sensed once again how distant the mass of women was from its leaders, here as elsewhere. What an abyss separated their resignation and sluggishness from her fervor! What dross continued to darken their timid souls! How long would it take for the warp of servitude to be definitive effaced from the furrows of their flesh?

On returning to her companions in the struggle, however, and tightening the links that connected her to her foreign friends, the hours of discouragement soon passed. She donned her harness of bravery valiantly, prompt to remember that, in the eyes of others, more or less favorably watchful under the superficial sympathy, in spite of her deep-seated internationalism, she represented French womanhood.

She knew full well, however, that no one among those delegates of worldwide intelligence was scornful of the true character of the female laborer, her qualities of devotion, honesty and cheerful courage, slumbering under the apparent mask as under the effaced visage. A few reckless braggarts of vice were no more Parisian than Hungarian, German, American, Italian or English. Did not all people see, day by day, as in France, mores undergoing a transformation of decline in the vertigo of luxury and increasing amorality? It was the fatal result of an epoch thrown, by a handful of profiteers, from bestial war into the rat race of peace.

On the last day's plenary session, before proceeding to the closure of the Congress that she had directed indefatigably, Annike had lunch with her guests, the President of the Magyar Council, Monsieur Ferencz and his wife, the Rohns, the Doctors Mousaloff, the famous criminologist Antonelli, Mrs. Sydney, the American to whom all the Mediterranean countries owed the creation of Heliomarine Institutions for children suffering from rickets, and Sir James Ramsay, the former Minister of Labor in the last-but-one British cabinet. London, Berlin, Rome, Moscow and New York thus linked, around Paris, the mobile network of their affinities.

Monsieur Ferencz, sitting opposite Annik, had just proposed a toast in the name of his government, associating with his gesture of hospitality the great absentee, Amédée Jacquemin.

Annik stood up, regretting that Claude and Sylvestre were not here. During almost the entire stay, separately or together, they had kept company with friends of their own age. She would have liked, at that moment, to have them by her side in order to materialize, by their presence, the image that she evoked verbally, in raising her glass of sparkling Tokay:

"To youth! To the true young woman and young men of every country! You won't hold it against me, Excellency, nor you, my dear friends, whose intelligence has not aged any more than your sentiments, that I extend my glass toward the sun in which all our hopes of realization will rise in the imminent future."

Everyone applauded. Mrs. Sydney, who, in consequence of having no children, aided those of others to live in thousands, proclaimed: "You're right. Our task is complete. The young require a new religion. You've formulated its precepts. There are now mothers everywhere who are beginning to acquire consciousness of their mission. And tomorrow, in accordance with your wishes, there will be fresh young troops in all nations."

"An army without weapons!"

"Brothers and sisters!"

"For the peaceful destruction of war!"

"For the harmony of the sexes!"

"For human happiness!"

Their voices intermingled, the mixture of accents forming an alloy in the fusion of beliefs. A great hope elevated them all, above themselves and the races they incarnated. Illuminated as Annik was, however, she could not see it any more clearly.

Undoubtedly, each of those surrounding her exercised a real influence on a quantity of women, and, through them, a number of men. Undoubtedly, the thirst—the need—to work in peace was increasing from pole to pole. However, the monster thus far eternal, the Beast of Violence, would not expire without a supreme backlash. It would only be suppressed after terrible convulsion if, following the examples set by Tolstoy and Gandhi, she had become a soldier, a humble but ardent disciple of Jesus, and did not prevail over the bloody sheeplike docility of peoples, where their stupid obedience would lead them to mutual slaughter.

"No, my dear Mrs. Sydney," she riposted, "our task is just beginning."

The Congress was on the point of ending, in the tumult of applause that was saluting with an interminable ovation the speech that Annik had just made, when a discordant voice rang out: "I demand to speak."

There was a murmurous ripple of disapproval. They were in haste to vote by acclamation on the manifesto that summarized, in a few directorial lines approved by everyone, the practical endeavors of the congress: resolutions commended in detail in each order of reform, whose declaration, entitled *Appeal to Mothers*, while awaiting the publication of the report, indicated the general feeling. The conference members had already taken cognizance of it, the text having been printed and distributed in profusion, like white butterflies.

In the middle of her group, Sylvestre was agitating, protesting against the protester. She had recognized the inevitable Véra Sélénosk, the Russian anarchist, and, knowing in advance the gist of her theme, was indignant at the idea of seeing returned to debate the very principle for the triumph of which Annik and her disciples had battled so fervently

She had had the proud joy of being the first to transcribe the words in which the new hope lived. She knew them by heart, like a *Credo*. She repeated them religiously as, in response to general demand, Dr. Moussaloff, the secretary to the Council, read the text in a firm voice.

Mothers,

If you believe in the possibility of a better humankind,

If you want your children to grow up in the happy labor of peace, alone fecund,

If you do not want your daughters to remain flesh-fodder and your sons to remain cannon-fodder at the hands of their masters,

Raise them to respect themselves and to love their neighbors,

Inspire them with a hatred of wars, all fratricidal,

And be persuaded that in affirming, everywhere and always, the inflexible will of your non-cooperation to the endeavors of cunning and violence, you will triumph over all evil enemy Forces, however powerfully they seem to be armed.

Elementary principles, which, translated into all languages, would be propagated and posted in all countries. The assembly saluted them with long hurrahs and bravos, almost unanimously.

"I demand to speak!"

The piercing voice rose up again. A clamor drowned it out: "Vote! Vote! Closure!"

Climbing on her chair and lacerating a handful of sheets of paper with the tips of her bony fingers, which fluttered above the heads as they were hurled, Véra Sélénosk proclaimed, in a shrill voice: "Silence, partisans of equivocation!"

A counter-rumor spread, unfurling all the way to the raised table where the Supreme Council was assembled, standing around Annik. Adjurations, now opposed, clashed. Many admirers of the fanatic cried: "Let her speak!" The majority, however, unwilling to reopen the debate, waved their raised arms.

"Vote! Vote!"

They were familiar with the theories of the integral communist, which she had been preaching for years against Soviet embourgeoisement. A former director of the Cheka, she had been unable, in the rigor of her mysticism to tolerate the fact that, accentuating Lenin's *Mea Culpa*, the opportunism of his successors had fallen into the dishonor of compromise with the reactionaries. She esteemed the sincerity of Annik's faith, but was even more scornful of her evolutionist naivety. As if one could expect anything of the future outside revolutionary means: the Browning, more expeditious than the guillotine; and the bomb, more rapid than the ballot.

Annik made a gesture of appeasement.

"At least let thought be free among us. Comrade Sélénosk has the floor..."

Small and thin—the body of a reaper, which the ardent brown face, radiant with a consuming flame, caused one to forget—Véra Sélénosk, still standing on her chair, barked rather than vociferating: "The proposition on which you are ready to vote is the renunciation of our hopes! You will not be liberated! You are holding out your wrists in order that they might be bound!"

Holding on with one hand on the shoulder of her neighbor, her Dutch ally Van Born, she shook her free fist at the Council, menacing Annik more particularly, with the delirium of a pythoness. "Listen to the song of the shepherdess! It's to the abattoir that she's leading you...and when you have been struck with a blow of the sledgehammer between your blind eyes, it will be too late—liberty will be dead! One obtains nothing by begging. On the contrary—strike first, and the gates of the future city will open. Do you believe that the masters, as your bleating claims, will release their golden keys unless by constraint? If you want to recover your wealth, kill, or you'll be killed!"

Boos rang out. They did not put her off.

"Is that not what one of the philosophers of Annik Raimbert's fatherland tells us? Your Renan,[23] one of the most skeptical among the madmen you call sages. 'Humankind only makes progress over ruins. The bridge of the dead is necessary to the march of the living.'"

She fell silent, as if exhausted, grim in the midst of the tumult provoked by her words. Already, Annik was calling for calm with a gesture. She had no need to raise her voice, so sudden was the attention as soon as he spoke.

She was no longer, as she had been a few minutes before, the celebrated advocate whose eloquence was attended by a grace that did not diminish conviction. A woman was speaking from the heart, with the irresistible accent that only maternal love can give.

"I know that Véra Sélénosk, if she had children, would persist in the same language that you have just heard. As she gladly is ready to sacrifice the lives of others, she would give her own. It is not, therefore, her courage that I doubt—it is the mortal danger of such courage. Like her, without lowering my eyes, I would accept death, but in order that our sons might live! So that a new order, thanks to their labor, might be realized! The brutal remedy that Véra Sélénosk praises does not cure; it makes matters worse. From one savagery to another, it is the river of blood that continues to flow. Murder appeals eternally to murder. Abduction founds nothing but abduction.

"On the contrary, let us oppose to the executioner the innumerable inertia of victims, and his rage is immediately impotent. The flock of sheep, if it is self-conscious, and only resists with head down, will triumph over the bad shepherd and his dog. One can do anything against the obstinate refusal of a few, but one can do nothing against the silent will of a people. The risks? The just crucified and imprisoned? So what? Only martyrdom, not murder, exalts the moral life that is the mainspring of existence. It was thus that Christianity

---

[23] Ernest Renan (1823-1892).

swept away pagan religion, and that India, free again, is commencing a new civilization.

"No, Comrade Sélénosk, behind your bloody mirage, there is nothing but ruined bridges. Violence, far from aiding, retards human progress. The law of life is not death, a passage that no one avoids, but from which we can at last recoil while embellishing the difficult road as we make our way along it. The law of life is love!"

Such persuasion emerged from her entire being. Her voice, although softly pitched, was penetrated by so direct an impetus, that the entire audience, rising to their feet, covered her pure profession of faith with acclamations.

Annik sat down and lowered her head under the storm of bravos. When they ceased their adulations, it was the vice-president, Mrs. Sydney who proposed: "A show of hands in favor of the manifesto!"

Uplifted by enthusiasm, the standing assembly pronounced. Only the anarchist and a few disciples abstained—wrecks lost in the irresistible flood.

Claude and Sylvestre, who were smiling at one another from a distance, felt the same pride welling up in them: a joy, a hope, magnifying the radiation of the moment before them.

Claude thought: *If Marise...*

And from a distance Sylvestre saw a joyful form floating, but without precise contours, which had the visage of her desire.

PART TWO

*It is a kind of happiness to know the extent
to which one might be unhappy.*
La Rochefoucauld.

I

"Have you read this, my dear? What cheek!"

Jean Cervier had irrupted so abruptly into the directorial office that an amazed usher gazed at him with admiration.

To enter in that fashion into Monsieur Turbot's domain! One might be a Minister, but it was necessary to be mightily sure of oneself to treat the Emperor of the Press in that fashion! It was true that Monsieur Cervier, one of the principal shareholders in the company, was somewhat at home here, but all the same! The medal-laden veteran who had been wounded in the assault on Vauquois trembled at the slightest frown of the Olympian eyebrows. Turbot I—as the thousand employees of the *Inter* called him—was the terror of his staff.

The ex-hero who had become a flunkey—one has to eat—closed the leather-lined door unhurriedly, and then the iron-clad door, not without cocking an ear. However, as majestic in his armchair as a potentate on his throne, Monsieur Turbot waited until he had disappeared, along with his curiosity and his scrap metal.

Jean Cervier unfolded a newspaper. Monsieur Turbot stopped him by raising his hand. The calluses of the former dock worker were still visible there.

"No need. I've read it."

An article by Amédée Jacquemin, which had appeared that morning in the *Universel*, was the cause of the banker-minister's excitement. It seemed, on the other hand, to have had no effect on the phlegmatic sovereignty of the *Inter*'s owner.

"And the textile strikes!" exclaimed Cervier. "Where are we heading?"

Originating in Roubaix and Tourcoing, the strikes were in the process of spreading to England and Germany, thanks to the international discipline whose rule the socialists were beginning to observe.

"That," conceded Turbot, "is more serious."

All thorax and nose, he was besuited with the grace of a rhinoceros. He was built only to be seen sitting down, ridiculous on legs so short that pedestal-heels might have been invented for him. Like this, and in spite of the enormity of his girth, he was imposing. By the coarse authority of a boor, and the millions that he was supposed to possess, without anyone being able to specify the figure, and, finally, by the glamour of a success of the printing presses in his basement, he had risen in ten years to the uncontested scepter of the great Parisian dailies: the director of the *Inter*, the President of the Syndicate of Independent Journalists, and, to complete the irony, a senior officer in the Légion d'honneur.

Turbot willingly told his intimate friends how he would have vegetated permanently if, one day, having been promoted to sweeper in the offices of the paper, he had not discovered a few secrets of which he had made good use. "Don't trust your own shadow!" he concluded.

It was thus that, thanks to an intelligence whose shrewdness was only equaled by its audacity, he had soon become deputy editor, and then editor, had acquired, after the publicity of the *Inter*, that of several large banks, and, by means of ever-increasing blackmail, had brought the paper to the point of fortune to which only an idea of genius, albeit simple, could have led—a genius that, because it was simple, had persuaded Jean Cervier and a few of his friends to its creation.

The *Inter*, in the miry depths in which the largest French newspapers then wallowed, dragging their platitudinous news to an information devoid of breadth, had broken with that key-hole gossip, and the base scheming of financiers and politicians. No more squashed dogs, violins or inexhaustible repeating revolvers. No more parrot cages in exchange for receipts for household goods or beauty products, the sickening stupidity of a bottomless puerility. No more feuilletons bleating romance or melodrama. No more claptrap about deep fishing in little purses. Instead a window wide open to the echoes of the entire world, accounts rendered with apparent impartiality of international activity in all is manifestations. The *Inter*, overnight, had veritably renewed the stinking air of its editorial offices, brought worldwide life into the narrowness of its lodgings and broadened the horizons previously limited by venal blindness.

Then, the competition having joined in, its success had relented. The old papers, while modifying themselves, had been able to keep almost all of their incorrigible clientele. New ones had been founded, like Amédée Jacquemin's *Universel*, which swept away an opinionated audience. It was then that Jean Cervier had associated himself with Paul Turbot, and, by a regular progression, the *Inter* had recovered its former sales figures of six hundred thousand and surpassed them, to reach a million.

International Finance, by the sacrifice of a small sum, had bought the most powerful of its business levers. In the hands of the master-blackmailer, the valuable tool was now worth more than all skeleton keys. Its masthead was ornamented by a slogan: *The Only Truth*.

"Jacquemin's well-informed," sighed Cervier. "The scheme's uncovered. The fellow is capable, when the Chambres re-open, of overturning us. He might see himself already as President of the Council in October."

"The *Inter* is here, my dear Minister," pronounced Monsieur Turbot. "Monsieur Jacquemin is counting without the gas jet—and what gas!"

Jean Cervier smiled. He appreciated the allusion to the secret trials that had recently been carried out. A brother of the eccentric who had discovered in 1872, two years too late, the bromacetic ether and chloracetone that had been able to reply to the German toxins in 1915,[24] the great chemist Louis Poncet, had just perfected a new substance whose toxicity was such that it could reliably neutralize, terrifying as they were, the Reich's latest inventions. The Minister had decided to have enormous provisions manufactured without delay. "The next war will be not merely electrical but chemical," Jean Cervier took pleasure in repeating incessantly to the Council of Ministers. He had almost succeeded in convincing Solmou of that evidence, even though the President of the Republic, a personal friend of Maréchal Lux, leaned toward old methods of generalship.

"You're like Lux, my dear director," said Cervier. "You dream of nothing but war!"

"Foreign to begin with and civil to finish, the former giving us the opportunity, given the certain revolt of the proletariat, to establish a solid base for the definitive domination of honest men. It's a program worth pursuing, you'll agree. All your forced smiles with Jacquemin are just a waste of time."

"Oh, I've given up on that."

"The strong hand. One can't make an omelet without breaking eggs." With that apothegm he rubbed his hands vigorously. Omelets! Turbot only liked them hot, applied to the lower abdomen by the expert hands of an inmate in a brothel to which, under a false name and wearing make-up, he went one afternoon a week, as regularly as to mass every Sunday. An innocent mania of which no one, not even the brothel-keeper, had any inkling.

Jean Cervier pushed back his armchair nervously, and while marching back and forth in front of the table over-decorated with bronzes, he said: "Let's begun by amassing, if

---

[24] Bromacetic ether and chloracetone were both employed as chemical weapons in the Great War, but to no great effect; they had been identified long before 1872 and it is not obvious who the "eccentric" cited might have been.

possible, a superabundance of eggs. There'll always be time for the breaking."

Now that, in consequence of his meetings in New York with the agents of Hartmann and Sudeky, the controllers of Westphalian and Rumanian oil, he had just completed the surreptitious purchase of magnificent deposits in Provence, he had not despaired of checking the maneuvers of the socialists in Parliament. They had resolved to table a proposal, without waiting for the next election, for the nationalization of mineral rights, retroactively applied to previous purchases. For him, that was the sensitive issue, which the *Universel* had just supported with a few inconvenient precisions. Bah! They would see! Was he not, in the final analysis, the stronger?

Like Cervier, Turbot believed that they were secure, with their army of blacks and the entire scientific arsenal with which plutocrats everywhere were equipped, in large measure unheeded by public insouciance, and sheltered in any case— Cervier supposed—from Jacquemin's gaze.

Boastfully, he said: "You know full well, old man, that since our association with the English and American financiers, and the fusion into a single Trust of Standard Oil and Royal Dutch, Hartmann, Sudeky and I are now the masters of all European oil supplies, not to mention those of Asia. What can that flock of poor devils do against that, and the rest— which is to say, our gas jet?"

"Let them finish organizing," Turbot observed, "and the flock will become a troop. Look at the textile strikes. Similarly, let those she-devils have their way...for a Raimbert is perhaps even more to be feared than a Jacquemin! The Budapest Conference has had an influence on public opinion that it would be childish to disregard. The elections—only five months away—will be fought on those two platforms: the female vote, which is to say, peace inevitably founded; and the nationalization of the subsoil, which is to say, property ruined..."

"With a few hundred thousand well spent..."

"Optimist! On that point, I agree with Lux. He's mistaken when he still believes in the rampart of breasts, and the perlimpinpin powder[25] of offensive miracles, but he's right when he declares that the sole means of imposing our peace once and for all is to go to war again. Oh, if we'd only entered Berlin in 1918 after having nailed all the defeatists to the stake, we wouldn't have been forced to return the Rhineland, and we wouldn't be facing all the recriminations of the world's blowhards. Social justice! Truly, that's a laugh! Their justice would be to put their dirty buttocks in my armchair, for a start. Thanks! Better, for a start, to shoot a few Jacquemins. And a good war thereafter!" He spoke those words coldly—which did not prevent him from bring his fist down vigorously on the glass with which the morocco leather of the desk was covered. "Max de Laume and Lux are right. Tighten the vice! If not, it'll all go awry."

"In any case," muttered Cervier, impressed, "it's necessary to convene a meeting without delay. I'll hop over to the Presidency of the Council. Are you coming?"

"No need. A Telephone call will suffice." He opened a drawer and leaned over the unmasked apparatus. "The Presidency of the Council."

Almost instantaneously, the call was answered. "For the *Inter*...is that you, my dear Max? Turbot here... Good, thanks... I'm expecting you at dinner this evening... Eight till one... The banquet of the Parliamentary Correspondents?... I don't care. Send another Minister...migraine...indispensable! Urgent affair... Good, that's understood. My house... Until this evening..." He broke the connection. "And that's one! On to Solmou...oh, no—he's hunting at Marly, that's true... I'll tele-

---

[25] *Poudre de perlimpinpin* [perlimpinpin powder] was a proverbial term applied to various supposed cure-alls, which had no benign effect, sold by the quacks and charlatans who flourished in the 18th century in France as elsewhere. The nearest equivalent American phrase, of somewhat later provenance, is "snake oil."

phone later this afternoon…or send someone to the Élysée. Don't worry about it. I'll take care of it."

These resolutions were made with a rapidity that permitted no reply. Turbot stood up and shook the hand of his shareholder and friend. "Until this evening!" The two Omnipotents parted, both satisfied, each believing that he controlled his accomplice, Turbot with his little documents, Cervier with his big bills: Robert Macaires[26] united by lucre and fear.

---

[26] The archetypal villain of 19th century French melodrama, based on a 14th century murderer but updated for that purpose.

II

That same evening, as His Majesty Turbot had decided, his old town house on the Quai Voltaire played host to the President of the Council and the President of the Republic, who had answered the summons.

Madame Solmou, nursing a chill contracted trying to play the huntress in the shoot in the old royal forest, was confined to her room. There were, therefore, no other women at the table than the inevitable Marquise d'Entraygues, accompanying Max de Laume. Jean Cervier never encumbered himself with his wife, and the host was a bachelor, like Maréchal Lux, brought by Solmou—"He's in my office now," he had proposed, when Turbot had invited him. "He might be able to offer some good advice."

"Of course he can come!" A blockhead, but right-thinking—a force not to be neglected.

Sitting opposite the rhinoceros and flanked by the two Presidents, the Marquise posed the head of a noble bird on a meager upper body. She was conscious, between the two mostly highly-placed individuals in the land, of the grandeur of her role. She was their Egeria.

Michelle had withered in growing older. The green fruit had become acidic, vices having turned gradually to virtue. Of the fresh girlish face of old, she only retained a little wrinkled skin over the bone-structure. Her hair, lifted up by way of transformation—she judged it more imposing thus—resembled a clownish tuft, and her shrill voice let oracles fall with an imperturbable abundance.

Of her mother, the dancer, nothing survived but the renown of the salon Jacquet, which had become the Cenacle d'Entraygues with Saint Max de Laume—a saint who invited the little girls to come to him. Michelle had made the said sanctuary the Sur-Quai d'Orsay as well as the Sur-Académie Française. Not only were old parrots nourished there, but their successors honed their beaks there. It was, above all, a kind of governmental Permanence, an occult Council of Ministers where the cuisine of the State was clandestinely elaborated.

As for the Marquis d'Entraygues, he was finishing dying, senile, in a sanitarium.

"Have a little more of the quail supreme, Monsieur le Président," she advised. She did the honors, with the same ease as if she were at home. A lackey in culottes, with silver buttons and a blue jacket—the Turbot livery—respectfully presented the silver platter to Solmou, but the President, who had had his fill of food, refused.

"Really, my dear Turbot," the Marquise simpered, in order to occupy the floor while the service was effectuated—for the Egeria was prudent—"You are an original! No one can match you as a man of progress, but you only surround yourself here with old things, including these candlesticks!"

Wax was burning in pyramids in the monumental candelabra, vestiges of the Hall of Mirrors at Versailles. Their soft light illuminated, on the gilded woodwork, the magnificent of ancient Gobelins, the famous suite of the Royal Châteaux. Coats of arms shone on the pink marble of the immense octagonal table, in which, especially in one carved by the elder Germain, French roses blossomed in sheaves.

"Yes," said Turbot, "it's a style."

"And the best," pronounced Solmou. "Without falling into the bad habit that consists of always opposing the past to the present, let's confess that the sense of elegance is gradually being lost. Classical culture..."

The Marquise interrupted him, touching him on the arm with her fan. Already she had turned to the President of the Council. Classical culture was terrain reserved for Max! Had he not once, at Public Education, reinvigorated, further reinforcing them, the Bérard decrees that had been abolished almost as soon as they were promulgated?[27]

---

[27] Léon Bérard was the Minister of Public Education in 1919 and from 1921 to 1924; the so-called *Bérard décrets* [Bérard

106

"You're right, Maurice!" opined the specialist. Since their debut, he and Solmou had addressed one another as *tu*, in accordance with the old fashionable habit of the Chambre: they sniped at one another behind their backs, but when they met they patted one another amicably on the belly. "Tradition is everything! Without Latin and Greek, how would we learn to think?"

"I beg your pardon," said Cervier. "Neither Turbot nor I have pored over dead languages. That doesn't prevent us from living, nor, I think, from thinking!"

Max de Laume got himself out of it with a pirouette. "The exception confirms the rule."

As for Solmou, he was floating in the obscure heavens of his digestion. Gluttony was his weakness—or, rather, as people claimed maliciously, his strength.

Turbot judged it polite, by way of a diversion, to try to extract Maréchal Lux from his mutism. With the dense appearance of a senior civil servant in a frock coat, he had thus far only opened his mouth in order to stick his fork in it. Like Solmou—it was their common bond—he liked the table, and his bed no less. Guzzling, and sleeping even more so, were his two passions. Of the rest, which is to say, *omni re scibili*,[28] military art included, he had only vague glimmers: reflections of schooling and received opinions. His veritable superiority was a perpetual amen to everything, except when is own inter-

---

decrees], among other instructions, made the teaching of Latin compulsory in State schools. Subsequent to the publication of the present text he served a term as Minister of Justice and was elected to the Académie Française. In 1943, in our very different world, he was Vichy France's ambassador to the Vatican.

[28] "Of everything knowable"—the phrase was made famous by a catty comment made about the Renaissance scholar Pico della Mirandola, to the effect that he knew everything knowable and a few other things besides.

ests were at stake. Then, like the wily Cévenol peasant he remained, he became ferocious.

It was thus that, a young captain of general staff at the commencement of the Great War, he had been able to profit from being the cousin of an army general, first to become a colonel in command of a brigade and then, quite naturally, in twenty-four years of peace, to reach the Maréchalat. Solmou's friendship had made him the generalissimo.

"Speaking of exceptions, Monsieur le Maréchal, what do you think of the Chambre's decision this afternoon?" asked Turbot, point blank. "Are you satisfied?"

The majority, in spite of Jacquemin's intervention, had refused to accord officers the political vote. The government had not even had to pose it, as the habitual question of confidence had decided it.

"Did I have a vote at the time of the victories of the Marne?" Maréchal Lux attested. "Do you see Messieurs the negro captains slandering us in the red rags? For it's necessary to recognize that the evil influence of the citizen army is beginning to poison black loyalty. What would become of us without our fine riflemen? They constitute the best of our infantry, and the infantry is not only the sole sovereign of battles, it remains, in spite of Monsieur the Minister of Finance, the great friend of electricians and chemists, and the best servant." He raised his eyes to the ceiling, a *Triumph of Mars* painted by Lemoyne.[29] "Everything is modernizing, even evil."

"Agreed with regard to the first point," replied Cervier. "Where would we be if subaltern, and even superior officers, started reasoning?"

---

[29] François Lemoyne (1688-1737) became the first painter to Louis XIV and painted mythological scenes on many of the ceilings at Versailles, but court intrigues and his wife's death apparently drove him mad and he committed suicide; the fashion of allegorical ceiling painting died with him.

"Obedience! One point, that's all!" affirmed Lux. "Think where we've come to, since the eighteen month law,[30] all the licenses accorded one by one! An officer is free today to take his meals wherever he wishes, to marry as he likes. Out of the electorate, and the uniform during periods of exercise, he's a civilian, just like the troops, since we've fallen into the Swiss system! With your simple military preparation, your service of three months, and your annual leaves of three weeks, there is no army anymore! Said without reproach, Messieurs les Présidents!"

In spite of the suppleness of his spine, Lux could not admit that Parliament should be allowed to sabotage the primary institutions. Oh, without the faithful black contingents and the powerful corps of career officers fortunately filling the offices…!

Madame d'Entraygues, who was bored by all technical conversation, changed the subject by asking Turbot: "Do you know whether Madame Reichmeyer's marriage to the Duc d'Altamira will take place within the next month?"

"The *Inter* knows everything, Madame. I can even tell you who will bless it at the Madeleine."

"The Archbishop of Hippo, Monsieur Audoin?" That was one of the regulars at her salon, an old houseguest of the Reichmeyers, who had for a long time, as a missionary in Libya, put out propaganda for the Grand Magasins du Tout Pour Rien and their shoddy goods.

"You're wide of the mark. A prelate of the diocese."

"The co-adjutor?" she queried, astonished and respectful. For, in growing older, she had discovered a religious vocation, as a chatelaine, alimenting the curé of Entraygues with holy

---

[30] The determination of the length and terms of national service was a perennially hot topic in French politics; the period in question had been settled by a parliamentary vote in 1923, but, as the author anticipates via Maréchal Lux's mouth, the determination only resulted in further piecemeal concessions and continued discord.

bread and offerings, not to mention, in Paris, the good works of the Archbishop, she was proud of being one of the pillars of the Church.

Turbot smiled. "Better than that. Monseigneur Chamelot in person."

"The cardinal!" exclaimed the Marquise, dazzled. "All's well that ends well."

Madame Reichmeyer, a widow of sixty, had just won on appeal the interminable lawsuit that her sons had launched against her, fearing to see the hundreds of millions that weighed upon their mother fall by way of a "scandalous" marriage into the hands of her latest lover, the pseudo-Duc d'Altamira—no more "Altamira" than Madame Reichmeyer was in her right mind, people said. The man in question having given proof, however, if not of disinterest, at least of a nobility that, by the adoption of the last Duc, went back as far as Charles Quint, passing via the servants' parlor, the tribunals had dismissed the case. Madame Reichmeyer had reverted from being a madwoman to an eccentric. Rich, she could buy herself the husband that suited her, and the great organs would play, under the lofty patronage on the Archbishop of Paris.

"I've always thought," Solmou concluded, "that Madame Reichmeyer was calumniated." He did not add that, once having been a donor to the rosette of the late Reichmeyer, he had long received in exchange liberal annual contributions to the electoral treasury of the Association of National Interests. It was, in sum, a little of the money of the "all for nothing" to which the solidity was owed of the party on which he had based the harmonious development of his career. Having reached the summit, Solmou judged it magnanimous to testify a certain gratitude to someone who had supported him, given that it cost him nothing.

The sumptuous meal and its conversation finally came to an end—everyone except the Marquise being in haste to get on to serious matters—with a surprise that rallied all votes; they repaired to the Smoking Room, where Turbot's personal taste blossomed in the gaudiness of an Oriental bazaar. A screen with a speaker and colored projections had replaced an admirable Persian carpet bought not for its beauty but its price—the highest that a carpet had ever attained.

"What have you done with it?"

"Sold it on! To a Museum in America. It didn't interest me—and with the profits I had this little showcase installed. The day's latest news…the *Inter* at home. It's the latest thing, or I don't know my own business. What do you think?"

Although Cervier had preceded him by some time with a similar installation—admittedly for other purposes—he joined in chorus with the Presidents and the Maréchal. They were all the more flattering because they thought less of it, but Turbot was, like them, one of those who, being adulated, necessarily lived on lies, while believing himself to be an incarnation of the truth.

They took their places in the hollows of divans bordered by low tables, on which coffee, liqueurs and tobacco were set out, along with the Marquise's chamomile tea, and were momentarily distracted by the announcements of the speaker. A sequence filed past of a train crash in London, a fire in the Refrigerated Docks at Bordeaux, the inauguration that morning by Solmou, at Bourg-la-Reine, of the twenty-seven-thousandth Monument to the Dead, with excerpts from the speeches, and the hunt held in the afternoon for the Diplomatic Corps at Marly…

Madame d'Entraygues applauded, with amicable warmth, the apparition of Madame Solmou, culotted and gaitered, beside the Soviet ambassador, and the reapparition of Solmou, wearing a felt hat with a pheasant feather.

"Our dear President is indefatigable," she praised.

He swelled up modestly. He was certain that the Republic of National Interests (Cervier, Turbot & Co.) possessed in him the model President. Irresponsible, and content to be— since the unfortunate adventure of one of his predecessors who, having tried to play the dictator, had been constrained to resign—he limited his role to that of decorative mannequin: the shadow of a monarch, good for making speeches at the

111

openings of exhibitions, banquets, centenaries and placing plaques, who had ended up, in good faith, mistaking the Élysée for France.

A sudden chill suddenly followed, however: Amédée Jacquemin was speaking at the Tribune in the Chambre. At the sight of the *bête noire*, the visages froze. The sound of the brazen voice, with its force and its rhythm weighing the phrases, seemed intolerable Turbot pressed a button. The speaker stopped, cut off. The screen became ash-gray again.

"He gets on my nerves, that man!" declared the Marquise.

"He's a public danger," snapped de Laume "One ought to be able to put such dreamers where they can do no harm."

"That's right!" said Turbot.

Solmou made no protest. The straight line always followed by Jacquemin was worse than a reproach; it was an insult to the curved line, in the opposite direction, that he had chosen. Jacquemin, a bourgeois liberal when Solmou had made his debut as an out-and-out socialist had, without ever deviating, gradually risen to the internationalism that Jaurès had incarnated thirty years earlier: the highest expression of the concept of fatherland. He was a traditionalist, in the sense that he only denied the dead weight of the past, because he thought that only the future could lighten all the chains of the present, but above all else, he was a realizer.

It was by virtue of that gift of government that he seemed infinitely dangerous to the traitors who, like Solmou, had changed camp, deserting in exchange for money to the holders of ancient privileges—the likes of d'Entraygues and Lux—and the new conquerors, like Cervier and Turbot, wallowing in their sovereignty as in a trough.

Turbot went on, peremptorily: "First of all, muzzle Jacquemin—not forgetting his wife, of course. The two are a unit. But make no mistake about it, their son is just as dangerous. It's him, more actively than the promissory eloquence, who is in the process of corrupting the people, who is putting its utopias into practice. Examples like that of Chesnay are deplorable. It's organized anarchy, a direct stimulation to revolt. With the taste for independence and wellbeing with which the inferior classes are now gangrenous, we're heading for a fall. We're already ruining ourselves with wages and soon, if we don't put things in order, the international strikes will end up expropriating us. Every day, the workers are getting a tighter grip on us. Now they have their towns, their gymnasia, and their swimming baths. Tomorrow it'll be our luxury…"

"Our shares, or dividends," Cervier added.

"And our places," sighed the Maréchal, horrified. "Monsieur Turbot has put his finger on the sore. Communism, that's the real enemy. If Monsieur the President of the Council wants my opinion..."

"An offensive, eh?"

"Exactly. And immediately. I'll answer for all the commandants of the military regions."

Solmou remained silent, ominously.

De Laume, a veritable protagonist, shrugged his shoulders. Having the custom of putting the President of the Republic in his pocket and only bringing him out to occupy the stage, he did not even consult him with a glance. In his dry voice, he pronounced, as if it were a verdict: "When necessary, I'll take care of the Jacquemins. But before resorting to…extreme means"—he exchanged a pitiless glance with Turbot and Cervier—"let's not forget that we are, parliamentarily, the masters. Our majority is loyal. Undoubtedly, the forthcoming elections will render it fussier, if it's a matter of questions as vital to democracy as to us. Even in our own party, the convictions that one could believe to the firmest are always ready to yield when the question of a new legislature arises. To be or not to be re-elected…!"

"You might even say, simply, to be or not to be," agreed Solmou.

An imperceptible snoring became audible. It was the Maréchal; only military strategy was capable of keeping him awake beyond the times routinely consecrated to repose.

Slightly vexed, Solmou coughed. It was a matter of the very destiny of the country—which is to say, the fate of National Interests. Lux was truly exaggerating serenity!

Madame d'Entraygues, who tolerated Lux because he to belonged to the Académie Française by the same mundane entitlement as the two Presidents, took pity on his glorious fatigue. She was feeling drowsy herself, having attended, charitably, the gala of the Petits Lits Blancs[31] the previous evening.

"I'll take our Napoléon away," she said. Going to sleep and waking up at will was the only point of resemblance that she admitted with the imperial genius. "Monsieur le Maréchal!" she shouted.

He opened an eye like a thinker extracted from some meditation. "Marquise?"

"We're leaving."

"At your orders. And yours, Messieurs."

Left alone, the four scoundrels talked without ambiguity. First of all, absolute silence in the major press. The order had, in any case, been given that morning by the President of the Council. It was necessary that the noise made by Jacquemin should fall into an oubliette. Then, if possible, buy the silence of the extremist papers. By exploiting their hatred of the proprietor of the *Universel* and his bourgeois socialism...

Cervier took responsibility for the delicate negotiations.

"And if the affair comes to the Chambre?"

"It will come, have no doubt about that," said Solmou. "I know my Jacquemin too well not to be certain that there'll be a demand for interpellation tomorrow..."

"We have means of persuasion in reserve. Oh, not for that fanatic, of course, but for many others," affirmed Max de Laume, tranquilly. He mentioned five names, which controlled

---

[31] The annual charitable *Bal des Petits Lits Blancs* [Ball of the Little White Beds], for the benefit of tubercular children, held at the Opera Garnier, was founded in 1918 by the journalist Léon Bailby.

a hundred votes. As for the small fry...he had a man for such work, Liéval, a former prefect capable of anything, who could work skillfully in the wings.

Solmou approved. Blackmail and bribery in all their forms, for the sum slipped from hand to hand to Madame's pearl necklace and Monsieur's old master painting, not to mention the distribution of places and election subsidies...the two Presidents smiled, thinking about the innumerable and elementary means of corruption. It was the infancy of the art...

Imperiously, a telephone rang. Turbot opened a nacre-encrusted box on a shelf, unhooked the apparatus and listened...

"For you, Cervier—your deputy."

The banker, his eyes and ears attentive, gradually assumed a serious expression.

"Good. Thank you, Lustand... No, nothing... I'll see about it tomorrow." He turned to Solmou. "You're a good prophet. Jacquemin's letter has just arrived."

"He's tabling a question?"

"Direct attack: "Is it true that foreign banks have bought, in association with a French bank, part of the national subsoil?"

"Denials aren't made for dogs," said Max de Laume, "nor procrastinations. Let's try first to drown the fish."

"And if he breaks the line?" asked Turbot, always precise.

"Then..."

There was a silence. Solmou lowered his eyes, careful not to compromise himself. Cervier, Turbot and de Laume looked at hm. They needed to specify the thought that was taking shape in them like a funereal larva. They were in accord.

"Then," Max de Laume translated, menacingly, "I'll see about it."

III

Claude stood up, in the section of the public gallery reserved for Presidents of the Council, from which he was listening, with his mother, to the debate of the famous interpellation, and waved his fist.

Cutting off one of Jacquemin's sentences at the very moment when the Chambre had calmed down, after stormy manifestations, to listen to his reply to de Laume, an interrupter on a neighboring bench had just cried: "Thug!" Vociferations, bravos and boos burst forth.

The tumult thus reignited propagated with instantaneous violence. From the balcony to the front stalls of the hemicycle, with the stage that Jacquemin, with his arms folded, dominated, under the desperate gesticulations of the President, the entire room had caught fire. One might have thought it a theater of lunatics in full battle. With the agitation of groups running riot, ushers throwing themselves between pugilists and the public leaping over the benches. A few revolver shots had been fired, drowned out by the cries that overlapped deafeningly: "Traitors! Wretches! Suspension!" There was only one vast din; many people, no longer able to speak, were using their hands.

Actors and spectators, playing pell-mell with the destiny of the nation, insulted one another and hurled abuse frenetically at the government, while at the table, surrounded by advisers as if by a cluster of flies, the President abandoned his futile hand bell. Coiffed in his top hat, he withdrew, while a picket of black soldiers, bayonets fitted, made its entrance.

Half an hour later, when the storm in the corridors had settled and the emotion in the galleries having calmed down, the doors were reopened, Claude, reinstalled next to his mother, was still shaking. She had succeeded in calming him down and Gine, who was sitting on another bench with Monsieur Blanchet and Sylvestre, was making him laugh by boasting about her prowess. She had broken her umbrella on the back of a huge imbecile. As for Sylvestre, she was exhibiting like a trophy a brightly colored decoration extracted from the hair of a neighbor clad in furs and pearls, who had had to be carried away in a fit of nerves. The interrupter had also been taken away with a broken rib and a bruised face—to teach him to make use of a Browning.

"Three shots—and aimed at father," Gine affirmed.

"They're not sure about that," said Sylvestre. "What is certain is that there was no need for the police to pass the tobacco. Everybody piled onto him. Not bad!"

"Come, come Miss Non-Violence!" Monsieur Blanchet observed, softly. "For it goes without saying, my dear Annik, that public sentiment is with you—which is to say, with Amédée."

She, like Claude, was sure that the "Thug!" came from further away, and that the incident had been carefully arranged in order to prevent the orator from completing his speech at all costs, and, since delays and various maneuvers of obstruction would only delay the debate for a few weeks, to hinder it by any means. Their clumsiness had overshot the target.

Annik did not, however, go so far as to think that it was a genuine assassination attempt—more the overexcitement of a madman.

Claude maintained his impression, however: "Bandits and, if necessary, murderers."

Since the collapse of his dearest illusion, he had changed, physically as well as morally. After the brief remission of the trip to Budapest, regret had gripped him again and was eating away at him. Sylvestre was alarmed to see him thinned out by the torment he was undergoing: the humiliation of being scorned to that degree, and, more painful still, the sentiment of not having shaken off the influence....

In vain he tried to deceive others, as well as himself. Sylvestre was not mistaken: he was still searching for reasons to explain and excuse Marise's behavior. Against Cervier alone, and his peers, he had deflected all the accumulation of his rancor. The rigor of a righteous hatred: he was now weighing upon everyone the suspicion from which, in spite of himself, he exempted the guilty party.

In despair, Sylvestre felt that he was ready, at the first lies, to fall back under the detestable charm, to yield to the penchant that everyone around her only wanted to favor. For two months, day by day, she had seen the efforts of her cheerful companionship go to waste: two months of despair, and defiant hope.

He had stopped seeing Marise, but seeing Sylvestre every day had sufficed for the former to become prestigious again, in becoming blurred, and for him to cease to render justice to the rare being with whom he was rubbing shoulders. A certain prejudice was even beginning to render him hostile to the manifestations, reserved as they were, of a tenderness that he only had to accept. He found being loved in spite of himself harder to bear than suffering from not being loved when he was in love himself. The satiety of certainty wearied him more than the uncertainty of his covetousness.

On perceiving the heavy mass of Cervier in his place, watching Jacquemin like a predator lying in ambush, Claude thought, in spite of himself, about Marise. He had only agreed to let himself be seen on one of the official benches in the expectation of her appearance. He had sought in vain among the flowerbed of faces for the rose of hers, and her golden tresses...

By means of a curious doubling, however, he heard the great paternal voice resounding, with its emotional warnings, over the disarray of its adversaries. A reversal of opinion was sensible. In the beginning, Jacquemin had only had the enthusiasm of his partisans with him, a minority founded on the assent of the benches in spite of the triage of their composition. Even by grouping the extremists, constrained by their principles to form a bloc on this occasion with the socialists, and what remained of the old radical party, it only added up to a third of the votes. However, the weakness and violent clumsiness of the governmental speeches and the redoubled blows that Jacquemin landed, riposting with the vigor of his heyday, had modified the situation.

From the increasingly sustained attention, and the involuntary movements that ran through the audience like the undulations of a storm wind, Claude sensed the disturbance increasing in the uncertain heart of the mass.

Elected on the equivocation of an impudent lie—"The parties of the left are war and ruination"—the bitterly reactionary Chambre had been invaded, in recent days, by the fear of the future: an interested commencement of wisdom, to such an extent that when Jacquemin spoke, agitating the electoral specter, the majority felt a sentiment of dread of annihilation entering into them. Might not obedience to the will of de Laume, for that majority, unprincipled beneath its vaguely republican label, be steering them toward certain defeat?

The country was weary of the scarcely-disguised dictatorship that the financier caste, with its bourgeois valets, weighed upon it. The immense sluggishness that the peace of Versailles and the metallurgical reign had submitted without reacting, and the transitional legislatures, had succeeded, previous socialist ministries having reawakened the popular imagination, by such a renewal of energy that it could not be suppressed for long without danger.

The Chambre, on hearing Jacquemin, was persuaded that the Cervier-de Laume reign was reaching its end, and, being primarily composed of old men with little or no interest in playing their guides' dangerous game to the end, was reluctant to gamble everything on the bloody trump card of a counter-revolutionary Terror.

Claude watched the progress of reason on the serious faces. Jacquemin, without pushing any further his advantage over Cervier—whose denials had not convinced anyone for an instant before the precision of his question posed—had risen to his feet almost immediately, to general consideration.

Europe had almost died, after the crippled peace, of the staunch partitioning of the protectionists, those sealed vessels of nationalities, great or small. The same masters of the game should not be permitted to broaden their field of operation under the mask of international customs unions. Treating the purchase of the oil deposits of Provence by the same Franco-foreign consortium that already owned those of Forez as an accomplished fact, he concluded by demanding, as a sanction of his interpellation, that the Chambre, in accord with the government, fix a date for the henceforth-inevitable debate on the nationalization of the subsoil. It was necessary to pronounce today, not on the principle, which Parliament would have all the time from February to May to study, but on its placement as soon as possible on the order of the day. Either his proposed law, first drafted years ago and brought back recently, would be taken under consideration, or, in the case of refusal, the Chambre must take its responsibility to the electoral body.

"And do not think, Monsieur le Président, that it will be permissible for you to find more subterfuges and sidesteps if, as I am certain, Parliament decides, in following me, to give satisfaction to public opinion. It wants to know, yes or no, whether your Minister of Finance has the right to deliver the territory of France to foreign masters; and whether, yes or no, international capitalism will make the law here, by reducing a nation, the owner of its land, to be nothing more than a mercenary to be exploited—worse than that, a slave to be despoiled. It will be necessary in the end for you to hear its cries of lassitude, and the ultimatum that I put to you in advance, certain of being the spokesman of veritable French thought. You and your majority will not escape its grip; either respond before May to the expectation of the people, or answer to them for your actions."

The threat was magnified in the silence, as the spreading ripples of a stone thrown into mud burst bubbles. Bravos and murmurs ran over the surface; profound sentiment was still reserved.

On the Ministers' bench, de Laume signaled to Cervier to sit down. "I demand to speak," he snapped, his voice gruff.

He was about to head for the podium when Jacquemin stopped him.

"One more word, Monsieur le Président, the last. It is affirmed that with capital whose origin the Minister of Finance is all the better placed to inform us, because it has been furnished to the Banque Cervier—I await further denials with tranquility—contrary to the stipulations of the Geneva Convention prohibiting the manufacture of toxic gases with any other motive than their industrial usage, a giant factory is presently under construction for the military exploitation of the patent that you have just bought from the inventor Louis Poncet..."

"That is a rumor unworthy of being brought to the podium," de Laume declared, from his place.

"Indeed! If the assertion were accurate, it would be a direct violation of the statute of the League of Nations—I would say a grave threat to peace, if your external politics did not *seem*"—he emphasized the word forcefully—"oriented toward the creation of a United States of Europe. I say *seem* because what you are working to form, with the collaboration of international banks, is merely a counterfeit, for the usage of your own interests, of that vital organism. The Confederation of the United States of Europe will be fashioned by the will of the people, not yours..." (Applause from the center left and the far left.)

"What are you trying to say?" asked the President, feigning a yawn.

"This: that one does not make a child's bed with gravediggers. Your external politics involves real risks of international war."

"You know very well that it is not so...!"

Jacquemin cut him off with brutal authority. "Then why, and against whom, are these enormous provisions being made, whose accumulation science might render useless tomorrow, in its ever-more-murderous search for the ray that kills and the gas that causes permanent sleep?"

"The Chambre will understand my discretion on the subject of this invention. The most elementary concern for National Defense, if we did not know that the speaker is an impenitent internationalist, would have forbidden him…"

"I take note of your confession, and offense at your accusation. I can easily deduce with what objective you have decided the employment and already commenced building stocks." (Murmurs and various movements.) "You are, I know, one of those who believes in fortifying peace by preparing for war—a tragic illusion, moreover; it is the disarmament of chauvinistic passions, not the eternal race to ruin and death, that can lay the foundation of peace. But you have recognized yourselves that no war would threaten the world if plutocracy were not ever ready to unleash it, for the supremacy of an internationalism more impenitent than mine.

"No? Is it, then, Monsieur le Président, solely for the needs of your internal politics that your precautions are being fortified? Know this, then! I give you this simple warning, in the face of the nation that is listening to you and can hear me: *nothing*—neither your arsenals of murderous gases, nor the black guards whose loaded rifles we saw appearing just now—will prevent us from snatching away from the *loups*-Cerviers[32] the prey that they believe they already hold, along with the French subsoil and those who covet it, and the organization of European resources."

Cervier, who was pale, had stood up, gesticulating in the midst of the indignant cries of his partisans, banging lecterns and brandishing their fists. "Censure! Censure!" howled de Laume's hired mamelukes. They were shouting themselves hoarse in the ovation that spread from bench to bench.

Jacquemin raised his arm. A relative silence was reestablished. Then he delivered the final blow: "The supreme hour is sounding for you, Messieurs of the majority. Capitulate or

---

[32] If Cervier is construed as a surname, then the additive *loups* simply mean "wolves," as per Jacquemin's intention, but the wordplay is based on the fact that the portmanteau term *loup-cervier* is the French expression used to identify the European lynx.

disappear. Capitulate today, as wise men who, foreseeing the future, do not despair of collaborating in it, or disappear tomorrow, swept away like wisps of straw by a high wind!"

Uncertain, a part of the Chambre hesitated, as if, unleashed by the threat, an irresistible wind were passing over their curbed heads. At the same time, half the députés acclaimed Jacquemin along with the almost unanimous public as he returned to his place in the midst of congratulations and handshakes.

Annik followed from a distance the sway of his strong stature. His white beard, curled round the broad face, brought out the color of his complexion, and his eyes were shining with youthfulness. He was assailed. Unexpected friends revealed themselves. Others, hostile the day before, brought him their apologies with a gilded smile for the new sun. The indubitable signs of a ministerial crisis had become manifest. A rush of sympathies formed an escort for the President of the Council designate...

Affecting disdain, Max de Laume, with a rage that would have committed murder if it could, went past the enemy as he headed for the podium with a rapid stride.

Annik and Claude only had eyes for their "great man", launching the tender darts of their admiration and joy at him. Before sitting down again, Jacquemin exchanged a satisfied nod of the head with them.

De Laume had begun his speech for the defense. In the amazement of finding himself unexpectedly condemned by the parliamentary cowardice of which he had so long been the beneficiary, unable to admit that it was his turn to fall victim to it, he attacked in order to defend himself. Such personal bitterness filled his insinuations, and eventually his accusations, with bile, that the aggression was weakened by it.

In vain he brought out the habitual clichés and brandished the images of yore: the man with the knife between his teeth, the crooked hand suspended over the peasant soil; the red torch and factories in flames. In vain he tried to strike, no longer at the imagination, but at the stomachs of his thus-far-docile clients. Their anxiety was more impressed by the dread of losing everything than by the hope of being able to gain more at a later date. By his intransigence, de Laume would lead them straight into the cul-de-sac of a revolution, of which the misery of Russian emigration and the first Soviet rigors had inculcated them with a holy terror when young. With Jacquemin—a revolutionary, no doubt, but whose political evolutionism did not reason *ex abstracto*, like that of the first mystic Muscovites—there remained, feeble as it might be, a glimmer of hope, the possibility of reaching an understanding. Throwing ballast overboard was better than sinking.

"He's shooting blanks," said Claude, on hearing de Laume fire at his fleeing troops the pistol of his eternal question of confidence.

"He's going down," observed Annik.

Meanwhile, nourished applause grew into a broken chorus. More by habit than privilege, the obligatory flowers and crowns were awarded. On scrutinizing the nominal list demanded by a final clumsiness of pride, the government found, instead of the feeble majority for which it had hoped, a deficit of twenty—a defection that rendered its departure inevitable

Under the storm of opposed manifestations—boos and bravos rumbling in a brief thunder soon interrupted by a general stampede—the Ministers quit their bench. In single file, portfolios under their arms, attempting to strut, they followed their leader.

White with repressed rage, Max de Laume displayed an indifference that he thought elegant, whose falsity was so evident that it generated laughter on the benches. To the faithful, who were thinning out he announced: "I shall inform the President of the Republic of my decision."

"The resignation of the cabinet?" groaned Cervier, linking arms with him. "Resign the game? That's crazy!"

But de Laume was bound, given his position, to abide by the constitution—which did not prevent him seeking a means to hang on, thanks to Solmou. An Élyséan message, deeming the vote to have been stolen by surprise, and not valid? A new debate, which might permit him to negotiate between now and tomorrow? One might be able to buy sufficient support by paying the price. Or convince the President of the Republic purely and simply to ask him to form a different Ministry?

But the wind of panic that had just bowled de Laume over had flattened Solmou merely by brushing him. Brave in inverse proportion to risk, Maurice the Pushover did not see any need to conserve de Laume, from the moment that he alone retained the authority that seemed as indispensable to the country as it was to himself. He made the utility of it evident to the vanquished.

"By refusing to accept your defeat, standing up against Parliament, I'd be assuming a responsibility"—he pronounced the word with a sacred terror—"for which…"

"You don't have the courage," de Laume concluded, bitterly, without being unduly surprised.

Majestically, Solmou attested: "I would have the courage if I didn't fear the result for our cause. To make use, on this occasion, of personal power, given that I, by definition as in fact, am not responsible"—this time the syllables flowered with honeyed softness—"seems, the more I think about it, to be less than politic. To be politic, here, is more than prudent; it's in our evident interest. Jacquemin will be President of the Council. So what? No one is eternal. He'll disappear, inevitably, sooner or later…"

He stopped, his gaze oblique. He avoided searching, in the eyes of his accomplice, for the thought that Turbot and Cervier had had one evening, and whose bloody larva had grown unconsciously within him.

He went on: "Given time, and favorable circumstances—who knows?—we can perhaps avoid a revolution over which you can't give me a guarantee, today, that you'll triumph. Let's wait and see—which isn't to say that we'll let things go. I know that you don't share my opportunism, but that's what got me to the presidential seat. It's a summit from which, believe me, one can see more clearly. In any case, there's one thing that you can't doubt, which is my attachment to your person and your ideas."

The ex-President let a harsh gaze fall upon his friend. They parted without cordiality, and the ritual consultations began. When he returned to the Quai d'Orsay, de Laume had reflected. Yes, perhaps apparent capitulation was the best course. One could not doubt either Solmou's experience or, as he put it, his "attachment."

Not all the payments of the Association of National Interests had been made namelessly. Evidence was slumbering, carefully filed in Michelle d'Entraygues' strong-box. Solmou knew that—and many others who had betrayed him just now, and whose insult de Laume was chewing over furiously.

He suddenly thought that it might be necessary to carry out a triage of those compromising papers. If many were of a nature to serve, some might be injurious, and dangerously so. Searches were so rapid! Jacquemin in power was, like him, a man who would not refrain, if not from burglary, at least from a legal investigation. What if he found the letters from Du Crêté?"

Du Crêté was the French ambassador to Berlin. There was an entire personal correspondence that testified to the transactions between the Quai d'Orsay and Otto von Wittelsbach, the ultra-nationalist Imperial chancellor. It detailed, with supportive names, the measures to be taken in the two countries in case of war or revolution: subsidies to be placed; socialists to be suppressed one by one—among them, naturally, Jacquemin, Rohn & Co.

De Laume promised himself to begin tidying up his archives, without delay.

IV

A cheerful family dinner at the Jacquemins' preceded the inevitable file of intimates. Madame Richou, the concierge, knew them well. The rest had been pitilessly shown the door. The telephone was also immobilized.

Claude and Gine, still trembling after the victory, were making, dismantling and remaking the Ministry, as if its composition had not been meditated and settled in advance by the victor in extraparliamentary discussions. Jacquemin reserved for himself, along with the Presidency of the Council, the Ministry of Foreign Affairs. In the meantime, he was enjoying an exceedingly pleasant hour of rest, like a haven after a perilous sea journey.

At the table, Annik strove to conceal the regret of sorts that she felt, this time as on previous occasions, at the changes that the heavy responsibilities of government that Amédée would assume the following day were undoubtedly going to bring to the intimacy of life. Not that they were thinking of quitting the old and cherished apartment in the Boulevard Raspail where they had woven the fabric on a daily basis, for twenty-two years, first in difficulty and then in joy, of the solid envelope of their happiness. Even when he was a Minister, Jacquemin returned there for dinner every evening, to refresh himself in the calm nest.

The couple had never been separated since Claude's birth, save for the travels that their professions sometimes obliged them to undertake in isolation: speeches by one or other of them in great cities, Annik's feminist propaganda and Jacquemin's official visits.

"This," she said, happy to remain in the house with Gine and Claude when a banquet or a reception constrained him to don formal dress for some inevitable ceremony, "is one of my petty benefits. But for free union I might be obliged to accompany you, to go and play the ape like the others..."

But he replied, teasingly, as he kissed her: "Do you think so? Have you ever done anything you didn't want to?"

"Are you complaining?"

"Of course!" And he laughed, benevolently, affectionately and wholeheartedly.

Life, instead of raising the hedge between them that looms up between so many husbands and wives protective of their egoism, had fused the equilibrium of their equality in a perfect understanding: an identity forged by reciprocal concessions as much as common ideals. Claude, Gine...the education of new couples! The expansion of human happiness...

When the first chime of the doorbell sounded, they had finished dinner, with the window ajar even though it was February. Every day, the glare of a precocious spring was radiating over Paris. A spacious odor rose up with the cool night air from the gardens opposite, over which Jacquemin loved to gaze when he went onto his balcony to breathe, at the mossy roofs of Madame de Chateaubriand's infirmary. *Les Mémoires d'Outre-Tombe* and *René* filled his memory with their magnificent racket at the evocation of the phantom who had walked there when alive...

"Adieu, my reading!" he sighed.

Everywhere, embellishing the walls with the variegation of their covers or the gilded leather of ancient bindings, the rows of volumes extended, invading the rooms.

At the sound of the drawing room door opening, the two women were hastily clearing the table.

"I'm sure it's Georgi!" Gine had said.

Claude had waited for his father to fold up his napkin. Taller than him, he had put an arm around him, marching affectionately in step with him. He admired him for the modesty of his science. That uncontested superiority, which even his enemies recognized—under the sole form, moreover, of eloquence—came from the eclecticism in admiration that the former pupil of the École Normale had refashioned in contact with the humble. Jacquemin had maintained the culture of Letters, but whereas a de Laume had only picked withered flowers and ashen fruit, he, Claude thought, had sucked all the generous sap from them.

"Why, it's Jules!" he exclaimed, on going into the drawing room.

The son of the chemist Louis Poncet, the man of the day, had come with Georgi.

"How is your mother?" Gine asked the latter, having immediately taken possession of him under Annik's tender gaze.

"Still suffering this morning—but it's not serious, since Sylvestre and Papa, who are going to a concert this evening, are going to come to collect me before going home. They want to congratulate your father, too."

Jacquemin listened with an expression of contentment to Jules Poncet's compliments.

"You nearly got me lynched by my father, Monsieur le Président, but I'm very happy. Thanks to you, our invention won't be used by the wretches who would have dishonored it. I did well to tell you. In our hands, I'm tranquil. And my father will console himself by thinking that his munitions, in changing their eventual target, won't go to waste. If they're used, it will be against the enemies of the people."

"Shut up!" said Annik, amicable. "You're horrifying me. You, one of Claude's friends, thinking of that monstrosity, the efficacy of Murder—and what Murder! The most terrible of all!"

"To kill murder, Madame, there's no better means than our gas, and if I weren't fearful of incurring your wrath, I'd even say that it's the only means. It's only when all the belligerents—and among them the greater number who don't fight—are equally threatened that violence has a chance of reaching its end. The day when all the men and women who, for one reason or another, lounge around in the rear while massacres are going on at the front—the gouty, the shirkers, the double-dealers, the very old, the very young, and women—sense inevitable death suspended above their heads..."

"The bomb of Damocles," said Jacquemin.

129

"On that day, believe me, it will be the end of war. It will die of the general fear, after having lived on the forced courage of a few and the sheltered cowardice of the majority. A salutary fear will have reckoned with gratuitous heroism. And the bravery of true heroes will be able henceforth to devote itself to less ingrate tasks..."

"Do you believe," Annik replied, "that we can't arrive at the same result without such weapons? Their danger is double-edged. The fear of their usage might perhaps be a brake I admit, but it's such a brutal brake that it risks breaking all the springs. Without the stimulant of a belief so beautiful that it imposes the acceptance of sacrifice at the required moment, we won't get out of the mire into which we're sinking. Fear has never engendered anything but cowards."

"I think I can convince you," said Poncet. "One example—tell me if I'm mistaken: last week, Claude and I came before the Revision Council. In October we'll be militarized. Let's suppose that, in spite of our hopes, the elections, thanks to our adversaries' large financial resources, have brought the war party back into power by then...and that one of those unexpected events that are, all things considered, nothing but the breakdown of a well-regulated piece of clockwork—one of these Sarajevo-like pretexts—confronts us with mobilization...Claude, me, Georgi, all of us. For, whatever Maréchal Lux might think, it isn't with shock troops, black or otherwise, that the question of war will be settled. *Finis Europae*, this time: all the nations going the way of their manpower, and the entire world to its ruin. What would our duty be? To refuse to obey, at the risk of being immediately sacrificed to your principle? Or to make use of weapons to go and destroy, with a well-placed volley, Berlin and a few other Munichs?"

"Are you listening, Mother?" Gine asked.

On hearing Georgi's name, she had drawn closer with him, while Annik, forced to respond to the friends who had arrived, was only paying partial attention to the discussion. Seeing Jacquemin surrounded, she came back, as the last words were spoken. Already, however, Claude had exclaimed:

130

"Duty, in a case of war like that? There's no doubt about it: it would be to abstain. No force, even that of a more or less specious reckoning, would constrain me to go and kill or be killed, for the greater glory of a Maréchal or the greater fortune of a Profiteer. A war of conquest or a war of rapine!" His gaze interrogated his comrades. "Well, don't you agree? And there would be hundreds of thousands of us, in all lands. Which would even rob us, shiverer," he added, addressing his sister in jest, "of the merit of running the risk you fear: a dozen so-called French bullets, or, which comes to the same thing, a revolver shot from some negro officer."

"Shut up!" she cried, hands extended to drive away the frightful vision.

Georgi reassured her. "Don't worry—that no longer happens, as in the time of the mutinies of 1917 or of the Versaillaise machine-gunners."

"Cadaver-mills," affirmed Claude, "would quickly cease to turn in the hands of the people."

"Agreed," Poncet approved, "but on one condition. That the people on the other side have also forsaken force. You and Georgi are reasoning as if all nations not only had the same age, but as if they had grown up together or aged wisely. There is, however, one case in which to refuse to obey wouldn't be a duty but a desertion. What if, tomorrow, without provocation, the Germans, the Russians, the Chinese—what do I know?—were to attack us? Georgi is free to think like Gine, but you, Saint-Just, against the defensive war that it would be necessary for us to fight..."

"The sacred union?" Georgi mocked. "The sacred union of strong-boxes, mattressed by our breasts?"

"Simply the Fatherland in danger."

Annik elevated the debate with a word: "One can always avoid a war no matter what."

"Assumption!"

"Truth. There would have been no need for your gas in 1915 if England had thrown her sword into the balance at the first threat...and if tomorrow, our Confederation of the United

131

Peoples of Europe, the only armed force, had its police. Adieu, Bellona!"

"Yesterday! Tomorrow! What about today?"

"No one would dare to declare and pursue an unjust war—and all of them are—even at the weak point of international understanding where we still are, against people who would courageously refuse the sword..."

"To let themselves be invaded and massacred?"

"Invaded, yes, to avoid massacre. I tell you that Non-Violence is the most powerful of weapons. The reproval against the aggressor would be such that, before universal revulsion and threat, he would allow himself to yield to the first pressure for arbitration."

"You're supposing the problem resolved and the world better than it is."

"No," said Annik. "But like Saint-Just whose testimony you're invoking against me via Claude, I'm supposing 'a general evil sufficiently great for public opinion to feel the need for measures appropriate to do good...' Remind me how it finishes, Claude."

"'That which produces the general good is always terrible, and seems bizarre when one begins too soon.'"

"Alas," Poncet persisted, "for a long time yet, Madame, not to say forever—and you won't deny me this time without putting yourself into contradiction with Monsieur Jacquemin, whose doctrine has never varied—the first of duties is national protection."

"The first of duties," opposed Gine, turning toward her mother a face illuminated by the reflection of her faith, "is to obey the highest law of humankind: 'Thou shalt not kill.' Isn't that so, Georgi?"

He hesitated, caught in a vice. All the force of his soul impelled him toward the religion of the future, but his feet stumbled over the traps of the present.

"Desertion for desertion, I believe that I'd choose the one that cost me the most..."

"Which is to say?" Jules Poncet demanded.

"To pass for an antipatriot."

"Letting France die, then! As if, in order for Humankind to be raised to a higher law of life, the blood of all Fatherlands weren't necessary! But it's Humankind I'm preserving with my murderous gases, if they give to France the means of living, while shedding the least possible blood..."

"Do you believe," Georgi riposted, "that I wouldn't shed mine willingly, to avoid even that effusion?"

"No, no," begged Gine, "don't say such things! The firing squad would be an imbecilic death, when, with a flap of the wing, one could be over the frontier, crying *beware*, raising the revolt of common sense, justice and life everywhere!"

Stubbornly, however, Poncet continued: "Death for death, and since nature informs us that the continuation of the species is nothing but a long hazardous battle in the selection of seeds, I'd prefer, for example, to destroy a few enemies of progress than to expose myself to being killed by them in honor of Saint Gandhi."

"He's right," said Claude.

Jacquemin, who had overheard the last words ringing in an interval in the conversation, came to stand beside his son. Annik, sitting on the large bench that blocked the fireplace, drew him to her, and said, tenderly: "That's right, come and support them, these men!"

A belief more absolute than Jacquemin's animated her in the purity of her mysticism. Like her, Amédée admitted the principle of non-cooperation with all ends of violence, but, Statesman that he was above all, and the head of a government rather than the leader of a party, he could not go as far as the rigor of integral application.

Thus, after having declared that small rural property ought, like large-scale land-ownership, become truly collective, he had been obliged, during his first Presidency of the Council, while imposing improvement by the nationalization of implements, to admit—at least for industry and commerce, mining and routes of communication—a system of wages that, in sum, allowed the former state of affairs to subsist, while

133

becoming more flexible and being modernized. A transmission still remained possible by sale or heritage, doubtless submissive to laws broadly preserving everyone's share, but maintaining the privilege of industrial labor.

Similarly, after his ardent campaigns undertaken against all the workers who, by toiling in the manufacture of cannons, shells, torpedoes and gases, were betraying the popular ideal, he had been obliged to take account of the fact that, in the bloody swamp into which the treaty of Versailles, a failure of the Wilsonian dream, had replunged human hope, it was necessary, if one did not want to risk being drowned, to manufacture sufficient cannons, shells, torpedoes and gases...

To the supplications of Annik, convinced that it would suffice for one people, the first, to disarm, for that the entire world, relieved, to follow its example, he had always opposed, sadly but with unshakable firmness, his conviction of an old man, raised in a traditional mold, and, in spite of all his generous good will, only escaping it in part. In vain, with the tenderness and pity of a wife and mother, Annik had launched forth into prophetic clairvoyance; he had held firm, he, too, hoping for the future, but hemmed in by contingencies as yet inevitable.

"You're both right," he concluded, placing his hand on Annik's knee, "and I believe sincerely that Georgi, enlightened by love, is, with Gine and you, in the truest of verities. There will come a day when struggles between fatherlands will seem as monstrously savage as a murder between brothers. Humankind—and more rapidly than we think on looking at its slow progress this far—will be raised to the highest law of all consciousness that Gine mentioned."

He smiled. "That is not, in my view, as it is, the one that you pronounced, my daughter: 'Thou shalt not kill!' There is, in any case, some illogicality in the instruction, for the carnivores that we are, and which, I fear, we shall remain for a long time yet, while waiting for Dr. Ladre and his pills to evangelize our physical nourishment definitively, as a mother nourishes us with morality."

He became serious again. "The most beautiful of maxims, not merely Christian but human, because it is not, like the other, a means but an end, and which contains the entire future in embryo, is 'Love one another!' There—that's better than good advice! It's the very law of existence: the ineluctable solidarity that reconciles, like it or not, the limbs and the stomach. In any case, while giving body and soul to the faith that we all have, it doesn't prevent us from diverging in our opinions with regard to the best means to serve it."

"Well," joked Annik, "deep down, you don't think differently from de Laume. You, too, believe that one can fortify peace by preparing for war."

"In preparing for peace," he rectified, "with the same determination. For there's one subtle difference: I only consider Poncet's gas as a kind of social insurance premium against the de Laumes and their wars. It is, therefore, peace and peace alone that I'm not only preparing, but ensuring, by making it so strong that it will impose itself, without there being any need for recourse to the violence that I hate, as you know, as much as you do..."

The arrival of Monsieur Blanchet and Sylvestre provided a diversion. The professor related the latest news. He had missed the second act of the play and had gone to the *Universel* in search of information. The Presidents of the Chambre and the Senate, summoned to the Élysée, had so clearly designated Jacquemin that Solmou, limiting his consultations, had just resigned himself to telephoning the newspaper, having been unable to get through to the Boulevard Raspail.

"He's expecting you tomorrow. His general secretary ought to be on the way here to notify you."

On cue, the doorbell rang. It was Solmou's envoy. Jacquemin received him in his study.

The joyful buzz in the drawing room continued. Gine had taken Sylvestre into a corner, worried by her sad expression.

"What's the matter? Is it your mother's health that's tormenting you?"

She blushed and replied: "Yes, she hasn't been well for some time..."

There was nothing to dread in that direction, however. Cardiac troubles, which only troubled with a temporary oppression a temperament so solid that her children and her husband, when Monique mentioned the sudden end that, she said, was imminent, always replied: "You! You'll bury us all!" A very different preoccupation was darkening Sylvestre's gaze. The nervous, vibrant enthusiasm of old had been succeeded by sudden bouts of languor, followed by a hypersensitivity so evident that Gine, without being able to divine the root cause, absorbed as she was by her own amour, had remarked upon it. Like Claude, Sylvestre had changed.

Gine thought it absurd for her brother to suffer over Marise, and that it was good of Sylvestre to be so concerned about a sentiment that, in sum, only affected her superficially. That was what she thought, at least, with Sylvestre, enclosed in the modesty of her suffering, having always avoided displaying, before anyone whatsoever, the entire depth of her wound.

Only Annik, for her son, like Monique, for her daughter, could read in their young faces the mute confession of their torment. They had often exchanged their impressions and regrets. Like Georgi and Gine, they would have liked Claude and Sylvestre to reach a mutual understanding. They cursed the unconsciousness of the heart that drives so many men to seek obstinately where it is not, a happiness that they have close at hand. Thus, Claude looked at Sylvestre without seeing her.

"Deep down," Gine said, casually, indicating to her friend the room, too small for the visitors, "this adventure irritates me. We'll no longer belong to ourselves!"

"We don't see you very often as it is."

"You're crazy. We've hardly been apart this week."

But him! Sylvestre thought. *The factory, the political and business meetings—he was never here! And when he was…!* Bitterly, she counted the recent times when her pleasure in seeing Claude had been spoiled, as it had just now, by the indifference of his greeting.

Indifference—that was putting it mildly. Under that banally affectionate abruptness, there had been a dull spite, the injustice of which lacerated her: poisoned thorns, the secret of which she kept to herself, a gangrene growing beneath the feigned stoicism.

Jacquemin came back into the drawing room, confirming the step taken by the Élysée.

"And now, my good friends," said Annik, "I'll throw you out. You'll admit that it's been a busy day…"

One by one or in groups, everyone withdrew, some with the hope of a portfolio, others simply rejoicing in seeing, with the triumph of their ideas, their man at the heart of things. Only the Blanchets still remained. The Professor was determined to be the last to leave in order to share momentarily the pleasure of being, as it were, at a family gathering.

Jacquemin took advantage of it to offer him once again the Ministry of Public Education, which Blanchet had refused during the last socialist cabinet. Again he refused, stubbornly.

"I'm not made for politics. It requires more faith than I have; Monique, who admires it in you, would detest it in me. And nothing, in my eyes, is worth as much as the security of our happiness."

"Georgi will represent the family, then, if he'd like to direct my secretariat with Claude."

"What about me, then?" exclaimed Gine.

"You?" said Jacquemin mischievously. "You'll be deputy secretary."

"Georgi's secretary! I'd like that…"

"While awaiting something better," said Annik, all smiles, and happy. A few days before, she, like the Blanchets, had received the young people's confidences. A union of free choice, which responded so completely to her desires as well as to her principles. Two healthy young people sharing the same hope: the straight line of a unitary life of overlapping parallels. It had been agreed that she would talk to Monique about it as soon as they met up, and that Georgi and Gine would then fulfill the formula of engagement, which, by establishing the identity of the contractants and their desire to unite themselves, was now sufficient, once transcribed in the registers of the civil estate, to validate the marriage.

A propagandist, by her noble personal example, for free union, she admitted intelligently that, Blanchet and Monique adhering to the old custom, and the grace of her influence having reinforced that of Amédée, the Code had ended up being profoundly modified in the chapters on Marriage and Divorce...

How complete her joy would be if Claude...!

While Gine and Georgi kissed one another on the cheek with a cheerful: "Until tomorrow," a dull echo of a voice cut short Sylvestre's adieux. She had retained Claude's hand in her own and had just said to him, mildly: "When shall I see you tomorrow? I won't have the good fortune to serve as your secretary, even temporarily...you've dropped me—that's not kind."

He had perceived, under the playfulness of the plea, the bitterness of the reproach, and replied hotly: "You annoy me!"

Mutely, Sylvestre recoiled as if folded up. Seeing the abrupt pallor that appeared in her sun-tanned face, Annik and Amédée exchanged a pained glance. Claude's unfortunate passion for Marise worried them. How stupid it was when, close at hand...

Monsieur Blanchet, who had not heard, clapped his hands to inform the lovers that it was time to go.

Annik drew Sylvestre to her, tenderly, and favored her with a long maternal kiss. The dolorous eyes met her consoling eyes.

With all her heart, the mother, who was still a woman, cried silently to that despair, the pride of which moved her: "Courage! Patience!"

V

For a month, an epidemic of flu had been raging—a savage flu, immediately diagnosed by the Faculty as very serious. Public opinion had outbid that: the disease was fatal. It was, however, nothing but influenza, otherwise known as Spanish flu, or more simply as infectious flu. It is necessary for maladies, like any other fashion, to change their name.

Monique had been confined to bed for a fortnight, on returning from one of her charitable visits to a poor unmarried woman with a six-month-old baby, who was dying. Her fever had immediately worsened.

The blow had been so abrupt that Sylvestre, frightened, had thought her doomed. Forty-eight hours ago, the oppression had diminished, and the lowering of the temperature had permitted the glimpse of a recovery, but it was at the moment when everyone shared the renascent hope after the scare, which her daughter envisaged, along with Dr. Fermot, supported by the employment of tonics, that Monique suddenly, by virtue of one of those mysterious warnings of the organism—one of those monitions that the soul perceives before the body—thought herself profoundly afflicted.

With curiosity and, in spite of her courage, with a little anxiety, too, she analyzed her condition. After a disturbed night, she thought she had become drowsy and begun to dream…what a bizarre sensation! It was a matter of consciousness, still keen, struggling with the body, the one trying to escape, the other to retain it.

Monique looked inside herself. Was she going to acquire a certainty dolorous for those she loved, to whom, thus far, she had consecrated herself so joyfully? Was she already seeing her…?

She stopped; her mind refused to specify the funereal word. A frisson ran through her. Was it…that *that* was announcing itself? Another frisson, more violent, shook her. It

139

seemed to her that, in contact with an invisible hand that was brushing her from head to toe, hairs emerged from the pores of her skin, to return thereinto immediately as the hand passed on. Yet another frisson…and during the interval that separated each fit, a strange serenity.

This time, she looked at herself squarely. She felt different: still alive, and yet already dead.

Death…why refuse to evoke it? At close range it was not as frightening as it was at a distance, when its name, merely its name, could chill you. Let's see, at this instant, what was she feeling? A doubling that surprised her without afflicting her. Her spiritual envelope outside her physical envelope…not beside it, but slightly above it…and a peace…an interior peace…unknown…sovereign.

How attached they are to little things, the living!

She watches her daughter moving back and forth in the room, on tiptoe. Sylvestre is bringing in a few items of delicate linen, in order to put them away in the chest of drawers. And Monique sees her past again: *How I suffered at her age! I was like her, ardent and savage…Lucien…that first disillusionment ravaged my entire youth. Sylvestre is also in love, and not beloved, Claude loves someone else…and I won't be there, I'll have gone, like Aunt Sylvestre!* A worrying parallelism.

Having finished her tidying, Sylvestre comes slowly toward her mother's bed. Monique follows her with her eyes.

"Oh! Did I wake you, Mother dear?"

Monique shakes her head negatively. The young woman leans over and kisses her tenderly. "How do you feel, my love?"

"Well."

"Ah!" A sigh escapes, along with all the dread that was within her.

"Sit down," Monique instructs.

"You don't want anything first? A drink?"

"No. Sit down and give me your hand."

"At your orders. Here it is, Madame." Sylvestre's tone is not the merriment of a veritable gaiety. It is a kind of sound thrown into the tranquility, true or feigned, of her "Maman." She finds the nostrils slightly pinched, the eyes widened, and an uncustomary acuity in her gaze.

Monique has smiled, but her visage has resumed its gravity almost immediately. "You resemble me today, I think, more than usual. That's curious. When I look at you, it's me at your age that I see. I know that I'm in my bed, and yet it's me that I see beside me."

Her voice has a strange ring to it. Sylvestre does not recognize it. How has it arisen? And why, if her mother contained it—that metallic voice, which clipped words—is she only hearing it for the first time today?

"How do you explain that phenomenon of doubling, Mademoiselle Doctor?"

Oh, how antipathetic and hostile that voice is!

"I can only explain it, Madame Convalescent, by means of weakness."

"No."

"What, then?"

"Lucidity. My spirit is outside my body."

"What do you mean?"

"Nothing, my child, simply that time is measured and that I'm contemplating us. I was like you at twenty: fresh, confident, loving…all ardent spontaneity…and that made me very unhappy."

"Because you hadn't had a Maman like mine to bring you up!"

"I had my Aunt Sylvestre, whom I loved as much as you love me, and who…left me at the moment when I needed her the most."

The child is troubled, and squeezes the invalid's hand. "You're talking too much. You'll tire yourself out."

Sylvestre's fingers surround her mother's wrist. The pulse is weak—so weak that it scarcely seems to be beating. Dread strikes her. Like a fearful animal, she scents the enemy, and tries to perceive it. But Monique continues: "Promise me that, if I disappear…you won't do anything in life without seeking advice from your father, and also…Annik."

Sylvestre tries to smile. "What do you expect to happen to you? Come on, shut up—don't say silly things, or I'll go away, naughty!" She wags her finger threateningly—but her hand is trembling.

"Promise me, my child, and don't forget that I made you promise."

"We'll talk about it when you're better. I'm going to let you rest now." She does not add that she is in haste to telephone Dr. Fermot. He will find the remedy! He will save her! She doesn't know what to do; she can no longer see clearly.

As she tries to get up, however, Monique holds onto her.

"Stay with me, and make the promise I asked of you. I would have so liked you to be happy, like your brother. Swear to me…if, one day…you're in too much pain…swear to me to take…before anything…your dear father's advice…"

"Yes, it's agreed, there! But you're tormenting me to the end!" Sylvestre's emotion rises into her eyes. "I'm going to send for Fermot right away."

"It's futile." Monique knows that her living hours are counted; she no longer has a moment to lose. Once the blow has fallen, her daughter, a courageous patient, will allow herself to be bandaged. "Neither you, nor science, nor anyone can save me now…I've been dead for an hour."

"Maman!" Sylvestre sobs, and stops her ears in order not to hear, and to hope for a little longer.

Monique extends a hand toward her. "Listen to me carefully."

"Maman, Maman!" She has become a little girl again, who feels ill and is calling for help.

"If you're afflicted by a great chagrin, don't live as I lived at the beginning of my life."

"You, my saint! My beautiful example!"

"What an apprenticeship I had to serve, before having the pride to be an example!"

"Let me, I beg you, ask Fermot to come immediately."

"Too late! It's my body that's speaking, out of habit...the rest is already far from human life."

"Don't leave me such a gnawing regret!" Sylvestre cries in a heart-rending tone.

"Let the chambermaid summon him, if you wish."

Sylvestre runs out. "And Papa and Georgi aren't here!"

"Oh, I want to last until they return. You can give me an injection of camphorated oil."[33]

While her daughter, after having feverishly telephoned the doctor herself, and ordered Nane to find and warn "Monsieur and Georgi," fussed around her, the moribund had collected herself, impatient to say her last words.

When the injection had been made, she replied: "No," with her gaze, to the supplicant "Be quiet!" and, gathering her strength, continued: "Listen. Even if you have to despair of your happiness, never be a rebel, at least against yourself. Whatever life reserves for you, my child... At your age, I, too, lost the person who loved me more than anyone else in the world, while a tragedy of love was consuming me."

Sylvestre has hidden her head in her hands. Monique gently caresses her forehead and her hair.

"Hope! Perhaps he'll love you one day!"

Those words unleash the hurricane of dolor. Sylvestre no longer knows why she is weeping. Despair abandons itself, within her, to the forces of Destiny.

"I've known a similar annihilation. Don't rebel as I did. Revolt is only healthy when one doesn't abdicate it. I denied everything, in order not to suffer any longer, and it was only then that I knew true suffering...that of diminished faith. Oh, if I hadn't met your dear father! Only act in accordance with his advice, swear to me. It's thanks to him that I understood the meaning of life and have been able to inform you. I've

---

[33] The author, like contemporary physicians, was unaware that camphor, administered internally rather than externally, is not beneficial but toxic.

143

always said it, and I repeat it to you one last time: act according to your conscience, without paying any heed to prejudices, traditions and habits. Oppose all routines, but nobly. Above all, don't suffer from love in sterility. Let one love console you for another, but above all, let work and devotion to others console you for love. You'll get there…you'll see…"

Monique was out of breath. She sensed her spirit drawing away, further and further, from her body. She murmured: "It's curious…my dear…I'm still in my bed and yet I can see myself going…going…"

One might have thought that she was following her already-distant image.

Sylvestre, moved as if by a spring, had stood up.

"Maman! My love! My darling!"

At the same time, the door opened. Georgi appeared on the threshold, followed by Claude. Nane's appeal had reached them together, at the Ministry, where they occupied the same room. Distressed, they had both come running.

Monique recognized them. A glimmer of joy traversed her pupils. Georgi had launched himself forward. Fraternally, Claude took Sylvestre's hands; the flow of her tears increased.

"And Papa, who hasn't come! And that accursed doctor!"

Monique drew her son toward her. "My good boy…hug me very tightly."

He could only stammer: "Maman!"

The paralyzed lungs gave the death-throes a brief and halting breath. Sylvestre cried: "Fight, Mother, fight! I beg you! Don't abandon us! Claude will fetch the doctor; he'll save you!"

With a weary gesture, Monique told him not to move; it was over.

"Tell your dear Papa…I…don't…"

A supreme effort reanimated her,

"Claude!"

He approached and kissed her hand. She raised herself up to point at Sylvestre, but her arm fell back; only her gaze went toward the young woman.

What she said was barely comprehensible.

"Love...her...for she l..."

That was all, Georgi made a sign to Claude to take his sister away, but she, understanding, threw herself on the body.

"Maman! Maman! I don't want you to die. Speak to me! If you love me, speak to me!"

Inarticulate groans followed. Sylvestre had fallen at the foot of the bed, prey to a nervous crisis. Georgi, who had thrown himself into Claude's arms, weeping convulsively, forgot his grief momentarily in order to take care of his sister, while Claude piously closed the dead woman's eyes.

At that moment, Monsieur Blanchet came in.

The blow was so abrupt that he stopped, his respiration cut off. It seemed to him that his heart, his entire being, was petrified.

Then, abruptly, at the first step, as a glass breaks, all his broken happiness shattered into a thousand sharp shards, which lacerated him.

He was at his wife's bedside. Mechanically, he kissed her forehead. Everything around him shuddered. He was so weak that he had to sit down, as if all his blood had flowed away with Monique.

VI

March had brought to Blanchet's mourning the irony of the first spring sunshine. It filled the old house with an irritating light, and the garden seemed all the more empty because the familiar asters, re-greening the décor, lacked the one who had been, and still remained, its soul.

The unexpected blow that had struck them all with an equal stupor seemed to have depressed Monsieur Blanchet irredeemably. He sat dreaming, his eyes always fixed on the same page of his book, or wandered restlessly from room to room, a shadow in search of a shadow. Sylvestre and Georgi, involuntarily occupied after the first days of prostration, felt, on contemplating him, another pain mingling with their own affliction.

They did not believe that they were less inconsolable. Sylvestre especially, in losing the most comprehensive of her confidantes, mourned an unparalleled source of consolation. For, good as Annik would have shown herself to be, if she had delicately touched on the matter of her double despair, the young woman felt that no tenderness could seem efficacious to her except for the one that, along with maternal support, she lacked.

Devoured by her chagrin, however, she still found, more than Georgi, who was diverted by his love, the means to be piously curbed beneath their father's grief. Filially, she tried to comfort the man who had protected her infantile weakness, and whose uncertain steps and arched back appealed for her aid now.

She also read clearly within her brother's heart, with the divination that suffering gives to those it illuminates instead of blinding them. One day, when Georgi had come back from Paris for lunch, accompanying Gine, who had come to spend the afternoon with her friend, Sylvestre indicated Monsieur Blanchet to them with a glance.

They had just got up from the table. The fuming coffee was embalming the air with the fine amber perfume of a cigarette lit by Gine.

"Poor father!" Sylvestre murmured.

Slumped in an armchair, he was following, from behind the windows in the drawing room, the shifting wisps of gold that the sun cast on the gravel through the young leaves.

"Why," she said, "don't you carry out Maman's wishes now? If nothing more remains of her than her memory, you won't offend it by realizing without delay what she had dreamed of seeing. If, on the contrary, she's not entirely dead, nothing could please her more than to see your happiness reflourish in the house. Replace her, Gine..."

Silently, Georgi joined his plea with that of Sylvestre, whom Gine, on an impulse, had hugged. They embraced.

"One thought torments me too much," said Gine simply. "That alone holds me back: the scruple of being egotistically happy here, when nothing can appease your grief."

Sylvestre shook her head.

"We need a true mistress of the house here, and, at the same time, a daughter who can surround Papa with a present, while, for my part..."

"What do you mean?"

"Nothing...a project. You'll know, a little later."

They pressed her in vain; she remained impenetrable.

"No, I don't want to, I can't. When my decision is made...then it will be time. Until then...don't pull that face, silly!" She added, reassuring her brother: "My project has nothing tragic about it. In the meantime, since we're in agreement, there's no more to do than for me to let Papa know. And in a week...do you know what you're going to do, Gine? Instead of spending the day with me, go back to Paris with Georgi, and ask your mother to come to dinner...your father, too, of course, if he's free. Let Annik come early, if she can."

"Understood. I know that Father's busy, but Maman—don't worry, I'll send her to you. And we'll both arrive, after...."

"And Claude!" exclaimed Georgi. "We're forgetting him..."

Although suspecting their disagreement, he had no suspicion of the extent, from one day to the next, to which his sister's wound had been envenomed. Gine, more sensitive, read alarm in Sylvestre's face, mingled with vague hope, and asked her, spontaneously: "Do you want us to tell him?"

She did not go any further, uncertain of what Sylvestre wanted, and exactly what she was thinking in a suffering whose bitterness she divined in full, but not its depth. She also feared engaging Claude imprudently. If he refused, offering the pretext of some obligation to escape the family gathering, what reproach would Sylvestre's entire person express, even mutely, in spite of herself? Certainly, he liked her a great deal—but was that not the most mortifying of alms, to the passionate pride of a woman in love?

After a moment of internal combat, Sylvestre replied: "Claude knows very well that he is always welcome—with all the more reason in his sister's house. He has only to come, if it pleases him. I've never constrained anyone..."

She did not add that she wanted him to come with all her heart. Since the funeral morning, the sinister moment of the incineration—five long weeks already!—she had only seen him three or four times, and only for a few minutes. Undoubtedly, like Georgi, of whom little more had been seen, he was lunching and dining with the Minister or in the Boulevard Raspail, absorbed in his functions—so taxing, along with his direction of the factory, led from the front, that only a few hours any longer remained available for secondary occupations.

What did she represent to him? Nothing but a camaraderie that was now superfluous, a habit in the process of easing, while every tug of the slackened bond irritated him. She had wished, ardently, that a benevolent impulse might bring them back together—how she would then have been able to soothe his hurt, care for him, and perhaps cure him! At the same time, though, she was sincerely afraid of seeing him. She did not want, for anything in the world, to force a sympathy that was refused. It would have been so easy for him to stop momentarily on his way to Chesnay, as before!

The effacement to which she had once resigned herself—when she had thought Marise capable of ensuring Claude's happiness one day and responding to his beautiful love as it merited—had soon melted away, as rapidly as snow, in the fire that was consuming her. By dint of watching Claude suffer a sterile pain, she had attempted once again to struggle against the enemy.

At present, in despair at her impotence, especially since Claude's last rebuff and the disappearance that had completed his abandonment, she had het herself go, a poor thing torn between dolor and pride. In vain she had thrown herself wholly into the refuge of her métier, doubly fatiguing since she had replaced her mother in all the hearths that Monique's charity sustained. The flu was raging with increased violence. Sylvestre multiplied her efforts against the scourge, exalted by despair to the point of total self-disregard, to an imprudence in which she was voluntarily reckless, as if she saw therein a possible means of deliverance.

Weary as she was when she went to bed at night, however, it was to give insomnia a prey that was less and less resistant. Then, in the darkness of her room, so thick that all of night seemed to weigh upon her nightmares, the insidious idea bored into her, gradually hollowing out its wormhole. To the beating heart of the clock, the precipitate pace of her own replied.

Death? The death that liberates all thought, which cures all suffering?

She thought about Poncet's marvelous inventions. A scrap of a sentence pronounced by Jacquemin—on the day when he had toppled the Ministry, Maman was still there—rang in her ears, not with the solemnity of a knell, but with the attraction of an appeal: "the gas that puts to sleep forever..." The sweetness—who could tell?—of suicide.

The idea soon became a project.

With the incomprehensible, if not inexplicable, facility of adolescence in submitting to disgust for life, when the extent of its desert is brutally revealed, Sylvestre could not find anything within her to react, to populate the future. Dreams, duties, beliefs—those guides, which progress before the strong like double beams projected by an interior light, illuminating the highway and the goals which always draw away as one approaches them—the poor ravaged soul could no longer even find a means of imagining them.

I'll kill myself a few days after the marriage, she told herself, *when Georgi's helic has taken him away, with Gine, into their open sky*.

She came back slowly from the platform, to which she had accompanied them, while Monsieur Blanchet went back to his study under the pretext of preparing the imminent resumption of his course at the Collège de France: a few notes to make. She went to see him, certain that she would find him, as usual, immobile at his table in front of his open books and his blank paper.

Oh, she would make arrangements to disappear so naturally that, when the further blow struck, he would soon scarcely perceive that a second face was missing from the house...to disappear in the manner of Aunt Sylvestre, so abruptly that everyone, even Gine and Georgi, would believe in the fatality of some accident and end up consoling themselves that way. Not as quickly as Claude! But more rapidly than they would have thought at first...

For a while, the promise made to her mother—she thought about it incessantly—tormented her. Yes, she had sworn. But what advice could her father give her in this matter? Was she going to torment him unnecessarily? What was the point, since her decision was made?

Sylvestre hastened her steps. First, make sure of her brother's happiness! Gine, better equilibrated than her, was truly the wife he needed---and also the daughter necessary to calm Papa's grief.

Her sacrifice made, Sylvestre felt, along with the peace of a lightened burden, a plenitude of joy, on thinking about Gine. A singular character, capable of such complete self-abstraction, at the very moment when it reached, via passion, the utmost depths of egotism...

"It's me, Father," she said, on seeing Monsieur Blanchet start. She had, however, taken care to come in without making a sound, as Monique did when she came to sit with him.

He passed his hand over his eyes; one might have thought that he was wiping away an image regretfully...

"I thought..."

He stopped, fearful of stimulating Sylvestre's grief with his own. He contemplated her, impotently, with a measure of involuntary rancor. Could anyone, with existence before her, torment herself to that extent for an amorous chagrin? Did she not sense, then, that there is only one irreparable misfortune: death! His materialism, equal to that to which Monique had long attached herself, impelled him in spite of himself toward life, bleak and diminished as it might be now that everything that he cherished, body and soul, was no more than a handful of ashes.

Sylvestre kissed his forehead tenderly and sat down facing him, gravely. She often came in that fashion, during Georgi's absence, to keep him company. They accorded their silences in the unison of their grief. But it seemed to him that a new idea had entered into them today, that a need to talk was impelling Sylvestre, but that nevertheless, as she was about to do so, she did not dare.

He was the one who questioned her. "Is it very difficult, then, what you have to say to me?"

He scrutinized her tormented face, gripped once again by the old anxiety. Visibly, another torment even more corrosive than the one he was suffering, had made her its prey. And as he loved her, if not more, at least as much as himself, he felt compassion for her, even though he was astonished by her weakness.

"It's Claude, isn't it?"

"No! No!" she cried, blushing with a reaction so abrupt that the father, surprised, took note of its violence.

The malady is even more serious than I thought, he said to himself. He reproached himself for not having followed its progress more attentively since the disappearance of the one who, seeing so clearly, had been incessantly preoccupied with it...

"Excuse me," said Monsieur Blanchet. "We might have respected your mutism, but we've shared your distress, your mother and I. Now that she's no longer here, I'd like you to know that her thought and mine remain united. To support you...my old wisdom isn't worth much, I know...I'd like you to be aware, anyway, of all the affection that animates it..."

Sylvestre contained her emotion, resisting the impulse that, if she had heeded it immediately, would have thrown her into the arms that were ready to open. No, she would not add her torment to the one whose traces she could see in the ravaged visage. She would disobey, out of pity, the oath extracted from her by maternal anguish. She alone was responsible for herself. Her pain was solely her own. She owed to others the joy that she was still capable of creating.

She shook her head. "Thank you, Father, but it's not about me that I wanted to talk to you. It's Georgi..."

He hid his dread as she hid her secret. He smiled. "Georgi? What does he want?"

Lost in his darkness, he no longer saw the dawn rising alongside him over Gine and Georgi, or the dusk descending over Sylvestre.

She hesitated, since he had not guessed.

Suddenly, he understood. "So he's not big enough to do without your intermediation!" A first surly reflex before that impatient happiness—which, by virtue of a return of tenderness, he wanted at the same time as he had forgotten it. "That's it, eh?" he added. "The objective of the embassy?"

"That's it, Father—but don't think that the idea came from Georgi. Neither Gine nor he has given it a thought. They were afraid, rightly, that you might criticize their haste. I alone thought that they could now be united without impiety. They love one another too much, and they loved Maman too much not to retain in their happiness the measure of their regrets. The house will soon seem less empty to us—to all of us—if a young Madame Blanchet…you'll say yes? I was sure of it."

Monsieur Blanchet murmured: "If the voice that has fallen silent could make itself heard, I sense that it would have joined its insistence to yours. It was your mother I saw while you were speaking to me. There are days when, different in appearance as you are, all of her soul of the old days, when I first knew her, is in your eyes." He sighed, and swiftly went on, as if chasing away a dolorous evocation: "She loved life so much that she would have rejoiced in seeing it reclaim its rights. A sterile pain ought not to sadden her memory."

Even though he was only thinking of himself in pronouncing those words, they struck and troubled Sylvestre. Grimly, however, she stiffened herself.

He continued: "Well, so let it be. The house is big enough for us all to live in it without importuning one another with our reciprocal egotisms. It's only a matter of fixing the date. The sooner the better!" *The sooner Gine is here*, he thought, *the sooner her presence will distract Sylvestre.*

She had risen to her feet, a pale smile distending her willful mouth. "Annik ought to be here soon. You have only to reach agreement with her."

"You won't be here? You're going to run from one sick person to another again, tiring yourself out? I hoped that Gine, today... Come on, stay..."

"I can't."

Monsieur Blanchet followed her with his gaze for a long time. He had sometimes regretted, but never as keenly as he did now, the abdication of the parental influence that the independence of children, which had become customary, had gradually removed from family authority. He could have none on the conduct of his own, except for the feeble ascendancy of affection, of which, at this moment, he understood the impotence.

He tried to apply himself to his work, succeeded for an hour, and, feeling a little better, went down into the garden. He always went to his old favorite corners, where he had always liked to repose, his chaise longue beside Monique's...

He arrived at the mossy bank under the sycamores, where one overlooked, as if from a hiding-place, the Avenue de Paris with its large expanse of sky, streaked by aircraft. He found Sylvestre there, her head in her hands, weeping. She had heard him too late to run away, and, surprised, displayed such distress that the father, emotionally, drew her toward him.

"What's the point? You've seen now, in spite of my efforts, how much I'm suffering...and you know why. I'm ashamed of it myself...."

"There's no shame in a certain amount of suffering. It's only misery."

Indulgent before such excitement, he coddled her, as when she was a child.

She hiccupped: "Oh, I've said it all...that Marise isn't worth this cowardly pain...that there are others than Claude worthy to be loved...but it's stronger than me now that Mother is gone...it's over. I can't any more...I can't any more..."

In the wildness of her gaze she perceived, fearfully, the extremity to which she had gone, the resolution that she had made. He hugged her, shook her hands...

"Sylvestre, listen to me. It's in Monique's name that I ask it of you...no! Don't tell me anymore. I've guessed..."

She kissed his forehead, obstinate—but he took hold of her head and forced her to look at him.

"So it's true! You've thought of that frightful thing? But you haven't thought, have you, about the repercussions of that new blow! You haven't had any more pity on me than on yourself?"

"Father!"

The grandeur of a life of pure and faithful love, the consciousness of a devotion never belied, gave Monsieur Blanchet's voice a tone forgotten by his equilibrating flexibility. "Do you think that if I hadn't thought of you, and of you even more than Georgi, since you're unhappy, that I would have hesitated, after losing your mother—more than half of myself!—to follow her? Like you. I've envisaged suicide. It didn't frighten me any more than it frightens you. But your image—that of your mother at twenty—stopped me. A duty more powerful than my right inspired me with the courage to live. For if there's a necessity, certainly, for the desperate act of which you're thinking, there's an even greater one to continue to do one's work...the poor, humble, quotidian tasks, sacred when they can be useful to others. You, my daughter, a scientist! You, who have youth, health, determination. You, whose profession is the most beautiful of all!"

He beseeched her so urgently that she lowered her eyes, troubled.

"You're at the age when, because one knows nothing of life, no more of its ugliness than its secret beauty, one gambles it without remorse on a bad card. What do you know about the future? What if Claude were to come back to you?"

"Impossible!"

"There's a long road ahead of you—and you'll let yourself go at the first corner? What about the unexpected that might await you at the next? Love—perhaps Claude's, who can tell?—will bandage love's wound, because life is its own remedy, because you deserve to be happy, because you have in your hand—yes you, and you alone, whatever you think— the elements of your happiness. Devote yourself! One only preserves oneself, truly, in giving to others. Death! It's necessary to struggle against it until the end. Where will Monique survive, without our memory? Before immolating yourself to a dream that might yet be realized, think of her, and all those to whom your presence and your care are necessary. And to begin with, physician, heal thyself!"

"How can I? I wasn't even able to save Maman."

"You can, by thinking about my grief—for if I didn't have you..."

Again she looked at him, shaken.

He embraced her again before leaving her to reflect, and drew away, less anxious.

Annik's visit, a second conversation with her and her father, the evening cleared up by the happy faces of the fiancés, and a night of meditation modified Sylvestre's resolution, if not in its dolorous depths, at least in its precipitate form. No, she would not betray the maternal memory. Her father would not have invoked it in vain, nor the sentiments of alarmism of which, she felt keenly, the best of her education had created.

In rediscovering enough energy to renounce killing herself, however, she did not abandon her desire to disappear. A little later, without it seeming voluntary. For want to the immediate, definitive departure, she would immediately quit the treadmill of an existence turning incessantly in its dolorous circle. Tranquil henceforth for those she loved—her father, Georgi—and certain that Gine would substitute for her perfectly in the house, she would leave Paris, Claude and opportunities for suffering.

A place in gynecology at the French hospital in Calcutta had previously been offered to her. She decided to accept it, secretly resolved not to go that far, to stop in Alexandria. An epidemic of the plague was raging there, the ravages of which an Egyptian doctor, a former comrade at the École de Médecine, had described to her. There was a shortage of physicians. She telegraphed her friend at the same time as India. By the time the replies arrived, the marriage would be concluded, Gine would be installed, and Monsieur Blanchet, recalcitrant at first, resigned.

With a simple valor, now that everything was settled, she had resumed her visits and her courses. She counted on departing without annoying Claude with the slightest explanation. As chance would have it, when she went to care for the Mureau girl, a friend of Nane's niece, who had fallen prey to the epidemic, she met him at the exit from Chesnay. She greeted him as if she had seen him the day before and nothing existed between them but their old camaraderie. He had the embarrassed expression of someone who has been the involuntary cause of a drama, and cannot do anything about it.

They talked about the latest news, of the hard work that the Ministry and the factory were giving him, and Monsieur Blanchet's health. Finally, as the conversation turned to her, he said, affectionately: "Maman tells me that...you're leaving?"

She looked at him breathlessly and saw that he regarded her going away as something natural, perhaps even desirable. However—he perceived it clearly—he felt sorry for her. And that was even crueler than if she had sensed that he was indifferent.

"I want you to be happy," she murmured.

"Sylvestre," he stammered, "I would so much have liked..."

Without waiting for the end of the sentence, however, she cut short his *au revoir* and his softening, feeling her pride weaken and fatality weighing heavily, and feeling that between them, for a long time, and perhaps forever, everything had been said.

VII

Claude is in Nice. The end of March is radiating, and over the evening of Mid-Lent hangs the blue-tinted freshness of a sky in which the stars are beginning to come out. He descends to the foot of the Avenue de la Victoire, threading a passage through the immense confusion that fills everything with the amalgam of its intersecting currents and multicolored tumult of its eddies.

The garlands of electric bulbs and luminous posters that are illuminated everywhere plaster a pale light over the advancing darkness. A fairground racket rises from the jostling crowds: crises, gibes, insults; an obscene squall punctuated by the explosion of fireworks, the stridency of trumpets and shrill mirlitons. A cloud of plaster dust floats over the battle of confettis. The trees give the impression of powdery prisoners beneath the network of multicolored serpentines.

Claude is revolted by the torrent of crazed individuals, the animal masquerade. The plebeians of empires in decline! He regrets not having gone directly from Monte Carlo to Paris once his mission was concluded. Oh, if only, on going back to his hotel the previous evening, he had not run into Marise, emerging from the Maund dance hall and arranged to met her at the Veglione! He marveled at the hazard that had unexpectedly brought them together. Destiny?

On seeing him she had immediately blushed with surprise, had rapidly come toward him, with a joyful expression in her bright eyes. The unexpected words were still stirring him:

"When did you get here?"

"This morning."

"For long?"

"Three days."

"That's not much. Are you still annoyed with me?"

"Except when I see you."

"Then see a great deal of me—I'd like nothing better."

"Really?"

They had walked for a while side by side. Mutual desires, which were measured, softens the words that one pronounces and those that one makes heard, as well as the radiant warmth of a beloved presence, which does not run away...he was still trembling at the memory of those subtle frictions, exchanging acceptance.

Marise had only quit him on perceiving her mother in the arms of Duc Laurenti d'Empeyta. An imposing group was following them: Comtesse de Huppel, Monseigneur Mhamady Kamara, prince and heir apparent of Oubanghi, and the Marquise d'Entraygues, whose lapdog was being carried by Max de Laume.

"You don't want to see those people, eh? I understand that. I'd like to see you, nevertheless, to explain. Tomorrow afternoon? Impossible—I have to prepare my auto for the Festival of Luminous Flowers. Come to supper at the casino in the evening, table 25, or, if that doesn't suit you, the ball afterwards...don't worry, I'll find you. Me, too, I have...a heap of things to say to you!"

What things? Stunned, he woke up as if after a night of fever, to a magical morning. A new Marise, the real one, had emerged from the decomposition of the other: a Marise who, seized by regret, loved him in return...

The genetic instinct had possessed him ever since, carrying him with an irresistible force above reality, even above his mission, above everything, suddenly transfigured.

Who would have thought, when he had leapt onto the Train Blanc—the luxury ultrarapid that had replaced the old Train Bleu from Calais to Menton—that a single minute would undo all that the last few weeks had done? The balm of laborious hours, the new skin of nascent forgetfulness, over the wound of his memory...

Since action had, in taking possession of him, returned him to himself, Claude had ended up almost becoming the person whose role had bent traced out for him by ambitions

159

and his dreams. The theatrical aspect of youth, which so easily clothes human simplicity and the nudity of life, had brought his heroes into play. Saint-Just had exorcised the faint-hearted lover.

Annik had helped in that. She wished, since Monique's death, that Sylvestre's marriage might follow Gine's. Satisfied with the progress accomplished in familial laws, she understood that even Amédée would, like Monsieur Blanchet, have preferred, instead of a free union, a liberated marriage more in accordance with custom, the obvious benefits of which she had only refused herself in order to make injustice more glaring.

Sylvestre! She felt even closer, perhaps, in her heart to that absolute child than to the equilibrated mind of her own daughter. She was sad to see Claude turned away, by regret for Marise, from his veritable companion. But had she not once been more attracted to Pierre Lebeau than to Amédée?

She had talked to Claude at length, affectionately, on the day after Gine's marriage and Sylvestre's departure—a day seemingly similar to any other, no ceremony having marked it apart from the journey of the newlyweds to the Mairie to register their reciprocal engagement.

"Doesn't that tell you anything?" she had asked him.

But he had shaken his head and replied: "You can't hold it against me, fundamentally, that I think as you do. What is marriage without love? Sylvestre, yes, I like her a lot. But be sincere: do you think that amity is sufficient provision for the journey, at the outset? No, you see!"

"You love...quite simply...Marise? Are you going to marry her?"

He had hesitated. She had left it at that. Of two seeds, one spoiled and the other healthy, which would germinate? She had confidence: the soil was good."

Claude had left, without thinking that in Nice, to which his father had sent him to confer in his stead with Sir James Ramsay, and then to Monte Carlo, with an emissary to Rohn, he might meet Marise. Only the political importance of his journey occupied him. Since he had tasted, alongside his father, the absorbing passion of power, the factory and his little workers' village had moved into the background. He hardly ever went to Chesnay any more, tranquil with regard to the direction of the establishment. Monsieur Lourmal was sufficient to a direction so well regulated that everything could run smoothly for some time in the absence of its true chief. In any case, Mureau came every week to report to him.

It was a minor matter, in the midst of his great preoccupations. The European situation had abruptly worsened since de Laume's fall. Of two reforms that the Jacquemin ministry wanted to conclude before May, one—the legislative vote and parliamentary eligibility of women—had been obtained without overmuch difficulty in a Chambre counting on clerical influence to neutralize the reform. The other—the nationalization of the subsoil—was about to enter debate. The Hartmann-Sudeky-Cervier consortium, supported by English and American banks, was striving by every means possible to excite public opinion, agitating the terrifying specters of communism and war. The information reaching the Quai d'Orsay revealed that the powerful financial parties in power in England and Germany were outbidding one another in provocations against the pacifism of France.

Sir James Ramsay, seen the previous evening, had it from a reliable source that incidents would be created before the elections, driving France into a conflict—where, the former labor minister did not yet know.

"But your father can be certain of being kept up to date; we have our own men in the Chancellery Council in Berlin." He had smiled, adding: "And in London, we're as interested as your father is in Paris, in the future of democracy! He can count on us, absolutely."

The same chime had rung in Monte Carlo, from which Claude had come. Rohn had warned Jacquemin to be careful of his personal safety. Letters inspired by Otto von Wittelsbach, advising energetic action against the socialist and communist leaders, had been addressed to Max de Laume. He knew for sure that Jacquemin, in spite of the replacement of Du Crêté, the former ambassador, by Fourquoy, a friend of his, was still being served poorly, not to say betrayed, by various diplomatic agents. A sweep of the broom in that direction, and a probe into the ex-President of the Council's papers...

Rohn, for his part, would remain on guard, preparing for the future. This time, the German proletariat would not stick its head in the noose, as in 1914...

Claude had just arrived, dusty and ill-tempered, in the Place Masséna, when a handful of confetti in the face reminded him of the pleasures of the moment.

"Oh!" he said, furiously, ready to hurl himself upon the aggressor. It was a pretty girl, who bared her head, sweating, and took evasive action, laughing and protecting her face with her bare arm. The brown down in her armpit and the bulge of her breast were uncovered, revealing with the musky odor an animal freshness...

He draws away, more disturbed than disgusted. The image of Marise chases away the impure vision. He sees her again as she was the previous day, on the Promenade des Anglais...

Now, from the window of his room, on the first floor of the Maund—where he is waiting for the Festival of Luminous Flowers to begin—he finds the city and the crowd, which sickened him a little while ago, sympathetic. He is no longer thinking about the noxious underside of that gala evening, organized by the reactionary newspaper of the département, the *Luminaire du Sud*, supposedly for the benefit of those wounded in the war. The *Luminaire* has only one concern: the pockets of the rich, preferably cosmopolitan. Of all this imbecile ostentation, once the expenses and bribes have been paid, how much will revert to the heroes providing its pretext? A pitfall for the foreign invasion, which extends the opalization of its corruption over the Niçoise mud like a thick foam...

Normally, Claude detests these nasty international locations, great markets of Decadence, in which all human vices adhere to the stupor of gambling in a frenzy of enjoyment, with the spasmodic incoherence of societies nearing their end. This evening, however, Nice seems dazzling, and its life beautiful.

The Promenade and the Jetée, the scintillating chandeliers and sparkling gardens, the walls of light with which the Casino limits the fabulous décor with a single rutilant embrace, over the black pedestrian swarm of idlers, noise and excessive... The latest discovery is being inaugurated: day in the middle of the night, thanks to the "helium" that stores solar light, with which the facades have been daubed. A rumor announces and greets the procession of autos. They go by, like chariots of animated gemstones, in the fabulous mass of their resplendent flowers.

"See you later!" cries the enchantress Marise as she passes. Yes, an enchantress, in the costume of a Persian princess, enthroned half-naked in her auto of a thousand-and-one flames, as if in the splendor of red roses...

A memory crosses his mind: he sees other roses...roses the color of blood, against the whiteness of a sheet, the line of a rigid body. The roses with which Monique's deathbed was covered... He sees her again alive, the day before...he goes into the bedroom with Georgi...Sylvestre is there, haggard... He feels the waxen hand placed upon him with the interrupted plea... Love Sylvestre? As much as Gine, yes! No more... Love! He is astonished that the same word can contain such different meanings...

The crowd is clamoring. Claude does not hear any of its servile admiration. He is extended in his silent joy; he can sense his own lightened heart beating.

Mechanically, he dresses for the ball—or, rather, undresses, antique costume being *de rigueur*. His tunic, his sandals... He has a desire to sing, to laugh...

As he goes down the stairs he whistles, glad of the amplitude of the overcoat that disguises his liberated body. The ground of the roadway has the elasticity of a trampoline. In order to get into the Casino he has to cleave a path through a hedge of poor people gaping before the arrival of their masters: the autos succeeding one another in the midst of mocking commentaries or hateful silences. As they get out, the women, scantily clad in veils, stand aside in order to show off their chinchillas and sables. In their ring-laden hands they clutch bags of real pearls with diamond clasps. Fashion is in furious flow. Some, laden with gems from head to navel, are reminiscent of reliquaries. The insolent arrival of Her Royal Highness the Comtesse de Huppel and her daughter, Princess Hélène, with the celebrated sapphires of the crown saved from the Bolshevik Revolution, causes a sensation.

Claude is astonished by the relative passivity of the curious before these she-apes wearing on their bodies the fortunes, health and lives of thousands of people. Are there souls in that mass of flies attracted by the gilded dung-heap? Doubtless those who would not have tolerated the outrage are not here. But he is not astonished at himself for being here, for the first time. His desire, in placing Marise so high as to separate her from her frame, isolates him, above the repugnant scene.

A domino and a flame-colored mask are handed to him at the entrance: a conventional uniform that one puts on when, after the supper, the lights dimming in response to a signal from the tubas, the great anonymous folly commences.

In the immense ballroom where people are already dancing under the harshness of electric light, there is a hubbub, a heat and a veil of smoke and odor that envelop everything, muffling the senses and the will. Around the perimeter of walkways encumbered by small tables, dinner at a thousand francs a belly has just finished, and in the midst of general excitement: the reek of dishes, the odor of tuberoses and perfumed skis, the bestial scent of sweat...

Claude is seized by the throat by a strange sensation of thirst: a thirst for iced drinks, for flesh quivering beneath a kiss, for he knows not what mysterious, intoxicating pleasure...

A new, unknown Claude is within him.

With a kind of embarrassment he follows the usher who guides him toward his box. More piercing than the glare of the electric bulbs, it seems to him that all those feminine gazes, sharp, mocking and acquisitive, are penetrating him, seeing inside him.

Finally, he retreats into is corner. He scrutinizes, with his lorgnette, the part of the hall that is visible, with its stages of restaurant-galleries and boudoir-boxes. Which, among those bare forms, is the one he seeks? Silks and lawns do not conceal anything, emphasizing, on the contrary, the cynical exhibition. He is afraid, and simultaneously wishes avidly, to discover Marise. His eyes, accustomed to sportive nudity, remain surprised by the revealed immodesty of all that skin, which is displayed for other objectives.

Where is she?

There, at the Cervier table, is Max de Laume and the Marquise d'Entraygues, very dignified. The Academician-Senator clad in a red toga, a crown of laurels circling his consular forehead. Mother Michelle sporting a matronly robe and, in her hair, her famous diadem, worth three and a half million…serious competition for the Comtesse de Huppel, whose sapphires are shining on her gray skin. Her Imperial Highness is next to her, with some people that Claude does not know: a fat man with a porcine head, flanked by a blonde Germania… And the couple! Jean Cervier, made up as a gladiator, talking animatedly to his neighbor, the pig-face. Of Madame Cervier, leaning toward the solid torso of Duc Laurenti d'Empeyta, Claude can only see a back like that of an American quilt, all blisters and grooves. The necklace of pearls and black diamonds appear in flashes when the rings of flesh around the neck shift.

The lorgnette turns away, searching…

"Ah!"

His mouth has hardened; there is a muffled, urgent pulse-beat in his temples. Marise, with an arm around the waist of Mhamady Kamara, is presiding over her habitual table. Louise Barlot, the three Hubertes and the three spherists, whom Hé-

165

lène de Huppel-Romanoff has deigned to join, with her two servants, Graby de Massugues, a Swiss, and John Ravelyn, an Australian. What a salad! Louise Barlot, dressed in a netting brassière and a girdle with two gold-laminated flaps, has annexed the Australian, while Hélène, disdaining the Belgian, is making eyes at the black prince. Laughing casually at Marise's enticements, Monseigneur is bulging his pectorals, the color of purple plums. His pale lips are drawn back from his canine teeth.

Is it to make him see this that she has invited him? What calculation is she making? What does she want from him? He admires her; he hates her, nude beneath her transparent peplum. All his rediscovered anger seethes in the blood that rises to his face, enfevering his need to crush…or to embrace…he does not know. The rage of the scorned male, suddenly dominated by the sexual instinct: all his respect for womanhood, and all the cult of adoration reserved for the Unique, has abruptly vanished. There are other Marises; he has only to lower himself, to make his selection from the docile troop of those who offer themselves.

He stands up, throws away his lorgnette and goes to mingle with the crowd, which, between two turbulent dances, is clapping hands to urge the orchestra to strike up again.

A voice hails him: "Monsieur Jacquemin!"

It is Henriette Legas, costumed as a slave: a petite actress, an old friend of Jules Poncet. With her large earrings she is charming, her torso delicately florid, her legs bare. They dance…and Claude knows, in the nudity that yields to him, the most intimate thoughts, at that moment, of Henriette Legas. They drink, and the sparkling champagne strikes him, in return, such a blow that he forgets the time and the dancer.

Intoxication takes possession of him, increasing as he passes from arm to arm and feels various breasts and legs pressed amorously against his skin. The tubas have given the signal for the masquerade some time ago. The particular cries that have saluted the pause of complicit darkness have become muted, in the renascent light, and the dominos are soon abandoned, in such a riotous orgy that Claude feels his head broken and empty, and his entire body vibrant, like a machine under pressure.

He does not see the curious gaze falling from the galleries, with which, returned to her table, Marise, who has been looking for him in the crowd and has finally found him, is following him...nor the even more curious gaze that has just simultaneously enveloped Jean Cervier, Max de Laume and the man with the porcine face.

The latter is the celebrated Hugo Hartmann, the owner of the Westphalian mines, whose head bears two crowns without majesty: the royalty of coal and the empire of oil. In accord with Cervier, he has just dictated to Max de Laume the will of the sovereign Consortium. Everything is ready, on their side, to set the gears in motion; the bomb, at such an hour, on such a day, will burst at the anticipated location—the French embassy in Berlin—in such a way that it will not miss the new ambassador, Fourquoy. The Chancellor will not offer any apologies, and will have the decree of Kriegsgefahr Zustand ready. France will thus be inevitably forced to mobilize—and mobilization, once again, will mean war.

Is Max de Laume ready to keep his promises? The suppression of Jacquemin, following that of Fourquoy? The ex-President of the Council, impassive but formal, has limited himself to replying: "The day after tomorrow, at the same hour; I have the necessary man to hand." The understanding is reached. The invisible ball is set rolling—red or black—in the sinister game, while Claude is spinning, unconscious of the eyes that are threatening him.

He was about to leave with Henriette Legas, having decided not to waste any more time, when, on going back into his box to collect his domino, he exclaimed: "What!"

A woman was lying on the chairs, set end to end, calmly smoking a cigarette.

"Marise!"

Send her packing, with a word? But it was her who, looking the actress up and down, uttered a harsh: "Go away!" which the slave, divining an irritated mistress, obeyed.

Satisfied, Marise had risen to her feet.

"You've abandoned me," she said, reproachfully,

"It's my turn. The negro's leftovers—no thanks!"

She put her arm around his waist, as she had Mhamady's a little while before. "You can see that it doesn't promise anything..."

He blushed at the contact of that young arm on his burning flesh.

"What's important," she said, "is..."

She did not finish. An image in her eyes passed so clearly that Claude saw himself coupled with it...

In a lower voice, she went on: "And that…is reserved..."

"For me?"

"If you want."

In her turn, under the mute covetousness, she blushed. The "act of love," the only one she had not yet accomplished, in her quest for strong emotion, tempted her, in Claude's features. A simple desire, which would pass, she thought, as soon as it was fulfilled. The obsession of it had pursued her since the scene at Garches and the retreat of the "enemy" that, for her as for "the Boss", Claude had become since Jacquemin's triumph.

She savored, in advance, the amusing experience. Afterwards, and promptly, *bonsoir!* Sentiment—no thanks! Nothing advertised the fact that an obscure daylight was about to dawn within her, at the end of the night, from which, by virtue of the most complete misunderstanding, they were both anticipating, with the same pleasure, such different joys. Claude, drunk, believed that he would conquer this woman, while Marise only supposed the revelation of the man.

"Come!" she ordered. "From this moment on, you belong to me."

He sensed that she had not lied. He would belong to her, as she would be his. A philter that set the blood ablaze, insinuating itself irresistibly into his heart and the smallest capillaries in his brain...

Three o'clock in the morning. The delirium of the fête is buzzing in his ears, and the gleams of the rainbow are blinding him. He is now seated at Marie's table, overlooking, like an indifferent young Bacchus, the Dionysiac saraband. Down below, the interlinked bodies are no longer dissimulating the orgasm that is agitating them, in the coupling of the dance. Other beings, powerful beneath their quotidian appearance, have released their veritable depths.

Madame Cervier is rolling, stuck to Duc Laurenti d'Empeyta. She is swooning as she feels the hand that is caressing her neck, and slyly evaluating the necklace. Another old woman, an authentic lady, whose skeleton is swinging pendants and bracelets, is pressing herself with crazed vehemence over a pale nauseated dancer, uttering sighs mingles with little squeals in her ecstasy. Bedroom noises are emerging from boxes whose doors are ajar. As at the famous balls at the Quat'z'Arts and the Internat, public coitus is practiced with tranquility, the sexes confused or inverted.

But Claude does not see or hear anything. Marise, her head on his shoulder, veils him with the gilded brushwood of her hair from the rest of the world. Hélène de Huppel is aspiring a nauseating mixture from a small jade pipe with a stem made from a long emerald, and sharing her favors between the delighted Monseigneur Kamara and Graby de Massugues, who is intolerant of the new chevalier. Louise Barlot, drunk, allows John Ravelyn to empty a bottle of champagne between her breasts, which Jean de Rancis intercepts at the navel. The three Hubertes have disappeared. Paul de Laume and Henri Chanteroy, isolated in their palaver, are philosophizing platonically.

At the next table, a young woman gets up on her chair every five minutes, prey to an obsession, and shouts: "I have lovely breasts, too!" She only consents to sit down after having displayed her flat chest, the despair of her days.

Gradually, the room thins out. At the table deserted by Jean Cervier, who has made off with Huberte the second La Mounine has abducted Duc Laurenti; only the Comtesse de Huppel remains. The quinquagenarian, habituated nevertheless to grand-ducal mouthfuls, is so drunk that she is singing a Slavic song, abruptly interrupting herself to cry: "Oh, I'm so excited!"

She pulls a wad of bills out of her handbag and waves it, cooing: "For an hour of love!"

A circle forms, rudely making fun of her. A Levantine even insults her in Syriac. But Jean de Rancis whom John Ravelyn has just roughly shaken to "teach him manners" has approached her chivalrously. "Would a dance suffice, Madame?" he sniggers.

He helps her to put the money away. He is applauded. Impassively, the adolescent merchant has pressed himself against the Comtesse, drawn her into the rhythm with one hand on her buttocks and the other supporting the generous hand she has given in pledge. The notes and the affair are in the bag...

"Stupid!" said Louise Barlot to Hélène de Huppel, observing the disappearance of Jean de Rancis. "At least, while abducting your mother, he could have left me my box of ouaba."

"There's some on the *Mah-ri-Tsé*," said Marise

Hélène proposed: "Shall we go finish the night there."

"That's an idea. The crew's been given leave. There's no one there but the watchman."

A languor had invaded her on contact with Claude. Their bliss, exchanging vague words, was floating above the Saturnalia...

"*Vive Mah-ri-Tsé*!" cried Louis Barlot. "Let's go!"

"What's that Chinese?" Claude enquired.

"My yacht."

She avoided saying "the Boss's yacht," knowing that Claude would refuse to follow them there. A need, not for pure air in the figurative sense, but for the free marine breeze, the sweeper away of fatigue, had reanimated her. There was not only ouaba but provisions aboard the *Mah-ri-Tsé*. There were, above all, cabins where…

She stood up. Claude retained her. She tottered, so dazed that she had to make an effort to overcome her intoxication "No, no! I'm still capable of walking on my own!"

But Graby de Massugues and Mhamady Kamara, full of solicitude, rushed forward, offering their arms. With a hard palm, Claude pushed the Swiss away, too visibly drunk, and said to the prince: "Go away, boot-polish."

Mhamady pretended to clench his fists. Marise appeased him: "Silly! We're all brothers!" And she beseeched Claude: "Tell him that, you who are a socialist!"

It was the first time she had addressed him as *tu*! Although vexed by having to share her with the oily-skinned prince, Claude was moved by that. A boundless indulgence drowned his arrogance, and even his pride. A vague fraternity—Marie was right!—caused him to admit, and even to find amusing, those foreign companions. He was living a dream and, without being astonished by its absurdity, only savoring drowsy delights. After all, it wasn't so bad to have a little fun!

As they went past the cloakroom, Marise burst out laughing. She had just bumped into a stout gentleman who was breathing heavily beneath his gold-braided carapace and who was helping Huberte the second to put on a magnificent mantle lined with ermine.

On perceiving his daughter, Jean Cervier seemed annoyed.

"Papa!"

"I'm taking Mademoiselle Poursaillon du Vidan home. She can't find her sister…"

"Lucky that you're here!"

An irritation passed through the feline eyes. He enveloped Marise with a singular gaze. "You're tipsy!"

He did not like to see her so naked, not with that retinue of dashing men. The virgin Jacquemin, fine, as much as she liked—not dangerous. But the Australian and the negro! A sentiment of propriety animated him, unconsciously doubled with an obscure species of jealousy. Marise was part of his wealth. There was nothing that resembled familial love, but a tenderness in which, without his being aware of it, mingled paternal authority with disturbed male admiration.

"Are you going home?" he enquired, authoritatively.

"Yes, Father; these Messieurs are escorting me back to the villa. Have a good time!"

"See you tomorrow!" he growled, discontentedly.

Outside, Marise squeezed Claude's arm. *There*, she thought, *we'll be tranquil until morning. The boss won't be finished 'taking Huberte home' until noon.*

Hydroplanes for hire were waiting on the quay, the caprice of partygoers desirous of sobering up in the fresh nocturnal air.

"To the *Mah-ri-Tsé*!" Marise ordered.

All the pilots knew the sumptuous boat moored in the old port, its landing-platform, its emergency planes and its American engines. The seven of them piled into the largest gondola. The electric headlights were illuminated, large resplendent eyes, and in the time that it took Monseigneur to modulate, amid idiotic pleasantries, the brief nostalgia of an African song, Marise and Claude, interlaced, saw the hydroplane take off, skim the water and settle on the low platform in the stern of the *Mah-ri-Tsé*.

Suddenly, the entire yacht was illuminated. On hearing the noise of the hydroplane, the sailor on watch, who was asleep, had just pressed the alarm button, switching on the lights.

"Switch them off, Yves! It's me..."

At the sight of Marise and her friends, the man took off his beret without surprise. He was accustomed to it, and, being well-paid, respected an originality that he found to his advantage.

"Switch them off, then," she repeated, not wanting them to be noticed, "and go to bed. The boat has nothing to fear."

Already, Hélène and Louise had dragged Graby de Massugues and Mhamady below decks, followed, with a stiff gait, by John Ravelyn. The Australian had drunk even more than the Swiss of the brandy with which Mhamady thought it advisable to reinforce the last bottles of champagne.

While the Monseigneur and Graby sprawled on one of the divans in the vast oval room that served as a saloon and dining room, Louise, an habitué of the place, immediately set the table, aided by Hélène and John, as serious as a pastor. Gravely, he removed the lids from some tins, and brought monstrous Guernsey grapes and enormous Tucuman peaches from the fruit cooler. Then, passing on from the cooler to the wines, he asked, at the sixth magnum: "Is that enough?"

"No," cried Louise, if one wants to drink a real cup…wait! In the cup of the Grand Prix de Cannes!"

She pointed at the gilded bronze bowl facing the stairway, reminiscent of a gigantic hip-bath, save for the Victory that surmounted it. Hoisting herself up onto the pedestal, she emptied the first magnum into it. Hurrahs uttered by the phlegmatic John caused her to totter.

"Idiot!"

She inundated him with the second magnum, which he had just uncorked.

"Your turn!"

But Claude and Marise, who had stayed on deck, appeared at the top of the mahogany staircase. Louise intoned the *Marseillaise*, accompanied by the percussion of forks on glasses and plates. Marise thanked them with a circular gesture of her arm. If Claude had not caught her she would have fallen down the steps. The cold air, after emerging from the steam bath of the Casino, had made her dizzy. Everything was spinning. She had not heard any of the litanies the Claude had just reeled off madly. Nor had she felt the kisses, timid at first and then bold, with which he had covered her arms, her neck, and finally her lips. She was no longer anything but an automaton, and, realizing that fact, made an effort to appear natural.

The table is satisfactory: caviar, sausages of *foie gras*, truffled pheasant. And the cup...a fine idea! Shrill cries—that's Louise, whom John Ravelyn, thoroughly soaked, is calmly stripping naked. He is getting his own back. The mesh, the loincloth...and hup! He grabs her.

"Into the cup!"

With the greatest calm, he executes his revenge on the drunkard. Without paying any heed to the wriggling of the plump body, he stretches out his hand, maintaining her by force. Louise howls at the touch of the chilled wine, and then bursts into shrill laughter under the flood that Mhamady and the Australian, uncorking magnum after magnum, delighted by the farce, pour over her neck, her head, her breasts and her legs, which she parts lubriciously.

"The fruits!" cries Hélène de Huppel.

All of them are brought into play. The velvety grapes, one after another, stain the skin that turns pink under the brutal hands. The peaches are crushed, their juices running into the sparkling wine.

"This is going to be good!" says Graby, reanimated, while Hélène, making use of her pipe as a drinking straw, sucks it in. She drinks so avidly that she is interrupted by a hiccup, and, over-full, she vomits.

"Not over me!" says Louise.

Relieved, Hélène de Huppel goes to sit down and, in order to fill herself up again, digs into the pheasant pâté. Louise caresses Mhamady's curly head, while he, good dog, laps up the foam. His white teeth bite into the fruits and the soft flesh at the same time. Louie is still laughing, hysterically. And the negro devotes himself to it, satisfied. He is taking his revenge on the civilization that exploits him, and which, for the moment, he is savoring while scorning it. John, even more disdainful, has turned his back and sat down at the table in front of the pâté, which Hélène, having relit her eternal pipe, recommends to him.

Marise lets things take their course. Nothing can any longer extract her from the torpor into which her soul has fled and in which her body is wallowing, unconsciously. Claude, lying alongside her, can no longer see anything of the universe but a pure white summit. It is the breast of which, with its pink button, the mysterious flower is offered to him. He breathes in the erect nipple, englobes the firm roundness with one hand, while the other, with a religious fervor, denudes and caresses the whole of the torso extended to the suction of his lips. An immense joy transports him... Breasts that quiver beneath the volutptuousnes that he imparts to them, adored breasts! Living communion of the man and the woman! Fruits of flesh from which, as a child, he drank nourishing milk. Beautiful fruits that will ripen, and where his son, one day...

Fluid words, ardent prayers and promises—an entire hymn is singing within him, while Marise sighs and, under the kisses that descend, she parts the final veils, mechanically...

Suddenly, Claude, sobering up, starts. He has just encountered a hand that is not Marise's.

"Occupied!" says a thick voice, with a satisfied laugh.

He palpates a man's arm, horrified. He leaps to his feet, and strikes Graby de Massugues full in the face.

"Dirty swine!"

The Swiss, lying along the divan, was taking advantage of his position to visit the ground floor while others occupied themselves upstairs...

That is what he attempts to explain, muttering: "Well, what! We're all brothers! N'so, Marise?"

She opens an astonished eye, sees Claude standing up, and murmurs: "Brothers! Of course! Come on, then!"

She extends her arms to them—but the spell is broken. Claude, horrified, has begun to recover his reason. It is to launch short-arm jabs at Graby de Massugues, who soaks them up conscientiously, and whose nose is bleeding. Hélène, John and Louise—who, emerged from her bath, is drying herself with a napkin—end up separating the combatants, not without receiving a few blows. Claude pulls himself together while his adversary, very dignified, has taken a card from his wallet and holds it out with a noble gesture. Furious, Claude takes it, and slaps him with it.

"You've fought enough like that!"

A duel with that slug! To kill? Wholeheartedly, yes! He would have done it just now if he could. But now...ha ha, honor, in all this! He laughs, dementedly. He had only one idea now—to escape, after having said to Marise...

He returns to the divan, from which rises a cry that fills him with revulsion. Stupor nails him to the spot. Marise is moaning—with pleasure or pain?—under the body of Mhamady, which is covering her...

Marise, polluted by that negro? A drunken nightmare? Reality?

He only knows one thing, which is that he is no longer in real life. The confused bodies roll onto the floor into the expanding vomit that, in trying to protect her friend against Claude's fury, Hélène, decidedly ill, is continuing to spew forth. Mhamady, nauseated, imitates her.

Claude does not move. He is thunderstruck.

Marise, semi-conscious repeats "Since we're... all... brothers..."

Is he going to fall over? Go mad? Thunder deafens him; lightning zigzags. With an immense disgust, he gazes once again at the two beasts hooked together, already torpid in their enjoyment and their dejection.

A last flash of consciousness agitates Marise, and lifts her up. "Claude!"

He pushes her away with his foot, and like a wounded animal, drags himself mechanically toward the stairway of the exit, the pure air, the daylight...

The daylight!

It is pale, a tragic dawn over the city and the sea. Claude has run to the bulwark. A lacerating combat is raging within him...the instinct of survival at odds with the desire not to survive his despair, his remorse, his shame... Life irredeemably soiled, love dead, all his beliefs corrupted... And yet, some unknown sentiment of deliverance in his nausea...

176

The black water laps against the flotation line. Claude is about to throw himself into it. Anything, rather than remain there an instant longer!

But someone comes up behind him. It is Yves, an early riser, making his round on the deck. He has seen them often, these fools who are incapable of digesting the good Lord's drink!

"Not a solid stomach, my poor Monsieur? Well, one can easily give the fish something to eat when one's had too much!"

"Take me ashore."

Claude is shivering. He is numb with cold, and feels ridiculous in his carnivalesque apparel in front of the sailor. Yves has already started to lower the dinghy.

The oars dip and rise again, rhythmically. Claude his eyes dry, watches the *Mah-ri-Tsé* draw away. The others, back there, are sleeping off their degradation. Is he any better than them?

Weary of his night's conclusion with Huberte the second, Jean Cervier has just quit the family *pension* where an apartment hired by the year provides him with the changes of clothing and the bachelor undergarments that he dares not install at the seigneurial villa at Mont-Boron.

He drags his feet through the dawn, mouth bitter and hips heavy. All the gold in the world, which permits him to buy the young and the old, cannot render his sixty years the miracle of adolescence...

He thinks about Huberte's ingenuous savoir-faire, and, by virtue of a correspondence into which he does not care to dig too deeply, the excessive independence of Marise. He will sort that out, tenderized in advance by the seductive protests with which she knows, the slut, to respond to his criticisms. The sensation of her little hand on his cheek...!

Aiee! A cruel jab in the loins warns him—the pain that he has when a lustful idea crosses his mind. But what is he imagining now? With a shrug of the shoulders he expels the confused image, and mutters: "Incest? Incest! What does that mean?" No moral constraint instructs him. He has not yet thought about it clearly, that's all...

A fiacre with two horses and a white umbrella, a vestige of olden days, passes with cracks of the whip. Hup! He installs himself, amused by the prehistoric vehicle. Marise would laugh...

He is in front of the little door of the villa. The gravel of the pathway crunches under his feet. A glance at the closed windows. Everyone asleep...no! As he passes by his wife's room he hears breathing punctuated by plaints. What is the matter? Moune is collapsed in an armchair, her dress and mantle thrown down any old how on the bed. Draped in a pink kimono from which she is overflowing, a bloated sponge of yellow fat, she is sobbing incessantly. Her despair increases at the sight of the Boss. What will he say?

She explains in a halting voice. "My necklace lost…my beautiful necklace of pearls and black diamonds."

Where? She doesn't know. At the ball? At the exit? Getting into the car? She knows very well: she remembers undoing the clasp and lacing the item of jewelry on the mantelpiece of the private room at Cacatoès, where Laurenti d'Empeyta... When she went to pick it up, no more necklace! Laurenti did not see anything, and was red with anger at the first word. A scene? She recoiled... Patience! She would make arrangements... In the meantime, it's necessary to explain the disappearance. And as the Boss frowns and mutters: "Two hundred thousand francs so well placed!" she moans more loudly and decides to faint.

Jean Cervier moves to ring but changes his mind. No point in making a fuss about the misadventure before the police... He goes to the door that communicates, via the dressing rooms, with the next rooms and calls: "Marise! Marise!" No reply. He goes through, knocks on the door. "Marise!" He opens it. No one! The bitch! She lied to him. Where can she be?

He comes back to the prostrate heap that is watching through one half-closed eyes and shakes her brutally. The eye opens entirely: a round, stupid eye. Then Jean Cervier seizes Moune by the arm, so rudely that she begins to cry for real, frightened.

"Your daughter! Your daughter who hasn't come back!"

Is that all? She breathes in, and tries to calm down.

"They must have gone to drink somewhere else…at Cacatoès or the Maund."

"That's all that it means to you? A child, who's already drunk too much! Left in the company of scoundrels..."

She looks at him, astonished. "Marise is old enough to behave decently. And then, you know, you haven't asked me to look after her. Marise, without reproach, is your concern. I have enough to do with the education of Mériane. Oh, children! If one knew, one wouldn't embarrass oneself with that burden. You'll get your Marise back. I wish I could say as much about my necklace!"

He scratched his head. "Where can she be?"

"How do I know? Perhaps, quite simply, on the *Mah-ri-Tsé*." Slyly she added: "You do enough partying there for her to want to imitate you."

The *Mah-ri-Tsé*? He wanted to clear the matter up. Disdaining to reply, he took out his watch. Eight o'clock.

A few minutes later, the big yellow and blue racing hydroplane, flying from Mont-Boron, landed on the platform of the *Mah-ri-Tsé*, at the same time as the launch came alongside, bring back the crew from their leave.

Yves, who had seen "the captain" clicked his fingers: "What if they get caught?" He thought it best to shelter his responsibility, and explained with convoluted excuses: "Monsieur the Minister's daughter...I couldn't..." Already, Jean Cervier, opening the hatchway to the staircase, was going below decks.

He stopped, suffocated by the ignoble odor and the unexpected spectacle.

Legs interlaced, Marise and Mhamady were asleep, exhausted, on a divan. Louise, Hélène de Huppel and Graby de Massugues were lying pell-mell on another, snoring. Alone, sitting at the table, John Ravelyn, as stiff as a pikestaff, was finishing a bottle of whisky...the unobtainable Edward VII whisky.

It was on the Australian that Jean Cervier, transported by fury, fell first. He laid him out with a blow of his fist, then rushed at the interlaced couple and woke them up with his foot. Mhamady, brought to his feet with difficulty, lowered his head at the sight of the father. He was so crestfallen that Marise, through her own emotion, found him grotesque...

No regret yet for her action itself, but suddenly, in the obscure depths of her heart, the regret of having forgotten, of allowing herself to be surprised in the arms of such a lowly partner. Without saying a word, she watched her father jostling the bewildered snorers on the other divan, and shoving them with the negro toward the narrow stairway, as to the door of a fetid stable.

"Wait!" ordered Jean Cervier. "I'm coming back."

She shrugged her shoulders. At ease! She even smiled at the thought of the five imbeciles letting themselves be thrown like parcels into the dustbin of the launch. She opened the porthole violently and breathed in a few draughts of air. The hull of the large launch was beneath her, where two impassive sailors were watching the singular cargo piling up. *Bon voyage!*

When her father, congested with anger, came back down, she had not yet emerged from the bathroom. She finally emerged, reinvigorated by a shower. Fresh and decent in the peignoir that enveloped her, she felt ready for the battle. She waited for the impact, drawn back into her pride: a soul that had not been washed clean, like the body, by the lustral water. She thought about Claude. What had happened? What had become of him?

"Little wretch!"

The ferocious eyes threaten her. Beware! They have changed color. The big pussy cat has become a tiger again. Brazenly, she gets in ahead of him.

"You're scaring me. I'm free."

"Even to have lovers?" He raises his fist, but lowers it before the clear gaze, which is mocking him.

"That's no one's business but mine." And insolently: "What has it got to do with you?"

He hesitated then, fearing self-analysis, cried: "You dare stand up to me, your father! Me, who had spent a fortune to make you the exceptional being of which I dreamed! A whore passing from one drunkard to another!"

"I was wrong to come here without telling you, since you're at home here with your champagne, your fruits and your drugs! One point, that's all." She pointed at the box of ouaba, respected by Louise, who was too drunk, and mocked: "I don't interfere in your affairs; don't interfere in mine."

He growls dully. "I do what I please."

"As is evident. Me, too. Loot and spend your millions as you wish, and don't concern yourself with the rest."

"The rest! Is it you, or me, who earns the bread that you eat? And when I say bread..." He pointed at the plundered victuals, and concluded: "You'll talk to me in another tone, until you're married!"

"Admirable! I'll have changed then, won't I?"

"Exactly! When you have another flag than mine, you can do as you like with the merchandise. Until then, you're under my roof. Respect it."

"Do you respect it, you and Maman? Rights? Since when do you pay any heed to me? You complain, when I'm only following your example."

"What are you saying?"

"I'm saying that if you didn't make a show of your mistresses, and mistresses of my age, and that if Maman hadn't brought to the house, ever since I could see, a collection of more or less rich and broad-shouldered friends, perhaps I wouldn't have been reduced to raising myself on my own! I have a lover? Yes, since last night—oh, not one of those you've just thrown out, not even that dirty negro, who won't ever have me! Yes, yes, I have a lover. So what? A lover that I chose, who can do with me what he likes. Am I more despicable for that than Huberte, whom you pay, or Maman with her Guimards and Laurentis?"

He fell upon her in order to hit her, but the supple body, molded in the peignoir, had slipped away. With one bound, Marise had reached the threshold of the bathroom. She shouted even more loudly: "And if that doesn't suit you, you only have to throw me out, like the others, jut now—one responsibility less!"

She burst out laughing before the hideous face that drew nearer to her.

"And now, *bonjour!*"

The door slammed so rapidly that Jean Cervier could only crash into it, after the click of the bolt. His fists hammered the hard wood.

"Slut! Little slut! Open this door!"

In his room at the Maund, lying on his bed fully dressed, Claude listens to the clock chime. Since the early morning, the pitiless sound has punctuated his headache. A circle of iron and fire is squeezing his temples...

With an effort that is as yet impotent, he tries to sweep away the memories of the night. Already, however, he is ashamed of the cowardly despair that laid him down, ill, when he returned to the hotel, until the gong rang for lunch. With his head buried under his pillow, damp with tears, the shutters closed and the curtains drawn, he has wept for so long in a childish distress that now, his eyes red and dry, he is incapable of movement, even of turning over.

A black route plunges before him, into which, bruised, he fears to go. He curls up, fearfully, in his own darkness. Dead is his love and dead his youth, with all the illusions with which he embellished the future through the prism of hope. As if for an burial, when everything ought to be meditation, silence and mourning, he refuses the light of day, ruminating his thoughts and his dreams of yore, as one sorts through the papers of someone who has died.

Kill himself? He has certainly thought about it, again— but a supreme instinct has protested: not so much the sense of self-preservation as that which the unconscious maintains pure and noble within him, obscurely reawakened after the anesthesia. Kill himself, for that? Life, even a desert, is worth more than such a death. He cannot think about Marise without a surge of disgust, a reignited hatred...

Three o'clock in the afternoon! It's time! He has to shake off his prostration if he wants to be in Paris before dinner. The Rome-London airplane leaves from Saint-Laurent-du-Var at four, and only stops for five minutes. Fortunately, he was careful yesterday to book a seat by wireless from the Palais Farnèse...

He is in haste now to repair his fault, to accomplish his stupidly-neglected duty without delay...

It seems to him that a century has passed since he left home. He does not forgive himself. When a danger—and what?—threatens his father, the man whose life is important to everyone and dearer to him than his own, to have failed in the most urgent, the most pressing...

He is also in haste to see his mother again, to rediscover her tender, consoling strength...

"Let's go!" he sighs, and, with a surge of rediscovered courage, he is reaching out to switch on the electric lamp beside his bed when two raps on the door of his room are prolonged in two dull thuds in his heart.

"Who is it?"

His voice is strangled, because he is sure that the person who is knocking, the person who is about to come in, is Marise...

Her dark silhouette, against the bright background of the corridor, appears in the frame of the doorway. Another bad dream? The nightmare continuing? It's her, her perfume.

At the same time, a fugitive sensation runs through him: the impression that the enemy that holds him there, oppressed and supine, is slackening its grip, that a glimmer of light in filtering through, that his youth, only wounded, is leaping up within him like a bird ready to take flight, and sing...

But Marise has spoken: "It's me, sorry..."

He is on his feet. He can no longer hear anything except the guttural, abject: "Brothers...of course...come on then..." He can no longer see anything but the whiteness of the submissive female and the black body agitating...

In vain, the ceiling light, angrily switched on, shows him a Marise almost similar to the one of the day before last, on the threshold of the Maund, who had reconquered him, a Marise in sober dress, with her decided but distant girlish attitude...

Almost similar? No. The woman he has before him differs from the Marise of old by an expression of dread, a timidity that no longer dares advance or retreat.

He gazes at her, very close and yet foreign, separated from him by a bottomless fissure. Finally, he murmurs: "You."

She perceives, beneath the astonishment, such a desperate, hateful reproach that all her boldness abandons her. *When did he go? What did he see? What does he know?*

A single piece of evidence strikes her: a different Claude appears to her, in the amorous man that she no longer recognizes, just as another Marise, anxious and at a loss, is in the process of emerging, painfully, from the chrysalis of yesterday.

That nascent Marise clings on with all her feeble strength to the mirage of her anxious hope, and tries to rediscover the old Claude in the new. And her eyes, in opening, discover that she is losing him at the very moment that her desire to reconquer him is redoubled.

"Claude!" she sighs.

He says nothing. Then, anxiously, without even daring to take a step forward, she asks: "When did you get back?"

Her question is tremulous. The dolor of repressing the impulse to kneel down, the thirst to be true, the desire to be pitied and simultaneously consoled…and she would like to cry out: "Forgive me! Forgive me! I've understood. I've brought you my shame, my remorse…from the depths of my unhealthy curiosity a Marise has emerged that I didn't know, a Marise who loves you..." But how, since he isn't helping her?

Her impotence seizes her by the throat. She begins to weep, her face hidden in her hands.

"Why are you crying?"

Finally! She seizes the buoy that is going to save her; she will be able to try to exculpate herself, to obtain his forgiveness, if he still loves her…but no. He said it with an expression so distant, a tone so weary, that she gives up. Deceit, struggle.… What would be the point? Too bad if he learns, if he does not already know, the full extent of her debasement. Let him scorn her, let him reject her. She no longer knows what she wants, or where she is. There is nothing in front of her but her nausea. What is Claude's unhappiness, compared to hers? His disillusionment, compared to her fall? He, aided by the benevolent hours that are waiting their turn, will be appeased. Perhaps he will even smile at it one day. Whereas for her, every day and every hour will render her regret more painful, will drive her, in order to forget, to other omissions no less odious...

And her sobs redouble, convulsively.

Claude draws nearer, troubled in spite of himself. The power of tears! The revenge, for him, of seeing the woman suffer who has made him suffer so much. The touching charm, also, of that unexpected weakness, that total disarray.

"Calm down."

Her nose in her handkerchief, she shakes her head. With a gesture of generosity he sustains her, leans her against him. Marise looks at him, gratefully: how sweet that relaxation is! If only the compassion that has just brought their perishable bodies together cannot refuse forgiveness!

"Claude...my Claude..."

He tries to draw away, but she retains his hand. "No! Let's stay like this...between suffering and hope... Oh, I'd like to die!"

For the first time since she came in, Claude looks at her less harshly. Has she, too, then, thought of disappearing? To redeem, by punishing herself, the pain that she has caused? A generous idea, by which he is moved.

Marise perceives the advantage, and, gripped by the semi-frankness of her exclamation, she shivers at the funereal invocation, entirely thrown back toward the enjoyment of being there, humble but alive, desirous and—who knows?—still desirable.

She straightens up, and tries to grip him more tightly.

"I love you...my Claude...I love you...only you."

As a spider coats its prey with glue before binding it, her desire envelops, her mouth advances...

Brutally, Claude pushes her away. "Too late!"

"Don't say that! Don't reject my tenderness! If I've disappointed you, I'll do everything henceforth to make you happy! We can still be..."

Prudently, she is now feeling out the ground. Is she not going too far? She fears that he might have seen in her excitement an unreserved confession. What if he doesn't know everything? And, throwing out the sound: "We were very drunk yesterday! Confess that you no longer knew, at the moment when I fell asleep, what you were doing..."

"You think so?"

The ground is cut away. Even so, she murmurs still interrogatively: "But...yes..."

"Enough deceit! Another has taken you...taken you like some random slut in a bar or a street corner. And what other!"

She stammered: "You know?"

She had collapsed on a chair, reassembling her scattered ideas.

"And you'd like me to make you my wife? The fervor that will surround the companion of my life, the mother of my children...the couple of which I dreamed? No, no! Impossible! After the image that you've just shown me!"

She attempted one last effort. "I'm not asking to be your wife, but to make of me what you will...I'm ready to leave everything, to live in poverty, alone...I'll learn to love everything that you love, I'll work..."

"A determination isn't enough. It requires an ideal..."

"Easy, perhaps, for you, whose high ambition isn't content with mediocre desires! I remember, you see! But me! My youth has been spent all alone, without a mentor, without true parents or true friends...and it's only this morning that I've understood that. If you truly loved me, save me!"

Tears bathed the sincere visage.

"I would have liked to, Marise. An offering such as mine has been is not withdrawn without difficulty..."

She grabbed hold of him, quivering. "Don't abandon me! Save me!"

"Save you? Would I want to even if I could? In spite of your presence, your perfume, your voice, everything that still disturbs me now, in spite of myself...."

"You see, you see..."

He made a gesture of helplessness in the face of the irreparable.

"I no longer love you, Marise."

The verdict was delivered without appeal. She bowed her head.

He gazed upon everything that was struggling within her, the knot of serpents in the depths of a cave, into which light penetrates...

No! In spite of all the pity...

He declared: "You'll always be the woman I saw lying there, squealing with pleasure in the arms of that negro. Forget? When one has loved jealously, with all one's being, body and soul?—as I loved you, Marise! There are memories that nothing can erase..." He read an incredulity in her gaze, the reappearance of the old Marise, the true one, beneath the good will that was searching, and plowed on: "...Stains that nothing can wash away. For you, and for many others, I know, the act of love is no more important than any other—you see, I remember, too. For you, it's a cigarette that one smokes, a random meal in a restaurant. For me, it's all of life. It engages it, models it, perpetuates it..."

She contemplated him from the other side of the precipice. She would have liked to reach out her arms, to take hold of him again. But what would be the point?

She spoke, inconsequentially. "Perhaps...! I didn't know...and yet, Claude, I swear to you, you alone please me. Certain things that you've said to me...your frankness, your strength...through you, in my unconsciousness, I dreamed confusedly of the love that has revealed itself to me now that I've lost it. One more minute, Claude, please! You're in a hurry? Paris, isn't it? Where you'll find calm...perhaps the woman you deserve....one minute, I beg you! I'd like so much for you to forgive me...or at least to retain a hope. I'm going to suffer so much, now..."

Touched, he took her hand. He pitied, in her, the incurable wound. He mourned and regretted, in her, the soul that, better fashioned, might have corresponded to his own, and the body that his desire suddenly re-enveloped: a flame extinct almost as soon as it flared up... Oh, if he had thought it possible to recover, to mark with another seal the indelible impression imprinted on the warm wax, that face burned by a new fire, whose harshness of expression had softened, melted...

But the unique moment had passed. Marise's face, refrozen, had resumed its dryness.

Sadly, he dropped the hand that he treated him so cruelly, within the glove with which education had covered it. Already, Marise was at the threshold.

"*Au revoir*, Claude."

"*Adieu*, Marise."

The door closed on the past. At the same time, he rang.

"For my valise...the auto."

He had just enough time to get to Saint-Laurent-du-Var...

The present entered into him again, like a traveler into an untidy room. Already, though, the future was reappearing, with cherished features. Annik, Gine...and, without precise contours, in the distance, on the ship that was carrying her away, a rediscovered sketch also floating before him: the affectionate face of Sylvestre.

189

PART THREE

The human race will last forever.
The fatherland must reach its end.
Diderot

I

"Hello!... Hello!... That noise!... You've heard?... Yes, come, that would be better."

Claude hung up. All the communications of the Presidency of the Council had been intercepted, since that morning. Where? By whom? A little while ago, with the Ministry of the Interior. And now with the Prefect of Police! It was at that point that Georgi, on Jacquemin's order, had just gone to the Central Telephone Exchange himself, to make enquiries.

"It's necessary to keep things tight," the President said. "De Laume still has his own men everywhere. I'm not sure that even here, in spite of Georgi's daily explorations..." He pointed at the walls, indicating the ears that might perhaps be lurking behind the tapestry.

At two o'clock in the morning, in the Boulevard Raspail, he had been woken up by the news of Fourquoy's assassination, transmitted by the *Universel*. A bomb in the embassy in Berlin. He had immediately run to the Quai d'Orsay. Mingled with the grief that the loss of a friend caused him, the sudden approach of bloody clouds filled him with horror. There was no official confirmation yet. Radio communication had been blurred, wires cut, on Wittelsbach's orders, isolating the embassy from the German frontier.

He went to the large French windows that were open to the steps leading down to the garden and breathed in nervous-

ly. A bright Palm Sunday was resplendent over the green ar-
bors and the flower beds. Ramsay and Rohn had been well-
informed! Three weeks had not gone by before the anticipated
incident; the bomb had exploded and, in an atmosphere so
overheated by provocations from beyond the Rhine that the
worst eventualities were to be feared. In spite of the watch-
word provided by the *Universel*, a part of the national press,
with the *Inter* at the head, was striving to reawaken and stoke
up chauvinistic passions. Even the papers that were not funded
by the Association of National Interests were half-hearted in
their campaign for moderation, stimulated by government
manna. They were squinting toward de Laume and Solmou,
the possible distributers of tomorrow....

Jacquemin examined the situation coldly. The most important thing was not to allow himself to be carried away by
the violence of the current. Determined, at all costs, not to fall
into the trap of the Profiteers' war, he was ready to do anything to avoid it. No mistake was possible: it was the debate
on the nationalization of the subsoil, fixed for the resumption
of the Chambres after the Easter vacation, which had unleashed the aggression. They wanted time to avoid its discussion, if possible, and, in any case, to precipitate events before
the imminent elections that would render them impossible. A
coup on the Bourse! And they would stop at nothing—not
even, if the ministry succeeded in not allowing itself to be
dragged into military conflict, a coup d'État...

"Lumel doubtless wanted to give me news of the
search."

At dawn, Jacquemin had summed the Prefect of Police
and the Minister of the Interior, Houdar, and decided a belated
sounding of the homes of de Laume and the Marquise
d'Entraygues. If Rohn's warning was exact, the letters exchanged between Du Crêté and the former President of the
Council would be an inappreciable asset aiding the work of
peace. By showing the evidence of an organized conspiracy,
including the plotting of the worst crimes, there would be
grounds to interest against a war of monstrous individual in-

terests not merely French and German democracy but the conscience of the world...

"Things are taking such a turn," he said, as he sat down again, "that we can still hope. If Lumel tells us that his hunt has been successful, all might be arranged in accordance with your mother's wishes. We'll have what we need to proclaim to the people that they ought not to fight, and why? Because Non-Violence will triumph of its own accord."

"You can be tranquil, Father; No one will march."

Jacquemin passed his hand over his forehead. A terrible problem! The most tragic that can be posed to a leader of men, who thinks... The duty to refuse to fight an impious war, sacrilegious if it is merely the servant of the Golden Calf... The sacred duty of war if it is, for a people, the condition of existence... He could be proud of himself, in any case, for having contributed without weakness to the realization of Jaurès' dream: the entire Nation armed, by militias strong enough to sustain to the end, if necessary, a war of life or death for the endangered Fatherland. And at the same time, reassured, he thought about the terrifying means that he had, with Poncet's gas, of abridging it victoriously, if it were inevitable.

"Telephone your friend Jules. Tell him to come immediately to receive my instructions. I don't want to be surprised in case of aggression."

Claude had just made the call when the usher announced: "The Prefect of Police."

"Send him in."

Jacquemin went to meet him, and read, in his anxious face, the disappointment.

"Well?"

"They've taken their precautions, Monsieur le Président. Nothing at Monsieur de Laume's home. In any case, he's not in Paris—left the day before yesterday for his property in Melun. And nothing at the Marquise d'Entraygues' home, where the strong-box was forced, in spite of her protests. Nothing, that is, except a sovereign budget in bearer bonds and jewelry..."

"It's necessary," Jacquemin said, "to carry out searches today at Melun, as well as the Banque Cervier and the *Inter*, and also at Garches and Turbot's home."

"I've prepared a list of individuals in whose homes it would be as well to take a look, Monsieur le Président. Here it is."

Jacquemin read it attentively.

"Although," the Prefect went on, "Monsieur de Laume is an old enough fox not to allow his earths to be discovered. His known affiliates are less to be feared than the others. In any case, Monsieur le Président, all measures have been taken, I beg you to believe, for your personal safety,"

Jacquemin made a gesture of resignation to fatality. He was one of those stoics who had made their own sacrifice and are only struggling tenaciously against the threat of evitable disasters for all. He stood up.

"As soon as the operation is over, come to give me your report in person, since the telephone..."

Monsieur Lumel raised his arms to the heavens. "It's not for want of surveillance! Fortunately, I believe that I'm on the track..."

He left; his shoulders stooped.

Before sitting down at his desk again, Jacquemin clapped Claude on the shoulder, smiling with all his paternal tenderness.

"The revolutionary times are here! The moment has come to open your eyes, Saint-Just!"

With a sideways glance he observed his son, who had sat down facing him again. When Claude had come back from Nice, he had been worried by his air of sadness, but soon tranquilized by the assurance that it was only a matter of an intimate chagrin and that "his boy" was valiantly making an effort to get over it...

Claude had not dared to confess to his father, any more than to Annik, the whole cause. He had kept it hidden within himself, like the secret of a truly shameful malady, which one does not treat overtly. At the moment, however, his mind was wholly preoccupied by the night's news. The dark hours that were descending had required all his attention. He had not even shivered when his father had pronounced Cervier's name. Now he was transcribing, for encryption, the dispatch addressed to the embassy in Berlin, which Jacquemin's serene voice was dictating. Soon, an aircraft fitted with a magnetic shield against blocking rays would transport a duplicate, while the original would remain in the documentary archives...

I engage you to keep extreme measures compatible with our dignity out of negotiations with the Chancellery. It is necessary at all costs to avoid...

At the same time, at the Banque Cervier, Marise went into her father's office, in search of news.

She had learned, on chancing to unfold the *Inter*—where she was looking for a report of the ball at the Barlots', to see whether she was appropriately mentioned—about the rumor that was causing a stir in Paris and the world. She had leapt out of bed, hastily donned pajamas, and had passed through the reception rooms without pausing outside her mother's room, to reach her father's study. It communicated by means of a secret stairway with the offices of the Banque.

After the assassination, she thought, war was inevitable! Anticipated, planned war! She had been hearing mention of it for a long time. An unavoidable settlement, perhaps even desirable—who could tell?—given the increasing insolence of the demands of the people...

"The people"—she lumped together, in that vague word, all the repulsions of a born millionairess, and also all her vague fear of something gross, malodorous but strong... The other word, "war," frightened her less. It was rich in victorious promises. And yet the risks, abruptly surging forth, worried her. *The Boss will soothe my anxieties...*

She had come back from Nice even more disequilibrated. The double blow of the scene with her father and the scene with Claude had left her prey to a bruising uncertainty. Obscurely she sensed, between her and the Boss, over whom she had recovered all her ascendancy, a troubled sentiment born and growing within her that astonished her, shocked her and also flattered her. One amorous man less, one amorous man more—unexpected, of course! She shrugged her shoulders. Not malevolent, at least, that one!

She could not think about Claude without a complex emotion. To reconquer him...and then, when she had him, how she would take her revenge! After the impulse that had driven her toward him, she resented the rigor that had stopped him stupidly in mid-route, the cowardly retreat that, after having left her rolling in Mhamady's arms, reproached her for an act that he had only wanted to accomplish himself. She resented most of all the fact that she continued, in spite of herself, to desire him, even though she had done everything, since then, to forget him—to desire him all the more because he was so obviously out of reach...

And with that, suddenly, this upheaval!

At the sight of the panel opening in the bookcase, with its shelves made of the spines of books, Jean Cervier started so sharply that Marise was surprised.

"Idiot!" he exclaimed. "One doesn't come in to people's offices like that!"

He was surrounded by piles of papers. Heaps of empty file covers were spilling from the monumental safe built into the wall. A huge fire was burning in the grate, fed by, instead of logs, thick wads of documents. They were reddening with heavy smoke, and then bursting into flames."

"You're cleaning up?" she said.

"As if I didn't have enough to do with my own papers! But it's necessary, into the bargain, that I stick my nose into de Laume's!"

"What are they doing here?"

He shook his head and explained. "Suspicious of that swine Jacquemin, who's capable of having him arrested, de Laume, whose papers were hidden in the Marquise's house, has gone to earth for a few days at Melun, and yesterday, warned that she was at risk of being searched herself, by reason of the tension of recent days, our friend had that stack brought here in the night by Liéval, so that I could burn them."

"Are they compromising?"

"That depends on the hands that sort them. There are autographs in there that de Laume wouldn't want to come under Jacquemin's eyes."

The association of those two names—de Laume and Jacquemin—struck Marise. The old sentiment of her rancor against the former President of the Republic was mingled with the image of Claude, a confused idea that still followed her. Perhaps there was a means of avenging herself for de Laume's disdain, which had once wounded her, and attenuating the scorn from which she was suffering today, in her pride? Even, perhaps—who could tell?—bringing Claude back!

Lightly, she said: "De Laume-Jacquemin. That's amusing. Show me."

He pretended not to hear, however. State secrets were not made for her pretty ears. He contemplated her, smiling. How pretty she was in those pajamas!

"What did you want?"

"Nothing…to see you…to know…this bomb?"

"Hasn't finished settling the matter. Since you're here sit down beside me. You can help me.

He set to work, passing her the papers for burning as he went along. He only retained those that might serve him as a personal weapon, if need be, against someone or other.

She put the first ones in a pile, scanning them with a glance, in the hope of finding some indication that might be useful to her, personally… Nothing. Then in armfuls, she carried them to the fire. Pink in the gusts of warmth, she came back to reinstall herself next to her father.

He muttered: "As if it weren't insane to keep such things! If they come here, the place will be clean. And if Jacquemin's police are clever enough to discover my hiding places, which I doubt, they'll only find things that might be useful to me, while harming others. Come on! To the fire! To the fire! The imbecile! There's enough to get us all shot, with this evidence!"

He passed Marise the Du Crêté correspondence—a thin file of a few letters. She riffled through them slyly, while he opened the next file, absorbed. The few words that leapt to her eyes were sufficient to convince her of the importance of the document: *Jacquemin...* Ah! *...must be one of the first to disappear. Those are the Chancellor's own terms...* Well, well! If it wasn't enough to get de Laume shot, much less her father, it might be useful all the same! Dexterously, she concealed her larceny under the reports that Cervier was holding out to her in a disorderly fashion, and when she was in front of the fireplace, she slid the letters under the jacket of her pajamas, between her chemise and her skin, at the same time as she threw the rest of the papers into the blaze.

She had picked up the tongs and lingered, in order to complete the pretence, stoking up the flames.

He had interrupted his examination, and was following her with a strange gaze, leaning over the fireplace in fashion that caused her rump to stand out. Now, the blood pounding in his temples, he was admiring her, her braced limbs molded in the supple fabric of the trousers. His eyelids fluttered, and, congested, he resumed his inventory, head bowed. Through the maniac's mind passed the continual haunting memory, the vision of the *Mah-ri-Tsé...* Marise naked beneath the bathrobe, behind the door on which he was knocking...Marise naked against Mhamady's black body...Marise naked...naked...

She leaned over him, without thinking about it, from behind. He felt her upper body weighing on his shoulder. Her fine hair caressed his cheek. The cleavage, visible under the lace, carried him away completely. He grabbed her round the waist, with an unintentionally brutal hand, and stammered: "Marise..."

He had come to his feet, still holding her, and swayed, as if he were unsteady on his feet. Amazed—because she had not expected such a direct assault—she recoiled abruptly, stinging him with such a "You're mad!" that he let go.

He turned away, mastered, babbling: "What! What? It's you that's mad! Your father can't put his arm around your waist?"

She was not fooled. She knew, having seen it on other faces, the wildness conferred by the irresistible savagery of lust. And, fearing anything, from a beast like him, with her hands advanced in a defensive gesture, she beat a retreat, without taking her eyes off him.

He had fallen back heavily into his armchair.

She rapidly regained the protective panel.

"Oh well!" she said, breathing out.

She only retained an amazement. Madmen! Madmen! They were all madmen! To the point, yes, of driving you mad yourself!

II

M. Claude Jacquemin,
Boulevard Raspail, Paris

Dear Claude,

My letter will surprise you, but in sum, it's necessary that I tell you once, at least, my sincere thoughts and the profound disturbance of my torn being. And if I am bringing my dolor to you like this, it is because I know that, being unhappy yourself, it cannot increase yours. It is because my misfortune is henceforth irreparable, because it is definitive.

Claude, you will never see me again. Or, at least, not before the future years have effaced the memory of the present years. Claude, I love you, as you know, but you don't know how much. The sad or joyful flame of my gaze, my vibrant courage, my comprehension of human misery, the ardent echo of my life responding to the appeal of life—you were all of that.

I write "you were" while the beating of my heart, and the tears that I can allow to flow far from you, are saying to me "he is all of that, and you're suffering and struggling, poor mad prisoner, without wanting to feel your wounds..." Yes, yes, beloved Claude, my dear Claude...oh, how glad I am to call you that without seeing your eyes darken! Here, you can do nothing. This paper is my domain. I can, at my ease, lean on your arm, place your hands against my burning cheek and murmur the thanks of my being in prayer...

Alas, that bliss you could not give me, because you were waiting for another. That's why, no longer sure of being able to live while seeing you, and having promised my beautiful extinct light, my beloved mother, and my father who invoked her, not to desert life basely and without profit to anyone, I have made the decision to stay away forever.

Papa doesn't know about my determination yet; I'm counting on habit to make him understand and accept it. Don't tell him about my letter. So far as everyone else is concerned, I'm bound for Calcutta. In reality, I've stopped at Alexandria because of the plague epidemic, which demands everyone's devotion. For you, know that was always the sole objective of my voyage, and that I shall not return.

Adieu, my dear Claude, with all my resignation to fate. I have offered prayers that your love might be more fortunate than mine. It is impossible that all the fervor that resides in me will ever disappear. I am counting on it to help you to be happy. Adieu.

Sylvestre.

Sylvestre! As he folded up the letter, Claude had the impression of holding her in his hands, alive. An emotion—still as strong as on the first reading—gripped him. He folded the precious piece of paper slowly, carefully, as if he feared that by crumpling it, he might wound the palpitating soul therein yet again.

Remorse, and a tender sympathy, had filled him on learning the depth of the gulf into which he had involuntarily thrown, without even perceiving it, the comrade of his childhood, the delicate friend whose eyes had opened at the same time as his own to the joy of living, to the beauty of the same ideal.

How had he not, quite naturally, followed Gine's example, drawn to Georgi? How was it possible that he had lived alongside Sylvestre, without her grace touching him?

The revelation of what she had suffered for him, and what she was suffering still, the dolor so absolute that she had not been able to imagine existence without him, the love that would prefer death to renunciation, made him repent the harshness that he had displayed, the indifference with which he had let her depart. There was shame, too, at the idea of Marise, the blindness with which he had pursued in her the chimera, until the monster was unveiled…a shame that grew as his recovered lucidity permitted him a clearer sight of the disproportion of the effects and their cause: time and sentiment wasted, his beautiful dream humiliated, his very faith afflicted, and, by repercussion, the crushing of Sylvestre. All that, why, and for whom?

An embarrassment, and at the same time, a pleasure, had invaded him a little while ago at the idea of finding himself in the presence of the dear victim. A few days after the letter he had received from her, a word from Sylvestre's friend, the doctor, to Monsieur Blanchet had summoned him unexpectedly to Alexandria, bidding him to come without delay to see his daughter, convalescent after an influenza that predisposed her to the epidemic...

They had arrived in Marseilles that evening. A telegram sent by Monsieur Blanchet from the ship that had brought them back had reassured Georgi and soothed Claude's anxieties. Sylvestre was very weak, but had returned safe and sound...

Standing under the chandelier in the dining room, where the set table was only waiting for Annik and Amédée to return, Chaude was closing his wallet again when his mother appeared. After a day spent at the *Maison de Toutes* sending pressing appeals to each foreign section of the International Council of Women in anticipation of a general intervention, if events—which had deteriorated since the previous day—took the bad turn that she feared in a definitive fashion, Annik was in haste to get back to her menfolk.

Claude's thoughtful gravity did not escape her, but, knowing nothing about Sylvestre's confidences, she attributed the preoccupation to the ongoing events.

"Your father isn't here yet?"

"There's a meeting of the Council of Ministers at the Quai d'Orsay. It will be a long session. He says not to wait for him."

"It's not going well?"

"No. Wittelsbach refuses even to express regrets. He says that nothing could prevent the assassination—that the

201

true provocateurs are the French socialists. My word! Yes, it's us who provoked the dock strike in Hamburg and the miners' strike in Westphalia! They want an end to it. Their decree of pre-mobilization is due to be promulgated any time now."

"It's frightful!"

She summoned up all her determination: to fight toe-to-toe to raise the common sense of the people against their tyrants.

"Sit down," she said. "I've eaten—two pills and my tea at the *Maison de Toutes*. I was exhausted. Eat—you only just have time if we're going to meet Gine and Georgi at the Gare de Lyon. Are you coming with me?

Although she, like Amédée, had observed with satisfaction the affectionate disturbance he had suffered on learning of Sylvestre's illness, and his joy on hearing that she was out of danger, she expected him to refuse, claimed by more urgent tasks. She was pleasantly surprised by the spontaneity of his: "Yes, of course!"

Who could tell, now? She had enough tact not to persist. She would hope for the resources of those young hearts. A small—very small—glimmer of light in the tempest of darkness that she felt, with all her antennae, that they were entering. She was stumbling around in search of exits, unable to see how they could get out of the circle that was tightening around them with every passing hour, if the cries of mothers did not make themselves imperiously heard, if the solidarity of women, standing up everywhere, did not bar the route to the march, as-yet-invisible, but which had already begun, sounding the dull tread of the blackest Destiny.

"There's the train!" cried Gine.

Already, it had entered the station. She ran forward with Georgi to meet it, waving the large bouquet of red roses that Claude had sent her for Sylvestre.

He was waiting, with Annik, at the entrance to the platform.

"That way, we won't miss them."

He shivered at the passage of the giant locomotive, its long carriages skimming the asphalt, and then searched among the confusion of the groups for the familiar silhouette...

He saw her, on Gine's arm: Sylvestre, clutching the welcoming flowers to her bosom. Behind them, Blanchet and Georgi were waving.

All six of them converge now. Accolades, questions, replies...

Chaude, who is shaking Monsieur Blanchet's hand, and Sylvestre, embracing Annik for a long time, have not yet looked at one another; they can only hear their hearts beating... It is so emotional to love, and be unhappy, and also to be loved, while remaining unhappy.

Thin and pale, Sylvestre is in front of Claude. She extends a timid hand to him, which strives to be firm. He does not know, as he takes that little hand, confidant of the secret that will bring them together henceforth, whether he wants to laugh or cry, and hesitates between a flippant or tender word. Stupidly, all he can find to say, offering her his cheek in a boyish manner that disguises his disturbance, is: "And me?"

Sylvestre is about to respond "You, too!" when she feels the fraternal kiss pose awkwardly on the corner of her lips. The shock is so powerful that her weakness cannot resist it. She becomes even paler, and would have fallen if Claude had not sustained her. Already she has opened her eyes.

"It's nothing," she affirms. "The fatigue of the voyage..." And taking back from Gine's hands the roses, which she has dropped, she says: "Thank you again, for the beautiful flowers."

"It's not me you ought to thank—it's Claude."

"Claude! Oh! That's nice..."

She envelops him with an ardent and pure gaze: a freshness of the dawn, when the sun is rising...but Claude turns away.

In Sylvestre's soul, darkness descends again.

The following morning, in the small room separating the office of the private secretariat from Jacquemin's office, which opens via a secret corridor—the Minister's Passage—to the interior courtyards. Claude and Georgi are riffling through the documents prepared for signature, the letters dictated by Jacquemin before his departure for the Council of Ministers, meeting at present at the Élysée…the time of which has been brought forward because circumstances have deteriorated since yesterday evening's meeting.

An usher brings a sealed envelope from the Office of Political Direction, containing a summary of the latest overnight dispatches. Georgi scans them…

"Rather somber! Confirmation from Geneva: the League of Nations impotent, divided between our influence and that of Wittelsbach… From London: England refuses any mediation whatsoever; the order of mobilization will be given to the fleet…

"Precaution or threat?" murmured Claude.

"Threat," Georgi replied. "The Red Army is massing on the Polish border…"

The usher reappeared. "A lady insists on being received. She says that it's very important, very urgent."

"For whom is she asking?" said Georgi.

"Monsieur Claude. She didn't want to give her name, and refuses to leave unless I give you this envelope."

Claude unsealed it, casually, and, surprised, passed the card to Georgi.

"What are you going to do?"

"It's odd! In truth…" He reflected. "See her…one never knows! For her to come here, at this hour, at such a moment…" He ordered: "Have her come in through the little door."

Georgi got up, discreetly.

"Stay!" said Claude.

They look at one another, intrigued. The door opens swiftly. Marise is before them, red with emotion. She does not bow or extend her hand.

"Pardon me for disturbing you, Claude. I have something very urgent and highly confidential to say to you."

"I'll leave you," Georgi said.

"I apologize for not inviting you to stay, but Monsieur Jacquemin alone ought to know. It's even necessary that, so far as anyone else is concerned, you haven't seen me. It's a matter of the life of someone...that you love... If not, I'll leave with my secret."

Georgi bowed before going back to his office. "I haven't seen you, Mademoiselle."

"Thank you."

They were alone.

Claude indicated a seat. "I'm listening."

She remained standing, however. "Claude, if I've acted badly with you, if I've caused you to suffer.

"I assume that it's not to talk about that..."

"No—be patient! I assure you you'll thank me soon."

She sat down. "I'm going prove to you that when I told you, in Nice, that the certainty of loving you had emerged from my confusion, I wasn't lying. Since then, I haven't stopped thinking about you...."

"I can assure you, Marise, that this remembrance is painful for me. Do you need my amity? Tell me quickly what service you expect from it."

"It's you who have need of mine, Claude! Your father is in danger."

He straightened up. "How do you know?"

"I have letters here that prove it."

"Show me."

"Wait! First, your word of honor that you will never reveal by what intermediary..."

"I give it to you!"

Marise took the packet of the Du Crêté letters from her handbag.

"Here..."

He read, rapidly.

"Oh, the wretches! The cowards!"

"They're important, aren't they?"

"I believe so!"

A decisive weapon—but perhaps double-edged? What if it were a trap...? The papers trembled in his hand. But no, they cried out, sweated authenticity. He looked at her, inquisitorially.

"How did you get these documents?"

"I can't tell you. Only know that if de Laume knew that they were in your hands..."

He did not ask what motive she was obeying, crediting her with an impulse of honesty, and of sympathy. Touched, he said: "Thank you, Marise. It's not just to us that you're rendering a great personal service—it's to the entire country, the world... When it hears of the crimes that these letters..."

She saw all the consequences of her action. She had only wanted to satisfy a grudge, preparing a revenge. Quickly, she said: "It's just that...I want you to give them back to me. It's sufficient that you know about them."

"Impossible, Marise."

"But my father in involved, in your eyes, with the criminals you hate. I love you too much not to warn you about a danger, but I love him enough not to take sides against him."

"I can't, however, allow my father and entire peoples to be assassinated!"

"You've been warned. Act henceforth in consequence."

"Even with these proofs, we'll never have proof enough!"

"Then swear to me that my father will be left out of it. I can't be precise, but in sum, you must think that if I have these papers..."

"He's the one who gave them to you?" He sniffed the bargain, and became firm.

"No, no!" she cried. "I alone..." She blushed. "Believe what you like."

An emotion, a desire had gripped her again before the lost love, the Claude of old, so young, so ardent. She stood up and moved closer to him. "In any case, my presence here permits me to demand of you that my father is left out of it. And now, Claude..." She sensed the moment passing, the minutes fleeting. She would have liked to stop them, to hold them back. "Know that I was only seeking one thing: to redeem myself in your eyes. Have I succeeded?"

Spontaneously, he held out his hands. "Never, Marise, will I forget what you've just done..."

"Then everything...is...forgotten? You'll render me your affection?"

"My gratitude has already done that. There is no longer anything in my heart but that proof of amity."

"Of love, Claude! Since...Nice, your memory hasn't quit me. That's why I'm here."

An embarrassment had gripped him. He would have liked her to be gone, now.

He confessed: "It's just that...since...Nice...I've had one thought in my mind regarding your memory: to rid myself of it."

"But now?"

"Count, I repeat, on my amity."

"It's your love that I want. As I did a month ago, I'm begging you: save me, if you love me a little."

"As I did a month ago, I can only reply, sadly: impossible."

Recaptured by the mirage, she no longer recalled the true motives for her action, becoming once again the delinquent, exhausted by fatigue and nerves, lost in the desert of her life.

"When I'm crying for you: Help! When I'm struggling to escape those who surround me! When I've come to demonstrate my devotion to you! You refuse to help me...that's bad."

"To help you? Oh, no, Marise!"

"Then tell me that I can still hope."

"Never."

The coquetry returned through the irritation.

"Am I no longer as pretty?"

"You're even more so; I've been admiring you since you came in. Only..."

"Only?"

He pronounced, glad of his victory: "The spell is broken. I don't desire you anymore."

She received the direct blow to her self-esteem.

The telephone rang.

"Excuse me."

Sylvestre's face appeared on the visor. Glad of the diversion, Claude took advantage of it to put that conversation, which arrived at an opportune moment, between himself and Marise, by way of emphasis. "*Bonjour*, Sylvestre... No, my dear, Georgi isn't with me. If he's not in his office, he must have been called away... Father? No, he's at the Council of Ministers; he'll be returning directly to the house for lunch... What should I tell your brother?... That you can't come to pick him up with Gine... Where are you?.... At Cochin, to see Fermot! You'll be better for the rest after that journey!... Not tired?... So much the better... Yes, that's right—see you soon!"

Marise was contemplating him ironically. How could she be mistaken, at the sound of that voice?

"I understand—I've arrived too late. The place is taken."

He defended himself, not so much against the affirmation as against the person affirming it.

"Indeed, no—what are you supposing?"

"That which is. As if I didn't know certain intonations!"

"Sylvestre's a childhood friend, a sister."

Already resigned, and malicious again, she snapped: "Then that will add extra spice to it!"

"Ah! It doesn't take much to recover the old Marise."

"That's true—forgive me, I yielded to an impulse of jealousy. After all, it's you, no doubt, who is right. Each to his route! Yours and mine had drawn apart from one another, then drawn closer again...and now..." She made a gesture of impotence. "It was probably fated. It's a wife like the Blanchet girl that you need...she's worth more than me. My virtuous impulses are too widely spaced and too fragile not to fold up at the first impact. I wouldn't have made you happy."

"Nor I you. But I've been very unhappy, before realizing that."

She divined that there was no longer any reproach in his thought. Like him, she sensed the separation of their lives broadening, the inevitable distancing already hollowing out the gulf, and forgetfulness...

A sudden stab of regret: the letters! If she had known...

She judged it inelegant to ask for them back. She had lost—too bad. After all, as long as she had his promise with regard to her father. De Laume? What did he matter? People, existence...

Her indifference, for everything that was not her, had gripped her again. With a little melancholy, even so, beneath her recovered assurance, she shook the hand that he offered.

"*Adieu*, Claude. You've sworn to me..."

Emotionally, he responded to the amicable pressure: "Don't worry."

One second of silence, in which the entire past resounded, and already, the intrusion of time, resuming its march... Their hands came apart.

"*Adieu*," he said, opening the little door.

She went out without looking back. He closed it again, and returned avidly to the desk where the letters were laid out. He picked them up. They were all perfumed with the odor that had troubled him for such a long time. He breathed in—and then, master of himself, his mind clear, riffled through them with the impression that he was turning a page of his life.

As he read, however, a horror mingled with dread and indignation swelled within him. Over the vanished face of Marise were superimposed the menacing, hideous masks of the purveyors of death. The words cut into him like blades:

Continued, this morning, yesterday's conversation with Wittelsbach... "the incident that will set fire to the powder," the Chancellor said to me, "is only a secondary maneuver. The primary necessity is the suppression, in our two countries, of the socialist leaders: to begin with, to make Jacquemin and Rohn pass for traitors. Public opinion believes anything one wishes. Then their assassination will no longer seem anything but an act of justice..."

III

"Dr. Mauloy? For a consultation..."

"Third floor on the right."

Jacquemin lived on the fourth. With a suspicious gaze, the concierge, standing on the threshold of her lodge, scrutinized the tall, thin individual with his head surrounded with a thick padded bandage, who was exhibiting a swollen cheek. In the most natural fashion in the world, he took the elevator.

Since the rumors of war had been circulating, and, guarded by uniformed officers and agents in plain clothes patrolling the Boulevard Raspail, the President of the Council's house had become a historic dwelling, a great pride, increased by the sentiment of her responsibility, had animated Madame Richou. Not for anything in the world would she have wanted any accident to befall her celebrated tenant. "Such a worthy man! Twenty-two years in the house!"

The sound of the elevator stopping on the third and coming back down reassured her. Tranquil, she went back into her observatory.

The pseudo-invalid continued going upstairs, stealthily. He cocked an ear as he went past Jacquemin's door. The blood was hammering in his temples. "Enjoy your rest, bastard!" he growled, taking the two carefully-loaded Brownings from his jacket pockets. Nimbly, he went up the steps to the fifth floor, and sat down on the top one. The landing was a good position, where no one would disturb him now. The apartment was locked, its inhabitants having gone to the country for the Easter vacation.

Hippolyte Lunain congratulated himself. Everything was unfolding in accordance with his calculations. Justice would soon be done! He was within reach of revenge for his life. That was well worth risking the loss of his skin. Forty years of disappointments, frustrations and hazardous poverty! With the shovel of his memory the wretch shifted that residue in the chaos of his brain.

An adjutant who had risen to the rank of captain, but always an alcoholic, first there had been the good years of the war, and then, too quickly, the peace, in which, as a civilian again, after having been dismissed from the regiment, he had looked for a position and drunk his pension. Rejected or sacked everywhere, he had dragged around the ball and chain of a wife and three children. Finally, his son having died of tuberculosis and his eldest daughter running aground in a brothel in Buenos Aires, he had been left alone with a semi-paralytic harpy and a kid who looked after her. For all his misfortunes, one thing alone was responsible: the rotten regime, this socialism, which, by ruining the army, had reduced him to beggary. A gang of thieves and traitors, synthesized by the man who served as their head: Jacquemin!

That fanatical hatred, similar to that which had once armed Jaurès' assassin, had been nourished every day, for ten years, by bile-filed articles published by the reactionary papers, against the apostle of the new era. He had missed its target once, during the session in the Chambre in which, after the revolver shots fired at Jacquemin, de Laume's ministry had been toppled.

The latter, on the eve of his fall, had used his still considerable influence at the Palais de Justice to ensure that the author, not of the "attempted murder" but of the "inconsequential prank," was released. An hour of conversation the following day between the *minus habens* and Liéval, who had come to see him in his garret with some money in his pocket, had sufficed for the ex-President to assure himself of the servant of which his interests, inseparable from National Interests, had need.

Hippolyte Lunain had quit Liéval impregnated to the marrow of his bones with the fluid of a sovereign will, fully convinced that he was a hero, and that he must, for the salvation of France, carry his mission through to the end: killing the filthy Beast, the sole obstacle to national revival. A hundred thousand francs in bills, deposited in trust in his name with Liéval's notary, to be collected by his wife in case of his decease, or by himself on the advice of the donor, had completed the removal of any scruple. If the plan succeeded, and he was able to escape his exploit, his old age would be assured. If he remained here, the future of his family was protected.

The sound of a door opening pulled him out of his reverie and brought him upright, muscles taut. No, it was on Dr. Mauloy's floor. He leaned over and saw an old lady calmly going downstairs. He sat down again, a Browning in each hand, in order to be ready to leap into action.

At that moment, comfortably installed in the smoking room of his Château de Boissise, Max de Laume, one arm resting on the broad arm of a leather armchair, was following the spirals of blue smoke that were rising from his cigarette. The cuff of his sleeve elegantly drawn back, he was holding a slender amber cigarette holder between the ball of his thumb and his index finger, in homage to Madame d'Entraygues.

Sitting facing him, the Marquise, who had just descended from her auto, was telling him about her drunkenness the other night, her awakening by the policemen, the strong box pillaged...

She was still trembling

"They hadn't stolen anything—that's astonishing! How is it all going to end?"

"Well," said de Laume, less tranquil than he pretended to be. "But you ought, with Liéval, to have burned all my papers yourself. Cervier will have done so, I think..."

His old friend's story spoiled all the security that he had promised himself, thanks to his alibi. He regretted not having expurgated the files himself before leaving Paris. Why put his trust in Cervier? De Laume was bound to him closely by ambition, but he despised him, not judging him worthy of such a fortune, when he did not possess one himself. Bah! He would soon be the master. At this moment, he thought, destiny was being accomplished.

If everything happened in accordance with his anticipations, Lunain, recharged by Liéval that very morning with all the necessary magnetism, could not miss his shot. As long as Jacquemin went home for lunch!

His eyes went from the clock to the telephone. Another half an hour and the bell would ring...

De Laume believed that he was certain thereafter to control, if not the events of which he knew full well that no one was the master, at least the men on whom they depended in the largest measure.

He would no longer rely, this time, on parliamentary methods and the platitude of those on whose constancy he had counted, too sure of his authority, having paid for their devotion. Fear, more surely than interest, would serve him tomorrow. Solmou? A balloon he would puncture, if it inflated to the point of resisting him. The others military or civilian flunkeys, were only waiting for a resolute dictator.

Without vanity—for he called pride that which, in him, was only a species of demented conceit—he was the man for whom France and History had been waiting, for want of a henceforth-impossible king.

The clock chimed. He shivered, his ears pricked up for the other ring. Still nothing! One by one, slightly more nervous, he went over all the reasons he had for hope: the plans made in the smallest detail, the certain complicities, the decrees drafted in advance, all the way to the positions anticipated, in case of riots, for occupation by troops. And tomorrow, in accord with Lux, who had declared himself completely ready, in the conviction that they would emerge victorious from the veritable war—the foreign one being merely a mask—mobilization would lower its iron curtain over the socialist rout.

He shook the ash from his cigarette into an old silver wine taster, and then brutally crushed the butt. He evoked Solmou in his study at the Élysée; Cervier in his office at the bank; on the other side of the Rhine, the same organization of the coup d'État...Hartmann, Wittelsbach...

"What are you thinking about?" the Marquise asked.

He replaced the amber trinket, still hot, in its case, and replied with a knowing smile: "The wisdom of the old proverb: *Dead the beast, dead the venom*."

As if a mysterious coincidence had animated the weapon, at the very moment when the veritable assassin concentrated his murderous will, Hippolyte Lunain, suddenly standing up, was taking aim with his Brownings.

Voices, a door opening, cheerful adieux. This time!

Monsieur Blanchet, who, with his children, had being having lunch with Annik, and had stayed with her and Gine for a moment longer, was telling Sylvestre not to overtax herself after her night of traveling.

She wanted to go down with Claude and Georgi, to accompany Jacquemin to the Ministry, which she had never visited.

"I'll come to collect you in an hour."

"And you, too," shouted Annik to Amédée. "Don't overtire yourself."

"Don't worry, my love."

He began to go downstairs, followed by the joyful group.

Suddenly, there are one…two…three detonations, like three slaps on the ears.

Claude has shouted: "Papa! Look out!"

The Brownings are still firing. Instinctively, they have ducked, but Jacquemin, struck in the heart, falls and rolls heavily down the steps. Claude, fainting with anguish for his father, has precipitated himself toward him, with Georgi, while Sylvestre has bounded toward the assassin. Lunain, having descended to the landing, fires again, but she has grabbed his arm and deflected it.

"Brute! Brute!"

At the same time, without worrying about Georgi, she shouts at Claude, bent over the recumbent body. "Look out! He might hit you!"

215

Doors open; clamors rise up. Three tremulous individuals run out of Jacquemin's apartment. Annik's face is distressed, covered in tears.

"Amédée! Amédée!"

"Is he wounded?"

Gine and Blanchet are panic-stricken. Their cries cover the tumult with which the house fills up.

"Papa!"

"Amédée!"

"Lift him up!"

"Gently!"

For a second, Sylvestre is alone facing the fanatic. He has thrown away one of his Brownings, and is hammering her head with the butt of the other. Half-stunned, her face covered in blood, she clings to him, waiting for help to arrive. He tries to get past to take advantage of the confusion to flee...

Claude, leaving his father in the hands of Annik and Gine, has launched himself forward, followed by the neighbors, beside themselves, howling: "Kill him!"

Finally, the agents are there, revolvers in hand.

"Don't let him go!" shouts Claude.

"I have him!"

But, with a supreme thrust, Hippolyte Lunain has freed himself, and while Sylvestre collapses, unconscious, he runs up to the fifth floor, darting a fearful glance behind him. The vengeful mob is about to catch up with him.

"We've got him!"

The ferocious animal charges then, in utter desperation. The die is cast. He knocks over the first assailants, and with a bound, leaps into the elevator shaft, and into the void, where he crashes into the roof of the elevator, fracturing his skull.

At the first words of the agreed signal telephoned by one of the agents charged with protecting Jacquemin, Max de Laume had flown to the Élysée in an airplane, leaving Madame d'Entraygues in the property she possessed close to his own. She did not care to expose her precious person to the emotions of such days any more than he wanted to subject her to them. It was no longer a matter of petty intrigues. The die was cast. It was now a matter of winning the great game. No middle course: it was the purse and life—or death.

When he went into Solmou's study he had a disagreeable surprise. Having left him in ignorance of the impending action, he expected to find him disconcerted by the accomplished fact. He had not foreseen such composure, nor, at the same time, such excitement.

At the first visits confirming the telephone call from the Prefecture of Police and the news that, in a tumultuous session in the Reichstag, the German Chancellor, insulted and wounded, had only been able to protect himself from the blows of the socialists by abandoning the hall, Solmou had thought the battle lost at the very moment that it was engaged. What was the point of killing Jacquemin if, in the two countries, a commencement of the agreed war did not provide, in Germany as in France, the necessary pretext for nationalism to realize in its ambition the common program: the provocation of bloody civil war in the two democracies?

Turbot and Cervier, prompt at de Laume's rendezvous, had in the meantime, used up their saliva in vain. Sinnoy, the former Prefect of Police, and Vincent, the former director of the Sûreté Générale sacked by Jacquemin, who had also been summoned, were fidgeting impatiently. Solmou refused any initiative, even envisaging the possibility of maintaining the decapitated ministry. If the socialists carried the day in Germany, why change harness in France at the same time? War? A better opportunity would never arrive. He was about to have Hurteau come in, who, after having been to pay his respects to Jacquemin's remains, had just been announced by the general secretary.

"It's crazy!" growled Turbot. "Wait for de Laume. It's three o'clock. He can't be much longer."

The door opened, shoved abruptly.

"It's high time!" sighed Cervier.

He had not calmed down since he had learned, a little while before, from Marise, about the abstraction of letters from the auto-da-fé and the insensate step she had taken in giving them to Claude Jacquemin. "Do you want to doom us all, idiot!" he had cried, while brutalizing her.

Far from defending herself, however, for only then had she discovered the full implications of what she had done, she had begun to weep, limp and abandoned, like a weakling. He had not dared either to continue hitting her or... Patience! Everything would work out. He had immediately tried to warn de Laume at Melun. Already departed... And, doubly anxious, no longer able to sit still, he awaited his arrival...

Having judged the situation at a glance, however, the true President, having swiftly shot the gilded bolt behind him, had already fallen upon Solmou, prostrate in his armchair. He placed the briefcase that he had under his arm on the desk and declared, in a tone that brooked no reply: "Hurteau, who is mounting guard on the other side of the door and who would have liked to prevent me from passing, has just told me that a German raid of gas-launching aircraft has set a part of Strasbourg ablaze." He omitted to say that it was in conformity with the decisions made in advance by Wittelsbach and himself. Then came the news capable of reanimating Solmou: "The Chancellor has dissolved the Reichstag and had the principal socialist leaders arrested..."

A stammer: "I...I...don't know anything yet."

"There's not a moment to lose. Fortunately, everything is prepared. The military government in Paris is only awaiting orders, and our friends everywhere a signal. The garrison is consigned and all the black regiments ready to march."

"How do you know?"

"By the presence of the captain commanding your guard of honor. His choice guaranteed me the certain execution of this plan, provided that you sign it immediately." He opened his briefcase and took out the decrees bearing the headings of the President of the Republic and the President of the Council. Solmou looked at them, vacillating.

218

"Sign what?"

"Simply this message to the Chambre and the Sénat." He read: "*By reason of the urgent gravity of the circumstances and in the face of the violation of our territory by our eternal enemies, I would be failing in my most sacred duty if, without waiting for the convocation of Parliament, I did not take the measures immediately necessary for the preservation of the Fatherland. I am therefore informing the Chambre and the Sénat that in replacement for Amédée Jacquemin, struck down by a criminal hand, I have invested Monsieur Max de Laume, the former President of the Council, with the task of forming a cabinet that will be responsible for the conduct of the war that is henceforth inevitable... Sacred burden that we will all, etc...*"

De Laume showed his accomplices and acolytes the back of the huge room, signaled to them to withdraw there, and, leaning over Solmou, he ordered in a taut voice: "Sign, Maurice!"

He had dipped the pen in the inkwell, and held it out to the hesitant Solmou.

"Sign there...the message...and there...the decree that covers you, since it passes all responsibility to me... Sign, and it's victory; hesitate, and we're doomed—but be certain: cowardice won't save you..."

Solmou turned the penholder round and round in his fingers, which had become as leaden as his complexion. Finally, with a deep sigh, under the imperious eye that was fascinating him with a tacit menace, he zigzagged, with an almost illegible endorsement, the first unconstitutional act that he had signed in his life, and then, with a further shudder, the second.

De Laume had no need to recall his servants; they surrounded him, attentive.

"Messieurs the Prefect of Police and Director of the Sûreté Générale can consider themselves as qualified to enter their functions immediately. I'm equally assured"—he addressed himself to Solmou—"of the ministerial cooperation of former collaborators. It's only a matter of mandating them.

The Council can thus meet in eighteen hours. In the meantime, you, Sinnoy, inform Hurteau that the resignation of the preceding cabinet has been accepted. Those Messieurs have only one choice: obedience or prison. At the present moment, all the Ministries ought to be occupied by reliable troops, along with the various central posts of emission. You, Vincent, alert the entire Sûreté Générale. The commandants of military regions on whom we can count have been advised, by superior orders, to be ready for any eventuality. The mobilization and state of siege, which the Council of Ministers will deliberate, will take care of the rest. As for the Press..."

Damn! thought Turbot, at that moment. He bowed. "That which is worthy of the name is with us, Monsieur le Président. As for the other...." With his callused hand he gave a significant gesture of turning a screw.

Cervier, finally able to intervene, exclaimed: "Pardon me! A word, Max—it's urgent."

He drew him into the embrasure of one of the French windows opening to the depths of the park, and rapidly told him—without betraying his daughter—about the disappearance—the theft?—of the Du Crêté letters, and their passage—how?—into Jacquemin's hands. At any rate, it was necessary to prevent them from making use of them, and immediately!

De Laume, master of himself as he was, had gone pale. "Damnation!"

He saw, under the blow of that revelation, popular disorder taking hold before the implacable laws and the military yoke could come down. Everything compromised, perhaps lost...

Without wasting time in reproaches he went back rapidly to Solmou's desk and telephoned the Governor of Paris' chief of staff, another of his pawns.

"Is that you, General? The Élysée here...yes, it's me, de Laume...send a contingent immediately to the *Universel*, Boulevard Haussmann...at the orders of the Commissaire de Police, it will find there... Good. Inform the Governor..." He hung up. "Did you hear that, Sinnoy? Go! That first, before anything else. Before anything—before even informing Hurteau! In any case, Vincent will take charge of that."

Left alone with Cervier—"Why, where's Solmou gone?"—de Laume sat down, in order to wait, in the large armchair with the sphinxes' heads on which, it was said, Napoléon had rested his hands during his last passage through the Élysée, and where, not without pride, he imagined himself striking an imperial pose...

"Where's he gone, that animal?" growled de Laume. "It's necessary, though, to finish reaching an accord before the Council..."

Solmou reappeared, still white, but relieved of his diarrhea...

IV

For an hour the cadaver has been lying in the bedroom, on the large bed. It seems that Jacquemin has just thrown himself down there, for one of the brief siestas that he likes to take after lunch. Apart from the jacket and waistcoat, he is not yet undressed, and, were it not for the blood staining his shirt, one might think that he is going to wake up at any moment.

Annik knows that it is all over. He's dead. Killed instantly, Dr, Feremot says, having arrived after Dr. Mauroy. She can't believe it. It has been necessary once again to draw her away from her unbreakable grip, from her supplications: "Amédée! Amédée! No, it's not possible! Answer me!"

Now she is beginning to realize, and stupor overwhelms her, at the same time as the immense void invades her.

After Sylvestre has been rapidly bandaged by Dr. Mauloy—"Rest! Immediate...or I won't answer for anything!"—Monsieur Blanchet has just departed with his daughter for Versailles. She has allowed herself to be led away, inert, exhausted by shock and effort. She does not want to encumber the house of mourning with the presence of an invalid—since it is necessary that she be put to bed, and feels the need.

She will come back as soon as possible; her entire soul remains suspended there. She has shared in Claude's grief. He has embraced her, saying: "Thank you for what you tried to do!" But she didn't do anything! She only followed, spontaneously, the irresistible impulse that threw her between her beloved and danger...

Now, in the motor ambulance that is taking her away, she is still mentally with Claude, sustaining him with what remains of her strength.

Impotent, with Gine and Georgi, he is witnessing, in the same lacerating fury, Annik's now-silent torment.

She has only let go of the already cold hand, which she clutched while kneeling, collapsed against the body, to kiss it as she rises to her feet. All of human unhappiness is unleashed within her. Gradually, light returns to her thoughts, filtering through the darkness that had submerged them. Stupor turns to indignation, desperation to rage. The letters! The accusing letters! Before mourning Amédée, avenge him!

"Go to the Ministry," she says to Georgi. "Bring back all his papers, his last dispatches, everything that can testify that he did the impossible to avoid the war. Perhaps they don't know yet; they won't have had time to make their move...."

She turns to Claude: "You have the letters? Run to the *Universel*, have them photographed. It's necessary that the prints appear this evening in a special edition revealing the names of the true assassins at the same time as the news of the assassination..."

"And the originals?"

"You're right. They'll try to get them back at all costs. It's necessary to put them in a safe place. Where...? They'll search..."

"If the revolution isn't immediate," said Claude, "they'll be the masters. A matter of days...and with a state of siege!"

"They'll stop at nothing!" Gine said.

Annik reflected: yes, the best hiding place would be abroad... She slapped her forehead.

"Madame Sydney! At Montreux."

"Perfect," said Claude.

"Find someone reliable. As soon as the photographs are taken, have the airplane take off."

"I'll go myself," said Georgi. "That's the best thing. The time to run to the Ministry, come back to kiss Gine, bringing everything back, and to take the letters to the *Universel*... Sapristi! My helic is at Versailles."

"There are airplanes at the paper."

Gine would have liked to go with her husband, but did not dare, before Annik's taut expression as she distributed tasks, to abstract herself from her filial duty to sustain her, even if it is impossible to console her.

"When will you be back?" she asked, anxiously, when her arms let go.

"As soon as I can. Tomorrow morning, at the latest."

"Be here, or I'll come after you!"

"Let's go, Georgi," said Claude, cutting short the parting. Claude hugged his mother.

They turned round on the threshold to give all the fervor of their devotion to the supine corpse. At the same time Claude gestured to his sister, indicating Annik, who had returned to the bed. With a glance, he confided her to Gine.

Having taken Georgi to the Quai d'Orsay, the auto reached the *Universel* in the Place de l'Opéra. Outside the immediate vicinity of the Boulevard Raspail, where the murder, already known, was beginning to create a stir, Paris was continuing its habitual life. Claude was astonished by the insouciance of people, the placidity of events. When they knew...!

At the *Universel* he found the place in upheaval. They had just heard. Telephones were ringing everywhere. Jacquemin was not only the guide and friend of the editor, but a kind of benevolent deity to the entire staff. An exasperation and a need for vengeance were exciting all the faces.

Claude lived through extraordinary minutes, in which the body and soul, although acting together, seemed to remain separate...

In a single surge he writes an account of the nightmare, in which the entire drama unfolded in hallucinatory brevity. He wants Jacquemin's name to cry vengeance for Jacquemin! He stands up, the living incarnation of the cadaver of the dead man.

He is called. He is in the photographic studio, then the darkroom. He plunges the plate into the developer, following the appearance of the denunciatory lines...

There they are, fixed in the galvanoplasty. Now he palpates the Du Crêté letters. There, in his wallet! The aircraft?

It's waiting on the terrace, with an experienced pilot. Claude climbs aboard, checks it mechanically... The magneto? Protection? Good...

He waits for Georgi... Here he is! He hands him the deposit...

The engine roars. They embrace. The aircraft has gone. Other aircraft are lined up, which will take off for the provincial distribution as soon as the issue is printed...

He goes back down into Jacquemin's office, takes with the editor-in-chief the necessary measures for Paris. Already, of their own accord, the vendors and the porters have arrived and are waiting...

At the same time, the imagination of all the unknowns, everything possible in the hours that are flying by, harasses him from the depths of darkness...

One by one, news items come in, fantastic, contradictory...

Then, falling together at a precipitate pace, the events striking Claude carry him away like a leaf in a cyclone...

Without a declaration of war, Germany has begun hostilities; Strasbourg has been partly destroyed, along with its population...

The German socialists will be masters in Berlin... But it's said that Rohn has been killed...or in flight...

What to believe?

"Hurry up!" Claude orders. "Are the autos ready?"

But a hubbub rises up in the vestibule, filling the entire building via the elevators. A Commissaire of Police stops the presses in the machine room. Upstairs, in the photographic gallery, another is carrying out a search. A company of Bambara riflemen has placed a military guard on the autos, where the first bundles were beginning to pile up, and, with bayonets fitted, are preventing anyone from entering or leaving. A section has reached the roof and immobilized the aircraft, and is standing guard over the pilots.

Too late! The letters are far away.

Claude, racing to the basement, swears at the man draped in his sash, impassive under his threats. The government? He knows no other than the one whose orders he is executing, received directly from the Élysée from the mouth of the new Prefect of Police. If the director or the editorial staff of the *Universel* opposes the accomplishment of his mission, he will have the regret of arresting the rebels, whoever they are. At the same time he indicates, through the windows to the street, the riflemen, of whom nothing can be seen but the feet and the butts of their rifles.

A flash of reason, warns Claude; he restrains his friends, and the furious group of workers. He will not give this brute the joy of serving all the hopes of his masters. He concedes, without ceasing to protest, clenching his fists...

And, leaving his collaborators the care of making up the evening edition if, as he hopes, the paper remains free—even censored—to appear, he returns, raging mutely, to the Boule-vard Raspail. The rumor of the assassination has spread now. Groups are stopping, discussing. An emotion is propagating through the nascent rumor...

Claude tightens his determination. Tomorrow, with the uprising of an entire people, he will avenge the victim...

The sinister vigil is about to conclude. In half an hour the body will be placed in the coffin. Taking turns, Gine and Claude have remained with Annik, who has not wanted to go to bed. Now, in the mortuary chamber draped in gray by the rainy daylight, Claude is caressing his mother's face piously, kneeling beside the bed. All her tears have been shed. Ardent-ly, fixedly, she is gazing at the handsome, placid face, and Claude reunites them in the same desperate religion. But for the moment, he has more hatred than love, more dolorous rage than dejection.

Annik, prostrated by the immense burden of the solitude that is beginning to enter into her and the nervous fatigue of the previous day and night, is no longer anything but a soul in torment, in the automaton of the body.

The door opens slightly. Gina beckons to Claude. He is needed. She whispers names. They are intimates, political allies of the dead man, who want to see him one last time. Since the news has spread, a thunderclap in the supercharged air, Paris in upheaval is converging on the Boulevard Raspail. All day long, and for much of the night, the apartment has been invaded by a crowd: an incessantly-renewed encampment in which stupor, indignation and tears bear witness... A flower garden is still growing of magnificent sprays and five-sou bouquets.

The file recommences, and a new murmur rises from downstairs: popular emotion, contained at a distance by barrages of agents, but whose dull plaint emerging from so many hearts unfurls all the way to the funereal bed.

Annik has understood. She turns her head. "No! A minute more! Go tell them, Claude!"

Gine approaches in order to replace him. "No! Leave us alone! Soon! I'll give him back to them!" She has put her hands together in a mechanical gesture of prayer.

The form of Amédée Jacquemin reposes majestically beneath the sheet, on which only a few violets are fading. The arms are extended alongside the body, like those of a sleeper after completing a task, but the closed eyelids, with the marmoreal forehead, behind which light and thought are extinct, imposing on the features, whiter still in the white beard, the rigidity that testifies to eternal slumber.

There is no longer anything there but matter in decomposition. However, Annik speaks to him as if he were still alive, as if a mysterious union still attached Amédée's soul to her own.

"You know what I'm thinking, don't you? You know what I've decided, what you would have decided yourself if you were in my place... What would love be worth, if it stopped with death? Yes, my darling, soul of my soul, I shall follow you soon, and rejoin you. I'm listening fervently to the advice that you're giving me, silently: 'Let your death, like mine, serve humanity.' In what way was it necessary to humankind that you die? I'm no longer rebelling, you see; my decision is made. I don't have to reflect, but to act. I'm simply asking myself why your eyes have been suddenly closed, when they contained so much light, so much love...

"Why, when we are all vibrant with the task to fulfill, are we forced to lie down, and become part of the immense mass of the dead? You must know, since your dear face is so calm... And since you've set the example for me, let their will be done! The children? Yes, I know full well, it's necessary to preserve a mother for them... Claude, already so dolorous, has need of one... But it would have been necessary for you not to leave me! Live, exist, without you? No, my love, you know that's impossible! Even if my flesh were pusillanimously re-signed to it, I'd seek you untiringly, with animal cries! I'd only be able to clamor my frightful solitude...the disgust of my clinging egotism!

"No. I remain as you have known me: faithful, intransi-gent. I've given you my life. I've said so a hundred times. It's not today, when you can't defend yourself, that I'll take it back. Before they take me away, I swear that I'll come to you soon. You know how impatient I am, you know that if I hadn't had to concern myself with your glory, your ideas, humanity and our little children, I would no longer be feeling anything but the death that the bullet, in striking you, has cast into me, and which is gnawing me away, savagely. I'm thinking about satisfying you, of understanding you, in order that you'll al-ways be more than proud of me. You're saying to me—and I can hear you—'Only choose a useful death...for the future of our children, for the peace of the new couples...in order that, more fortunate than us, they'll be able to go on together to the end of the road.' I promise you that, my soul, my life...

"*À bientôt.*"

V

To the excited insistence of friends who wanted to give the martyr a grandiose funeral, in the dolor and indignation of the people, Claude had opposed the parental will: rapid, silent incineration with no one present but the family. He almost regretted it himself now, the new government having made it known that, in view of the circumstances, it would not tolerate manifestations around the interment taking on a revolutionary aspect, at a moment when all the nation's thoughts ought to be directed toward the war. The transfer would only take place after nightfall. But Amédée Jacquemin, before de Laume, had given orders, and Claude Jacquemin obeyed.

As soon as the news was known, all those in the party who were not attained by the mobilization or had resolved not to answer it had undertaken a pilgrimage to the mortuary dwelling. An enormous flood, rising from the faubourgs and extending to the suburbs, had come to break against the cordon of order. All day long, while a small guard of honor surrounded the coffin and took shifts in the apartment, it had rumbled, until, with dusk, individual concerns had dispersed it.

People returned to their immediate interests. Fear also emptied the boulevards and streets: not so much the panic of the fugitives—the crowd of whom had laid siege to the railway stations since dawn, mounting assaults on the trains—as a vague, immense, universal terror at the idea of enemy aircraft and their bombs, perfidious layers of gas or invisible rays, killing at a distance.

It was only in pitch darkness, via a small street intersecting the Boulevard Raspail, that Annik, Claude and Gine, in an open carriage, were able to remove to the crematorium of Père-Lachaise, the corpse that was all that still remained to them of the man who was gone. They had followed, with a supreme surge of emotion, the disappearance of the mortal remains into the Fire. They knew full well, Annik included, that since the blow that had struck them, the great soul vibrated in them, in all the memories fecundated by his example. Hours that had been no less atrocious...

They returned to the house, exhausted, and took a brief rest there. It seemed to them that it was so much stolen from the irreparable time that was passing vertiginously. They had woken up after a few hours, and set to work again. Annik—who, until the departure for the cemetery, had emptied the house and shut herself away to work in the study with Gine and a few secretaries, collaborators with the International Council of Women—had gone to install herself at the *Maison de Toutes* in the Rue Saint-Antoine. She was in a hurry to get on with the burdensome take commenced a few days earlier. With Georgi's auto, driven by Gine, she could come and go...

"And when I've rejoined Georgi," said Gine, "You can take young Richou."

Not seeing her husband return at the appointed hour, she had taken advantage of everyone's confusion immediately after lunch to run to the American Embassy and have a wireless message sent to the radiographic station at Montreux, addressed to Madame Sydney: *Tell Georgi to wait for me. Arriving tomorrow*. She would be able to get there by mans of the helic that was still at Versailles. Her mother had approved. Georgi would be more useful to everyone in Switzerland, especially if, as the news had given out, Rohn had been able to reach Lausanne.

In his little amphib, Claude had returned to the cooperative printing works at Belleville where a workers' newspaper and cooperative publications were normally printed. By virtue of its modesty it had escaped the dictatorial forethought. The Paris garrison, reduced by the necessities of mobilization, was scarcely sufficient, in spite all the black troops it had conserved, for the exercise of surveillance and the maintenance of order. Partial riots had broken out in places, immediately suppressed.

Claude feared, in view of the torpor induced by the stunning blow, that popular indignation would not react as quickly and completely as he hoped. As rapidly as the guarded or blocked roads permitted, flying when necessary, he reached the workshop where his friends were waiting for him.

Shutters closed, at the back of a courtyard, the printing-works, in the hum of its machines and the odor of hot oil, was operating flat out. Copies of a black-lined poster were rolling off the presses incessantly, headed: *The names of the assassins*, followed by the most striking extracts from de Laume's letters, the irrefutable, explicit confession of the premeditation of the crime…and then a few moving lines of universal appeal.

The fury that possessed them rendered them confident. It even calmed their excitement: they wanted, without delay, to provoke the riot that was the only thing that could soothe it. But Claude, although he was appealing to everyone to join the revolution, did not want to compromise it by too much haste; it was necessary first to form the conviction of the greatest number, by revealing...

During the seizure carried out at the *Universel* the day before, he had been able to save a few proofs reproducing the crucial document. That had permitted him, without any news as yet from Georgi and the Swiss newspapers to which he would unfailingly have transmitted facsimiles of the originals, to proceed with the immediate composition of the posters, which twenty devoted men would soon stick up on every wall that they could.

At the paper itself—under military occupation, along with the Place de l'Opéra, under the pretext of defending the *Universel* against the aggression of patriots—Claude had not been surprised to find a delegate of the Ministry of the Interior installed. The morning issue, riddled with blank spaces or splashed with large black patches, had only been able to give strictly limited information. A pitiless censorship had been imposed by the Place Beauvau, from which all the subsidized press had to take direction, while at the five or six opposition papers the proofs were checked and plucked to order.

Claude had briefly considered suspending its appearance himself, but after the odious maneuvers launched in the morning in the *Inter* and continued by the afternoon papers he had, in accord with the editors and the staff spared by the call-up, decided to hold on, to appear no matter what the cost, until the day when, victoriously, they could proclaim the truth in the re-liberated *Universel*.

In the meantime, it was necessary, for a few more hours, to gnaw at the bit, to tolerate the wretches, attempting to do everything with journalism to dishonor the victim of the assas-sination. Lunain, sacrificing himself to save France, was hailed as a hero... There was proof that Jacquemin, reconciled with the extremists, was a traitor, that a vast international con-spiracy had been hatched, in which French socialism, duped yet again by the promises of Social Democracy, was preparing to stab the Fatherland in the back... All the Germans were, as in 1914, under the flags of their revenge. A few madmen al-ready reckoned with or fled, like Rohn, had not been able to prevail against the nationalist spirit... The spirit of salvation against which the crime of a Jacquemin, in France, would not prevail...etc., etc.

Monstrous calumny, through the eternal beat of the old drum! It had ended up rendering Claude beside himself, with the insinuation that had begin to show its point, a preventive move against the publication of the Du Crêté letters: "It is believed that, not recoiling from any weapon, the party of treason has not hesitated to direct the most ignoble accusations against the great patriot that Max de Laume is. Forgeries are already circulating, so grossly fabricated that no one will al-low themselves to be taken in by a diversion as base as it is stupid... While inclining before the dolor of a widow and her children, the public conscience will rise up to denounce the supreme infamy of the traitors who, having wanted to leave the country defenseless against the enemy nation, are the first to drive it toward civil war..."

Patience! Soon the posters would be ready, displayed, declaring the truth! They would see whether it would stand up against the assassins of the popular revolt; whether, inflamed by the blow, the timid hearths of mutiny—ignited by the mobilization in a few Parisian barracks and affirmed in several provincial cities—would not propagate the irresistible conflagration of will power! And whether, against any assault, sheep-like docility, the force of prejudice and inexcusable ignorance would paralyze those crowds resigned to the hereditary massacre and the pseudo-fatality of the scourge, it would then set an example, refuse to obey the anticipated order for the mobilization of its class that was expected at any moment.

How would the de Laumes, the Cerviers and the Turbots hesitate over a measure so simple as to advance from October to May of a gathering of recruits, when they had just postponed the imminent elections and adjourned parliament, now in recess? Since the unfortunate lesson of 1914, when, for want of preliminary regulation and by virtue of a false conception of duty to the representatives of the people, a party of députés had been able to play the officer when public salvation demanded the most severe military control, the Chambre ought, in time of war, legally to be in permanent session. De Laume, respecting the principle, had neutralized the effect.

The sole master as long as he was given free rein, it was necessary to fear anything on his part. The Poncet factory, militarized on the evening of the assassination—and where he was searching rancorously for the author of the indiscretion that had contributed to the toppling of his ministry—had put into his hands the most terrible power that any tyrant had ever had at his disposal against the enemy—the People!

Jacquemin had seen clearly and Claude was not mistaken. The proof was that after the initial German raid on Strasbourg, there was a calm. Paris was still waiting, chilled by fear, for the rain and wind of death that would already have fallen if the hostilities had been real: evidence that they were not directed against one country or the other but against a common adversary: the domestic millions.

233

No! That in Germany as in France, the presidents, chancellors, maréchals, themselves lackeys of the kings of finance should triumph over the force that was still spare and searching itself—impossible! Imbecile crime would not defeat all the energies of life!

Annik's faith transported Claude. Without violence, simply by imposing inertia, by refusing to march, the murderous machine would be immobilized! The Juggernaut would finally stop before the insurmountable wall of the massed people, the obstacle of the arms folded over their breasts. *I shall be the first to cry duty to those of my class, to the uncertain comrades, if they are summoned to form convoys toward the training camps and the prison parks...*

An awakened dream, which he lived entirely while supervising the departure of the bill-posters, and accompanying the squadron that he had reserved for the arrondissement personally. It was necessary, for preference, to reach the very heart of Paris, the workers' quarters, the ant-hill of the little people. Crammed into the amphib, they drove around. Briskly, while he kept watch, his men, choosing the best locations as far as was possible, stuck up the posters. They were able to exhaust their supply without attracting the attention of patrols. By daybreak, everything was finished.

Exhausted, Claude retained them briefly in a bistro owned by a friend of one of them, who opened the shutter, yawning: "Won't say no, M'sieur Claude!"

While they were having a bite to eat, he drank a hot coffee. "That'll do you good!" said the bistro owner, who, having come to sit down with them, joined in with the others in surrounding him with admiring compassion. Claude sensed a boundless good will in the devotion of their simplicity and their rude interjections. He left them regretfully, after having shaken their hands.

"Tell the friends that I'm at the *Maison de Toutes*, Rue Saint-Antoine, if anyone needs me. Keep someone on permanent stand-by at the printers' for liaison. Make your arrangements with the International Syndical Federation so that if our friends are, like me, pursued and arrested, even if the printing-works is closed down, there'll be another safe corner in Belleville where we can meet up. And courage! We'll have them!"

"It'll be done, M'sieu Claude…"

"We'll let you know at the Rue Saint-Antoine when the place is found."

"We're behind you, for the storm."

The enthusiasm of the brave men gave him heart, accompanying him as he flew over the network of rolling sidewalks around the Place de la Bastille and landed on the terrace of the *Maison de Toutes*.

In spite of the early hour, the entire building, from the residences on the ground floor to the communication center and the lecture halls, was buzzing with wide-awake activity. The night-shift was giving way to an ever-increasing troop of new arrivals. Annik, installed in her office well before dawn, like a captain at the microphone of command, had dictated the most urgent letters, corrected the proofs of her Women's Manifesto, and read some of the post—a pile of telegrams and heaps of letters—that had been pouring in from all over France and Europe since the tragic event. The Post Office had not yet received orders to isolate the *Maison de Toutes*; it was still being forwarded from the Rue de Grenelle.

Suddenly, at eight o'clock, when the secretary of the French Section asked to be connected to Montreux, complete silence. They rang and rang in vain, using other apparatus. Annik's efforts would henceforth be blocked, rendered semi-important by the adversary's precaution.

She immediately envisaged other means. Multicopy duplicators began printing the Manifesto on the spot. The addressing-machines typed envelopes non-stop. As soon as they were stamped, employees and boarders carried them, disseminated in small bundles, to different offices, in order not to attract attention.

When Claude arrived, he was glad to find his mother completely self-controlled, coming and going, giving orders with the apparent calmness with which she was long accustomed to discipline her nerves.

Gine was agitated, unable to keep still. She welcomed Claude with a "Finally!" which he understood was addressed to him less in the joy of seeing him again as in the haste to put him to work.

Scarcely had Annik finished interrogating him with "The posters?" and informing him: "The Manifesto is ready," then Gine demanded: "The amphib?"

"Up on the terrace. Why?"

"To take me to Versailles. I'll take the helic from there. I'm leaving...to join Georgi."

"He'll come back!"

"No, since he wasn't here at midday yesterday. I've had the American embassy notify him that I'll rejoin him this morning."

He did not immediately grasp the whole of her thought. He was convinced that Georgi's return was only a matter of hours. That he had stayed in Switzerland, and that Gine, deserting her filial duty, approved and was encouraging him, surprised him and pained him. There were better things to do.

He was about to say so bluntly when someone touched him: it was Sylvestre, pale beneath her circular bandage, her eyes seemingly widened in their dark rings. A square-jawed man with a resolute expression, in a pilot's costume, was with her, carrying a heavy parcel under his arm. While she embraced Annik and Gine, Sylvestre named him: "Monsieur Zierfel from Lausanne, who has brought Swiss newspapers and news, in Georgi's stead...."

"He's...staying out there?"

Sylvestre detected the ill-disguised criticism beneath the astonishment. "Yes, and here I am, instead."

Claude directed a suspicious gaze at Sylvestre. What did she mean?

She blushed, sensing that he had not understood her remark. "It's necessary to substitute for Gine, since she's leaving with Monsieur Zierfel!"

"But how do you come to be here together?" he asked.

"He left the *Universel*'s airplane at Versailles. Georgi was afraid that if he came down in the Place de l'Opéra, he might be caught in a trap. We came by the electric without being noticed. Quickly, now—let Monsieur Zierfel tell you what Monsieur Rohn..."

"He's alive!" exclaimed Annik, hope reviving.

She had just opened the package brought from Lausanne to unfold the accusing newspapers. They had all published reproductions of the letters on the first page, with long obituaries. Simply, in a few precise words, after saying that Switzerland "and every other country" shared in French mourning, the emissary repeated what Blanchet and Sylvestre had been so delighted to hear: Rohn and the principal leaders of the Social Democratic Party had escaped imprisonment and nationalist assassination attempts. Berlin was in full revolution, divided between the former officers of the Imperial Army and the militia supported by the popular quarters. Westphalia and Saxony against Munich...

In sum, the game was so far from being lost that Rohn, before returning to Berlin, had asked Georgi to remain in Lausanne, to centralize the French propaganda there, in close cooperation with the efforts of all the socialists making common cause for the first time against the other Internationalism, that of de Laume and Wittelsbach...

Annik shook Zierfel's hands like those of an old friend, and asked him for one service more: that of dictating the good news himself into the autocopying recorder, at the same time that one of her stenographers made a summary of it. Claude would take it to the printing-works right away, for immediate distribution via posters, while she would start a new dactylographic duplication, addressed to all the female workers of France. She took him into the next room to install him.

When she came back, Sylvestre had sat down, tiredly, on a corner of the desk. Claude's welcome had crushed her. He was reflecting, immobile, in front of the window. He turned round when his mother came back in.

Gine, who was putting on her hat, also turned, and said to both of them: "Why don't you come with me?"

"Never!" snapped Claude.

"No, my daughter," said Annik, more gently. "We can't go."

"Why not?"

"Because Georgi and you are sufficient to serve the human cause out there, and that same cause has need of us, here."

"Of you, Mother, perhaps—I recognize that. But Claude?"

"My presence is no less indispensable."

"You're going to fight?"

"No."

"Then you'll be killed, like Papa."

"At least I'll have held, until the end, the torch he passed on to me."

"You can raise it just as well beyond the frontier."

"No, it's only in my country that it can shine. Just as, before knowing what hate is, I loved all people, without that preventing me from cherishing you; I love all countries, but cherish my own above all, because in its origins, its genius and its language, I began to be conscious of myself; I'm part of it, to the point that I wouldn't be able to understand myself, and to serve it better, anywhere else."

"Serve it better? By giving de Laume a pretext to kill you more easily!"

Without daring to intervene in it, Sylvestre followed the argument ardently. There was a ferment within her; she could not discern her preferences. But Gine took her as a witness.

"What do you think, Sylvestre?"

She started.

"I don't know! Everything is dangerous, and everything is necessary. I'd certainly like to see Claude out of here, but I'll understand if he fights beside us. We're at a moment when, if we want to launch ourselves out of our petty lives to serve universal life, we ought not to choose; we have only to

238

follow our instinct—the idea of human love—wherever it leads each of us."

Her eyes searched Claude's face for an effect. They brightened on hearing it.

"Sylvestre's justified me!"

"And Georgi, and me. Did you think that his absence and my departure were running away?" She had tears in her eyes. "Are we cowards?"

"No!" cried Annik. "Of course not!"

But Gine continued, ardently: "We're risking as much as you. We won't be imprisoned by the lie, that's all. As in Germany and in France, it will be just as perilous to keep on going, wherever it's necessary, to sow the truth in the open air. If Georgi were here"—she looked at Sylvestre—"and he's not your brother for nothing, he's say: 'This isn't a matter of preserving my life. I've dedicated it to the unfortunate, to their education. To serve! Yes, but the common cause! And as intelligently as possible! If I come back, I'll be called up. If I refuse to fight, to kill, I'll be killed. And afterwards?'"

"Perhaps she's right," Sylvestre murmured. "What will become of Claude if he remains here?"

Gine gladly added her support: "You'll immediately have your hands tied. You'll be arrested, imprisoned, perhaps shot, and your death will accomplish nothing but our greater misery."

Someone knocked on the door.

"One second!" Annik shouted.

But the door opened. Monsieur Zierfel's head appeared, worriedly. "We need to leave. Every minute's delay increases the risks."

"Wait for me," shouted Gine. "I'm coming." And when the door closed she turned to Claude: "You decision is final?"

"Irrevocable. I'm staying with Mother, to link my action with hers, as our father would have done."

"Thank you, my child. I believe you're right—and Gine, too, when she thinks that Georgi will be more useful to us all by virtue of acting as he has. There are heroic tasks for all of us, in the hours we're going through." She held out her arms to her daughter. "Go on, my child. Do what you have to. But don't risk your life needlessly. Promise me?"

"Understood! One way or another, we'll meet again soon. We'll be tortured if we don't have any news."

Sylvestre, who had collected herself, kissed Gine in her turn. "Kiss Georgi for me…"

"How hot your hands are! It's you, Sylvestre, that I ought to take! In the state you're in, the calm of Montreux would be better for you than the emotions of Paris."

It was Claude who replied, spontaneously: "Her father needs her…"

Sylvestre said nothing, prey to the confused joy that those words, without her knowing why, had just filled her.

"She'll be as well at Versailles," said Annik. "And I'll be glad to have her closer."

"*Adieu*, then, Mother…and forgive me for leaving you; I can no longer live apart from Georgi."

"I understand."

Her tone was so grave that Claude and Sylvestre exchanged glances. Gine tried to make amends: "You're necessary to me, too—one only has one Mama."

It was Sylvestre's turn to darken her expression. Whichever way one turned, the dead appeared.

Gine hugged her friend again. "Forgive me, my sister." She pointed at Annik. "Be a daughter to her; you know that she loves you like a mother." She embraced Claude tenderly. "Be prudent, my elder. And keep me up to date whenever you can."

But Annik called her back, with open arms, as if she was never going to see her again. "Kiss me one more time, my love."

"Maman!"

They hugged, tears that had been too long held back mingling.

"Be brave, my child, always be brave." She collected herself and shoved her daughter toward the door, where Mon-

240

sieur Zierfel was waiting, resignedly. "Thank you, Monsieur," said Annik. "Show them out, Claude."

Before disappearing, Gine blew her another kiss.

Annik followed her with a long, last farewell gaze. Pensively, while waiting for Claude to come back up, she went back to sit at her desk, after an affectionate glance at Sylvestre. Each of them was searching within herself to discover the palpitations of her destiny. They collected themselves, their souls tumultuous and oppressed.

Sylvestre, bruised by so many shocks, could not succeed in materializing the hope that Claude, with his unconscious desire to keep her close to him, had sown in the dolor of her convalescence. At that heart-rending moment, when the men were in danger, she no longer wanted anything but to help Annik and save Claude. Her will was limited to that.

Claude reappeared, his expression preoccupied.

"What is it now?" asked Annik

"Nothing."

But she could read it in him as clearly as Sylvestre. What bad news was he trying to hide?

He thought it unworthy of him, and of them, not to associate them with the sentiments that were agitating him.

"Something it was necessary to expect!" he said. "My class has been called to the flag as from tomorrow. The notices have been put up this morning, it appears. And it's necessary to believe that they'll pay particular attention to my compliance, since here's the individual summons that the cyclist from the Recruitment Office has just delivered to the Boulevard Raspail. Young Richou has just brought it to me."

Annik and Sylvestre had stood up, both pale. Twenty times over, since the day before, they had envisaged the eventuality of that anticipated call-up. It had emerged at the moment when they were not thinking about it, all the more disquieting since that abnormal personal summons seemed to be aimed at Claude in a particular manner, pursuing in him the most dangerous enemy, resuscitated.

"Well," said Claude, "the circle is tightening."

"You won't go!" exclaimed Annik. "If I'd known…and I held you back just now! To think that you might have left without knowing…"

He shook his head. "I knew, when I decided to stay, that my class would be called up. It could only be a matter of hours. My resolution is made. Tomorrow at eight o'clock, I'll be at the barracks at the Château-d'Eau, from which we'll be sent to some training camp. And when all my comrades are together with me, I'll inform them, Mother, of what you've taught me. I'll make them understand where their true duty lies, the most useful fashion of serving."

"And what if they kill you?" cried Sylvestre.

Her distressed face moved Claude more than the silent torment that was ravaging Annik. The storm, unleashed, had completed the sweeping away of his sentiments, his habits, all the quotidian deposits. He suddenly measured his attachment to Sylvestre, laid bare… The letter from Alexandria! The bond toward the assassin! A double memory that abruptly caused to reappear, more tender and more complete, the old fraternal affection. He did not confess it to himself as yet, thinking, like her, that it was too late, that he was going to die: a certainty that gave his voice a new tone.

"Sylvestre, we're envisaging the worst at this moment, naturally. Sylvestre, if I'm killed…"

Annik raised her head. "What are you saying?"

"Don't be alarmed, Maman. It's necessary to look the future in the face. The dark hours have begun, with my dear Papa's murder…" His voice choked, while Annik closed her eyes in order neither to lose nor give anything to the visage that was there, behind her eyelids…

"It's our turn now, the young men. Mother, I'm asking Sylvestre never to leave you. I'm asking her to live."

"Not without you, Claude!"

A cry in which hope was bleeding, with despair, in which love and death were exalted and confused, pierced Claude's failing courage. With his head in his hands, he collapsed on the desk, weeping like a child. Sylvestre, pale, did not have the strength to move, but Annik had run forward. Stubbornly, he would not raise his head, groaning: "Let me alone! Let me unwind, finally. This minute of weakness will do me so much good. I can't do any more, Maman, you understand! This chaos in which we're struggling…this madness without issue. My father is dead and I haven't yet wept for him, since it was necessary to defend him. The war is going to take me, and it's at the moment when I've glimpsed happiness…"

Heroism buckled under the excessive weight of regret. Youth, at bay, refused, with all its strength, to perish.

He wiped his eyes and said, more calmly: "Do you understand, Maman, do you understand? It's hard to think that one might have been able to live happily, in a peaceful era. It's hard, at twenty, to renounce everything!"

He looked at Sylvestre, at the love that had come too late. Annik hugged her son against her, weeping with him.

"Yes, I know, my dear child. It's necessary not to despair, though, as long as we, the others, haven't made our effort. Do you believe that, like the mothers in the last war, we're going to allow our children to be massacred? Don't you think that, to preserve the flesh of our flesh, the happiness and future of humankind, we wouldn't sacrifice ourselves first? You're talking about catastrophe…and it might, in fact, be produced. Since you've made a testament of sorts, listen to mine. One never knows, my dear children—one thinks about death, and it's the other that comes. If, as I hope—as I demand—my turn is the nearest…come here, Sylvestre."

At a hesitant step, which emotion caused to tremble, Sylvestre obeyed.

"With you, my son, this is the true repository of my thought, of my ideal. Personally, I have no more to do here, without your father, for whom I, too, haven't had the time to weep. Both of you, continue your task, by doing, like us, everything that you can. Promise me."

In front of her, Claude extended his hand to Sylvestre, Annik secured and tightened the timid grip. And all three of

243

them, mute for the moment, remained thus, elevating their souls above their destiny.

Claude broke the silence first, anxiously interrogating his mother; "But it's understood that, no more than we'll flee death, we won't seek it out?"

He understood Annik's final statement more clearly now. What was she going to do?

"You'll see," he went on, "if we come through this horror, how we shall love one another! Swear that you won't seek death!"

Sylvestre begged: "Oh, that it's necessary to swear to your son!"

"Don't worry. I'll only do what it's necessary to do."

VI

The squadron of gas-launching triplanes to which Jules Poncet is attached—even though he has not yet been militarized for the moment, any more than Claude has—is lined up on a lawn at the Château de Mahire, near Verdun. The airfield extends its aviary into the surrounding meadows. An entire army is massed around the new town where Maréchal Lux has established his General Headquarters in the subterranean bunkers of the old citadel, familiar terrain to the bombardments of 1916.

In a dawn as dreary as the one that is simultaneously enveloping Paris, the young engineer is nervously inspecting the giant machines, whose cargoes of bombs, enormous mysterious tubes, are stowed six to an aircraft. What are the eighty terrible machines waiting for before taking to the air, flying to Berlin and dropping the devices *en masse*. The bursting of one alone, on touching the ground, is sufficient to put thousands of people to sleep forever. Spreading their toxic gases in a cloud, how great will the hecatomb be?

Poncet closes his eyes at the idea of all those innocents who will pay for a few guilty parties. He has faith—an absolute faith—in the murderous power of the invention. Adhering to the ground to a height of ten meters, over a surface area of twenty thousand square meters, the odorless layer—the charge of a single tube—will numb almost immediately with a painless asphyxia: a sleep from which one does not return. The open air trials carried out on the Breton heathlands, on sheep and distributed at various distance and heights, leave no doubt about it.

What is Headquarters thinking? Why, since Tuesday, when, without even waiting for the declaration of war, German aircraft destroyed Strasbourg with Ludwigshafen's incendiary gases, had Lux not riposted immediately? Only a few flights of biplanes have placed ordinary bombs in centers of enemy concentration. Yesterday, all day long, the tremulous Poncet walked back and forth in front of his arsenal of slaughter, the condition of a future without war. All through the night, he waited, feverishly. He is booted, helmeted, ready to depart. He intends to try out the family invention personally.

Now, he thinks about Claude. What has he done since the fatal moment, and what is he doing? Jules Poncet sees the mild masculine face of Jacquemin. He hears the supreme advice ringing in his ears: "Love one another!" However, it was on Jacquemin's own orders that, on the eve of his assassination, he left for Verdun, driving the first truck in the convoy that carried the first shells toward the frontier.

He knows, better than anyone, what the great patriot's last thought was: to defend national integrity if enemy Hatred and the victorious forces of the Past, attempted to ruin therein one of the factors of future Humankind. No matter how monstrous the crime was to which Claude's father has fallen victim, the act of a madman has not changed the duty that Jacquemin, alive, recognized himself, consenting to necessity.

"By executing the orders of the new government," Poncet said to himself, "I shall only be following the path traced by the preceding one. The de Laumes and the Solmous I despise and hate, along with the interests they represent—but at this moment, when the conflict that I would have liked to avoid with all my might is a fact, when the present life of the country is at stake, I cannot worry about whether the hand holding the flag is clean or not. It's for France that I'm fighting. It's my country that I'm serving..."

The force of hereditary sentiments had not possessed him to the point that he had denied any of his mystic ideal. Yes, it was to save millions and millions of human lives that he was about to sacrifice a hundred thousand, deliberately and coldly. It was to ensure the new order that was going to crush the old, in blood and in fear. What was that insignificant ransom, by comparison with the foundation of Peace? Every day, on the surface of the globe—and without any benefit to the general

246

good—death levied that sterile toll. Centuries of labor, henceforth fecund, are well worth that extra sacrifice...

"Monsieur Poncet!"

He shivered. Was this, finally, the order? His heart beat faster. It was the captain commanding the squadron, with another officer...that one with a tricolor brassard. He ran toward them.

"Captain?"

"Colonel Ledant, from G.H.Q. Maréchal Lux is summoning you, immediately."

"I'll take you," said the Colonel. He looked at the young man without amenity. A specialist in artillery, Colonel Ledant did not look kindly on anything that prospered outside his own weaponry. Aviation, yes, all very well for reconnaissance, and, exceptionally, for certain destructive raids...but if it was now to be charged, not merely with abridging, but suppressing wars! The appearance of Jules Poncet, at first sight, did not modify his impression. He was only twenty years old, and claimed to be revolutionizing the world.

A more attentive examination, along the way, completed his indisposition. Hollow chest, a sly hint of the seminarist, and spectacles! It would not have required much more, as they reached the foot of the château, visible through its clumps of maples, for the deputy chief of the Bureau of Operations to be persuaded that the rumors that were going around about young Poncet might have some basis in fact.

An enormous auto with a small white flag fringed with gold—the Maréchal's personal vehicle—was waiting, parked in front of the entryway. The colonel went to shake hands with his comrades, grouped on the balcony to watch the departure. Poncet, standing beside the door of the car, was surprised to see that he was the object of general attention. Only the two drivers—the banker Merceau and Henri Chanteroy—were contemplating him with the distant arrogance of the privileged individuals who were worthy to embellish the top of the military tree.

"Climb in, Monsieur," commanded a dry voice.

Poncet, not understanding anything, made himself small in a corner of the spacious vehicle. It was fitted out for long journeys, with a folding table, doubtless for the rolled-up maps with which the satchels were full. For unless they were bottles... As for the rear seat, with its elongated footrests, it was so deep and so vast that the Maréchal must be able to sleep there in comfort, dreaming about his offensive strategies... But what a singular expression that colonel had, with his sidelong glances! Poncet had the impression of being examined, like an accused suspect...

He was so bewildered that, without him perceiving them, the camps of the machine-gunners and the heavy artillery flew past, villages of tents so swarming with negro infantry that one might have believed oneself in the heart of some Dahomey, and finally, the streets of a town, transformed into an officers' promenade. The auto was engulfed by arches.

"We've arrived," said the colonel.

Preceding Jules Poncet, he traversed a courtyard, and then another, went into a somber building where footsteps resounded along the corridors. Poncet looked round. Two gendarmes were following him.

"Wait there!"

And suddenly, the kepi barred with five small stripes disappeared.

What's happening? Poncet wondered.

Colonel Ledant had put between them the dry click of a door, on which a label could be read: *Bureau no. 2*. Although not well versed in military arcana, the engineer knew enough history to recall the bad memories evoked by that denomination. To the service, along with espionage, a legend remained attached of a secret tribunal held behind closed doors, in which the officers acting as judges and litigants were not always determined in accordance with the rules of common sense, or even simple justice.

With a mistrust that had not yet divined the imbecile suspicion of which he was the object, Poncet could not think without a vague anxiety about the discretionary power with which the war had just increased an authority that was already redoubtable in peace time.

There was great emotion among the military magistrates. Since Ledant's departure for Mahire, a German aircraft had flown over the citadel, dropping a white rain of leaflets, which contained tendentious information—also implausible, according to Colonel Hardye de la Mettraye, the chief of Bureau no. 2.

"What do you think, Ledant? It can only be a ruse of war? The German railways sabotaged by communist gangs? Mobilization hindered everywhere by parties allied with the Social Democrats? False information that the German G.H.Q. is doubtless sending us to delay our offensive in preparation: the irresistible impact of the black troops and your heavy cannons. I have, however, drafted a note for the Maréchal's office."

The door opened again.

"Come in," ordered a young lieutenant. Addressing the two gendarmes, he added "You stay there."

Poncet found himself suddenly confronted by three officers seated at a long table with a green baize top, covered in inkwells and stacks of paper. They were staring at him. At other tables, in the corners of the whitewashed room, other officers were working. They scarcely raised their heads from their writing. Colonel Ledant said to the central individual, who seemed to be presiding over the hearting: "I'll leave you. Don't forget that Monsieur le Maréchal wants to see…Monsieur Poncet himself, after you've interrogated him."

He went out, responding with the most courteous smile to the salutations of the scribes, rising from their chairs.

The president directed at the young man standing before him—who did not know on which leg to rest his puzzlement—a gaze even less benevolent than Colonel Ledant's.

Slowly he said: "Do you know…Monsieur Poncet…of what you're accused?"

"Me, Monsieur?"

"Colonel, if you please."

"Pardon me—I didn't know what rank..."

The chief of Bureau no. 2 pulled down his sleeve in order to display the insignia more clearly. "It's true that you must be myopic, to judge by your spectacles." He paused. "What use are they to you, then, if not to see?"

The man's mad! I've been mistaken for someone else. Of what am I accused? The ideas floated, anxiously, in his stupor. What should he reply? He hesitated.

"Aha!" said the Colonel. "If that question embarrassed you, I'll ask you another. But first, take off those spectacles. We won't permit you to hide anything here! And without your smoked lenses, perhaps you'll perceive more clearly the consequences of a revelatory silence or explicit lies."

"But Colonel..."

"Silence! By virtue of what order were you, who are not even militarized, able to bring to Verdun, for the aviation service, trucks containing bombs charged with explosive gases?"

"By the order of the President of the Council of Ministers, Monsieur Jacquemin himself."

"Naturally!" The three officers looked at one another. No more doubt!

"You admit it?" said the Colonel, as he made a note.

"Admit what?" Jules Poncet was racking his brains. How could he have imagined that his secret mission, his unexpected presence at Mahire had been denounced as a criminal machination by Jacquemin? Was he suspected of being an instrument or an accomplice?

Colonel Hardye de la Mettraye pressed him: "An order, you say? A written order...? No? Aha!"

"I had a safe-conduct for the aviation. I gave it to the commander of the squadrons when I arrived."

"Let's admit that. So much for the bombs. And the triplanes specially designed for the launching of your bombs? Will you tell me why, on the same day that you were sent to Mahire, they followed you, when they were at Le Bourget, the place indicated for their assembly by the mobilization plan? A plan established under the previous de Laume ministry, which had not been modified, so far as we know, by…Monsieur Jacquemin."

"It was only natural—at least, it seems so to me—that the gas-launching triplanes would, in the eventuality of unexpected hostilities, be placed within range of their bombs."

"I warn you that your case is suspicious enough. Don't aggravate it with your insolence and irony!"

"But after all," exclaimed Poncet, exasperated, "what is this about and what do you want with me?"

"You'll find out! One more question: is it true that the power of this invention is in conformity with the results of which you have boasted?"

"If you'd tried it out two days ago, you'd know!"

"The Bureau of Operations knows what it's doing. You're here before Bureau no. 2. And what you have to answer for is not the projects of the General Staff but those of the traitors you serve. You're accused of having, knowingly or not, taken part in a socialist plot..."

Poncet opened his eyes wide, and stood there open-mouthed.

"The objective that you were pursuing was not the destruction of the German army or cities; it was that of the citadel of Verdun—the brain of France."

"What!" he murmured.

Dazed, he tottered. His hands had fallen, involuntarily, on the green baize of the table. The colonel and the two officers had risen to their feet. Such a collapse was worth more than any confession...

Swiftly, one of the scribes with two stripes had run to the door. The gendarmes, entering in haste, took hold of Poncet. He looked around him, bewildered, as if in a dream.

"The council of war will decide. You'll have time to reflect, between now and then, in a cell. Gendarmes, take the accused to Monsieur le Maréchal's study. I confide him to you."

Insults were foaming on Poncet's lips. He wanted to shout: "Idiots! Brutes!" to blast them for their insanity, their blindness. The idea of the revolvers in the policemen's holsters stopped him. He would have no difficulty in exonerating himself before the Maréchal.

Escorted by his guards, he went back along the corridors, recrossed several courtyards, and had just arrived at a high grassy bank in which, flanked by monumental stones, a small armor-plated door opened, when detonations rang out, so forceful and so close that the gendarmes stopped, their faces distressed, and looked at one another.

German aircraft? The deluge of fire?

Poncet clenched his fists. The unused triplanes back there!

At the same time, a group of a dozen men appeared, running toward the entrance of the bunker, shouting. Young or old, the same fear possessed them; they went past in their blue horizon uniforms, bending their backs and ducking their heads. In spite of the dangers whose menace was materialized by the fleeing men, the gendarmes snapped to attention before kepis sparkling with golden oak-leaves. They had recognized the Maréchal at the head of a number of officers of the General Staff. Already, swallowed up by the entrance to the cellar, they had all disappeared, as if sucked in by the protective bunker.

They were just in time. The detonations were getting closer, with the purr of powerful engines. Flames were already rising high into the air, from what must be the direction of the church. Screams, a mephitic odor...

The instinct of self-preservation gripped Poncet in his turn. He launched himself forward to flee...but one of the two gendarmes, seeing their prisoner escaping, instinctively drew his revolver, took aim at Poncet and shot him.

He fell, like a hare felled by a hunter.

There was no longer anything on the ground where the Maréchal had been taking his hygienic stroll a little while before but a cadaver, on which a bomb fell, emitting a jet of flame so vertiginous that it licked the roofs of the neighboring buildings, enveloping the bunker in a black and red whirlwind, under which the charred bodies of the two gendarmes curled up.

Down below, twenty meters underground, in the new cellars hollowed out in the heart of the rock beneath the old subterranean working, the Maréchal was suffocating, surrounded by officers of his general staff and a few lieutenants. They had the habit of thinking for him, but at that moment, the emotion and surprise were so forceful that no one could think about anything. There was one single haunting thought: when would it end? The thickness of the room and the reinforced concrete walls was such that all immediate peril seemed to be set aside.

None of those men, the majority of whom were brave and accepted as a professional risk the death in which they dealt, was ashamed of have felt panic all the way to their entrails. War, in changing its form, had created a new mentality. The amplitude of its catastrophes contained something superhuman, imbued with a sacred terror—especially among its direct beneficiaries, previously more accustomed to advantages of every sort than to the inconveniences of a similar risk.

The Maréchal could not get over it. An indignation rose up within him. Was it a reprisal of the German socialists—if, as the leaflets dropped a little while before said, the power of the Reich was in the process of changing hands—or a unqualifiable procedure of the regular army?

Such an attack was no less odious no matter what its origin was. Attacking a G.H.Q. now! Where would it end? War would no longer be possible, if those waging it no longer played by the rules.

Sylvestre is sitting on the mossy bank in the shadow of the sycamore. She has taken off her bandage, which made her look ugly. From her hiding place, which overlooks the Avenue de Paris, she searches the distance with her gaze for Georgi's auto, which Annik has kept. She sounds the sky, where aircraft are flying at top speed toward their invisible goals. But Claude's amphib does not appear.

Standing behind his daughter, Monsieur Blanchet is in torment. "What's become of them?"

Sylvestre shakes her head, dolorously. She last saw Annik at midday, in the Boulevard Raspail, Claude a little earlier, at the *Maison de Toutes*, where a worker had come to ask for him...

"The printing-works at Belleville was invaded by a contingent of Annamites. It's locked and guarded. The posters! It was fatal. He left in his amphib with the man, after saying to us: 'Go back to Versailles. I'll try to join you there in the morning.' As for Annik, I repeat, although someone came to warn us shortly after Claude's departure that they were equally under threat, she absolutely insisted on calling in at her home and going in for a moment, without me. Papers to put in order...rather, I thought, to spend brief interval alone with her despair and her memories. Oh, she won't be long, since she has the car, and little Richou...but Claude!"

She was suspended on her thought, like a gymnast on a flying trapeze over the avalanche of a Niagara. If that support gave way, she would fall into the abyss! With all her strength, she clung to the precarious thread of existence...

Since the confession wrenched from Claude by the excess of misery, since the pact of union sealed thanks to Annik's maternal will, Sylvestre had glimpsed, with the grandeur of the task that had been delegated to her, the possible magnificence of the future. It opened up before her, like an unknown land: a land ornamented by all her dreams, since the awakening of affection in childhood. And a sky also ornamented by a mysterious voluptuousness, since she had felt the fluid fire of the kiss on her lips: Claude's first maladroit kiss, the evening of her return from Egypt.

The hours went by. No one.

It was not until the end of the afternoon that Annik arrived. Her first words were to enquire about Claude. His ab-

254

sence plunged her into the same mortal anxiety as Sylvestre. The evening newspapers brought the obscure incoherence of their information, without succeeding in extracting them from their anxiety. What did the bombardment of the General Headquarters by German socialists and the popular action progressing in Berlin matter, now that the Government had declared its intention to pursue the politics of national war no matter what the cost, and to respond to the German provocation on the G.H.Q. and the incendiary bombs annihilating Verdun after Strasbourg, with a mass attack, a unanimous effort of all the French forces?

For the first time, Annik began to despair of the triumph of her work. She saw Claude sacrificed, perhaps uselessly, after his father, to the principle of Non-Violence whose sovereign force the still-enslaved crowds were incapable of comprehending. Was Véra Sélénosk right? Was resignation, easier than revolt, about to lie down in its eternal servitude again, beneath the iron heel of the gilded boot?

Blanchet still sought, in vain, after the long wait for dusk, and after the bleak dinner, to find reasons to explain Claude's absence.

A prolonged ringing of the doorbell in the night brought their alarm to a peak.

"It's the front door," said Blanchet. "Go and see who it is, Nane"—but the two women had already run to answer it.

They soon came back, somewhat reassured, to the Professor, who had followed them, dragging his heels involuntarily.

Louise Mureau, breathless, had told them that Claude was hiding in their house. He had arrived at the factory after the shift, and sent her to tell them. He was waiting for them.

Leaving her father, who also wanted to come and embrace Claude, at the house—"No, it's best if you stay, in case anyone comes here to arrest him!"—Sylvestre had taken the steering wheel, in the place previously occupied by Gine. Annik, by her side, hastened the progress of the auto with her impatience, its crazy speed still seeming too slow for her taste.

255

Louise Mureau and young Richou, in the back, were chatting feverishly about events. They both had only one thing in view: their adoration of "Monsieur Claude."

After an afternoon spent in a tragic and all the more passionate game of hide-and-seek, in which he had succeeded, not without difficulty, in avoiding pursuit and going to see a few socialist leaders, who had all told him of their hope for eventual success, Claude had decided to go to earth at Chesnay, sure that there, if the factory was not in enemy hands, he would be able to spend his last night of liberty tranquilly. Annik and Sylvestre could meet him there as soon as they were notified, whereas at Versailles, as at the Boulevard Raspail and the *Maison de Toutes*, he might fall into enemy hands at any moment.

He intended, in order to give the premeditated action its full significance, to present himself at the barracks of the Château-d'Eau of his own accord. It was only by responding spontaneously to the summons that he would confer an impact on the display of his refusal of obedience, of which preventive imprisonment would rob him.

Mureau was on watch. On perceiving him through the open windows of the Office, he had run to meet him, his arms raised.

"Oh, Monsieur Claude! What a joy! Here you are, safe and sound!"

"As you see, Mureau..."

"I've been looking for you everywhere, this afternoon. Things have happened here since I saw you yesterday morning!"

The foreman had come to the Boulevard Raspail with his daughter, the day after the assassination, to bring humble flowers from their little garden, the first narcissi...

"You can tell me all that in a minute. First, telephone your daughter; tell her to leave immediately to inform my mother, at Mademoiselle Blanchet's house... Good. Now, the overseer that's due to relieve you—tell him to take your place. And let's go."

"Is it because they're looking for you, Monsieur Claude? Oh, the scum! Let them come here! They'll find us all..."

"No, Mureau, no violence, still. So...here?"

"Oh," said Mureau, "first of all, in spite of everything I could say and do, too many people left for their filthy war. The young ones especially. They don't know! They imagine it's a sport! They said that once they were *en route*, we'd see...oh, it's necessary not to count on them to complete their five years, or even five months..."

"It's not a matter of months, Mureau, nor even of days, but of hours. Everyone is pregnant with incalculable consequences. If all the workers have done their duty..."

"Be certain, Monsieur Claude, that if it only depended on me...so, today, Monsieur Lourmal came. He's changed his tone, the cayman, since he's obtained for the war, it seems, an order for a million grenades. As if there were still going to be trenches! Barricades, I don't say no! He gathered all the overseers together and gave us orders to dismantle some of the machines. It seems that others are due to arrive tomorrow, all ready. German, too! A machine is money, isn't it?—not the Fatherland. He wasn't able to get to the end of his speech, that Bazile![34] Then he ran away, saying that the night would bring counsel and that he'd come back tomorrow, with what he needed to make us do as we're told, if we remain stubborn. He can come, with his blackamoors. They'll be well received! That's what everyone's talking about in the town. Already the lads wanted to set out this evening to find you and, if necessary, to defend you."

They had arrived at the first houses. Claude was immediately surrounded and acclaimed. If his catechism of Gentleness had not convinced all those souls to the point of raised them to a cool abnegation, it had at least given them an affectionate respect for its apostles. When they knew that, being hunted, he had come to seek refuge at the factory, and that he

---

[34] The reference is to the music-master bribed by the Count in Beaumarchais' *Le Barbier de Seville* (1775).

intended to go toward danger the following day, to deliver—along with all the young disciples of the religion of Love—a battle on which everyone's fate might depend, the agitation became stormy.

Mureau summed up the general sentiment; "Rendezvous at the Gare de l'Est as soon as we've sent the grenade-merchant and his retinue packing. That won't take long. Let him come—I have my idea, and unless they have cannons…!"

Claude, exhausted by fatigue, had had nothing to eat or drink since the hot coffee in the bistro that morning. Having filled his stomach, he waited for Annik and Sylvestre to arrive with more serenity.

They finally arrived. Mère Mureau, her husband and the *"p'tit gars"* left them alone in the kitchen-dining-room, rejoining Louise and little Richou, proud to recount once again, with his own embellishments, the various adventures in which he had played a role...

When the two women had embraced Claude, they started talking feverishly. They exchanged their news, and, keeping silent about their fears, strove to be unanimously hopeful. Soon, however, no more words were exchanged. The cup was not entirely empty, but they all kept the dregs to themselves. There was nothing but a silence, in which their three hearts were beating, in the mystery of their destiny.

With an equal determination not to allow themselves to become sentimental, they enjoyed the bitter joy of being together again, perhaps for the last time. Sparse words fell heavily. They measured their range, following their rebounding fall into the black well of their thoughts. They were like as many moments detached forever from the unique hour.

When Claude sensed that Sylvestre could no longer control her emotion, he looked at her for a long time, as if to impregnate her with strength. Their courage must not buckle.

He called little Richou: "Get going—you drive."

Gently after kissing them both again, and again, he helped Annik into the car, and then Sylvestre. And when he saw them both seated, holding one another by the arm, their faces desperately turned toward him, he said to the boy: "Go!"

With its headlights switched off, the auto drew away, and disappeared into the darkness.

VII

What day is it? Claude no longer knows. What time do the black hands of the clock indicate? He does not know, scarcely able to perceive the shadowy circle in the corner of the room. He leans out of the wagon, and sees other hallucinated faces at the windows, all along the train that is going to carry them away: the cattle-train, lined up with other trains, equally full, in the immense hall of the Gare de l'Est. The platforms are swarming with mobilized men joining them, dejected or overexcited relatives, penned recruits and riflemen with fitted bayonets, gazing, with fixed smiles on their faces of yellow or black wood: the suicide of civilization.

The dial of the pneumatic clock—still obscure a moment ago—is gradually illuminated, as if by confused daylight. The hours are legible now. The nineteenth is finishing in a wan twilight when, at the same time, all the electric lights come on, red dots in the fog of dark smoke.

Day dawns in Claude's consciousness: a day of limbo in which death and life are quivering simultaneously.

In the morning, when he presented himself at the barracks, it was obvious that they had not expected to see him. After various long telephone calls—he had been in the adjutant's little office for an hour—he had been taken to join the others. He had sensed that he was under scrutiny. He had said to himself: *They don't dare kill me immediately, like my father; they're waiting until I'm out there.* He is waiting, too, having prepared his seed, to bring forth the good grain of revolt as soon as he had sown it there, Tomorrow, at the training camp, when he will have made friends of these strangers, he will be able to say to the officer whose face he could picture, the words that will awaken profound echoes in their sheep-like souls. He is preparing them, rehearsing them.

All day long he has been trying out their effect, whenever he could. At one moment, not long ago, he had almost shouted them, while they were being herded into the wagons reeking of livestock. No, let his gift not go to waste!

Now he is thinking about yesterday's farewell, about the cherished faces that plunged into the darkness, their imploring expressions. But he does not want to, and must not, weaken. Bleakly, he chases away their image at the very moment when, driven by the supreme instinct, Annik and Sylvestre, possessed by love, are coming to his rescue, at the head of wives and mothers.

Annik has quickly found out from which station, at what time, Claude would be leaving. It is Sylvestre herself who went to the barracks and, outside the gates, mingling with the dolorous crowd of wives, mistresses and sisters, obtained the information from an obliging junior officer. She went back to Annik, reinstalled in spite of the risk at the *Maison de Toutes*. They distributed the tasks, and also the leaflets that they had succeeded in having printed and typed since the previous day. The truth in a few lines, the latest news of the popular progress in Munich, Frankfurt and Dresden…Wittelsbach shot…the French and German General Headquarters bombarded simultaneously by the socialists of the Reich…

They have divided into two troops the quivering good will and courage of the hundreds of women assembled there, and now, toward the Gare de Nord and the Gare de l'Est—for the two troops had swollen as soon as they took to the streets—an irresistible moving force.

Annik and Sylvestre are in the first rank of the principal body. They are marching with heads held high, singing the *Internationale*. With a grim grandeur, a religious faith, the hymn of revolt and human hope rises up from their frail breasts, taken up and reverberated by a growing chorus. The stupefied agents stand still. A few men mingle with the procession, lined up by a discipline. A Senegalese barrage is overturned. The assault column, around which the crowd thickens, advances slowly but relentlessly.

Annik and Sylvestre, through their illuminated eyes, see nothing but the goal. Around them, torsos and heads, the white hair of old people, the tresses of the wives and daughters of the people, the elegant hats of bourgeois women, and, as they get closer, faces...some hateful, others fearful, as if imploring...the majority poor, having only one expression fixed upon their skin, gazing with bleak, unseeing eyes.

"Make way! Make way!" someone cries. Bodies jostle, elbows dig into ribs and backs. In the boulevard filled to bursting, the crowd opens up like ripped paper. To the vibration of the refrain, as the winged hymn unwinds, everyone feels palpitating, in the depths of their inner being, that which the obstacles, the struggles and the necessities have covered up, and which every being, even the most denuded, possesses: a glimmer of heaven, a breath of hope, an impulse to surpass life.

The visionaries continued to advance.

People were attracted by curiosity, scenting something. A few women touched them to see whether that dedicated flesh was flesh like their own. Others, when they had passed by, followed them, as if that example had revealed a vague, imperious mission. Jolted, pressed, cleaving the surf, the wave unfurled all the way to the station.

The employees had been swamped and the black troops drowned by the multitude. It alone was sovereign, and yet obedient, drawn toward the goal that the demonstrators want to attain: the trains.

The songs had ceased. There was no longer anything but a great tumult, in which voices and cries were confused. Untiringly, the propagandists of the *Maison de Toutes*, distributed their leaflets, the provisions of truth, insufficient for all the hands that were reaching out.

Annik hesitated on the transversal platform where the parallel tracks end. Which of those human cargoes contained Claude? It seemed to her, suddenly, that a mysterious magnet attracted her. She plunged straight ahead.

Sylvestre was the first to see Claude's face, in the turbulence that carried them toward the front of the train. It was pressed, with ten others, to the gap between sliding doors, guarded by a sentry. Had he seen her? She thought not. She told Annik immediately, but it was already too late to turn back. Forward! Their true post was at the front...in front of the locomotives, across the tracks.

Sweeping past the impotent soldiers, the solidifying mass had now succeeded in forming a block around Annik. Her name spread with the instantaneity of an electric current: "Annik Raimbert...Jacquemin's widow." Hoisted up onto shoulders, and clinging on to the headlights of the locomotive, she spoke: a tenuous cry, no matter how ardently was it launched, of which only a few syllables could be heard beyond a range of twenty meters.

"People! It is in the name of the great death that has been laid down, better to crush you, that I am here. People, I am appealing to your vital instinct, since reason and justice are no longer anything but words..."

Annik perceived in front of her, trying to slip through to the front rank, soldiers who had been able to force the doors at the front of other trains. Still in civilian clothes, they were already wearing the helmets of the other war. She searched with her eyes for Sylvestre; an eddy had borne her away. A few beardless recruits, projected there, made her think, while she continued her vehement adjuration: *If only Claude could hear me!*

He was there, on the platform, with the others from his compartment, who had rushed outside, but was separated from her by the compact, impenetrable, living magma. He had no doubt that Sylvestre was only separated from him by fifty meters or so. Who was speaking? Annik? He did not know, unable to see or hear.

The voice swelled: "Men, will you quit your wives, your children your mothers, to enrich the profiteers and murderers of all nations? Do you believe it necessary to go and fight against poor people like yourselves, who have done nothing to you? Because the forgers of gold and glory have extended themselves beyond frontiers to maintain the hatreds from which they profit!"

Various movements were agitating those who were listening, communicating with one another, from group to group. The interjections, the laughter, the *shut ups*, overlapped in the commencement of a relative silence around her.

"And you, women, does your entire being not revolt in seeing them depart? Will you permit the fruits of your loins to become cannon fodder again? Are we under attack?

"Yes!... No!...Enough!... Shut up!" But a stronger will gradually got the upper hand: "Let her speak"! Let her speak!"

"No, my friends, no! We are not under attack. You've seen the latest news from Germany, the documents proving that the international bankers alone have prepared and organized the slaughter! You're nothing to them but cattle, sold before the abattoir!"

Murmurs rose up again, but died down almost immediately, in the species of expectation that had gripped the crowd, and made them attentive, under the vast hall filled until then by a rumble of clamors.

"I'm addressing the hearts of mothers! Shall we allow ourselves to be mutilated, when German women are in revolt? Will you reserve your tears, like the mothers of 1914, for the charnel-house? Is it to wish your sons *bon voyage* that you are here, or to prevent them from leaving?"

The emotion was legible in the twisted faces. A cripple raised an arm and shouted: "Listen to her! I was in the last war! When I came back, I had one leg less and no more family, except for my twelve-year-old kid, abandoned..."

"Boo hoo!.... He's right!... Cuckold!"

The cripple brandished his crutch. "I found him again at seventeen, without education, without a métier. They only want him today for the butchery!"

Annik had managed to haul herself up onto the front of the locomotive. Standing there, with her hands gripping the headlights, she shouted:

"You hear! Mothers, don't fatten the ogres! On the other side of the frontier, your sisters are sabotaging the tracks. Do as they are doing! By attacking the General Headquarters, the

German socialists weren't attacking the country, but the accomplices of the crime. The burning of Strasbourg was agreed in advance! This war is nothing but a financial game, in which every proletarian cadaver consolidates the bourgeois strongbox! You've created young plants in order for them to blossom, in order that they can be fecund in their turn, not so that a savage gardener can plunder the nursery!"

The sentences flew into the distance, stirring hearts. Sylvestre, imprisoned on the platform between chests and backs, tried to stand on tiptoe, to see better, in order not to miss any of the message of peace. She repeated it, propagated it—an ecstatic face, amid the ardor of others...

A brief pause, streaked by flashes; the sound of an acclamation. Scarcely three minutes had gone by since Annik had begun to speak, and the crowd swelled, rocked, undulated with stirring rumors.

Cries of fear rose up: "Look out! The train's going to leave!"

A shock spread. Howls resounded. An order must have been given: a contingent of Arabs had succeeded in surrounding the engine; a few fanatics were threatening the mechanics. Spontaneously, however, a surge of the audience assailed the locomotive, and began to demolish the wagons. Shots rang out.

"No, no! Don't break anything. Violence only leads to violence! Form a wall of flesh! Everyone, in front of the trains, in order that the rails will be nothing, all the way to the front, but a living track!"

"Look out! Look out! The train's pulling out!"

In a frightful tumult, in the midst of insults, vociferations and pleas, one of the mechanics had fallen under the bayonets.

The machine was moving...

A cluster of women suspend themselves from it. The Arabs strike out, the bodies fall, immediately replaced by other bodies. The train is blockaded.

A melee, in which nothing can any longer be distinguished, spreads in all directions. Two currents are distinguishable within it, one fleeing, the other blocking the way. Faces are bloodied, lamentations are sobbed.

For one tragic second, during which the train, immobile, releases its steam, Destiny is in suspense. Upright in the white smoke, Annik exerts all her pity, all her exaltation, wishing that the fire that animates her might take on body, that the light with which she is radiant might impregnate these lunatics, that those fists might unclench, that hearts and minds might join together...

She attempts, in a hoarse, strained voice, one last effort. Clinging on with only one arm, she gesticulates as if to hurl the words at the ears that can no longer hear them.

"Don't fight! Let the religion of Love..."

The locomotive's whistles rip through the air. A song responds to them. The train has resumed moving. The hymn rises up, launched toward the welcoming tomorrows. The *Internationale* springs forth, victoriously, from the wall, reformed, demolished and re-formed again...

> *This is the final struggle*
> *Let's unite and tomorrow*
> *The Internationale*
> *Will be the human race!*

Blood spurts. People are knocked down, people are trampled. Amid the insults, the maledictions and the plaints, in the terror of splintering bones and crushed flesh, the machine moves forward. Annik weakens, but, almost voicelessly, continues singing.

Suddenly, her hand loses its grip on the headlight and her feet lose their point of support. She is thrown down face forward, onto the heaped up bodies that the buffer is flattening and the wheels are crushing...

They finally stop.

Annik's flesh and blood are mingled with the mangled flesh and blood already shed.

VIII

From the moment when he relocated Sylvestre, when his convulsive arms seized her in passing, in the formidable pressure of the demented crowd, and since they were able, both of them, to reach the place where Annik was lying, crushed and misshapen, under the black mass of the inert locomotive, Claude has had no more memory than a grain of sand rolled by the sea.

The strange sensation of the previous day—of one machine that is acting and another machine that is recording—has taken possession of him again. An irresistible flux of gestures, words and actions carries him away. A vertigo drags him...

Empty of its cargo of fresh meat, the train has retreated, uncovering the horrible pulp.

With words of inarticulate rage, superhuman lamentations, Claude has fallen upon the heap, which he searches in vain, trying to recover some shred...

Sylvestre wrenches him from his hypnosis, from the madness that has overtaken him. She drags him away, haggard.

Around them, a band of fanatics is agitating, in which he recognizes faces seen once...and others that are familiar...liberated comrades, workers from Chesnay, Mureau, the p'tit gars...They're there, a hundred of the faithful, and one, two, three thousand new friends.

Where have they come from, the factory workers? Later, he will discover that after having put Lourmal and his reinforcements to flight, scythed down by jets of icy water from the big fire hoses, they have collected up the rifles and they have come, in the trucks that have escaped requisition, and everything they have been able to find in the way of weapons and tools...

Of weapons there is no lack. They have been torn from the hands of soldiers, policemen—rifles and revolvers, truncheons and knives.

A cry rises up: "To the Élysée!" sprung from an unknown mouth, repeated by all, inflating and rumbling like a sudden thunderclap...

Claude and Sylvestre are lifted up, thrown by the wave from the depth that carries them away. Behind Claude for whom the workers form a guard, Mureau supports and carries Sylvestre. The p'tit gars has picked up a small red flag in passing, which he raises up, waves, and to the short staff of which, in order to make the symbol stand out more clearly beneath the blue light of electric arc-laps, a big fellow fixes to the end of a cane...

They pile into taxies. They draw away to the strains of the *Internationale*, now intoned by a hundred thousand pairs of lungs.

On the Boulevard de Strasbourg, where the crowd opens up before them, forming a hedge, they advance like war-chariots, surrounded by companies of volunteers.

Several columns have formed instantaneously, all of which have, like Claude's, tacitly elected their leaders. One goes up the Boulevard Magenta to lend a hand to the mutineers of the Gare du Nord. With a lightning rapidity, the events that have unfurled at the Gare de l'Est have propagated their ripples.

The socialist députés and militants who, although hunted and pursed, have been able to escape the repressive firing squads that de Laume has set in motion in the course of the afternoon, reappear, taking charge of the organization of the movement in all the arrondissements, at the Féderation de la Seine, the Bourse du Travail, the Maison Syndicale et Internationale du Peuple, reoccupied after a bloody struggle, the resistance is finally organized.

Unleashed by the immolation of Annik, the mob has become the Revolution...

At the intersection of the great boulevards, level with the Eldorado, the trucks from Chesnay and the troops surrounding them are halted by a panicked reflux. Above the roadways, on the quadrilateral of rolling sidewalks, which have not been rolling any longer since the morning, contingents of machine-gunners have just lined up, threatening to rake the avenues. They are the troops finally massed, in response to telephone calls sent from the railway stations, taking up their positions.

Without any preliminary demands, the sinister rattle bursts forth. The hail of bullets smashes into the trees, whose twigs rain down, and enter like a swarm of wasps into the soft bodies, which fall, punctured by stings.

"Lie down!" Claude shouts to Sylvestre, perceiving the blacks about to commence fire. He holds her down in the back of the truck, her nose flat to the boards, while he remains standing, offering himself to the fire, hurling the challenge of his hatred and despair.

"Cowards! Brutes!"

But with a somersault she has freed herself and is standing, holding onto him.

"Long life the free people!"

Other explosions crackle; the blacks panic and flee under the grenades that are aimed at them from windows and balconies. It is a militia battalion, which, sent in support, has gone over to the people and has sent a few men to climb to the upper floors. Soldiers and civilians fraternize...

The column resumes its march. It is still growing, along the way, in spite of the solitude of the roads, the desert that extends as it approaches the wealthy quarters: the facades are blind and deaf facades, shutters and the iron curtains of shop-fronts closed.

Bombs can be heard exploding in the direction of the Gare des Invalides: the bombs of governmental aircraft. Their lights can be seen, little shooting stars against the black sky. Undoubtedly some attack against other demonstrations. More distant still, there are other detonations—and suddenly, complete darkness. The electricity has been switched off every-where.

What hand, for what advantage has cut off the current? It is the workers, in the orders of the Féderation. Darkness diminishes the risk. The filthy swine, partially blinded, will not kill so many! And tomorrow, at dawn, a population, if not the entire population, will be upstanding, also armed, at the emplacements of the inevitable battle.

The remainder of that night, the two days and two nights that follow, and one further day—minutes? centuries?—Claude and Sylvestre traverse, without living them. They are tossed back and forth like corks in the chaos of troubled waters. They go at the whim of events wherever Hazard takes them, confused and dissociated—in a turbulence that rises and falls, like motes of dust in the grip of a crazy tempest.

Actions without consequence, snatches of exhausted slumber, one evening at the Boulevard Raspail, one at the *Maison de Toutes*…meals taken on the move, at irregular intervals, morsels of bread and oddments from tins, gulps of water…an existence on the wing, setting off again as soon as it pauses. A nightmare seen and felt, in which they have been in close proximity to murder twenty times over, in which they have not even had the energy to protest, or the indignation of pity, in which they have forgotten everything in the order of gentleness and the religion of Love for which their Saints have died.

Of the immense terror under which Paris, after the noise of the aerial bombing, has been buried—the end of the world that the capital believed was coming, at any moment, with the approach of rays and gases, the determining reason of France rising up in alarm against the warmongers, and also the suddenness of the popular victory, rapidly outlined and then affirmed—neither Claude nor Sylvestre has even been able to take account. A haggard unconsciousness unites them and separates them…and they find one another again without surprise at having been apart.

Was it yesterday or today that they learned of the death of de Laume? He has been dragged outside his office at Foreign Affairs by the workers from Chesnay, then strangled by Mureau, furious because his son had been killed by a stray bullet. A harpy castrated the cadaver with a paring-knife before it was thrown into the river like a dead dog.

Was it yesterday or today that they went through the reception room of the Élysée and saw Solmou lying on a Beauvais sofa, shortly after he had been taken out of his study? He had been found dead of an embolism, in a jacked striped with the great sash and his trousers down, the tail of his shirt covered in the excrement of terror.

Was it yesterday or today that from the terrace of Station B, at the Tuileries, they saw the Banque Cervier burning, with the crackling of its petrol-soaked woodwork, and the flames spurting from the broken windows?

If Claude had been able to think, what would he have said of learning that in those heavy plumes of red smoke, unknown to anyone, a yellow and blue hydroplane had taken off, saving, along with his boxes of foreign bonds and jewels, Jean Cervier and his daughter, clinging to one another in their egotistical terror, while la Mounine, who had gone back to her room to look for a forgotten brooch, remained trapped on the lower landing-platform with Mériane, in a broken-down elevator, where the fire roasted them, the little she-monkey shriveling up beside the fat one.

They no longer know, and no longer have, at the end of that day and week swallowed up in the depths of the abyss, any but one idea. An idea? Not even a pious, unconscious reflection. They incline the confused energy of their lives, at the end of their immense lassitude, toward the memory of their dead. From Annik, from her frightful remains collected along with all those of the sublime communion, they have separated their footsteps, but not their grief.

Tomorrow, in the solemnity of a national funeral—which Berlin will celebrate at the same time as Paris, to render homage to its own martyrs—the coffins will be taken from the Infirmary of the Gare de l'Est to Père-Lachaise. Their august contents will be incinerated there.

Claude and Sylvestre are going, hands joined to the cemetery where Annik will rest, in the colombarium that already holds the paternal ashes, while awaiting the perpetual monument that will soon be erected to the two noble memories.

They go there in the falling dusk, through the peaceful streets. They are going there for the funeral vigil, in the bleak splendor of that Easter spring. Religiously, they go along the pathways where, in the thickets of young verdure invisibly woven together by mauve shadows, the old garden conceals the ugliness of magnificent mausolea, forming the face of the profound park. The tombstones disappear, with their melancholy paving, beneath heaps of freshly-cut flowers. It is the unreal continuing, the dream for which the nightmare substitutes, weighing them down with distress and a nameless fatigue...

Now they are wandering, lost in a maze of tombs, and a scattering of box-trees and hyacinth, whose excessively strong perfume is sickening, afflicting their nerves. They cannot go on any longer; Sylvestre is so exhausted, hanging on Claude's arm. He is obliged to sit her down against a tree, but she slips from his grip and falls full-length on the ground, semiconscious. He lies down beside her, tries to reanimate her, and feels her burning breath on his face.

Instinctively, she has taken him in her arms; she draws him to her, sobbing.

"There's too much mourning, misery and catastrophe!"

Life rises up within them, from the bosom of the death that has penetrated them, and surrounds them, the unconscious protest of instinct. Their bodies interlace, their mouths come together.

Everything is abolished. Everything recommences.

The couple that has disappeared is succeeded by the new couple.

IX

A fortnight later. Eleven a.m.

Monsieur Blanchet, his steps heavy, heads toward the kitchen where Nane is preparing lunch, while muttering to herself, in accordance with the mania that solitude has given her. She starts at the sound of the door opening.

"Oh! You frightened me!"

"It's only me," says Blanchet.

Since the recent events, while Sylvestre has been absent, he has acquired the habit of coming to chat occasionally, but the moment is ill-chosen today; Nane does not want to spoil the lunch, the first one at which the four children will be reunited.

They will be seven, including Claude, whom Sylvestre has asked to come to live in her father's house, the dwelling in the Boulevard Raspail being too distressing for his dolorous heart; the good Roussot, their guest for a week; and Rohn, who is bringing Georgi and Gine back from Berlin.

"They ought to be here by now, don't you think?" sighs Blanchet. "As long as Georgi isn't too grievously wounded."

"His wife wouldn't have let him travel if he were."

"I hope so. What are you making them for lunch?"

"You'll know soon enough. Don't come prowling around my saucepans! It annoys me. You know me…"

"Yes, yes..."

Regretting having exploded, she watches him head for the door, compassionately, with his sad expression, and gives him what he came to seek.

"Don't torment yourself, now! You're going to see him, your Georgi, in a better state than you think..."

But Blanchet could no longer hear her, hastening toward a certainty. He had just perceived, at a distance, an airplane descending over the lawn. He took the shortest route, through the kitchen garden.

Gine ran to meet him. "Bonjour, dear…Papa."

For a second, she had hesitated. Could she use that word, which belonged to a dead man? Mentally, she added: *Dear Papa Blanchet…*

He kissed her on the cheek, holding her by the shoulders.

"How is he?"

"Much better. And the others?" *The others* were Sylvestre and Claude.

"They wanted to go, as they do every morning, to the *Universel* and the *Maison de Toutes*. They'll be here…"

Rohn had joined them, his honest face blossoming, with an emotional glimmer in his eye as Blanchet hastened toward his son. He was lying on a stretcher carried by the German pilot and mechanic.

The embrace of the two men reknotted all their past emotions. Only then did Blanchet hold his hands out to Rohn and thanked him for having consented, in spite of his occupations, to have lunch with them. The new President of the German Republic had to confer with the Executive Council, to which Hurteau, the provisional head of the government, had handed over power, but he had insisted, before then, on rendering Jacquemin's children that mark of affection.

Under Gine's direction, the stretcher-bearers headed for the house. Rohn reassured Blanchet about his son's condition.

"He lost a great deal of blood because the femoral artery was damaged. The femur was only grazed, fortunately. He needs complete rest, but in a month's time, he'll be on his feet."

Georgi had asked to remain under the acacia until lunch time, while Gine, leaving her husband to the two men, went upstairs to freshen up.

"I'm all right!" murmured Georgi, enveloping the old house, trees with the thick foliage and the pure sky, gilded by the May sunlight, with his gaze.

And airplane passed overhead.

"But that's my helic!" he exclaimed, pointing at the bird that floated silently toward the hangars.

"In that case," said Blanchet, "we're now complete. Claude and Sylvestre are bringing Roussot, who wanted to finish his sketches of the ruins before returning to Gaillarde. Fortunately, apart from a few banks and barracks...there's progress with the Commune. It's necessary to render justice to the people."

"How could there not have been progress," observed Rohn, gravely, "since there has been education?"

Gine had run down in haste to throw herself into her brother's arms, and both of them, to one side, were weeping without being able to say a word. Then they drew away, Gine wanting all the details.

Blanchet, Roussot and Sylvestre, seated around the stretcher, listened to Georgi.

"I'd had plenty of luck in the first two days. Five trips over Coblentz, Munich, Dresden, Stuttgart, Hamburg, Bremen, Berlin and Leipzig to drop leaflets giving the French news—the real news, not the official! I'd escaped all the electric snares...and then, on the Thursday morning, during the bombardment of the German G.H.Q..."

"You were there?"

"Yes."

"What he isn't saying is that he has simply been heroic. While our first squadron was bombarding Lux at Verdun, he insisted on being part of the second. Wounded, he replaced the pilot killed at the steering-column and, in spite of his hemorrhage, brought the apparatus back..."

"Well, I didn't want to stay there, with the smashed remains of those Messieurs! Of course, I've no idea how I landed..."

"What he's also not saying is that before the expedition against our G.H.Q., it was him who came to bring Paris the news of the crushing of the Mothers at the railway stations of Munich and Berlin..."

"Shh!" said Sylvestre. "Here come Claude and Gine!"

Rohn shot her an understanding glance before looking affectionately at the children, silent in their mourning dress.

From the dining room, the chambermaid announced that lunch was ready.

Claude and Blanchet picked up the stretcher and arranged it beside Gine's chair. Standing around the table, they all waited for Blanchet to sit down. On finding one another again like this, they were all subject to the same concentration. It was Roussot who interrupted it cordially.

"At any rate, we finally have the victory without the war. At a price, it's true!"

"Yes," said Rohn, sitting down opposite Blanchet, "A great social victory. The reign of the people is arriving anyway, you see. It isn't yet the epoch of Non-Violence for which, after our dear Jacquemin, the great Annik Raimbert died—but thanks to them, we're a little further along the road, still so short and yet so old, of the religion of Love."

Gine was about to begin passing the *hors-d'oeuvres* disposed on the white tablecloth—one of the beautiful items of linen that Monique loved—but Rohn, having half-filled his glass with the generous Bordeaux that Blanchet had carefully chosen and uncorked personally, raised it in a pious gesture.

"Let's drink in memory of those whose are absent, and to the faithful who have fallen for the same Ideal."

Everyone stood up, and with tremulous hands, clinked the frail chalices. Blanchet and Roussot, in touching Rohn's glass, felt, even more profoundly than the two young couples the symbolism of that elevation of hearts, evoking the sacrifice of the two reconciled peoples. Beyond France and Germany, young people were entering at a confident pace into the new Humanity. The philosopher and the painter, one old and the other broken, remained, in spite of their good will, on the threshold at which their stage of the journey was finishing.

It required all of Blanchet's good grace and all the forced enthusiasm of Roussot to produce a little relaxation, to render to the lunch the calm that, after all the tears, everyone was instinctively glad to recover. They talked about the details of the revolution in Paris and Berlin, about the absurd death of Jules Poncet, whose courage and faith had deserved better, of

Lux's platitude, offering the provisional government the devotion of the army, and, finally, the even-more-unexpected volte-face of Turbot. He had taken to the sea on seeing things going awry, and with the moribund Paul de Laume and the immortal Marquise d'Entraygues had waited on his yacht, cruising in the Mediterranean, until the *Inter*, by virtue of a savant conversion, had prepared the possibility of his return.

They had just left the table when Nane, after having brought the coffee and liqueurs into the garden, deposited a voluminous package of letters and telegrams on a chair. Every delivery brought as many to the *Universel*, the Boulevard Raspail and the *Maison de Toutes*. From every corner of France and the world, expressions of sympathy flowed and the homage of liberated peoples rose, in touching terms, toward the children of the Liberators. That morning, Claude had received two touching notes from James Ramsay and Madame Sydney. It was not only the former enemies on the two sides of the Rhine who were fraternizing, there was England, too. The workers of the entire world were celebrating, after the bloody dawn, the irresistible rise of the new sun.

While the family formed a circle around Georgi, Rohn linked arms with Claude and drew him toward the chestnut trees.

"Before you go back to Paris," he said to him, "I have a proposition to make to you. At the same time as the League of Nations is being transformed, becoming the League of Peoples, and while waiting for us to be able to constitute in a definitive manner our Federation of European Democracies, we would all be glad, since you're not yet of age to exercise a political mandate, if you'd accept the secretariat of the new International Workers' Bureau. Your industrial experience, the authority of your name..."

"I must refuse."

"You can't."

"I thank you, I thank all of you who have done me that honor, but nothing can alter my determination."

Rohn was amazed. "Why? Come on, my friend—it's a position that requires a man like you..."

"My dear Monsieur Rohn, I'm renouncing political life forever."

"You! You're fleeing the struggle? Impossible."

"Fleeing? No, on the contrary. But in accordance with my mother's wishes, it's purely in the moral order that I'm going to strive."

"That doesn't exclude the political order."

"Yes it does! Too much mediocrity diminishes thought there. I've found among Annik's papers a book on which she was working without our knowledge: *The Philosophy of Gandhi*. It will henceforth be my guide and my faith."

"Gandhi? Certainly, I admire him, but that's the Himalaya! Before attaining the summits lost in the clouds, let's climb the slope."

"Exactly! I've read more fully, and understood more fully, since I found in the echo of his doctrine the soul of the creator. We've entered by the low door of Violence—yes, more quickly than by non-cooperation—the country of the future that the cooperation of all in the new labor and Non-Violence will make better. Violence suppresses the intelligence and makes brutes of humans. I've decided to combat it with all possible examples."

"That's not incompatible with the position I'm offering you."

"Yes it is, because in a few days I'm going to leave, accompanied by my wife—I'm marrying Mademoiselle Blanchet..."

"Oh, my dear friend, I'm delighted!"

"Yes, she's an admirable person. We've learned the law of suffering at the same time. We know that no one can escape it, and we also know that one can work to purify it."

At that moment, seeing Rohn smile as he looked at her, Sylvestre approached. The worthy man took hold of her hands. "Claude's just told me. I congratulate both of you. Now, I'm asking you to make him understand that he ought not to abandon our cause."

"Abandon it? But we've never thought of doing so. On the contrary! Hasn't Claude told you about our organization of propaganda? We're leaving for a series of conferences in Europe."

"You can do that later."

"Our itinerary has been planned for six months," Claude objected. "Letters exchanged with all the affiliates of the *Maison de Toutes*...even some countries where they don't exist have asked us, already knowing about our plans, to stop off in their Universities."

Sylvestre had passed her arm tenderly beneath Claude's. She added: "We'll do the same every year; and the other six months, we'll spend here. Claude intends to resume his work at the factory and help me to continue his mother's work at the *Maison de Toutes*."

"In that case," said Rohn, "we'll let things take their course; you'll come back to us."

"But we're not leaving you!" Claude protested. "While plowing our own furrow, we're following the same route. I merely believe that before fixing the rules of work, it's necessary to teach the religion in which Humankind will one day fuse souls..."

The beautiful words of the Hindu Sage sang in his memory: "Every man is a stream, every people a river. They must follow their bed, limpid and without pollution, until they have reached the sea of Salvation, where they will all mingle."

"The religion of Love!" repeated Sylvestre, fervently.

Rohn enveloped them with an affectionate gaze.

"A beautiful dream, worthy of your couple. Let's do everything we can to make it a reality."

Saint-Maxime-sur-Mer
September 1923-May 1924.